Drawn to Perfection

For Eleanor,
with much love,

Victoria Owen

Drawn to Perfection

By

Victoria Owens

Hookline Books

Bookline & Thinker Ltd

Published by Hookline Books 2011
Bookline & Thinker Ltd
#231, 405 King's Road
London SW10 0BB
Tel: 0845 116 1476
www.hooklinebooks.com

A CIP catalogue for this book is available from the British Library.

This book is a work of fiction. Names, characters, places and incidents are either a product of the author's imagination or are used fictitiously.
ISBN: 9780956847683

Cover design by Donald McColl
Printed and bound by Lightning Source UK

To David with much love

Chapter One

Whenever she crossed the low bridge, Caelica would lean out over the parapet. Rolling up her sleeves like the countrywomen, she would rest her weight on her elbows and gaze down at the waters as they poured through the dark arches. Habit died hard, and although it was late, she paused at the bridge's mid-point.

There had been little rain in the past weeks, yet the river was swollen and fast-flowing. She could guess the cause of the surge. In the hills above the town, men seeking lead would dam up the streams for weeks together. When they broke down their barriers, the great head of unleashed water scoured away the earth far beyond the stream beds to show where the veins of mineral ran across the flank of the hill. They must have released nigh on a lake full for the current to run so high.

For a time, Caelica stood above the cutwater, the fury of the waters holding her as though by magnetism. Turning downstream to where the glutted river divided itself around a great stone, she noticed that the rock looked larger than she remembered. A solid shape, prominent even in the dusk, rested against it.

Staring, her focus sharpened. That black bulk had human form – a head hanging forward with face down and a torso curving towards a sagging mound of what looked like skirts. The thing – she would not call it a body – must have jarred against the boulders. In the thickening light she could not be certain of the skirt's colour, but if she narrowed her eyes, she could believe it was the same blazing colour as the gown Hannah Hallet had worn that morning.

Hannah had left the parsonage in high anger. Perhaps it made her careless. Perhaps she had fallen into the stream, the ungainliness of her pregnancy putting her balance awry. Caelica caught back her scudding thoughts. In all likelihood what she could see was another woman, a living woman who had tried to ford the stream, as people sometimes did when they did not want to wait while a long pack train clopped its way over the narrow bridge. No doubt the traveller regretted her recklessness now, for she was evidently exhausted. She might well rest on that rock to recover her energy – but surely there was no question that she was alive.

To rush would set the seal on Caelica's worst fears. Therefore, deliberate, she walked along the path by the river until she was level with the shadowy object midstream and then, wary, edged her way down the bank, her feet skidding on the mud beneath the thin grass. Close to, the shape might turn out not to be human at all – just a massive piece of debris thrown up by the flood. Later, with her father, she would laugh over her mistake. Even her mother might smile a little.

But standing at the water's edge and looking towards the dense heap in its resting place, utter certainty that it was Hannah Hallet hardened in Caelica's mind. Even by moonlight there was no mistaking the deep red which swathed the spreading bulk. In the quiet parsonage parlour, it had shouted out, brazen, beside Caelica's mother's mourning garb. If only Hannah would move – not just shift with the tow, but stir, breathe, rise and make for the bank. Anything to show she lived.

Sometimes in droughts the more daring children of the town would try to cross the river's central channel without wetting their feet, leaping from stone to stone. Now the waters ran so high that, except for the jagged outcrop against which the dark form rested, almost all the rocks were submerged. Guessing at where they lay, Caelica stretched out her hand under the water's surface until her stinging fingers brushed against something massive and hard. Finding its top wide and flat, she straightened, then stepped forward onto it, and at once looked for the next firm foothold. Her sight had adapted with the nightfall so, marking a point where the smooth patina of parting water indicated the presence of another drowned boulder, she reached it with a second, lunging stride. It was harrowing, this progress – so slow, so uncertain. At last, her shoes, stockings and skirt all sodden, she found herself some two, perhaps three, feet away from the torpid mass.

'H-hannah?' she called above the flood's roar, 'C-can you hear?' Shifting a little, Caelica put her hand on the fleshy shoulder. It was cold and quite motionless.

Was this death? Unwilling, Caelica looked at the woman's splaying limbs, her swollen unblinking eyes, her vacant face. Let it be no more than a faint, Caelica's wits urged, a loss of consciousness following exhaustion, drenching and shock. People recover from shock. It may make them ill or drive them to lunacy but better by far to be sick or mad than a corpse. Perhaps, deep in the woman's frame, the embers of life still kept their heat.

Stricken, Caelica blundered back over the wet stones and up the bank. She must find help, and it could not be the help of any passing townsman, but rather from someone she could trust. Running to the house where her tutor lodged, she struck the door with her fists. 'Mr Russell – Mr Russell,' she shouted. For answer – silence. Again she pounded on the wood and called his name. Why didn't he come?

The heavy door scraped open. By the pallid candlelight from within she saw him, the familiar lank hair falling across his brow and a look of astonishment in his red-rimmed eyes. It was plain that he wanted to ask what had happened, but to her own surprise she seized his ink-stained hand and headed, mute, towards the river.

Uncomprehending and cold after having spent a raw afternoon over his books, Thomas Russell went with her, trying to guess what could have happened. To find his quiet pupil grown so bold defied belief.

Yet her hand shivered in his and the thin moonlight showed streaks of tears down her face. She must have been in the river, for her dripping skirt clung about her ankles and her sleeves were muddy to the elbow.

Instead of keeping to the high ground before swinging left to cross the bridge as he expected, she took the path that ran under one of the dry arches. At her side, trying to catch her torn words, Thomas thought she was saying that someone was in the river.

At once he understood her panic. When the miners released pent-up waters from the hills' heights, no one could hope to stand against the flash.

Stumbling, he slid down the bank at her side. Following her eyes, sure enough he saw a huddled female form downstream.

'Y-you see?'

He nodded without speaking.

Some rash woman must have tried to ford the river at the worst time, and although the hope of finding her alive was minuscule he could not let it pass. Looking at the stream's broil, he decided to risk wading out to the stony ledge where she lay. It would be dangerous, but he would sooner let himself in for an honest soaking than try to balance on the slippery stones, only to miss his footing and fall headlong.

'Stay where you are,' he warned. 'Don't follow me.' The stream bed gave good purchase he knew, having occasionally made the crossing on horseback; even so, the force of the current took him by surprise. Although he was near the bank he still had to brace his limbs to keep upright, and the cold tore him to the bone.

When at last he reached the woman wedged up against the rock, he took her head in his hands and looked into her face. It was blank, her eyes fixed sightless on the stars; her limbs stiff and chill to his touch. She was stone dead and, he saw, with child – her clinging wet gown making her condition conspicuous.

'She stopped breathing some hours ago by my judgement,' he called, and at once wondered if he should have softened the truth of it. 'I'll retrieve her, though. Poor reckless soul – you'd think the sight and sound of the river in spate'd make her think better of fording it, especially with the bridge so near.'

'Now - we must accord her fitting respect. Is there somewhere at the parsonage where she' – the word was wrong,

4

but he did not want to say 'it' - 'that is, where her body can rest until we have found her people?'

He could not hear Caelica's reply though he thought he saw her nod.

Moving with the greatest care, he leaned forward, trying to raise the lifeless woman from her resting place. To his bewilderment, she proved much more cumbersome than he had expected; it was as though she positively resisted his efforts to lift her. Shifting his feet on the riverbed, he tried again. Some unconscious faintness of spirit must be hindering his strength. It might be sad work but it was surely not beyond him to carry a woman's corpse. Pregnant she might be and a strong, hale woman besides, but this heaviness was excessive, unnatural even.

'I cannot raise her,' he called at last.

After a fractional pause, he heard Caelica call back.

'C-could there – could it be that something is holding her limbs beneath the water?'

'Perhaps.' Reluctantly, he began to feel around the submerged part of the body. It was unseemly, this probing; he had no business to touch the woman's legs and belly, dead though she be. Just when he was about to stop, his affronted fingers made contact with something burdensome and solid that hung from her hips under the water.

Almost insensible with cold, he closed his hand upon a heavy cloth pouch. It was tied, like an extemporised pocket, to a band around her thick waist. Was it, he wondered, full of coin? A heavy purse of sovereigns, perhaps? Or a hoard of jewellery? Whatever it was, it explained her weightiness. But what folly, to cross the torrent carrying such a load.

His fingers were too numb to untie belt and bundle here. Nerving himself, he at last positioned her clumsily against his shoulder and clasped her trunk to his chest. Unsteady against the river's buffeting, he bore her with cautious steps to the shallows and set her down on the bank.

At that moment, the thin moon broke through the clouds to show a strip of linen, bone-white over the red dress, knotted around her waist. From it there hung no fewer than four heavy pouches, each secured in a square of cloth. Kneeling at the woman's side, Thomas rubbed his hands together to restore a little feeling, picked one of them up and – although he knew the coroner would condemn his meddling – began to slacken the knot at its neck. Whatever its content was, it had none of the smoothness of coin. It beggared belief to think anyone might take the chance of carrying jewels in so many makeshift pockets on foot across a rough river. Working the cloth loose under Miss Hearne's silent gaze, at last he pulled it open to find inside not gems and gewgaws, but common stones – shards of slate.

Abrupt, he dropped the pouch, stood up and took a step away from the body. The thought of the woman gathering the pebbles into squares of cloth, tying them round her body, then seeking out a secluded place under one the arches of the bridge and plunging – the very idea was shocking, a wild, groundless fantasy. He could not know what had happened.

'It's Hannah.' The quiet words cut into his conjectures.

'Who?'

'Hannah Hallet is her name. She was afraid her mother and father'd turn her out when they saw she was with child.'

'Miss Hearne,' the certainty in her voice surprised him. 'How do you know this?'

She gave no answer, but turned away, bent forward and retched. Dismayed, he moved towards her. She only shook her head, hunched her shoulders and retched once more. When at last she faced him, she was quite grey and her speech fractured on every word.

'She...she came this morning. T-to the house. She spoke with my mother.'

She said no more. About to prompt her, he stopped himself. It was unkind to make her speak when speech caused her such trouble. She would take up the story in her time. With all the tenderness he could bring to bear, he rested Hannah's body over his shoulder. Mute, Caelica picked up the stony pouches. Together, they crossed the bridge.

'She said –' climbing the track that led up to the parsonage Caelica found speech once more. 'She said she and Ki- Kit –' For a few paces, she left the words hanging.

'She made out she and Kit were lovers,' she said at last, as they rounded the low mound on which her father's church stood surrounded by tombs. The clouds were dispersing, and the moonlight grew. The angular roof of the parsonage stood out against the wedge of starry sky between the steep slopes of the hills. Thomas realised that what she was saying embarrassed her, but somehow she must have rallied.

'At least, she did not say quite that ex-exactly,' Caelica continued, 'b-but she came to ask where my brother now lodged and to say she needed to see him. M-mother – w-well –' Again her voice tailed away.

Thomas thought he understood. In the eight weeks since her son had been arrested on a count of forgery, Mrs Hearne had sunk into a melancholy bordering upon madness. She hardly ate, hardly spoke and had taken to wearing mourning. The whole parish knew how the rector feared for his wife's health. Had he not called upon his son's accuser earlier that week in the hope of persuading him to drop the charge?

Bearing the stones at his side, Caelica – the gentle, unassuming pupil of whom Thomas was fonder than he cared to admit – took up her tale once more.

'Hannah asked mother for – for some money to live on, and for something of my brother's. As a keepsake – until he should come back to her. I – I offered to fetch one of his books, but mother said no.'

That was credible enough. When Mrs Hearne cared to break her stony silences, her words were often harsh.

'Does your father know of this?' he asked.

She nodded. 'Do you suppose,' she asked, stopping short and facing him, 'do you suppose that she – she k-killed herself by t-tying those stones around her body?'

'We cannot know for certain.' He did not want to believe it.

Trying to quell the misgivings her question prompted, it struck him that if the allegation concerning her brother was true, then the child – the unborn child in the dead woman's womb – was the Hearnes' kin. Although her father was an aloof man who watched over his parishioners with scornful eyes even he, surely, would not condemn his grandchild to the shame of a self-murderer's roadside grave? But would he countenance burying mother and infant in the sanctified ground by the church, where every day their resting place would remind him of the slur that hung upon his son? Even if it were untrue it made a foul tale and once it spread, the outlook for the Hearnes would be bleak indeed.

'Bu –'

His thoughts were running too fast for him to heed her struggling attempt to speak.

'Listen,' grave, he faced her. 'I understand that a young woman's death and the death of her infant is a time for sorrow.' He paused, disliking his prim speech. Though he burnt with compassion for her, it would not do to show it. He must not unbend, must keep his proper distance, even in the face of her distress. 'Since chance has led you to find her body, Miss Hearne, you have, perforce, obligations to fulfil.

'Not only will you have to help prepare her corpse for burial but also, in all likelihood, you shall find yourself having to explain to your brother's accuser the circumstances and condition in which you found her.'

That was just the dry language her father might use. He had not known he could sound so pompous, yet perhaps the heavy warning was not ill-placed. From the few previous encounters he had had with Bevan the coroner, he foresaw that any interrogation she had to face from him would be ruthless, if not downright harsh.

'Your evidence may be material to his conclusions as to the cause of Hannah's death. Testifying to the inquest may be distasteful to you.' Her expression told him it would be worse than distasteful; it would be repugnant. 'But by law and morality you have been thrust into a relationship with this dead woman that you cannot sever.'

He was, he noticed, turning prim, yet she met his eye straight, as though his sternness heartened her.

'Sh-shall you tell Mr B-Bevan what I have told you?' she asked.

For a moment, he was silent. He could hardly lie upon oath, but he had no wish to turn tale-bearer.

'I was not present when this woman called at the parsonage, and therefore nothing that I might presume to say about her visit would be direct evidence,' he reflected. 'Of course if he calls me as a witness,' he added, thinking as he spoke, 'I shall have to give true, full answers to his questions.'

'I would not expect you to deceive him,' she replied. Her earnestness and the sudden defiance of her speaking smote him to the core. It must have cost her dear to watch while he retrieved the weighted corpse from its watery perch and then accompany him upon this joyless journey. Here he was, playing the tyrant pedagogue, yet he had been glad of her presence at his side. He was always glad of her company.

They had reached the parsonage and the light of many candles shone from its windows. No one had yet drawn the shutters and he could see figures moving inside. He looked at Caelica, yearning to make amends, but not knowing how to begin.

'Miss Hearne –' he faltered.

'What is it, Mr Russell?'

But Thomas could not find the words he wanted.

'I think your father has returned,' he said.

Chapter Two

Candle in hand, her father opened the door, and at once paused in visible surprise at the sight of his pupil bearing a dead woman on his back, and his daughter half carrying, half dragging four heavy bundles. Without saying anything, Thomas adjusted his burden so that Mr Hearne might see the woman's face. In silence, the two men looked at one another.

'There is,' said Mr Hearne at last, 'a legal requirement that a dead body be left where it has come to light until the coroner has inspected it. Now I shall have to summon Bevan here, to my house. He will complain about the irregularity no doubt, and everything else besides, for that is his way. Let us hope he does not allow his grievance against my son to colour his conduct of the inquest.'

Shaking his head, he told Caelica to leave the stony bundles by the door and get his prayer book.

It was clear he did not want to arouse the servants' curiosity. He went through to the kitchen and she could hear him apologising to Anstice and Robert for the disturbance. Then he returned carrying two of the settles that usually stood at the fireside. Robert's hoarse voice enquired from behind the kitchen door whether the master needed any help, but her father declined, taking the settles himself to a small, stone-floored chamber that opened off the hallway.

Crossing to the dining room he took one of the long wooden shutters off its hinges and placed it lengthways across the settles so that Thomas could at last put the body down. It must have been a weighty load and ridding himself of it a relief, yet he rested it upon the makeshift bier with the utmost gentleness. Abashed by his care, Caelica retrieved the stone-filled cloths and laid them quietly on the floor at the dead woman's side before fetching a blanket with which to cover her. Only when her father was satisfied that they had quite hidden both her face and her distinctive red dress and then arranged her on her side so as to conceal her pregnancy did he summon the servants to join in prayers committing the unfortunate creature's soul to God. Of the unborn child he said nothing, although Caelica noticed him pause more than once in the middle of a phrase, as though he wanted to change its wording, but then thought better and continued.

The sound of his steady, unimpassioned voice held her calm, but although she knew that he despised tearful women, after their final *amen* she began, quietly, to cry. Frowning, he watched her try to hold back the tears. She knew he was hoping that she would succeed in gaining possession of herself. But it was vain, and he must have decided that her grief should run its course, for soon he put a stiff arm round her shoulders and remarked that she was cold and no doubt hungry. Anstice would surely find her something to eat and set stones by the kitchen fire ready to warm her bed, he added, glancing at the housekeeper who nodded at his words. Anything more Caelica might want to say could, he was certain, wait until the morrow; kissing her on the forehead, he turned to ask Thomas what he knew about the hapless woman's family.

John Bevan, coroner for Carterford, Brynwardine and Pwllfechan, came grumbling to the parsonage next morning. Even while he mumbled his terse greeting, his small hands clenched and unclenched as though he could not hide his resentment of the way in which his legal duties interrupted the day's hunting; rank peevishness glittered in his small eyes and he kept smiting his riding crop against his boots in mounting impatience.

Affecting not to notice his prickliness, Caelica, Hearne and Thomas followed him into the stone-floored chamber to inspect the body. She had no wish to accompany them, but since the law in the ferrety-faced person of Mr Bevan required her presence, she was ready to submit to its obligations with good grace.

Bevan, it was clear, did not intend to spare her blushes. Striding up to Hannah's body, he pulled down the blanket, thrust her onto her back and then, brisk and peremptory, rent open her dress and shift to show her bare breasts and swollen stomach. Caelica's face, neck, back broke out in a sweat of shame, but Bevan only narrowed his eyes to scan Hannah's pallid flesh while from the high window beams of mild sunlight played over her face and torn hair.

At last the coroner looked round.

'No mark on her body other than light grazes,' he said. 'Five – maybe six months with child,' he went on, his consonants ferocious, 'and see here, no marriage ring on her finger.'

His severity goaded Caelica's wits. Was there any legal necessity for him to know about the allegations concerning the infant's paternity? Kit already stood deep in trouble, and her mother took it very ill. The scandal of his fathering a child upon a girl from the town could destroy her utterly. It threatened them all, for the bond linking priest and people in Llanmichael was weak and brittle. Her father loved to make himself stern with his parishioners; it would take little to make their shaky, reluctant respect for him splinter to nothing.

Bevan prodded at Hannah's white abdomen with a stubby, grubby forefinger, musing aloud over how he should direct the inquest jury.

'Self-murder. That is what it is, I am certain,' he remarked, distaste plain in his hissing sibilants. 'Think of the evils it will spawn if we do not condemn it straight out, Mr Hearne. By my conjecture, this young woman sought to elicit compassion. Perhaps she thought that by procuring her own death, she might make people pity her plight instead of reviling her sinfulness.'

'I take it,' Caelica's father asked slowly, 'there can be no question of a homicide?'

Unfriendly eyes contracting further, the ferret deliberately surveyed the pouches of stones. Thomas, who had been silent till now, explained how he had discovered them tied around her belly. Bevan gave a knowing sniff.

'Self-murder it is, I tell you. She bears no mark of strangulation, look you, nor yet wounding by weapon. And see that white at her mouth?' He gestured with a nod, 'it suggests drowning. Oh, I can tell the tale of her actions clear as day. It is not homicide, Mr Hearne. No, she tied the stones round her body and drowned herself, the jade,' and with a contemptuous tug at the blanket he covered her nakedness once more.

'When her father and mother come before my inquest – see here, if we hold the inquest tomorrow the body will not have decayed overmuch; your parsonage'll serve for it as well any other place. Now what was I saying? Aye, when her father and mother speak, they'll say she'd been dreamy and maundery for days. I know it, for I have seen these cases before. And maybe she will have left a note making out that the world was too hard on her. But if the world is hard on evildoers, is that not cause for the righteous to rejoice, eh, Mr Hearne?'

He gave a rough laugh and a drip of moisture which had formed at the point of his nose fell onto the exposed skin of Hannah's right shoulder. He took no notice, other than to grimace and wipe his nose with the back of his hand. He was an educated man and a lawyer, yet he was content to treat Hannah's body as though it were carrion. Thomas, who had insisted that they accord her respect in death, now asked quietly if he should let her parents know about the inquest. He had, he explained, called on them the previous night to inform them of the body's discovery.

'Who are her people, anyway?' the coroner snapped.

'They are new to the district,' said Caelica's father. 'Mr Russell here tells me they live in one of the caves beyond the town.'

'You parsons always know everyone and their business,' said Bevan with another dismissive sniff, adding that yes indeed, someone must call on them to ensure that they attend.

In a pacific voice, her father enquired whether he too would be required.

''Tis your daughter you say found the corpse,' returned Bevan, bending to tighten a buckle on his boot. 'She's the one whose evidence counts for most. What is your name, young woman?' he asked without looking at her.

'She is Caelica,' answered her father before she could speak, and pushed her squarely before the testy coroner's sight.

'Chay-? An outlandish name, to be sure,' he observed, acknowledging her curtsey with a jerk of his head.

'It springs from my sentimental fancy,' her father explained, 'and it means "heavenly".'

'Well, you are the first finder,' Bevan said, ignoring the rector's affability. 'Therefore the jury must hear your testimony in full. It is the law's requirement.'

Bevan's boorishness was not so much contemptible as frightening. How she would give her evidence to the inquest jury with his hot eyes watching her and his voice rasping out rapid questions, she could not imagine. She tried to smile as a token of good will, but when the coroner only stared back, his grim mouth unyielding, the smile died on her lips. At least he had made no mention of the man who had fathered the child, the hapless child who now lay dead in its dead mother's womb, the child she believed to be her own kin.

For the most part the inquest took precisely the direction Bevan had foreseen. The dead woman's parents, a wizened, unhappy couple, surveyed the tall young woman who lay lifeless upon the shutter and after a long silence confirmed almost inaudibly that she was indeed their daughter, Hannah Mary Hallet. A jury of local landowning men stared upon Hannah's remains under Bevan's irritable guidance to satisfy themselves that her body did not bear any sign of assault, to mark the coroner's instruction that white marks around the mouth betokened death by drowning and to inspect the heavy stone bundles beside the bier. Then they shuffled into the sombre dining room and seated themselves around the table while Bevan, impatient at the table's head, set about questioning his witnesses and noting down everything they said in a great leather-bound book.

No, haggard Mrs Hallet asserted, she had not known her daughter was with child – had not known she had a lover even.

Hannah had left no note; she could not write much, except her name. But she was a good girl, always mindful of her parents and a great worker who'd been earning a steady wage. True, there had been some weeks last summer when she'd been out every evening, but why not, in the long light evenings? As to her big belly, while it might show plain in that gaudy red dress there hadn't been anything amiss to see when she was in her working duds, and that was the truth of it.

John Hallet, a wiry man with dark hair turned grey, echoed everything his wife had said without adding anything new.

'We reach,' Bevan announced, 'the circumstances in which the corpse was discovered. Where is the first finder?'

'I-it i-is I.' Rigid in every nerve, Caelica went to the opposite end of the table, and gripped its surface so hard that her knucklebones glared white. On either hand the jurors' keen eyes in their fleshy faces pierced her like pins. Bevan slouched facing her, his mouth sullen, elbows on the table and his aggressive chin in his hands.

Once she had taken the oath, his questions fell sharp as hail. Where? When? What had she been about at the time? Her tongue rebelled and immobilised itself. She faced him, feeling herself make mouths like an idiot, all the while stark dumb.

Only at her father's soft questioning did her speech begin to unlock.

'What can you tell us, daughter?' he prompted.

'I – I w-was coming home,' now, despite Bevan's irritable intake of breath at the interruption, she could begin her tale. 'It w-was g-gone f-four – p-perhaps five in the afternoon a-and nigh dark. I saw it – her – the b-body, that is – fr-from the bridge. I st-stood a-at about the m-middle arch l-looking downstream.'

The jurors put on benign smiles, as though to encourage a timid child.

'Sh-she was a-against a ro- rock in the river w-with no more th-than her head, h-her shoulders and – and upper body c-clear of the water.'

15

Instead of staring dead ahead into her eyes, Bevan had glanced down to make a note in his ledger. Perhaps she could be a little easier. Soon her testimony should be done.

'I thought her hurt perhaps or faint. I – I b-believed she m-might yet live.'

But the thought of Hannah with her fair hair in her red dress gathering the stones and tying them in the lengths of cloth was altogether too shocking for her to strain into speech.

'And what else did you think, Miss Hearne?' Now the coroner was glaring straight at her again, probing and jabbing with the needlepoint of his malice.

'I –I –' she stopped. 'I –c-ca –' again she stopped.

'My daughter has been inclined to stammer from infancy.' Her father rose. 'I once thought I had cured the affliction by making her read poetry aloud through a mouthful of pebbles,' he gazed from Bevan down the rows of jurors, 'but as you gentlemen can see, the remedy has proved imperfect. While her fluency is immeasurably greater than it used to be, her speech still falters at times of excitement. You will have to be patient with her, and let her take her time.'

There was a murmur of understanding from the stolid jurymen, who looked as though they were in no hurry. But Bevan was incredulous.

'She is a grown woman, is she not? She must understand the law's requirements. Come Miss Hearne –' he raised his voice. 'What else did you think when you saw the young woman against the rock in the water?'

In truth, she had thought of her mother. When Hannah had called at the parsonage her mother had been full of indignation, her cold anger jarring against Hannah's rough sobs. 'Insufferable presumption,' her mother had pronounced as Anstice had escorted Hannah out of the house. Then, through the open window came Hannah's breathy voice from the garden: 'Where d'you leave your charity, mum? Up some tinker's arse?'

But no misgivings clouded Caelica's mother's conviction that she had done what was right.

'I shall defend Christopher to the last,' she told her husband in high satisfaction over their midday meal. 'Others may traduce him and drag his fair name into the mire...'

'My dear, the case against him is compelling.' Her father had spoken mildly, but her mother flared as though at an insult.

'How can you be so disloyal and unloving as to suggest that our son should have to answer in court for a trifling prank committed in high spirits?'

'Could I not see his faults for what they are, dearest, my love for him would be a poor thing indeed. And it was uncharitable of you to send this poor woman away.'

Despite the censure, he had risen and gone to her side, making as if to put his arm around her in pardon, but she had shaken it off. Caelica had been shocked. Her mother might be distraught, but it was gall to see her reject the forgiving embrace. Wishing she were elsewhere, Caelica had closed her eyes, wanting to banish the sight from her mind. Her father, whom she loved with all her heart, must have understood the ugly confusion in which she found herself because he had asked her to take a letter down the valley to the parson at St Cadog.

She could hardly tell Mr Bevan these things, especially here in this same dining room, now full of honest townsmen in their musty-smelling best clothes, leaning forward to listen. She'd known them all her life – pasty-faced Mr Gleeson the carrier, Tobias Greene from the Golden Lion Inn, his hands clasped over his striped waistcoat, her father's enemy Emrys Parry the Dissenter who gave her a quick, warm smile.

Encouraged by his unexpected kindness, she tried again to speak.

'I-I th-th –' she started, but straight away her tongue hardened, rigid as metal. She shook her head, unable to shift the weight of words.

'Miss Hearne, you have informed the inquest that you saw the body in the river lying against a rock.' The coroner's eyes stabbed her. 'See here, it is the law's requirement that you testify. Compose yourself, mistress. Say what precisely you did upon finding the body.'

'F-fet –'

'Yes?'

'F-fetched M-M –'

'Miss Hearne, I would remind you that my jurors and I have many demands upon our time. I cannot gentle you through the proceedings like a groom with a filly-foal.'

'M-mr R-ru – Russell.'

'And who is Mr R-R-russell, pray?'

'Come, Bevan - do not mock her affliction.' *O father, at last.* 'You must see that the stammer precludes her from testifying. She has told you plain enough that she fetched Thomas Russell. As you know, he assists me upon my parochial works and reads with me. He also tutors her. He lodges in Gleeson's house by the bridge so he would have been nearby. He is here, if you wish to hear his testimony.'

But once Thomas admitted under oath that he had removed the body from its resting place in the stream, rather than ask further questions, Bevan only reprimanded him.

'Even though the town uses the river for its water supply, Mr Russell, yet the law is still the law and it states that any dead body be left where it is found until the coroner's arrival. By moving the corpse, you have acted most presumptuously. You may stand down, sir.'

It remained for the jury to determine Hannah Hallet's state of mind at the hour of her death. When Bevan stalked out of the dining room, Hearne went after him, plainly eager for talk, and Caelica followed.

'Whatever decision the jury may reach,' he said, crossing the hallway at the coroner's side, 'it is my earnest wish that you release her body for Christian burial.' The significance of the request burst out upon Caelica, like the earth opening under her feet. *Burial, perhaps, of our own close kin.*

18

He must have caught the sound of her indrawn breath, for 'Come daughter,' he invited, motioning her to accompany them, 'you shall join us. Mr Bevan and I will be in the library.'

She had no wish to comply, but he had saved her from Bevan's mockery so she followed the gentlemen upstairs to the austere library her father used for discussion of subjects that he deemed too grave for the parlour. Books piled high on the shelves covered the best part of three walls, on one of which a stark-faced clock spoke of time's inexorable passage, hastening them all to the grave. Sitting down by one of the west-facing windows, she thought she should be inconspicuous, although Bevan half-turned to give her a brief, ill-tempered glance over his shoulder.

'I would have the dead woman buried in the churchyard.' Her father seated himself deliberately at the massive oak table as he made this extraordinary request. She knew that if the jury should decide that Hannah was clear-witted at the time of her death, then Bevan would have a legal duty to order her burial in unhallowed ground and he could be very hot to uphold his legal duties when he chose. Yet her father would argue hard for the child – the child to whom his wife had given no thought when she had turned Hannah away, and to whom he sought to show what belated kindness he could.

'Even if your jurors should hold her death to be self-murder and make out that she was sound in her mind when she died,' he said, 'yet I will not gratify the primitive backward-looking cast of mind by denying her a place within my churchyard.'

To hear him made the sweat prickle on her brow, as though she were feverish. Bevan had now sat down on a low chair across the table from her father. Looking sideways from her window seat Caelica saw how he shifted his weight back and forth, his small mouth puckering. He did not, it was clear, care for the request.

'You are not a local man, Mr Hearne, are you?' he asked after a restless pause.

'Not by birth, perhaps, bu–'

'Well then, you will not know the weight of feeling people hereabout attribute to right and proper justice, see,' and he parted his lips in a brief grim smile that showed his brown teeth. 'I know you to be a faithful minister of the Church, a man of book-learning and dignity.' He was a guileful opponent, knowing so well when to flatter. 'And you are conscientious, highly conscientious, in your pastoral care,' he allowed. 'These things I respect, for all that you are a *saesneg*.' Her father nodded politely to show his understanding of the Welsh word for an Englishman. 'But see here,' the coroner went on, 'by your own admission you have not lived here all your life – you do not know what thinking sways our hearts.'

'Really, sir,' and the argument came in the mildest manner, 'in such a case as this, determination on what is best is a matter in which the law of God, not the customs of men, provides the surest guide. Our Lord enjoins us to show mercy...'

'The law will not have it and the people will not like it, Mr Hearne.' Bevan's obdurate voice cut like an axe blade cleaving a tree trunk. 'Unless my jury find that she had taken all leave of her senses when she drowned herself, you will have no business to bury her among the virtuous people of your parish. It is my conviction,' he rasped, 'that that evil cat of a Jezebel died in her sin and took her child, the fruit of her wickedness, with her.'

'Pray have a thought for my daughter's presence,' her father interposed, at which Bevan glared at Caelica as though he wished she might melt, then scowled down at his boots. Bending her head low, Caelica's mind's eye saw the fair-haired labouring girl in her red dress.

Her child. Perhaps my nephew or my niece. If so, then almost my child too. And, O father, your grandson or grand-daughter.

'The people will not like it, Mr Hearne,' repeated Bevan, his eyebrows meeting low across the bridge of his ill-tempered nose.

'Surely you would not have it said that you were unmerciful,' her father urged. 'The girl's parents would not wish to see their daughter bundled under-ground at the junction of the roads after dark and hear foolish folk babble about her sad ghost blighting the country round. Not when she might take her last rest under the wild cherry boughs by my churchyard wall. Have pity, I beseech you.'

He could be very winning in his speech but Caelica was not sure that he would win round Bevan. Stubborn as a schoolboy, the coroner had picked up his riding whip and started to twist the lash around one of his fingers so tight that the yellowish flesh darkened and went livid.

'O, now Mr Hearne,' he was saying, 'it is my place to enforce the requirements of the law. That is what the people want, see. The law makes no mention of mercy.'

'Come, Bevan, we all hope for God's mercy when He sifts our souls in judgement.' Her father paused. Then before Bevan could answer, he straightened in his chair.

'I had hoped you'd heed courteous persuasion, sir,' he continued abruptly. 'Since you show no wish to take a forbearing, compassionate view of the matter, let me put my request in a new light.' His manner was no longer emollient, but bleak and stern.

'You have conducted this inquest in great haste,' he said. 'What's more, you made a mock of my daughter as she strove to give her testimony, though I urged you to show patience. These things give me cause enough to go to the Justices and ask whether I should consider framing a complaint against you. If you will agree to what I ask, I shall say nothing about your curt manner with the witnesses nor your over-zealous direction of the jury. Otherwise – well. Think about it, sir.'

Bevan made no immediate reply. From her place at the window, Caelica watched as his face flushed dark red and a tide of unease spread across his mottled features. From the twisting of his petulant mouth, it was evident that her father's change of tone had surprised him. Some lingering respect for the authority that a clergyman might wield with the Justices must have made Bevan consider the wisdom of his stance, for at last, with yet another ugly sniff and a grimace of distaste for the whole business, he gave way.

'Have it as you wish.' He spat out his agreement like a sour plum.

For answer, Caelica's father expressed his heartfelt thanks for Bevan's well-judged discretion and magnanimity.

'This deed will win you no friends in Llanmichael, Hearne,' warned Bevan, rubbing at the brass mounting of his riding whip with a restless hand.

'As to that, I shall have to bear whatever consequences arise,' Caelica's father replied, just as shouts from downstairs indicated that the jurors had reached their verdict.

When the jury's spokesman announced that they found the woman had died *felonia de se* without there being anything to suggest that she was of less than sound mind at the time of her drowning, Bevan gave a bleak nod.

'I thank you for reaching your decision so fast. She procured death at her own hand while sane in her wits. It was grievous sin indeed, and yet your rector Mr Hearne asks me to drop the usual order that the body be buried in unhallowed ground. Now I do not care to wrangle with parsons, be they never so capricious in their whims. If you do not like his request, you must address yourselves to him – not to me. I have reminded him of the law's ordinance and told him where he offends against it – see here, I have done my duty. The inquest is concluded, gentlemen, and I thank you for the services you have given. *Diolch yn fawr.*

'Now, hounds were to meet this morning at Carterford Cross, and they may be drawing the coverts as I speak. So now, good day to you all,' and Bevan took his leave.

'At least,' pronounced her father when the last juror had gone, 'we may accord compassion to mother and child in death. For this small grace, daughter, we must be thankful.'

Touching his hand, she found it hot and tremulous, and knew that the worries of the last hour had wracked him through and through.

To avoid stirring disturbance, they buried Hannah Hallet at daybreak when few people were around. While her father read the burial service, Caelica stood near Thomas and the two of them joined him in throwing clods of cold earth into the grave where Hannah's body was to lie. Mr and Mrs Hallet kept their distance at the edge of the churchyard, as though afraid. The cloud hung so low, it might have been resting on the very turf. In her light cloak Caelica soon began to cough and saw her tutor turn towards her, concern in his thin face. She ignored him and gave all her attention to following the stark black print of her prayer book.

Chapter Three

After Hannah Hallet's burial, winter grew more vigorous. Wind rose and rain fell in honest showers dispersing the damp that had hung in the air through autumn. Advent passed. Christmas came and went. Caelica knew her father had tried to show the Hallet parents some kindness and had once bidden them to the parsonage to talk and pray with him. She had let them in, the stick-like woman with her gruff, dark husband at her side, but she never saw them in the house again. Perhaps they found the scholarly atmosphere of her father's library, its shelves piled high with books and the clock sternly marking each second, too severe for comfort.

Her father said little about his plans, but one grey January day he told Caelica he was going to visit Christopher in gaol and set off to Hereford. Promising to cheer her mother in his absence, Caelica had waved to him and watched as his mare tossed her head and forged up the steep path behind the parsonage that joined the drove road. Returning to the house, Caelica thought of her brother, five years older than she and never much of a companion. How would he take the news of Hannah's death?

Hearne reached Hereford in the evening and put up overnight in an inn near the Cathedral. The following morning, in exchange for a small sum a co-operative turnkey took him along the dingy passages to seek out his son.

Christopher was not in a cell, but a wide, dark room. It had a low ceiling and, apart from a small fire at one end, the only light to enter the room came from a grimy window high in one wall. The air of the place was stale. Four men, Christopher among them, sat round a rickety table by the hearth playing whist.

'He can stay here because he hasn't been charged on indictment yet,' the turnkey explained in a low voice to Hearne's unasked question. Thanking him and handing over a coin with the request that he wait outside, Hearne turned his attention to the card players. Evidently the game had reached a critical stage, for not one of them had lifted his eyes as the door opened and closed.

Watching, Hearne realised how little he knew about prison hierarchy. While it was still uncertain whether Christopher would have to stand trial, he must be permitted more privileges than he would if he were serving a sentence. In time – it could be as much as a year hence – twenty-three landowners, all friends and acquaintances of Bevan like as not, would assemble for a day's justice in their grand jury room by the courthouse. Bevan would tell his tale against Christopher with the witness Allardyce on hand to flesh it out. Once the jurors had considered, they would send the prisoner word of their decision on a scrap of paper bearing either the term *ignoramus* – 'we do not know' – which meant Christopher would be free, or the phrase *billa vera* signifying their belief that there was a true count against him for which he should answer to a judge and jury. In Hearne's mind, there was little question but that his son should end up in the Assize court. And then, he reflected wryly, Christopher might face a fine, or perhaps prolonged imprisonment; transportation, maybe, or even, since men took a heavy view of forgery, the noose. One way or another, conviction would put an end to the comfort of being able to warm himself by a fire while gambling.

Table thumping and exclamations signalled the game's end. Christopher must have started out in funds, for now he reached into his breeches pocket to hand over a fistful of coins to the balding man who had been facing him across the table. Turning, he caught sight of his father.

'What brings you here?' he asked, plainly surprised and in a wary voice.

25

'Good day to you, Christopher,' said Hearne, looking his son up and down. 'I am glad to see you looking so well.' It was true. The boy did look well. Despite the scant light and fetid air, Christopher's bearing was vigorous as ever. He wore a fine ruffled shirt and tossed back his hair as though he wanted to show how much he was at ease in this place, with these companions.

'What brings you here?' he repeated. Exchanging glances, the three other whist players retired into the room's far corner.

Aware of having intruded where he wasn't wanted, Hearne found himself momentarily at a loss. Fatherly affection had never found ready expression with him, and he could not easily subdue his distaste for Christopher's swagger. Unwilling to touch his son on the arm with those three fog-thugs watching or call him 'dear boy' in his old way, he baulked at the prospect of opening a disagreeable conversation.

'Be seated, father,' Christopher invited at last, indicating a chair. 'Now – why have you come here?'

'First,' Hearne prevaricated as they both sat down, 'I must tell you that your mother misses you much. Have you any word for her? It'll cheer her spirits much.'

Christopher gave a short laugh. 'Must my mother have me dance to her every caprice, if she is to know any happiness?'

'It is but natural fondness...'

'Natural spleen, more like.'

A biting snub sprang to Hearne's tongue, but he somehow kept himself from voicing it. Instead he took up the chief business of his visit. 'There is a most pressing matter...'

Christopher raised his delicate eyebrows and sought to dislodge some morsel from his teeth with a forefinger. 'Did you ever know a young woman called Hannah Hallet?'

Hearne thought he saw his son start.

'I think not,' Christopher answered, suave and sure.

'I beseech you to give my question your most thorough consideration,' Hearne insisted. Christopher only picked at his teeth again. 'Did you – might you – have any acquaintance with a woman of that name?'

26

'Father, you goad me.'

'I must have your certain answer.'

'Why I should put up with your quizzing when you come here unbidden?'

'Kit,' using the short, affectionate name somehow made Hearne lean forward and touch his son's hand. 'Are you sure you never heard of her?

Christopher sighed. 'I suppose I may have run across some such chit,' he said in a bored voice. 'I enjoy the company of adventurers and where bold men gather, women flock too. Not the chilly sort of woman who keeps to her books like my sister, but women who welcome pleasure where they find it.'

'Might Hannah Hallet have welcomed pleasure where she found it?' Hearne persisted.

'Father, I cannot swear to know anything of this Hannah Hallet with whom you keep taxing me.' Christopher ran his hands through his hair in stagey exasperation. 'Believe me, if I knew her, as you aver, and she and I were fond, let us suppose, and perhaps lay together – why, then I'm certain she liked it well enough at the time.'

Rising, he strode across the room to where a heap of garments lay upon a straw bolster, picked up a coat, put it on and turned deliberately to the other men.

'Stay!' Hearing the pulpit voice the card players looked round at Hearne, open-mouthed. Addressing the tallest, he took a softer tone.

'I crave your indulgence, gentlemen. Pray let me keep my son from you a little longer.'

'Listen, the woman called Hannah Hallet is dead.' He would question his son no further – just tell the story as best he could. 'At the inquest, the jury concluded that she died by her own hand, having freighted herself with pebbles and cast herself into the water beneath Llanmichael Bridge. She was great with child.'

He paused, spreading the palms of his hands wide in question – *do you still deny all knowledge of her?* – and faced his son in silence.

'Well, Father,' at last, Christopher met his gaze, his face full – overflowing, indeed – with filial frankness. 'It pains me to see your wits so exercised by this Hannah Hallet, whomsoever she may have been. That her end was lamentable, I do not deny. But, believe me, of this unfortunate woman I know nothing.'

Hearne looked at him closely. Despite the bridling and glib denials, it was possible that Christopher spoke the truth. If he were in fact lying, he went about it with great guile. Avowing that he had no memory of Hannah Hallet did not rule out the chance of his having come across her at some time, and perhaps remembering her in the future if it suited him.

'Does her death touch you so little?' Hearne demanded.

'It is, as I say, lamentable.'

'Would you call your attempted deception of your employer lamentable?' pursued Hearne. To wring an admission of wrong-doing from this prodigal son, together with a few words of penitence and remorse, would count for much.

But Christopher only flicked his long hair out of his eyes and laughed.

'Oh, to be sure, I bungled most lamentably in the business with Bevan. Why else am I here? Yet,' he continued, unabashed, 'he could well afford to lose the trifling sum for which I touched him. After all, his duties as coroner must earn him many fat fees. Anyway,' hitching his coat up his shoulders, he gave a broad smile, 'I always meant to pay him back in time. Had he not been so much the bear, always growling and snarling, I should have begged him straight out for a loan.'

'There is more about Hannah Hallet,' said Hearne, although he knew by now that the purpose of his visit had miscarried. 'Because the circumstances of her death – hers and her child's – pained me much, I have defied the wishes of my parishioners and the advice of Mr Bevan to give her a Christian burial. She lies in my churchyard.'

There was a little grim satisfaction in seeing his son fall silent at last.

'Will that not cause affront?' Christopher reasserted himself almost immediately. 'And why must you provoke Bevan?'

'It is hardly fitting in you, Christopher, to complain of affront arising from my conduct.' Deliberate, Hearne straightened his stock, severity taut in his fingers. 'There are indeed powerful voices that speak against me,' he admitted. 'In time they may condemn you too.'

'But father...' There was no trace of dissimulation in his wide eyes. 'Why should anyone condemn me because a pregnant girl does away with herself?'

'Is that all you have to say?' But Hearne knew the answer before it came.

'My last word, dear sir. Allbright, Carr,' Christopher summoned his companions. 'My father has done. What about a hand of *picquet*?'

Vacating his chair, Hearne heard them arguing about who should deal the next hand. His contempt for his son was limitless, equalled only by his scorn for his own inability to break through Christopher's bluster and wring some confession from him. The aftertaste of this offensive conversation would, he knew, sour his memory of his son for months to come. But for now, he made his farewell – Christopher barely acknowledged it – and called to the turnkey once more.

The morning after his return, glancing through the window in the parsonage hallway Hearne saw his pupil approaching through the garden with the commentary he had been writing on Philemon under his arm. Plainly, he was expecting to talk about it. Out of sorts after his long ride the previous day, Hearne longed for a morning's leisure.

'Ah, Russell,' he hailed him from the door. 'I see you have brought me your treatise on Philemon. Would you mind if we were to postpone our discussion? I must give some time over to composing a sermon.'

The young man's face fell. Taking no notice, Hearne hastened to explain that he had found a copy of Tertullian belonging to the vicar of Pwllfechan upon the parlour shelves only that morning.

'I had agreed that he should have it back by Michaelmas,' he added. 'But my memory must have slipped and my good friend Aylmer has been too courteous to request its return. Would you, if you please, be so kind as to ride over to Pwllfechan vicarage with it?'

'Indeed, Sir, I shall return it for you,' said Thomas, pocketing the book.

'You may take the mare,' Hearne offered.

From her bedroom, Caelica watched the light breezes stir the leafless branches of the trees in the orchard and faced the empty day. She had been expecting a Latin lesson later that morning, but glancing towards the stabling, she saw her tutor mount the keen bay mare and ride away towards Pwllfechan. Plainly, there was a new plan for the morning. She was sorry, because she enjoyed teasing terse Latin phrases into civil English under Mr Russell's instruction. When she first met him, she had not known what to make of the serious scholar who corrected her errors with such cool precision and rigid detachment. Before long, she found herself liking him. Her parents – well, her mother at any rate – took little notice of what fired her interest. Mr Russell had rare skill in teaching – skill enough to stir her enthusiasm even for a dry discipline like geometry. If he could show her the satisfaction that came from distilling one of Horace's knotty Odes into plain English, or setting forth the exact relation between a small circle and a grand cycloid as they rolled along the same notional line, then it was no wonder that she valued his company. What was more, in her lessons, her stammer almost disappeared. Not that it ever vanished entirely, but at least she got better purchase on the slippery words and managed to make them more submissive.

With time on her hands, she remembered how the Hallets had never returned to the parsonage after their one visit. Would it be fitting for her to renew her father's efforts to befriend them in their distress? Considering, she went down to the parlour where her mother sat, listless and remote, stitching with black thread upon black cloth, her father grave at her side.

'M-might I, with your per-permission, father, c-call upon Mr and Mrs Hallet th-this afternoon?' she asked. At her request, he smiled.

'It is a kind thought, dear daughter. My words, I think, did nothing to lessen their grief. You maybe can bring them some solace.'

As he spoke, his gaze turned again upon her mother. By custom it should be she who went to comfort the mournful, taking with her a cheering gift from her garden or kitchen. A visit from the parson's wife in her silks and satins counted for far more with the parishioners than a call from his daughter who dressed no differently from themselves and who stammered or was silent by turn. Once Caelica's mother would have done what was right, and bidden Robert drive her to visit the bereaved taking them dishes of curds or bloomange. Now she would not stir.

Since it was a dead season in the garden, and Anstice, short-winded and short-tempered, disliked anyone's taking preserves from the stillroom, there was little available to take as a present for Mr and Mrs Hallet. Chancing the old servant's hard words, Caelica filled a basket with apples they had put by in autumn and stored in straw.

She had never visited the caves before. From the parsonage she could just make them out – a dark line of habitation above the woodland and pastures that extended over the lower slopes of the great hills across the river. Beyond the bridge it would be a stiff climb, but the cloud cover was breaking to reveal a thin crack of pallid blue. After the still air of the house in which her mother's sorrows hung so heavy, the prospect of a walk pleased her, even if it had a melancholy destination. Tugging her cloak around her shoulders, she set off towards the town.

As soon as she reached the bridge she found a pack-train crossing from the western side. So she paused while twenty – twenty-five – a total of twenty-seven sweating ponies jogged past her, muzzle to tail, deep panniers of ore set across their withers.

Behind them rode a youth wielding a whip with a long lash. 'Watch where you walk.' He was as brash with her as he was with his beasts. 'This bridge gapes like a beggar's breeches.'

He must be new to the district. Of course you had to tread carefully on Llanmichael Bridge and avoid the places where you could actually see the snarling grey-white water through the stonework beneath your feet, but all the local people knew about the holes in the fabric. It was a wonder the fractured surface gave these heavy-laden packbeasts so little trouble, for their steady pace had never faltered. Once they had gone, she walked across and turned into the town's one street, exchanging greetings and smiling as she went, before heading along the steep track that ran up the hill.

Her father had said that the place was on the left-hand side of the cliff, so once she had reached the high-lying flat ground below the ridge's summit, she stopped to regain her breath and look about her. There, upon the ruddy rockface, were scraps of muslin nailed into the soft sandstone to cover the gaps that served as windows for folk who dwelt in the very flank of the hill. She marked a door of rough planks swinging on its hinges across a jagged opening. It was so low that although she was hardly tall, she could see she would have to stoop to enter.

Cautious, she called out. 'G-good day – is anyone within?'

'Who is that?' A woman's cold voice answered.

'It – It is M-miss Hearne. F-from the parsonage.'

'What brings you here?' The speaker did not show herself.

'I came but – but to bring you a gift of apples, ma'am. A-and to t-talk with you a little. Sh–should you wish it.'

At last, Mrs Hallet opened the door. She was a shrunken and weathered woman, her eyes dull and her mouth a sour curl. She grasped a broom in her left hand, the skin taut across the bones.

'Come in – if you must.'

Crossing the muddy threshold, the damp in the thick air gave Caelica the sense of stepping into a shelter for beasts. It was dark and the mingling smells – trapped smoke, rancid fat and human sweat – made her eyes water and caught at her throat. Although there was a fire in one corner which gave off good heat, it burnt with only a dull glow and no flame.

'You may sit down,' said Mrs Hallet, pointing to a rickety stool beside the hearth. Wiping her eyes as she sat down, Caelica peered into the murk. Mrs Hallet must have adapted to her twilit existence, for there was a bunch of grasses thrust like a posy into a pot on the table.

'What was it that you came to say?' The hard tone reminded Caelica she was an uninvited guest. She might be sitting down, but Mrs Hallet stayed standing, her eyes slits and her mouth straight.

'Only – only th-that I was sorry. Ab-about Hannah. And to bring you f-fruit.' Her hands shook as she held out her basket of apples. The gift, this show of parsonage bounty, felt wrong. She wished she had not brought it.

'You're sorry, Miss Hearne?' As she spoke, a chill, faint light lustre kindled in the extreme depths of Mrs Hallet's eyes. She might be old and thin, but she looked as though she had all the strength and elemental endurance of the hillside gorse. Her voice grew rougher.

'Sorry, you say,' she repeated.

'Most tr-truly s-sorry, ma'am.'

Mrs Hallet said nothing.

'Y-you kn-know it was my father who said that Hannah should be buried in the churchyard?' Caelica wanted this silent woman at least to know how her father had argued with Bevan about it. 'Th-the coroner sought to refuse her any place in holy ground.'

Mrs Hallet only sniffed. 'What does it matter where she lies? I'll never see her again.'

Caelica saw she was aggravating the pain she meant to salve. She should have been wiser than to think Mrs Hallet would care about the efforts they had made on her daughter's account.

'Ma'am,' once more she tried to find words with which to lighten the desolate mother's grief. 'In your Hannah's d-death I too have l-lost – felt the l-loss of – of a woman b-but l-little

33

older than myself.' The phrase *perhaps a niece or nephew besides* almost reached her tongue, but she thrust it back.

Mrs Hallet rounded on her. 'You think it counts for much that you should mark the death of a girl the same age as you? Call to mind, Miss Hearne. I have lost a daughter – a true, quick-hearted girl I'd brought to birth and reared, only for some callous man to have his way with her then cast her aside.'

Christopher? My brother?

'And you think your apples can take away my sore?' Mrs Hallet demanded. 'Or the parson's prayers make good her loss? Or that I should mind your sighings for a babe who never saw the daylight?'

She fell quiet, her face locked in contempt. Cowed, Caelica rose and took up her basket.

'I don't want your charity,' said Mrs Hallet watching her. 'I can feed myself and my own well enough without the leavings from your table. I will have nothing from you. Nor from your father who made John and I listen while he read the Bible, nor from your mother who keeps her distance from poor people like us. Eh, why didn't she come to see me, if anyone had to?'

'She – she is not well.' The statement hardly skirted the truth but Caelica could not begin to describe her mother's sick melancholy.

In answer, Mrs Hallet gave a brief bark of something like laughter. 'Not well? Whatever can ail a woman who has lived in comfort all her life? Get away with you.'

Rising, Caelica pulled her cloak round her shoulders and hastened to the door.

'You can tell the parson,' said Mrs Hallet, hands on her hips at the threshold, 'he shall not see us in his church again. We follow the new worship – Mr Parry's worship – with prayers from the heart instead of out of a book.' Her hand on the door, she shut it with such decision that Caelica found herself impelled outside as though by a force of nature and standing on the hillside once more, under the wide grey sky.

Tears rose shaming to her eyes. To check them, she stared at a horseman far away on the road below – a solitary fair headed man riding towards Llanmichael from Brynwardine. By watching him as though he were immensely important to her, she might just keep her composure. Once, his horse threw up its head as though to resist the curb and she saw him strike it with his whip, so that it flinched and plunged forward. But her tears did not wane and before long she was crying so hard she could see man and beast no more.

Near blind, she retraced her way down the track, feeling the sharp stones through her shoes' thin soles. Wiping her eyes she could just discern the outlines of the town's small grey houses huddling together as though the massive hill frightened them. On her way up, she had had the wind at her back. Now she walked into it, the cold stung her face.

To go on weeping was sheer self-pity. Deciding it was the raw air that made her eyes so watery, she trained her sight upon the distant rider once more. He must have set spurs to his horse's side for he had covered much ground and looked likely, if he held his present course, to pass her before she reached home. It was unusual to see anyone so well-mounted in these parts. Even from this distance, she could tell that his dark grey steed moved with more power and grace than the plodding cobs and ponies on which the farmers went about their business, their wives often perched pillion behind. It was the sort of horse Christopher liked – fast, spirited and highly bred. The fair-haired man must be one of the wealthier landowners of the district, or his son maybe. He must have much confidence in the animal's sure-footedness to spur it over the rutted road at such a pace, flourishing his whip as he went.

Not many people were about when she reached the town, but one or two acquaintances nodded and bade her a good afternoon. She nodded without speaking, not wanting to encourage anyone to draw her into conversation, let alone ask why she should have carried six apples on soft hay in a basket up the mountainside and down again.

Nearing the bridge, she saw the horseman about to cross from the opposite end; the two of them looked likely to pass one another mid-way across. But the grey horse had turned stubborn. Plainly its manners did not match its looks, for it jibbed, half-reared and then wheeled round, refusing to set foot on the stone structure. Caelica watched the young man urging it on with voice, spurs and whip. Some horses, so she had heard, always disliked water; others, people said, wouldn't go near swine.

At last, the young man's goading went beyond the beast's endurance. Snorting and curvetting, it advanced, eyes wide, nostrils dilated and ears pricked taut. Caelica made for one of the cutwaters, so as to be out of the way. Passing her at a thrusting trot, the fair-haired horseman turned in his saddle, smiling as he called his thanks.

She watched till he was out of sight and then glanced down at the river. The miners must have loosed another head of water, for it was even fuller than it had been that morning and reached almost to the bridge's parapet. No wonder the grey horse should be nervous. Still, the stream had often run high in the past, but it always subsided in time. Even so, she could not help thinking of the young packman's warning as she looked down at the holes in the bridge's fabric. Had it really grown so beggarly? There had been gaps in the stonework for as long as she had lived at Llanmichael; yet could there be more of them, and yawning wider than she remembered? Standing above one of the middle piers she saw a fissure, just a narrow crack, run straight across the path from side to side. For a moment, she wondered whether the solid structure was shifting with the tow and pulling away from its foundation.

She checked herself, abashed to own such foolishness. The bridge had stood firm for hundreds of years. It might wear with age, but there was no reason to think it would ever give way.

Chapter Four

Over dinner, Caelica told her parents about Mrs Hallet's assertion that she and her husband would attend the parish church no more. Her father sighed. Before long he pushed his fricassee of mutton to one side, rose from the table and said he would go in search of Thomas who, despite the late hour, had not yet returned from Dr Aylmer. Caelica had the idea that in truth he wanted the chance to think alone in the quiet of night. It was now eight in the evening and had been dark for the best part of four hours.

'Wh-where shall you seek him first?' she asked. Riding in the dark could be dangerous; it would be reassuring to know what direction he planned to take.

'Oh, I shall cross the bridge and then head west to Pwllfechan. I expect he stayed with Aylmer to dine. Aylmer keeps a good table – a very good table indeed. My hungry pupil may be there even now, with never a thought of the time.'

Caelica doubted it. This reasoning did not fit her conscientious tutor at all. Perhaps her father read the doubts in her face.

'Yet it would be well to make certain no mishap has befallen him,' he added. 'And there is the mare to think of. You help your mother with her embroidery, Cherry. Don't fret for me on my cob – I'll not meet with any harm on that fat nag.'

He donned his coat and was about to give her a parting kiss when the sound of hooves and voices reached them from the stable. A few minutes later, Thomas came in rubbing his hands, his face drawn.

'Forgive my late return, sir,' he looked bloodless and white. 'I was almost home by dusk, but Llanmichael Bridge is down and the river's running far too fast for safe fording. I had to turn about and cross at Pwllfechan.'

Although he tried to make light of it, he was plainly exhausted. Caelica pulled a chair up to the fireside so he could warm himself while her father called to Anstice to bring food. They let him eat in peace, and then asked what had happened.

After leaving Dr Aylmer's house, Thomas told them he had taken his homeward journey slowly so as not to push Hearne's young mare. By the time he was a mile or so from Llanmichael, it was dark, and the moon just rising. In its gleam, he saw that where once the bridge's seven pointed arches had straddled the river supporting the road like a ribbon, waters were surging through great jagged gaps in the masonry. One arch stood intact at each end, with a solitary third in the middle of the stream. Of the rest, only broken piers and rubble remained.

The growing moonlight left no room for doubt about the extent of the damage. Even so, he had struggled to believe the evidence of his eyes. The bridge's fabric, he supposed, must have given way under cover of darkness. The men he passed outside Tobias Greene's inn on his way through the town only moments previously had bidden him a civil goodnight, without suggesting anything was amiss. Since there were no signs of agitation – no outcry, no pointing, no worried watchers gathering on the bank – he supposed he must be the first person to know what had happened.

Caelica did not find it surprising. The townsfolk were a chary lot who did not venture far beyond their doors after sunset. Few travellers ever had cause to cross Llanmichael Bridge in the dark.

Yet there must, Thomas was saying, have been quite a splash when the crowns of the arches fell. He could only suppose the rushing river's noise had grown so familiar to their ears that the sound of stone crashing into the current somehow went unnoticed. Or people took it for nothing more than the rumble of boulders shifting in the tow.

Deciding that to raise a general alarm would only cause needless anxiety, Thomas had ridden to his landlord Gleeson who acted fast, summoning neighbours to put up hurdles and wattles as a barrier to stop anyone straying onto the shattered structure overnight. On the morrow, they agreed, they could take more permanent measures. Thomas had then retraced his path, urging the flagging mare all the way back to the bridge at Pwllfechan before riding downstream to Llanmichael parsonage on the east bank.

Caelica's father hoped that that the long ride had not damaged the mare's tendons or her wind. You could not be too careful with horses. Perhaps it would be well to use the cob on future errands, it being a tougher beast. Recollecting himself, he observed that they could hardly expect Thomas to make a third journey round by Pwllfechan – this time on foot – in the one day. He had better stay overnight at the Parsonage.

Caelica looked at Thomas, sitting by the fireside, avid with hunger as he tore apart a piece of yesterday's bread to dip into his broth. Her father could not mean to be ungracious, but she thought he might have thanked his pupil, who had not only returned Dr Aylmer's book, but also taken wise precautions to ensure that no one should come to grief on the broken bridge by night. Rising, she asked them to excuse her and went to lay a fire in the spare bedchamber, and make it welcoming with candles.

'Stop mammocking round with those lights, Miss Caelica and pull that corner tight.' Anstice was making up the bed in the small room, and Caelica had brought candles – good tallow candles that burnt with a steady flame – for the mantel shelf. Having no wish to increase her ill-humour, Caelica obediently tugged the sheet taut around the bolster, ignoring the surly tone. It was understandable that the old servant should turn short-tempered, being disturbed once dinner was done. When, in a hesitant effort to make conversation, she mentioned the bridge, Anstice was unimpressed.

'There'd be none of this pother if your father hadn't given that worthless little blower a Christian burial after she'd done away with herself.'

Caelica stood straight and looked at her. 'An-Anstice – '

'It was too good for the like of her.' Anstice rolled her sleeves up to her elbows, showing forearms mottled with purple.

'B-but for-forgiveness...' Caelica began, trying to think of soft words with which to turn away wrath while she smoothed down the linen.

'Oh, forgiveness...' Anstice pummelled the bolster with hard, red hands. 'That's just church prattle. It may do very well for your father up in his pulpit or that fiddle-faddle pupil of his, but it won't serve for us who make our way by graft and sweat. That Hannah should be lying where four roads meet. With all those paths to confuse her she'd stay still and quiet and harm no one. Now your father's gone and put her in the churchyard, she'll rise up and do us no end of mischief. The bridge is only the start.'

'You d-don't th-think Hannah Hallet's burial made the bridge fall?' The idea was preposterous. Caelica straightened, staring into Anstice's sunken eyes. 'Y-You can't think th-that?' she asked in disbelief.

'Why not? It sounds likely enough to me. She's blighted it by seeking her death in the river so nearby. And like I say, your father's heaped trouble upon trouble by giving her a churchyard grave. Evil gives way to fresh evil. It's always the way.' Anstice looked around the room, then snuffed out two candles with finger and leathery thumb. 'That costive Mr Russell won't need all this number of lights. It's not as if he's the bishop, and we've already put more than enough time and effort into readying a room for him.' Giving the fresh linen and thick woollen bedcovering a last, sour look, she told Caelica to let her go down the stairs first and to be sure to hold the candle steady so she shouldn't miss her footing.

The following morning, the river still ran high. Over breakfast Caelica's father decided to take the cob down to the old fording place and ride across the river to the town. For the local people the loss of the bridge could prove disastrous. It was his duty to give what succour he could. Thomas at once offered to accompany him on foot, but he waved the suggestion aside.

Watching from her bedroom window as the cob made its stolid way through the waters, Caelica guessed that her father had a restless longing to be seen alone to care for his beleaguered parishioners. Something in the abrupt, overly-commanding tone in which he had dismissed Thomas's help, ordering him to attend instead to Caelica's Latin, spoke of a desire to see no one else usurp the role of faithful shepherd to the Llanmichael flock.

Looking down on the dull garden, Caelica stopped herself short. What business had she to judge her father in this impious, undaughterly way? A strand of her hair came loose from its coil, and she thrust it back, twisting and pinning it in place with fierce fingers. She must restrain her disloyalty. Her father was a good man, a clever man, a man of rare learning. She might wish he exercised his care with a softer eye and a gentler voice, but it was fitting that he and he alone should bring God's solace to his people at this time.

She watched him cross the river, the old cob forging ahead, sure-footed and confident despite the current. Reaching the far bank, it heaved itself up and shook like a wet dog before neighing vigorously, as though pleased to be on firm ground once more. Her father dismounted without agility. Then he looked round as though expecting to find people approaching, but no one was at hand. No doubt they would talk to him in time, but she knew he would like more immediate acclamation. Turning away from the window, she sighed and went to the parsonage library for her lessons.

"*Nil mortalibus ardui est,*" read Caelica from Horace's *Odes*.

In his months in Llanmichael Thomas had grown lonelier with every day that passed. The townspeople were as wary of him as they were of Hearne – more so, in fact, because while they were used to their rector's aloof ways. When Thomas addressed them in the scholarly, precise voice that belied his lank hair and shabby clothes, they would stare in a way that betrayed their surprise and mistrust, uncertain what to make of this learned man who was poorer than they. The unassuming goodwill and native intelligence of Hearne's daughter thrilled him to the core, but to return her wide and lasting smile would be perilous. As she stumbled through the poem, he listened in stern silence.

'Well?' And what sort of fist might she make of translating it?

'*Mortalibus* – "to mortals". Or should I say "to men"?'

'It is my conjecture that Horace addresses a largely masculine audience.'

Holding himself bound to keep the lesson on a staid footing, he gave his answer in all seriousness before it occurred to him that there might have been a suggestion of quipping in her question. How lacking in humour he must seem to her. But it was too late to bite the words back. 'Pray continue.'

'"*Nil*" – nothing,'

'Umh.'

'"*Ardui est*" – is difficult?'

'Or arduous. Or "too difficult." Perhaps "too arduous". The poet castigates humans for their arrogance in undertaking labours which, he says, lie properly in the province of the gods. He derides puny mortals for over-reaching themselves.'

'I don't care for that way of thinking,' she began.

Mr Hearne's library faced west and in the mornings, the daylight was subdued; even so, he couldn't help marking the zest in her face and her gleaming eyes inviting him to dispute. But where might it lead? God forbid she should fathom the depth of his fondness for her.

'Continue, Miss Hearne, if you please,' he said.

Holding her book up in front of her, she read with great care.

Caelum ipsum petimus stultitia neque
Per nostrum patimur scelus
Iracunda Iovem ponere fulmina.

She stumbled only over eliding 'Cael-ipsum' and 'Iracund-Iovem' as anyone might. When she was not stammering, her voice was lyrical, her reading full of subtlety and nuance.

'Construe,' he commanded, bleak and blunt.

'"*Stultitia*" – in our stupidity?' she began gently.

'Well, yes. Or even in our obstinacy.'

'"*Petimus*" - we seek, *caelum ipsum* – heaven itself, *neque* – and –'

'Remember it's a negative.'

'Oh, indeed, Mr Russell,' she flung him a smile. 'This poem, I see, is full of negativity, so that is no shock.'

Had she any notion what it cost to hide his laughter?

'To your construe,' he insisted.

'And *per nostrum scelus*' she sighed, 'by our wickedness, I suppose I have to say.'

'You do indeed, Miss Hearne, though I might allow you "evil" or "vice" in place of "wickedness". Pray continue.'

'And by our vice, then, *ne patimur*, we do not allow – there's your precious negative, Mr Russell.'

He allowed himself a flicker of laughter. 'Proceed, if you will.'

'*Iovem* – object, Jupiter, *ponere* – to put, to place, to place down? Put down, perhaps?'

'You might best say "to lay aside".'

'To lay aside, then, *iracunda fulmina* – his angry thunderbolts.'

'His wrathful thunderbolts indeed, Miss Hearne, which signify those instruments the gods favour for crushing overweening man. So our passage runs thus: "In our obstinacy, we seek heaven itself and by our vice, we do not allow Jupiter to lay aside his angry thunderbolts." Horace makes out that our aspirations are a ceaseless provocation to the gods. That was his theology and I daresay that these present days many parsons, magistrates and coroners find great merit in it.'

What recklessness was this? He could feel the heat in his cheeks. By laying the ground open for talk, he was flying in the face of his own wisest precepts. His future career depended on his remaining in good standing with Hearne; therefore he must not indulge in this treacherous affability. Who was to say where it might lead?

'Your poet writes bad sense, however elegant his verses,' she pronounced, the fire of her rare forthrightness making him long to encourage her and tease out her thinking.

'Why shouldn't mortal men and woman make use of their talents?' she rushed on. `What gives your Quintus Hora - Horatius Flaccus,' she gave a brief gasp of amazement at getting the full name out, 'any right to expect the likes of me to reverence him, when he calls our wish to turn our abilities to useful ends stupid or obstinate?'

This spirit was nothing like the habitual meekness of her conduct towards her parents. Flecks of gold which he had never noticed before danced in the brown of her eyes. He burnt to take on her question, but instead, sitting back on his hard chair he replied in dry terms.

'Horace's *Carmina* have been valued by the schoolmen for something approaching two millennia, Miss Hearne. Of what weight, set against such learning, is an ignorant girl's assertion that she finds his poetry inadequate? Mr Dryden, in his translation of these lines, has Horace tax mankind with audacity which compounded the sin of Satan, did it not?'

'Without daring, we achieve nothing,' she answered. 'You're welcome to your Horace, Mr Russell. I d-don't care at all for his pr-precious *C-carmina*.'

She must have taken his snubbing hard for her stammer to return.

'Ha -have you no other Latin for me to read?' she asked.

He frowned, hoping his pretended exasperation concealed his longing to bid her come and walk on the hills, where they could talk and talk, and she might recover that lovely eager fluency. But it wouldn't serve at all.

Keeping his voice chill, emptying his wits of all thought of friendly conversation, he announced that they might as well turn their attention to prose. Scanning the shelves once more, he picked out a volume of Cicero's speeches, found what he thought a likely place and told her to write him an English version.

While she worked, he rose, walked across to the window and stared out. Llanmichael's geography and spirituality had combined in a way that did the place no favour. With the cold little church on its promontory and the snug parsonage in a fold of the hills behind it on the river's eastern side, the faithful in the squalid town on the west bank had scant incentive for worship. Even when the bridge still stood, its very existence marked the great gulf that severed them from God and His henchman the rector.

The actions of the parish's incumbents over the years had emphasized the magnitude of the chasm that severed them from their flock. When the Cistercians had bridged the river long ago, it had pleased them to build a chapel on the promontory at the water's side, where they might pause in prayer on their way to the abbey of Fons Sanctae Mariae in the fastnesses of mid Wales. While their small church had never had much beauty, its stark height on the mound above the river was eloquent. It turned people's thoughts to judgement, especially if they recalled its dedication to Michael, the archangel of the end of time, his sword drawn to exact retribution on sinners.

Once, it was said, there had been a house for a priest in the pastureland at the stream's side. Prone to flooding, the clergy had abandoned it long ago and the valley farmers had pillaged its stones for their walls and barns so that in time the only sign of its existence was a stony outline on the ground. To replace it, some comfort-loving rector had put up the present square parsonage in a sheltered hollow nearby. It looked onto a fine garden and stood well out of the wind. Spacious and pleasing, the building was not showy but impressed any observer who chanced to compare its clean lines with the sagging roofs and irregular windows of the town's impoverished hovels.

Llanmichael had never known much prosperity. Before the discovery of lead in the heights it had had no sustaining industry except agriculture. All the wealth from the new lead mines would assuredly go to their owner, Sir Rowley Curwen from Birmingham. Had he not given up his great manufactories and fine town house expressly so that he might take up residence in a commanding pile called Menston from which he could survey his miners as they worked?

At least Sir Rowley's mining concerns gave the town some hope of riches. Before he began to take an interest in the area, the small tradesmen and shopkeepers of Llanmichael made what living they could from the passing trade. Often packsmen would pause in the one street before urging their trains of freighted horses across the river and heading either east with copper and coal for the trows at Carterford or west with gewgaws and buckles to Pwllfechan, but they never spent much. Men coming in to excavate veins of lead ore were a different prospect. With their proud wives and hungry children at hand and their wage monies in their pockets, they could transform the place. But for this transformation to happen, the bridge was crucial. Because the old structure had stood much as its builders had left it for over four centuries, Llanmichael had expected it to serve its needs for ever. It pleased the townspeople to credit the Cistercians' bridge with the steadfastness of the ash trees from which the men cut their staffs or the wizened bushes over which the women aired their linen. Now, after successive generations had crossed and re-crossed, it had given way at last, while the sullen river ran on through its fractured arches and between its desolate piers.

Hearne came home early in the afternoon. He had spent more than three hours going from house to house, gleaning what he could about the bridge's disintegration. As young Russell had intimated the previous night, no one had witnessed the precise moment of its downfall; nevertheless, everybody had a theory about what caused it. While parishioner after parishioner babbled the most arrant nonsense at him about the circumstances that caused the calamity, their rector, his horse's reins looped up in his hand, struggled to contain mounting impatience. When at last he had been through the whole town, listening to his parishioners' absurd notions, in high frustration with the stupidity of the people he was bound to serve, he remounted and came home.

While Robert unsaddled the cob, Hearne went straight to the library. There was his dear daughter, busy upon her Cicero under her tutor's eye. Surveying her at work, Hearne wished she would not frown so. The lines forming on her brow were over-grave and unsightly. Clearing his throat to announce his arrival, he suggested that for that morning, his daughter's lessons had gone on long enough. Russell, he was pleased to find, had the discretion to leave at once, pausing only to commend Caelica's diligence and thank Hearne for his hospitality of the previous night.

Having tidied away her books, Caelica came to his side.

'W-well, father,' would she ever overcome that stammer? He doubted it – 'w-what do people say about the bridge? D-did anyone see it fall?'

Hearne sat down in the great chair at the table's head.

'No one,' he said, 'although many of the townsfolk claim to have seen rocks and branches wedge themselves under the arches as the water level rose. Strange as it may seem, they had thought nothing of it at the time.'

If his voice should sound sharp, she had wit enough to guess why.

'Catherine Gleeson – you know, the carrier's daughter – asked me why the current didn't just bear them away,' he added, his hands tensing with irritation as he remembered the way Miss Gleeson had stared, moon-faced and open-mouthed, at his attempted explanation. Having picked up a broken quill and torn away some of its barbs, he looked up at his daughter once more.

'She couldn't understand how the debris would compact together until it formed a dam.'

'Y-yet she must have s-seen how p-pressure was building all the time be-behind the arches un-until th-the waters sh-should force their way through.'

'So you might think.' At least his Caelica showed swift understanding. 'Yet Miss Gleeson was most insistent that there could be no connection between the ruthless motion of a stream choked with refuse and our crumbling bridge's collapse.'

'H-how so? Father – is it not?' She stopped mid-speech and looked at him.

'Self-evident, would you say? Listen,' he lent forward on his elbows, 'everyone I've spoken to this day believes that the bridge gave way because of poor Hannah Hallet. While I can see how this account of events might appeal to the gullible Miss Gleeson, it surprises me to hear the same interpretation from an astute soul like Tobias Greene at the inn. Not a word has anyone said about the how the bridge was ill-maintained, with no funds invested for its repair. We all know it was grown too weak to take much battering. Yet, despite its long neglect and ruinous condition, people persist in saying that the unhappy young woman's self-murder and my decision to inter her in the churchyard precipitated its fall.'

The early brightness of the morning had passed. As though to sharpen his words, a spurt of rain lashed the windows.

'Tell me, Cherry,' he did not want to ask this question, but some inner compulsion drove him on. 'Do you think that dead girl had fair ground for accusing your brother of getting her with child?'

Caelica reddened and looked away. 'I do n-not kn-know, father,' she said at last, in a voice softer than a whisper.

Hearne rose. 'I do not know myself,' he agreed, shaking his head. 'Christopher will neither admit that he knew her nor yet deny it. Your mother cannot bear to think he might be in the wrong. In truth she is grown so contrary and distracted I cannot bring myself to over-ride her in anything, lest it drive her into a decline. Let us find her now and hear how she has spent the morning.'

It was Hearne's custom, at the end of each day, to ask the servants to join his family for prayers before their evening meal. They sat around the table in the oak-panelled dining room,

Hearne with his back to the windows, his unhappy wife on his right hand side, his daughter on his left, Robert beside Caelica and Anstice facing. Hearne felt the edge of a draught begin to tease its way beneath his neck-cloth; Robert had not yet replaced the wooden shutter that had served as Hannah Hallet's bier. No wonder that the candles on the table should gutter so.

'*And an highway shall be there and a way, and it shall be called The way of holiness; the unclean shall not pass over it,*' he read aloud from his great Bible.

A pane of glass in the window behind him shattered. A hard object deftly thrown hit the panelling beside the fire place. As Hearne looked round a second missile flew through the air to land on the table by Robert, who leapt backwards, knocking over his chair.

'God damn...' the startled servant began, seeing the sharp-edged stone in front of him. Then he caught Hearne's eye.

'Leave this room at once,' Hearne ordered, pleased to see that Anstice had risen to shepherd his wife out of danger. In truth, he minded Robert's blasphemy less than the alarm it caused. Usually Llanmichael people expressed their affront by banging sticks on pots and pans, and had they brought their clatter to the parsonage, it would have been disagreeable enough. But stone-throwing was worse. Could they have got wind of the notion that Christopher had fathered Hannah Hallet's child? If so, they would find it harder to forgive than forgery.

'Leave,' Hearne repeated, seeing Caelica and Robert linger by the door. He must make certain of her safety. Robert, a man of obstinacy and gristle, could look after himself. Cautious, Hearne edged towards the broken window.

A pebble hurtled past him.

'Who's there?' he called.

'Where are you hiding, parson Hearne?' taunted a voice from the dark. Someone, perhaps more than one person, must have forded the river to lie in wait in his garden. Hearne peered into the night. Except for the familiar shapes of the ash trees, the gate and the wall that bordered the road he could see nothing.

'Come and face your accusers, you who spend your time reading pagan poets instead of attending to the word of God,' another voice cried. 'You who pollute God's holy acre by burying vile sinners within its sacred bounds.'

'Why this outcry?' he called.

His question rang unanswered in the cold air.

'Had you listened,' he went on, raising his voice above the sound of the wind in the ash trees and the river's headlong rushing, 'you would have heard me read from Holy Scripture even now. And my learning does you no harm, nor yet my compassion. Why should it distress you?'

Somewhere from the depths of the parsonage garden came a volley of laughter.

'Where are you?' he shouted. At once the laughter ceased.

'Who are you? What do you want?' he asked, but for answer he heard only wind and water.

Getting no reply, Hearne came back into the light of the candles and the warmth of the fire. Perhaps, having seen how easily they could frighten him, his enemies had retreated, thinking their work well done. But lest they should linger in his garden, he decided to abandon the household prayers and put his Bible away. Was Parry the Dissenter behind this outrage? Hearne thought it highly likely. Well, he wouldn't give Parry the satisfaction of seeing him complain to the justices. It would only make him look small-minded, and he was already unpopular enough. About the evening's events, he would maintain a stoical silence.

All the same, it would be well for the townspeople to have something new to think about – some venture that would banish the memory of Hannah Hallet from their minds and stop them speculating about his miscreant son. Llanmichael needed another bridge. That prospect surely should fire their wits. Full of resolution, Hearne went in search of his family to suggest that they might dine, and to ask Robert if he would please replace the window shutter without delay.

Chapter Five

No-one in Llanmichael knew who was supposed to take the lead in repairing the bridge. Hearne reckoned that the duty of administering the town's business lay between the vestry – himself and his churchwardens – and the landowners who struck the rates and sat as justices. The justices viewed the vestry party as contemptible tithe snatchers and God-botherers; the vestry regarded the justices as a small-minded set who clung, cavilling, to undeserved privilege.

Dislike them though he might, Hearne couldn't overlook the fact that the justices held the purse strings. While highways and therefore bridges came under the vestry's charge, the vestrymen had to exercise their authority at the justices' pleasure, and the justices were set against the vestrymen on principle. Thinking of the rivalry and bitterness between the two groups, Hearne decided it would be to everyone's advantage if he could somehow secure finance for a new bridge without going through the regular channels.

'W-wh-why should there be so m-much d-difficulty in achieving any ag-agreement b-between the justices and th-the vestrymen?' Caelica asked over breakfast when he was digressing upon the intricacy of his negotiations. 'Th-they are all grown men who understand the ways of money – wh-when it concerns a-agriculture or shop-keeping. If the t- town is ever to have its bridge, th-they must see the need to c-combine in their thinking,'

'Do not vex your father. Don't you see the impropriety of quizzing him?'

'Christina, dear wife,' he could not let such severity go unchecked. 'Caelica's question is no matter for rebuke. Indeed,

51

it touches on difficulties that stand at the very root of my ministry.'

'Only think, daughter,' he said, 'of the differences which sever man from man in this parish. When the Churchmen push out their chests, don their fine raiment and stroll up to divine service of a Sabbath morning, they take every care to avert their eyes from the spectacle of the Dissenters trudging out to sing psalms with Parry in the fields. The English families will not converse in any ease with the Welsh, who take refuge in their own language to share the secrets they wish to keep from their neighbours. Rich men enjoy the company of equally rich men, but barely speak to the middling sort, let alone to the field hands. Then there all sorts of old grievances that fester in men's hearts – grazing rights or fishing rights not respected, bad bargains struck, works ill done.'

He paused. Caelica's eyes were thoughtful; his wife's stormy. Her worries made her more cantankerous with every day that passed.

'Of course,' he resumed, 'there are times when people come together. Births, marriages, deaths. Even the Dissenters attend my church to see their infants baptised, to wed or for burial, so from time to time I behold the populace of the place gathering, one and all, to make their common supplications, as the prayer book has it. But experience leads me to think it'll take more than a few shared services to unite the factions of this quarrelsome town.'

For a moment he watched his wife's frown deepen as she faced Caelica who crumbled her bread in silence. Poor child, he mused. She was always at odds with her mother these days, yet her only fault was to be safe under their roof while Christopher lay in prison.

'It is well, Cherry, that you ask me about these things,' he said gently. 'God bless you for it. It does not vex me in the slightest.'

Rising from his place, he stroked the back of his wife's white hand. 'And I trust, Christina, that you too will find your share of blessings this day.'

That day, Hearne planned to call upon Sir Rowley Curwen. It was a fair morning which promised well for a ride over the hills. Putting on his hat and coat, he found his thoughts still turned upon his daughter. Although he had the habit of regarding her as a child, in truth she had reached an age when she should be contemplating matrimony. Marriage would make her happier. To whom, he wondered, easing the linen stock round his neck, should he offer encouragement? Strictly speaking, the question of finding an acceptable husband for Caelica was less pressing than the matter of choosing the right words with which to persuade the prosperous manufacturer turned mine owner to put some money towards rebuilding Llanmichael Bridge, but it was also far more entertaining. Therefore, crossing the parsonage garden he let himself muse upon possible suitors.

He was not sure how much he cared for the landowning squires and their sons, whom he took as his equals in standing, but his inferiors in learning. Once in a while they might invite the parson and his family to share a meal, but they unbent little. More often he saw them swaggering through the district in their fast, low-slung chaises or riding their long-legged blood horses over the lowland pastures after foxes. At their quieter times they might try angling, or go after the game birds with a fowling piece. Their pleasures lay in the chase and the kill, these knowing, keen-eyed young men, hard as soldiers. Their element was the savagery of battle and in peace, they sought occupations that promised to remind them of the thrill of war. Without exception their families had lived in the same area for generations, though tending towards its English rather than its Welsh side. Once the sons of the squires had made a dutiful tour of France and Italy collecting paintings that combined religion and eroticism in the continental way, together with a marble statue or two for show, they would come home resolved never again to venture more than a dozen miles from the place of their birth, unless it was after hounds at a hand gallop.

His hand on the gate between herb garden and stable yard, Hearne remembered his distaste for their conversation which he found dull and their manners, boorish. Yet he did not think them stupid. In his estimation they possessed wit in abundance; their mistake was to anchor it solely to dogs and horses. Of the books and the poetry that he loved and had taught Caelica to love they knew nothing and cared less. He did not suppose that their company could hold much charm for his graceful, clever daughter.

He took a more favourable opinion of the mercantile men - those who earned their wealth through keen brains and hard hands, rather than inheriting it from their forebears. Sir Rowley's manufactory, Hearne reminded himself, had prospered vastly even before Sir Rowley decided to turn his energies to mining for lead. Not only would a man of Sir Rowley Curwen's stature be a good friend to the cause of the bridge, but he might well have sons. If so, Hearne wanted to make their acquaintance.

As he entered the stable, Robert grunted a greeting.

'She'll need shoeing soon, Mr Hearne,' he said, scowling at the bay mare. Bending to put his shoulder to hers, he picked up her nearside forefoot to show how thin the iron had worn. 'Aye, or she'll go slipping about on these paved roads, I shouldn't wonder...'

'Easy, my pigeon,' said Hearne patting the mare's warm neck under her black mane, and pleased to find her questing nose nuzzle his coat as he inspected her shoe. He was not much of a horseman, but he was always flattered by her way of whickering and pricking her ears when she heard his voice. Besides, she was an appealing creature with her small, graceful head and fine, wide eyes. Calling her his pigeon went some way towards convincing him that she was calm and placid, which was not entirely true.

'Will they last today, would you think?' he asked Robert, who sucked in his brown cheeks without saying anything. 'I have a call to make on Sir Rowley Curwen, you know.'

'Might do, sir. Then again, they might wear clean through. Is that the Brummagem gentleman as has moved into the big house that looks like a boil?' asked Robert straightening.

'You're blunt today,' Hearne observed.

'Well, I'm sorry if I speak out of turn, sir,' said Robert. 'But in this place, the stone's grey, the sky's grey, the river's grey – oftentimes even the hills are grey. A house built of blood-coloured bricks shouts out that it has an owner who's rich and pleased with himself.'

'Pleased with himself? How so?' Blowing into the mare's sable nose meant Hearne could hide his somewhat improper enjoyment of this gossipy exchange.

'Stands to reason,' and Robert began to twist a handful of hay into a wisp. 'Why would he choose to live where every eye turns to him if he didn't think he'd done well for himself? He wants to garner up praise. That's a sin, isn't it, sir?'

'Well, the gospel enjoins us not to heap up riches,' Hearne allowed, adding that he doubted whether compliments and adulation could be stored and counted in quite the same way.

Rather than ride the stout cob to the Curwen residence, he decided to risk the mare's shoes. Disapproval contorted Robert's face as he saddled and bridled her, and then led her out to the mounting block, but Hearne ignored it. Looking up at the high cloud scudding across the sky from Wales, he wondered how long the fine weather would last. It would surely rain before the day was out. Bidding Robert goodbye, he mounted and urged the mare forward.

When Hearne arrived at Menston, as the brick-red house was called, Sir Rowley Curwen proved to be at home, and happy to meet the rector of Llanmichael. A manservant ushered Hearne into the library – a large room, panelled and carpeted, with a modest coal fire burning in the grate. Fine, oak shelves lined the walls, but Hearne was disappointed to see how few books they held. A man of Sir Rowley's means could have amassed several volumes, including works that Hearne might have wished to borrow. To be on book-borrowing terms with a man of Sir Rowley Curwen's standing would be a fine thing indeed. Perhaps country life would give the manufacturer and mine owner more leisure in which to buy books than he had known in his town days.

Sir Rowley Curwen motioned Hearne into one of the harder chairs in the room while settling himself on a large, soft sofa. Observing his host's striped silk waistcoat, well-powdered wig and soft leather shoes with gleaming silver buckles, Hearne marked how everything about the manufacturer spoke of satisfaction. He was pleased with his success, pleased with his brick-red country house, pleased even with his ill-stocked library. Surely the only thorn to puncture his buoyancy would be the occasional twinge of gout.

'Fond of grounds, are you?' asked Sir Rowley abruptly. He leant back at a comfortable angle, his hands at ease upon his lap, but his eyes shrewd and keen in his slab of a face.

'Grounds, good sir?' Hearne could not conceal his bafflement.

'Don't be obtuse, man. Fine grounds, you know, to set off a fine house. The house is well enough – I chose it for its elegance – but all it has for formal grounds are a few borders round a lawn, a kitchen garden and an orchard.'

He sounded well-provided for, this city gentleman who had chosen to make his home high above a tumbling river on the remote verges of Wales.

'I want a park,' Sir Rowley spoke of it with fervour. 'A park, running towards a glade of trees at the river's margin. Nature does well, Mr Hearne, but the exuberant elements run unchecked.'

To Hearne's mind, the absence of formal cultivation encompassed much of nature's wonder, but seeing his companion lean fiercely forward as though to secure agreement on the need for spade husbandry, he wasn't inclined to argue.

'I would like each window of my house to look out onto a magnificent vista,' Sir Rowley announced. 'A scene composed with artistry, like a painting by a great master. It is well that your town, sir, the appearance of which as I recall has little to commend it, lies in a bend of the river well out of our sight.

Throughout my life, Hearne, I've dwelt in towns. Fine places too, mark you. Ever been to London?' Hearne admitted that once he had indeed been to London. 'Then you'll know what I mean,' said Sir Rowley. 'But a man grows tired of streets and churches. He wearies even of manufactories, when they thrust themselves into his sight, despite the wealth they bring. No, I yearn for acres of parkland in which to walk when the mood takes me, or to gaze upon to refresh my eyes.'

Biting the inside of his cheek to contain his impatience with Sir Rowley's rustic enthusiasms, Hearne wondered how he was going to introduce the subject of the bridge.

Just then, the library door opened to admit a woman. She was perhaps in early middle age; dark-haired, slight and, to judge from the cut and sheen of her dress, assuredly not a servant. A minute spaniel scampered at her heels.

Smiling – even if she were no longer youthful, it was not as if her charms had faded – Hearne rose. It had been his understanding that Sir Rowley was a widower. Could he be mistaken? Was there a Lady Curwen after all? Or perhaps she was his younger sister, or some other female relative.

'Ah, Alice, this is Mr Hearne the rector,' said Sir Rowley, standing also. A slight almost imperceptible wariness clouded his bluff manner as he spoke. 'Hearne – this is Mrs Whatmough – she was married to my late business partner. She's spending a few days in the country, you know.'

Hearne extended his hand to Mrs Whatmough and greeted her with sedate good will.

'Good day to you, Mr Hearne.' Her eyes were lively, her voice laughing and clear.

'I will not interrupt your conversation,' she said. 'My own business can wait. Only tell me, Rowley, are we to expect Edward here this evening? Mrs Lavery wanted to know.'

Rowley, thought Hearne, not Sir Rowley. For a guest of only a few days, this personable young widow was very much at her ease.

'Edward?' mused Sir Rowley. 'Ah, yes, or so he gave me to understand.'

'Thank you. Come Pippet.' Calling her dog, Mrs Whatmough gave them a fleeting smile of intense warmth and withdrew.

'My condolences, sir, upon your sad loss.' To express his sympathy was only correct, although whatever emotions Sir Rowley might have experienced at the time of Whatmough's demise, he showed little sign of sorrow now. Nevertheless, Hearne judged, if he were to secure his new neighbour's friendship, he must proceed with the utmost propriety and discretion.

'Aye, well,' Sir Rowley cleared his throat as though to hide a spasm of confusion, 'William Whatmough died some months ago. He was a good man. His son Charles and my stepson John run the manufactory for me now.'

'Whatmough's son by the lady who has just left us?' Surely elegant Mrs Whatmough was far too young to have a son at the helm of a thrusting commercial enterprise?

'No, no. Alice was the second Mrs Whatmough. Charles is Whatmough's son by a previous marriage.' Sir Rowley spoke with great vigour, as though set upon putting the subject of Whatmough's relict behind them.

'He's very able,' he went on. 'In fact he and John are among the foremost manufacturers in Birmingham. John has a large family to provide for, so it's just as well he prospers. I've a younger son of my own, too. Edward. He is unmarried.'

Having ascertained that Sir Rowley indeed had an unmarried son, Hearne thought his morning well spent. Leaning forward in his hard chair, he glanced towards the high south facing windows, marking how the soft blue of their curtain-drapes chimed with Alice Whatmough's eyes, and smiled.

'Your proposal, sir, to surround Menston with parkland interests me greatly,' he said. 'Indeed, it flatters me to find you so ready to take me into your confidence and discuss your plans.' That struck the right note – companionable, but not over-familiar. 'Allow me, dear sir, to tell you of a pet venture of my own.'

'And what, parson, might your venture be?' Sir Rowley spoke without enthusiasm. He was plainly a man who preferred to talk than to listen.

'To build a new bridge for my townsmen,' said Hearne outright.

Within the fleshy folds of his face Sir Rowley's eyes narrowed.

'I knew Llanmichael Bridge was down.' From his breeches pocket, Sir Rowley extracted a fine large snuff box from which he helped himself. He did not offer it to Hearne. 'I take it that the town has no funds for its repair,' he said.

'That is true.' Hearne could not argue. 'While, sir,' he continued, anticipating that Sir Rowley might snub him to silence at any second, 'I apprehend that the business of my parish must be of small account to a great man like yourself, yet I thought the enterprise of constructing a bridge might commend itself to your forward-looking and adventurous spirit.'

Sir Rowley gave a harsh laugh. 'I need no chart to follow your reasoning, parson,' he said. 'You hear that I am a rich man and a landowning man. You know that anything I say or do will sway the minds and actions of other men in these parts. Therefore, you listen mousy quiet, bide your time and bite in your blether while I talk about my plans for a park. The truth is, you'd rather have me with you than against you. In fact, you want me in your party at all costs. I'm right, aren't I?'

'Right indeed,' Hearne admitted. The fire in the grate had been welcoming when he arrived, but now the flames had died down.

'I am no lover of flattery and cajoling,' Sir Rowley rasped. 'So you can forget your talk about forward-looking adventurous spirits. I know the lie of the land in Llanmichael. The truth is that it galls you to think of your congregation waiting on the river bank of a Sabbath morn for a ferryman – not that he'd have any business to ply his trade on the Lord's Day, by-the-by – to row them across.'

'While I like, indeed, to see a full church,' Hearne admitted, 'there are other...'

'You're full of a fret that folk'll go running to schoolmaster Parry's services out on the hillsides instead of heeding your sermons' said Sir Rowley, who had a gift for the carrying interruption. 'I've heard my servants speak of it – Parry's worship, I mean. They like the singing.' A rather ugly smile crossed his florid face, as though he enjoyed exposing Hearne's self-interest and holding it up to the light.

Rebuffed Hearne half rose, wondering if he should leave without more ado. His appeal had fallen on stony ground.

'Sit down, parson,' said Sir Rowley, as though reading his thoughts. 'Just because you come at the thing slantwise, doesn't mean it doesn't have some merit. How will Llanmichael fare while its bridge stands derelict?'

'Ill, if I tell truth,' Hearne answered, trying to keep his voice steady in the face of this unexpected gleam of hope. 'There are men who'll ferry travellers across the river for a fat fee, and as you'd expect, they'll no wish to lose their trade to a new bridge. But packhorse trains cannot be rowed across and when the waters run high they cannot ford the river safely either. If our town should lose all trade, it will lose its standing too. The people will grow poorer and the parish's means of providing for them diminish. If Llanmichael is to survive, it needs its bridge. '

'I see.' Was it his imagination, or did Hearne sense that the wily manufacturer found the idea of proving a benefactor to Llanmichael somehow to his liking?

'A man can put a deal of money into a bridge,' said Sir Rowley at last, 'but unless he has the right to take a toll, he'll never live to see any return on it. You can rule out any question of levying a toll upon the people of Llanmichael. They won't stand for paying to drive their beasts over the river from pasture to pasture and I don't suppose you'd want them to have to pay to get to your church.

'Now, as it happens, I don't care to see my ore delayed on its way to Carterford. If the pack-beasts have to go round by Pwllfechan, it will lose me much profit. If– if, I say – I were to back your venture, it'd cost me dear,' said Sir Rowley thoughtfully. 'And yet the money might prove well spent.'

He gave a sardonic, self-deprecating laugh. 'What do you think your justices'll say about it?'

'They'll dispute any part of the cost they have to bear,' Hearne warned, hardly able to believe the turn the conversation had taken.

Sir Rowley grunted. 'I've no love of committees and their interminable talk,' he said, zeal lighting in his hooded eyes. 'But I'm no mean hand at slugging it out with justices when I have to. Now let us think of a stratagem by which we may season your plan to their palates.'

He paused. After a moment, he gave Hearne a wide grin. 'We'll make it a contest,' he decided. 'We'll have notices printed and put up all round the district. They'll invite submissions for the design of a bridge that'll withstand storms and any floods my miners raise when they scour the earth for new ore. We'll pledge a cash prize for whoever produces the best design, and we'll find some man of parts and power to decide who deserves it. Yorke Aislabie'd do it. He and I have seen good and bad times together, and I've always found him obliging. How say you, Hearne? This'll prove a deal cheaper than commissioning an engineer to make costly surveys. Is it not a fair answer to your prayers?'

Relief hot beneath his stock, Hearne nodded. 'It is indeed,' he mouthed.

This goodwill was the finest blessing he could ask. Not only would Sir Rowley provide the means of paying for the new bridge, but the idea of having a contest and inviting an acclaimed engineer to judge it was a clever way of bringing the structure to public attention while keeping its costs down. And he, Matthias Hearne, was in large measure responsible for this happy outcome. Perhaps when they learnt of his efforts, his parishioners would take him to their hearts once more.

'I like the idea of winning a bit of support from the landowning farmers,' Sir Rowley continued, helping himself to more snuff and this time, offering Hearne to take a pinch too.

'I'm thinking of standing for Parliament at the next election, you know.'

Hearne did not know, but to show his interest he uttered an encouraging 'indeed?' and almost heard the raw glee pounding in his veins. That gibe about missing his congregation had sunk his spirits for a moment or two, but Sir Rowley's wish to secure a sound short route for his ore had made Hearne's task of persuasion easier than he could ever have imagined.

'If you've a mind to it,' Sir Rowley was saying, 'we'll seal this compact some time and drink to it. Not now though. I have an appointment with Rendle to speak of my park – Rendle the improver, you know – and I wish to keep my wits clear. Perhaps when the days turn longer, we'll confer again. I'll send word.' And with that, Sir Rowley summoned a servant to escort Hearne out of the library and waved him away.

Riding home in high elation, Hearne marvelled at the morning's triumphs. Not least among them was the discovery that Sir Rowley had an unwed son. It was a most excellent augury for the future.

Just when he was nearing the highest, bleakest point of his homeward ride, the mare started to limp on her nearside fore foot. Cursing, because the high cloud of the mild morning was lowering and rain starting to fall, Hearne dismounted to see if there was a stone in her hoof. There was none, but the worn shoe had broken clean across giving him no choice but to lead her the rest of the way home.

Chapter Six

With certain knowledge of Sir Rowley's support, Hearne put the contest in hand. He decided to dispense with canvassing the opinions of his fellow-vestrymen who would only argue over the wording and size of print in the announcements. Instead, he told them that plans for the new bridge were advancing well and he took the matter before the justices. Having indicated that a local landowner of wealth and repute was willing to finance the construction of a new bridge, he added with some satisfaction that the wealthy man was on good terms with Yorke Aislabie – the country's leading civil engineer, no less – who had agreed to judge the competition. He would even modify the winning bridge if necessary, to ensure it should meet the needs of its users for years – nay, centuries – to come.

The justices took this news with exactly the sleepy, unquestioning goodwill for which Hearne had hoped. Before long, bills advertising the contest appeared throughout the district.

Caelica sat in the narrow church, trying to give her attention to her father's sermon. These days, his congregations had dwindled almost to nothing. Few people cared either to ford the river or to pay avaricious Luke Vaughan the ferryman to row them to church in his coracle. Yet Sabbath by Sabbath, her father would mount the worn steps, lean out over the edge of the carved pulpit, and preach with his accustomed erudition.

A shaft of spring sun filtered through one of the windows above the aisle and cast its light across the stones of the floor in front of her. Against the sunlit patch danced a shadow from the ash trees that shielded the south side of the church. The bridge competition, she knew, had been open to entrants now for some two months and it pricked at her curiosity like a thorn. With her father's voice lulling her, as he held forth upon the theme of obedience, she let herself wonder what entries might already have arrived. What sort of structure, indeed, did the entrants think fitting to serve Llanmichael's needs for the future? She knew how much her father cherished the prospect of establishing a new and better bridge in the town, but whenever she tried to ask him about it, he dismissed her questions with the most cursory responses.

Her mother had said she was too ill to come to church that morning, which meant she had to forgo her Sunday worship – they had recently abandoned the accustomed evening service – and Anstice had agreed to stay with the invalid. In his wife's absence, Robert sat by himself on one of the backless benches in the north aisle, his mouth glum and eyebrows converging towards one another as though he were finding the sermon as tough as old mutton to digest. Every so often his worn brown hands moved towards his coat pockets, then, just as he was on the point of pushing them comfortably in, he would arrest their motion, clenching his fists hard and clamping his arms to his sides, as though it affronted his sense of piety to put his hands in his pockets in church. Perhaps, Caelica speculated, watching him stir and straighten his back on the hard bench, he believed there was something virtuous in being uncomfortable. Besides Robert at the north door, Joseph Watkin – churchwarden and overseer of the poor – sat, stooping, a little ahead of her while her tutor, formal in gown and bands, clasped his hands on the litany desk by the chancel arch. She, alone, occupied the parsonage pew. Otherwise no one came to hear her father preach but the sunbeams and the church mice.

Reflect, my brethren, her father exhorted, as though addressing a bench of bishops, *how the constellations show the beauty of submissive order. Are the stars not a true type of obedience, shining as they follow their heavenly paths, the meek daughters of their almighty father?*

Some shade of vacancy must have shown itself in her face, for her father leant forward in the pulpit and stared straight at her, as though he surmised that her thoughts were beginning to stray and signalled to her to pay attention. She curved her lips in a deliberate smile at him, but before long her eyes wandered back to the dancing shadows.

His sermon done, he bade his listeners join him in reciting the *Te Deum*. As he lifted his voice, Caelica shrank. *We praise thee, O God* the words began, but what praise could the stilted sound of a few embarrassed, voices yield? It overwhelmed her with shame. Even if she should manage not to stammer, she had no wish to hear herself adding to the thin murmurings of dutiful thanksgiving. If this strained prayer with the few participants puckering their faces in shyness was devotion, she wanted no part in it.

She could not remember ever having marked the rhythm of rebellion in her pulse before, though she recognised it plain enough. Galled to find herself so at odds with her father, she tried to subdue her mutinous thinking. She looked at bent-backed old Watkin, tidy and respectful in his worn coat. Surely no defiance gnawed at him, for he was saying the words in a hushed, abashed voice. Mr Watkin was a humble man, gnarled with age and a habit of deference. He agreed with her father in everything. Up till now, she had agreed with her father in everything herself.

Still uncomfortable, she found herself looking at Thomas and saw he was reading the words with distaste in his eyes. Did he too dislike having to speak out bold in the nigh-empty building? He had none of Mr Watkin's shambling humility. Sometimes she had heard his voice in the parsonage library, raised and ringing as he clashed with her father in hot discord. Thomas, she thought, understood more about rebellion than he cared to admit.

The congregation were still intent upon the *Te Deum*.
Day by day: we magnify thee.
It was not wholesome to dwell on the theme of defiance.
And we worship thy name: ever world without end.

Think rather how local men were answering the invitation to submit their plans for a new bridge to replace the old one -

Vouchsafe O Lord: to keep us this day without sin.

- which had been crumbling for as long as anyone could remember.

O Lord have mercy upon us: have mercy upon us.

It must be vast pleasure to draw up the design of a bridge -

O Lord let thy mercy lighten upon us: as our trust is in thee.

- and then witness your pen strokes taking solid form in stone.

O Lord in thee have I trusted: let me never be confounded.

Her voice came out far louder than she meant. Her father glared at her while the others visibly stiffened. Since there were no musickers on hand, they had no hymn, but only a final blessing at which she knelt, thankful for the chance to hide her hot face in her hands.

As she left the church, Thomas, who surely should have been discussing church business with Watkin and her father, came to her side, shaping his steps to keep pace with hers. Pleased, she reasoned he must mean to escort her home, but having tucked her prayer book under his arm, instead of making towards the lych-gate facing the parsonage garden, he headed towards the gap in the churchyard wall above the river. Walking beside him, wondering where they might be going, she could not stop herself from turning to glance down at Hannah Hallet's grave.

In all likelihood Hannah would never have any tombstone or memorial. The turf over her burial place still had a raw unsettled look; perhaps as summer drew near, Mrs Hallet would come here to remember her daughter, to think of her grandchild and put flowers on the rough grass where they lay. Or perhaps she would avoid the place. Given the local people's feelings, she might not want to be seen here.

Letting Thomas help her over a heap of stones where the wall had collapsed, Caelica put the Hallets out of her mind, enjoying the walk and the fine morning. The track that skirted the churchyard would eventually bear them to the back door of the parsonage below the wooded slope of the great hill. It was well enough trodden for its surface to have worn smooth and easy under foot; at the same time it was peaceful and rather lonely.

'I have not been here since summer,' she remembered.

He looked up at a hazel, a bush that had expanded itself over the years into a venerable tree of more than ten, perhaps twelve or even fifteen feet in height. 'That'll be in full leaf before long.'

From it hung flowers, new and young, which showed a slight golden sheen in the sun. When she touched one, the deep yellow pollen came away on her fingers.

'Your father might well make a sermon upon that.'

Was there something not altogether serious in his voice as he made this outwardly proper remark?

She gave him a quick, searching look and they both laughed. 'Indeed he might – most like he will.'

It was not so much for the comedy of the thing that amused them, but the complicity in which at the same time they marked her father's custom of drawing morals from the world around him. As they walked on, she had a strong sense that her grave tutor was no more impressed by her father's commendation of the stars' passivity than she had been. Just now, he wasn't even grave. He was still half-laughing, his bony, irregular features alight and his eyes full of irreverent mirth. Why did he make himself so severe with her when it so clearly went against his grain to be stern and solemn?

'Shall you,' she asked him, friend-to-friend, as the path lead them round towards the house, 'submit an entry for the contest of which my father spoke and seek to devise a new bridge?'

'I have not the skill,' he replied. 'Besides, because your father does not want competitors disturbing his labours, he has stipulated that they should deliver their work to me. I am charged with the safekeeping of all the entries submitted, and I am not sure I could discharge this duty faithfully if it were known that I were a competitor myself. Other entrants might suspect me of mislaying their drawings on purpose.'

'Have there been many entries?'

'Indeed there have. The contest has been open for a clear four weeks and I have amassed quite a number.'

'I – I should dearly like to see them.'

'Why not? I had agreed to meet Luke Vaughan at the jetty around noon. He'll have room in his boat for you, I'm certain. Provided he has no other business, he can wait for you at the river bank and return you to the parsonage when you are done with the drawings. But your father may...'

'My father will make no objection.'

This statement was untrue. While her father might send her on parochial errands, she knew that he would not care, except in high emergency, for her to visit her tutor in his lodgings without an escort or, for that matter, to entrust herself to the coracle of sullen Luke Vaughan whom people accused of lying with his sister. But the seed of disobedience which had entered her spirit in church had rooted itself too deep for swift excision. She wanted very much to see what manner of bridge men thought would serve Llanmichael. She wanted also to stay out of the parsonage, well away from her mother's plaints and her father's fussing. It was better by far to enjoy an hour or so of sunlit freedom and unexpected comradeship.

'Since you are so certain of your father's good will, let us go.' Tucking the books more securely under his right arm, Thomas offered her his left, and they retraced their steps past the overgrown hazel, back around the outside of the churchyard, down the steep slope of the mound and towards the river. To Caelica's relief, her father was nowhere in sight. Either Joseph Watkin was talking to him inside the church, or else concern for her mother had already drawn him home.

As soon as they reached the rough stone jetty Thomas saw Vaughan's round, flat-hulled coracle approach, Vaughan himself propelling it with a pole. Thomas called a greeting to which the ferryman responded with a grunt and once the boat was close enough, put the books down to assist Caelica to embark. Although Vaughan was quick to pocket the proffered coins, he was plainly not going to exert himself on his passengers' behalf. Picking up the books once more, Thomas then embarked himself and sat at Caelica's side on the narrow cross bench.

Despite the light on the water and warmth in the air, it was a disagreeable passage. Downstream the old bridge stood forlorn with its broken piers and shattered stonework. Of the seven arches, the central three that spanned the deepest channel must have taken the greatest punishment although the middle one, strange to say, survived like the limbless trunk of a body. On either side, the arches in the shallows closest to the banks were still intact, but where the structure had given way the gaping bare stones appeared to reach out to those parts of the bridge that remained, as though the fabric yearned to heal itself. Glancing to Caelica, Thomas saw that her feet in light shoes were growing wet. From her tense face he guessed that she expected the boat to be swamped at any second. To distract her, he pointed to the ruin.

'You can see,' he remarked, swathing the books in his cloak to protect them from the splashing of Vaughan's pole, 'how the abutments took the greater part of the strain.'

'Yet it was the arches that collapsed,' she observed. 'My father thought the branches and refuse building up beneath them must have been like a dam.'

'Yes, finding their passage blocked, the waters would thrust their way through whatever stood in their path.'

'Of course,' she said slowly, 'if there were but one arch, it should not choke.'

'Well, but its span should be vast – almost inconceivable,' he replied, not caring to quench her eagerness. 'See how far it is from bank to bank.'

As she turned to gauge the distance, it struck him that there was something most appealing about her pointed chin and the way it bore witness to her spirit. Despite her stockings being wet through, her eyes had taken fire and once again he noticed the minute flecks of gold ringing their pupils. But before he could talk more, the coracle's movement ceased. They had reached the jetty on the river's Welsh bank.

'Ah, thank you, Vaughan,' he said. 'You have brought us across the river in safety and neither Miss Hearne nor I are more than passing damp.' Thomas looked down deliberately at his companion's sodden shoes and his cloak's dripping hem. If his gratitude came tinged with irony it was no more than the churl deserved.

'Will you please wait upon Miss Hearne's return?' he asked.

'If you make it worth my while,' answered Vaughan, and another coin changed hands.

The room where he lodged shocked her to the core. Looking round the dingy walls, she realised she had expected her tutor's dwelling to resemble, to some extent, Llanmichael parsonage. It would be less spacious, of course, and humbler because her father had been a clergyman for many years whereas Mr Russell was just setting out, but its character would preserve that essence of scholarly comfort that had pervaded every house in which she had ever lived. Yet here she stood in a hovel.

The dark, the damp in the air and the stench of decay almost made her draw back on the threshold. It was not at all what she had expected to find in the accommodation of a man whose learning lent him, even now, some standing in the parish. People – not only her father, but people in general – expected him to assume apparel and deportment befitting a man who would before long find himself ordained and presented to a curacy, if not a living. Then he would not just read lessons and line out psalms, but he would preside at the Eucharist, say the daily offices of matins and evensong, would baptise infants, marry betrothed couples and bury the dead. He would preach sermons, take a share of the tithe and have a handsome house provided, but for now he dwelt like a mole in a hole.

Great stains scarred the rough plaster, pieces of which had flaked away to leave glaring patches of visible stone. Through her shoes' thin soles, Caelica could feel the flags' cold – cold with a damp edge. It was no surprise to see a veil of green scum on the floor, much like the moss that covered the rocks in the river after it had run high. This place could never dry out. Although there was a grate against the wall facing the door, it was minute, far too small to hold a fire large enough to warm the room through. Anyway, except for a few ashes, it was empty. One of the casement windows stood in the wall facing onto the street; the other, much closer to the ground, looked to the bank behind the house. Both of them were small as though they begrudged letting the daylight enter. Indeed, although outside it was bright, her host was cheerfully putting rush lights in a stand on the table which, to judge from the pewter ink pot on one side and loaf of dry-looking bread on the other, must serve him both for dining and work. When he struck a flame from his tinder box, she saw a box bed curtained off against the wall standing closest to the bank on what must, she guessed, be the chamber's dampest, coldest side. Those threadbare drapes would not keep out the draughts, and nor would the warped window frame. Looking up, she noticed the threatening way in which the sagging ceiling bowed, as though it might collapse at any moment. Seldom, even in the homes of the poor – even, indeed, in Mrs Hallet's cave – had she met such cheerlessness.

Yet he did not seem to notice the squalor and gave no sign of resenting the fact that one mean room must serve him for kitchen, library, dining room and bedchamber.

'Come,' he invited, courteous and genial. 'I'll show you the drawings, if you care to sit down. Oh...' Realising that a tottering pile of books occupied the seat of the one chair, he broke off and put them on the bed.

'As you see,' he explained, 'there are no shelves here and even if I were to pay the joiner to put them up, Gleeson my landlord doubts the walls would support them for long.

'Now please sit down, Miss Hearne' – how come she had never noticed his slightly uneven smile before, the left hand side of his mouth spreading before the right? His eyes – ochre brown – shone and his voice was warm. She hoped he had not noticed her dismay at his dwelling.

'Here are the drawings submitted so far,' and he produced a sheaf of papers from the lower window sill and proceeded to hand them to her, one by one.

Caelica hoped and expected that the draughtsmen would possess not only artistry, but also high vision. Llanmichael might be a poor town on the remote fringes of Wales, but there was no reason why its inhabitants shouldn't prove ingenious spirits, full of creative fire. Yet looking at one drawing after another, she began to grow disappointed.

'Well?' he asked.

'I do not – Mr Russell, there is something I can't understand.'

Wondering whether she had judged the sketches too harshly, she took them up for fresh inspection. It did nothing to shake her first impression. Every draughtsman had set out to replicate the old bridge. For the future, they offered only a version of the past. Why otherwise should they all show such fondness for cumbersome pointed arches with heavy cutwaters like a jaw of gaping teeth? Some entrants had even bedizened their bridges with carved heads that scowled upstream; surely no one could be so foolish as to suppose an ugly bridge would cow the rising waters?

'Why should all of them favour these undersized arches under a heavy parapet? See here,' she extricated one of the offending plans and thrust it under his sight. 'This squat stonework straddles the river like a great ponderous beast. Your geometry lessons often puzzle me, Mr Russell, yet for someone with a surer grasp of the principles, might not mathematics guide them towards producing a bridge with – ' she hesitated, uncertain how to frame what she wanted to say. 'Well, more graceful proportion?'

Silent, he bent over her shoulder to scan the drawing.

'It is as though,' confident of their friendship, she spoke her thoughts without waiting for his answer, '– as though the men who made these drawings are frightened. Frightened of breaking away from the style of our old bridge with all its small arches, or trying anything new. See – the bridge in this drawing would choke with debris in no time.'

For a second, she imagined that single, great arch that would sweep from bank to bank. Facing him, she realised how much she wanted him to share her thinking.

For answer, he said nothing, but one of his tawny eyebrows edged upwards. The mute challenge stopped up all her words. Her brief command of speech must have sprung from sheer vanity, for what else could lead an ignorant young woman to make so free with her opinions? And what did she know about bridge building?

'The competition remains open until Whitsun, Miss Hearne,' he observed at last. 'These drawings may not show the style you hoped to find, but perhaps the more adventurous contestants bide their time.'

Only a few brief moments previously he had talked to her as a friend; now he turned dry and scholarly once more. His vein was kindly, to be sure, but it was also detached. All the warmth and gusto with which he had cleared his books from the chair and bidden her sit down had gone.

'I have no wish to hasten your departure,' he continued, formality settling round him like cloud on the hills, 'but Vaughan is neither patient nor reliable. If you want to get home dry-shod, it would be well to make him wait no longer. And your father too may begin to stir with concern.'

Sighing, she rose and picked up her prayer book. Mindful of her resolve to think before she spoke and conscious too of the change in his mood, she said nothing as they returned to the jetty. There was Vaughan, hunched glowering amidships and when Caelica tried to say how much it had pleased her to see the drawings, her stammer came on so thick that she could not get the careful phrases through her lips.

Waving her words aside, her tutor's smile returned in all its unlikely tenderness. Then his expression changed. 'Make haste, Vaughan,' he urged. 'I can see Miss Hearne's father on the far shore. He is, I judge, looking for his daughter. The way he keeps raising his hand to his eyes as he paces along the bank suggests that anxiety gnaws at his very soul.

'Miss Hearne, I have no wish to make you conspicuous by shouting to tell him you are on your way, but should he rebuke you for your absence, you may assure him that all blame in the matter rests with me.'

Chapter Seven

Next morning, one of Sir Rowley's servants arrived at Llanmichael parsonage bidding the rector and his family to Menston on the following Saturday. Should the Hearnes wish to take luncheon and hear the celebrated landscapist Mr Rendle discourse upon possible designs for a park, Sir Rowley would be happy to send his carriage for them.

'If Sir Rowley desires our company, then we should certainly go.' The invitation pleased Mr Hearne enormously. The previous afternoon he had scolded Caelica in round anger for going to her tutor's lodging without a chaperone; now he stood serene and smiling with his back to the empty parlour grate, folding his arms in buoyant good humour, ready to answer any argument against visiting Menston that his womenfolk might raise.

Caelica and her mother faced one another across the walnut wood table. Outside it was mild but gusty; through the window Caelica could see the branches of the ash trees rising and falling in the wind. She was not sure how much she wanted to meet the great Sir Rowley Curwen. His august presence would bring on the worst of her stammering. Her mother, to judge from the shadows of unease around her eyes and mouth, viewed the prospect of calling on this new acquaintance with equally little enthusiasm.

Quick to dispel their forebodings, Mr Hearne drew up a chair between them. 'Christina, dear wife,' he urged, smiling. 'You surely cannot wish me to decline this friendly offer. It promises to be a most pleasing diversion,' he ran his thumb affectionately across her knuckles. 'Come, you used to enjoy society,' he reminded her. 'We see little enough of it nowadays. Besides, Curwen has a son not many years older than Cherry.

And she is, beyond question, ready to move in more exalted company than anything Llanmichael can offer.'

Caelica noticed her mother give him a swift, sharp look, her thin, contemptuous eyebrows lifting somewhat, as though in question. Then, as though satisfied with his unspoken answer, she agreed that of course she would accede to her husband's wish to dine with his worthy new friend, though she doubted that the occasion would bring her much pleasure.

Despite her initial acquiescence, when the day came, Mrs Hearne prevaricated and complained about weakness in her legs.

'Rouse yourself, ma'am,' insisted Mr Hearne when he saw her sink onto the parlour sofa. 'The change of scene will lift your spirits and I shall be on hand to attend to you. Besides, my love, Sir Rowley is a humane man and advancing in years himself. You may be sure he will take every care to see that your frailty is not taxed beyond endurance. He may even supply a sedan.'

Under the teasing, Caelica could see how set upon the visit he was. Although he had not spelt its purpose out to her, she could guess what he had in mind. Some scheme which related, no doubt, to this son of Sir Rowley Curwen's who chanced to be so close in years to herself. In the past, he had encouraged her to keep to her lessons, while her brother enjoyed the social round. Now he was anxious to thrust her into the light. Did he hope she might be on the way to finding a husband? Girls often wed around her age. To see a daughter set up in a household of her own was a blessing to impecunious parents, and while the Hearnes were reasonably comfortable, no one could call them rich. The day before, Caelica had felt rebellion on her pulses; now she tasted cynicism in her wits.

Leaning on an ebony cane, Mrs Hearne unsmilingly permitted one of Sir Rowley's footmen to assist her inside the Menston carriage. Then she sat, ram-rod stiff upon the hard seat with its red cloth covering, looking straight ahead while her husband and daughter climbed in to join her.

76

Her mother's rigidity made Caelica all the more conscious of her own unease. Anstice, who had a good servant's instinct for what her employer wanted, had brought greater than usual care to the business of assisting her to dress. It was fully evident that her father hoped she might make a favourable impression upon the company. But the twisting and pinning of her hair, the gold necklace that she so seldom wore, the frock of grey-blue rather than her usual dove grey all gave her the sense of being thrust into disguise. The fine feathers were urging her to behave, to think, even to speak in new ways and she disliked their insistence.

The journey required a lengthy detour to cross the river by the bridge at Pwllfechan but after two hours' jolting, they drew up in the sweep of the carriage drive at Menston. The brash ruddiness of the Staffordshire bricks from which the house had been built struck their eyes at once.

'To think that not so long ago this dwelling was no more than a fortified manor built of grey Welsh stone,' mused Caelica's father, glancing up at the ugly, magisterial house. 'It won't take much rough weather to take the edge off that florid shade.' He leant forward. 'Robert called the place a great boil,' he confided, and laughing, reached out to touch his wife's hand. 'Sir Rowley,' he remarked, 'has ridden the currents of worldly fortune with consummate skill.'

At that moment, Sir Rowley – for he, surely, was the gentleman in the fine blue coat – came out to meet them, walking rather gingerly as though the gout ravaged his large, slippered feet.

'Ah, Hearne,' he said. 'Your humble servant, ma'am.' bowing to her mother. At this point, there was some difficulty with Mrs Hearne's cane. Being a new rather than a confirmed invalid, she had not yet discovered the best way to greet an eminent manufacturer while descending from a high carriage. In the event, she had to allow her host to hand her out of the narrow door before requesting Caelica to retrieve her cane. But before Caelica could pick it up, Sir Rowley had already advanced.

'My dear Miss Hearne,' he began, and to her surprise, as his vast hand engulfed her own, she realised it was not white and soft as she expected, but reddened, worn and furrowed. Clearly Sir Rowley had no nice scruples about leaving rough toil to his workmen. If he had laboured himself in his time, she respected him for it. She might even come to like him. Shy, she scanned the rugged clefts of his face, and found in them traces of true kindness. To her relief, her voice held steady when she exchanged his greeting. The cane remained in the carriage.

A lady stood a little behind Sir Rowley and to one side. Mr Hearne greeted her with every sign of affability, as though she were an esteemed and long-standing acquaintance, before turning to his wife. 'This is Mrs Whatmough, my dear – Mrs Alice Whatmough, the wife of Sir Rowley's late business partner. Caelica, this is Mrs Whatmough.'

Caelica took the small, proffered hand and curtsied.

'Miss Hearne, what a pleasure it is to make your acquaintance,' murmured Mrs Whatmough, fragrant in a shimmer of azure silk. Looking into the charming oval face, in place of friendship Caelica found a veil – a soft, impenetrable sheen across the limpid eyes. Mrs Whatmough's words were warm and her manner gracious, but something about her brought on all Caelica's wariness, much as though she were crossing a marsh by night, knowing that at any moment the firm ground might yield beneath her feet.

Just as they were admiring the brick-built porch, a tall young man sauntered up, extending his hand to pat one of the sweating carriage horses. From the cut of his grey broadcloth coat, it was clear he was no servant. Swallowing, Caelica steeled herself to return his greeting.

This time she stammered badly, but instead of looking away in embarrassment, he smiled at her, hearty and genial. He was tall – taller than his father and broad withal, his colour high and his eyes the clear blue of a summer sky. When he spoke, it was with the total ease and assurance of someone who knew he would be welcome in whatever company he found himself. His utter self-belief reminded her of her brother.

As she offered hesitant replies to his questions about their journey, she saw him frown as though something about her puzzled him.

'I remember you,' he said suddenly, 'the girl on the bridge.'

Here was a revelation. 'You – you rode p-past me on a gr-grey horse,' she recalled, surprised at her memory's power.

'Aye.' He lingered happily over the syllable, his face lighting up as though the discovery pleased him.

'How remarkable,' he went on. 'You're quite right Miss Hearne. It was grey Hesper. He showed the devil's own obstinacy that day.'

The horse had baulked, she remembered, and he had whipped it hard.

'Perhaps some instinct warned him,' the young man said, 'that the bridge was soon to fall. To be sure, it took all my efforts to coax him out of his jibing. Yet in my mind's eyes I can still see the meek young woman who waited so patiently for us to pass. She had a basket of apples on her arm, as I recall, and was no doubt bound upon some act of charity.' He laughed. 'And she was you?'

'Sir, she – she-' But the statement 'Sir, she was,' proved too cumbersome for her. Something, be it the embarrassment of that wretched call she had paid Mrs Hallet in her cave, or the knowledge that Mrs Whatmough was watching her, muffled her tongue like cloth round a bell-clapper.

'How remarkable that you two should already have met one another,' Mrs Whatmough unexpectedly intervened to smooth away Caelica's awkwardness. 'Do you believe in portents, Miss Hearne? Edward? Your chance encounter must surely be an omen of the happiest and most lasting friendship between your two families. Now let us all go into the house.'

As though Menston were her home, she gestured to the open front door beyond which Caelica could see into an imposing hallway with flanking marble pillars and a fine patterned carpet on the floor.

They sat round a vast mahogany dining table to share what Sir Rowley described as a modest repast and what, to Caelica was sheer surfeit. The food was more elaborate than any she had seen before. It gave the impression of being presented for their delectation only once its creator was satisfied with the artistry of its appearance. Each dish possessed perfect symmetry; decorations adorned the precise place where an eye that craved regularity would expect to find it. In the face of such lavishness, she could not help but recoil. To find herself confronting so much of everything unsettled her stomach. Worse, every course announced itself by smell long before the servants bore it to the sideboard, and the aromas lingered and mingled, so heavy upon the still air that she had the sensation of half-suffocating. One of the servants helped her to a wing of cold fowl and she picked up a knife and fork, weighty with decoration, and tried to follow the talk that flowed round her.

Sir Rowley to Mrs Hearne, chewing vigorously while he talks: 'You see, Ma'am, I've lived in Birmingham all my life. It's a grand place to make money, ma'am, - may I help you to a little of this turbot? – which is all I've ever cared for. When I was thirteen my father bound me apprentice to a button maker. But I craved for bigger things than buttons, ma'am, and bigger profits than buttons could bring. Once I'd learnt my trade and made every quarter farthing from it that I could, I joined forces with another man to buy a foundry.' *He takes another mouthful.*

'A foundry, mark you, which was progress indeed. But at first, d'you know ma'am, he wouldn't have me going in with him. He even said folk'd laugh if they knew his syndicate included whip-snapper button makers barely out their indentures. But I kept on at him and he changed his mind in time.

'That's the way of it, ma'am. Even when I was just setting out in the world, I knew that if you just hold fast ready to sing out your song, you'll find someone waiting to hear it in time. I had a good song to sing and sure enough, a day came when the man who'd set me at nothing decided he might as well listen after all.'

Mrs Hearne, overwhelmed by her turbot and not making much attempt to follow: 'Indeed, sir, and are you deeply fond of music?'

Mr Rendle, the landscape-architect, to Mr Hearne: 'You see, reverend sir, it is my purpose – I would not disdain to say my vocation – to enhance nature. Nature scatters her beauties with abundance, but she does so without any feeling for decorum or discipline. Therefore it falls to men like me to school her.'

Mr Hearne: 'But my dear sir, have you never considered the workings of the hand of God? Isn't He the supreme artist? And doesn't the man who dares think he might improve on the divine handiwork show a touch of presumption?'

Mr Rendle, nettled: 'You speak as befits a clergyman. It is true that I have before now encountered the objection than I am "gilding the lily." My answer is that, to my mind, every wanton bloom in prodigal nature stands to benefit from adornment by the skilled hand and discriminating touch of an educated man.'

Mr Hearne: 'That is a fair answer indeed. Can I invite you, sir, to partake of these elegant kickshaws, adorned as they are by the skilled hand and discriminating touch of Sir Rowley's educated cook?'

Edward Curwen to Mrs Whatmough speaking softly: 'Your silence is enigmatic, ma'am, and the thoughts that you harbour tease my spirit. Pray what did you mean by your remark upon there being safety in crowds?'

Mrs Whatmough equally softly: 'Edward, this is hardly the time or the place... For myself, I am looking forward with the utmost eagerness to hearing Mr Rendle expound upon his schemes for developing your father's park.' *She deliberately faces Caelica, seated at her right between herself and Sir Rowley:* 'Miss Hearne, you stay very quiet. Perhaps, after an arduous carriage journey, it is only to be expected so I shall not press you to speech. But I would commend to you the pineapple

–it is very fine and its piquancy may well revive your spirits.' *She turns.* 'Rowley, pray assist Miss Hearne to a little of the pineapple. She is so wan and quiet that she might almost be a spirit rather than a living woman. Do you not think her gold chain graceful?'

Brought to the party's attention Caelica felt herself redden. But before Sir Rowley could pass her a wet-looking yellow triangle of pineapple, a diversion occurred. At intervals throughout the meal, Mr Rendle had been clicking his knuckle joints and tugging at his ill-fitting wig, plainly impatient for them to give their full attention to his schemes for Menston Park. Now he caught Sir Rowley's eye and Sir Rowley obligingly abandoned Caelica and the fruit. Instead, he began to shepherd them outside onto the wide terrace, from which they might survey the land surrounding the house and to hear the landscapist's plans for its improvement.

Would Edward Curwen, Caelica wondered, attempt to draw her into conversation at this comfortable after-luncheon time? Evidently not, for he had offered Mrs Whatmough his right arm and sauntered along the terrace at her side, a small dog gambolling between them. As they passed, Caelica caught the words 'filly' and 'town plate'. It sounded as though they were discussing horse-racing - a subject about which she knew nothing. Disappointed, she sat down on the low wall that bordered the lawn composing herself to listen to Mr Rendle.

'You see before you, ladies and gentleman, a vista of the wild.' He pointed at it accusingly with a stick.

'High amid the umbrage and foliage on yonder southern slope – southern, dear lady.' Her mother was looking the wrong way. 'There, follow where my finger points,' urged Rendle, 'and you will see where a stream pours itself over the native rocks.'

In her peripheral vision, Caelica observed Mrs Whatmough and Edward had reached a wide bed planted with tulips and grape-hyacinths. The dog began to dig with its forepaws, but they did not notice. Instead, as though to emphasise a point in their conversation, Mrs Whatmough laid her right hand on Edward's in a gesture so intimate, Caelica would have preferred not to have seen it, but the tumbling lace on the lady's cuff was too abundant not to catch the eye.

'We would tame this impulsive waterway.' Rendle, smiling and pointing with his cane, was tireless. 'It might furnish an attractive fountain, let us say, within a stone-girt trough. Though rather better, I aver, would be an ornamental rill, the construction of which would give me the deepest satisfaction.'

Mrs Whatmough and Edward stayed absorbed in talk. Caelica's mother, her back turned upon Rendle, now appeared to be counting the ornate Menston chimney pots. Only Sir Rowley and her father paid the architect any attention.

'Otherwise it might, with some benefit, be diverted to form a subterranean reservoir whence in time waters might accumulate wherewith to meet all need for irrigation within our – how shall I term it? – *wilderness of artifice.*

'As for the surplus vegetation,' the excitable voice continued, 'I should clear it, although I should preserve the more healthy and massive of the trees to enhance the vista.'

Mrs Whatmough's hand was no longer on Edward's now, and the two of them were strolling back to the house, deep in talk. If Caelica's father still had hopes of her forging some friendship with Sir Rowley's son, they plainly had little chance of fulfilment. From out of the empty air, the thought of Thomas taking irreverent measure of her father's preaching rose in Caelica's mind. Trying to banish it, she heard Edward break off what he'd been saying to call to his father, at which Sir Rowley nodded in an absent sort of way, as though he had not fully heard. Reaching the door, Edward opened it for Mrs Whatmough and the two of them went inside together. To hide her disappointment, Caelica gave all her attention to Mr Rendle, who was listing the reasons why he preferred larch trees to elms. Although meeting Edward and realising that he was the spirited horseman who had passed her on the bridge had at first brought on all shyness, she liked his broad smile and easy laugh. It was understandable that he should wish to make himself attentive to his father's house-guest, but she could not help wishing she too could talk with something approaching Mrs

Whatmough's sparkle and vivacity. Why, then he might have spent more time with her, and her shyness might have vanished.

Ten minutes later, while Mr Rendle held forth on the subject of sunken fences, Edward and Mrs Whatmough returned. They must have shut the dog in its kennel, for it was no longer with them, and Mrs Whatmough had exchanged her fine silk shawl for a warmer woollen one. Graceful, her silvery smile encompassing Mr Hearne and Sir Rowley, she walked up to Mrs Hearne, took her by the arm, to Caelica's amazement, and led her, in the most amiable manner imaginable, towards the sun dial, chatting as she might to a dear friend. At the same time, Edward bowed to Caelica.

'My dear Miss Hearne,' he said, his blue eyes bright, his voice inviting. 'You really must see my horses. You've heard quite enough of Mr Rendle's talk for now, I surmise.'

So, he had sought her out after all. Such a turnabout, she could hardly believe. In sudden happiness, she took his proffered arm and went at his side towards the cobbled stable yard.

On the journey home, Caelica scarcely noticed the discomfort of sitting with her back to the horses. Thoughts of Edward Curwen filled her mind – he had shown himself to be so amiable a companion, his talk so diverting and his manner so frank. Not only had he shown her his fine grey horse munching hay in its stall, but also the plot where Sir Rowley hoped to grow roses. While she had never taken much interest in horses or gardens before, to find herself in the company of a young man who so loved to laugh and who spoke of subjects other than God and learning was a new and delightful experience. She liked the way he talked without waiting for her response; it meant she did not fret lest her stammer get in the way of her replies.

His unaffected, artless intimacy charmed her beyond measure. As they walked together across the wide lawn, whenever he spoke, he had smiled down into her eyes, as though he cherished her company. A sensation – strong, warm, pleasant and hitherto quite unknown to her – came over her, so that, despite her diffidence, she wanted to laugh and sing. Here was no tepid, polite friendship. This was surely love. True, it was as yet in its infancy, but in time it would surely grow as rich and gorgeous as the crimson heart's-ease he had twined in her hair.

What was more, he was coming to stay at the parsonage. It wasn't an idle pledge of unfixed intention, but a firm appointment. Sir Rowley, it emerged, was hoping to install a pumping engine to keep the lead mines clear of water. Scouring the flanks of the slopes for mineral veins and digging into them was all very well in the early stages, he averred, but now the time had come to disembowel the very hill itself. When the elements resisted their efforts, his engine would fight them with pistons, pump rods and an immense oak beam. He had already had a specification for it drawn up which he and his mine manager were both eager to see. If Edward were to collect the plans from the coach office at Carterford, might he then break his homeward journey with the parson and his family? It would make for a lighter day than riding the full distance between Menston and Carterford twice over. Besides, the company of Mr Hearne, his hospitable wife and accomplished daughter would surely give him a pleasanter welcome than he would get at an inn.

To Caelica's satisfaction, her father saw the sense in the suggestion at once. Marvel of marvels – Edward Curwen was to spend the following Thursday night under their very roof.

Nearing home, they saw Anstice running up to the carriage. Before it had even stopped, she thrust a folded paper in the window, her face pouchy with apprehension. At once, Caelica's father called to the coachman and the horses halted while Anstice, panting, explained that old churchwarden Watkin had been that very day in Carterford. Seeing a letter for the rector at the coach office, he had brought it back with him.

Caelica's father rent it open, spread wide the single sheet, scanned it and handed it to her mother without a word. Pale already, the last vestiges of colour drained from her face as she read the brief note. At last she folded it, her hands shaking, and gave it back to her husband, all the strength in her bearing – there was never much – seeping away in front of their eyes. Before they could say anything, she opened the carriage door, climbed down and headed past Anstice towards the house, her stick forgotten.

'My dear,' blinking as though with anxiety, Caelica's father went after her. 'It is not good news, I grant you. Yet the court may show clemency.'

Wordless, she shook her head, her eyes closed, her lips compressed and near grey.

Picking up her mother's ebony cane, Caelica got down and tried to thank the impassive Menston coachman without stammering. The letter must concern Christopher. To judge from her father's words it confirmed that the grand jury had summoned him to face trial at the Assizes.

Chapter Eight

On the day of Edward's visit, Caelica's father decreed that she should have no lessons but instead help Anstice prepare for their overnight guest. Anstice, who had been so truculent about readying a room for Thomas, took quite a different attitude towards putting things in order for young Mr Curwen of Menston. She threw open the heavy oak presses on the landing to seek out the sheets in which the scent of lavender was strongest and which had the fewest darns, while Caelica, catching her fierce energy, shook the curtains of the airy east room to dislodge the dust and then swept the floor. Once the two of them had made up the bed, far from carping about candles, Anstice suggested that Caelica rubbed up a full half dozen pewter sconces with gritstone and vinegar, so that the guest should have plenty of light by which to dress and read.

All the time she worked, Caelica could feel her mother's misery, seeping through the house like the smell of festering fruit.

'Why, daughter, must you rush about so?' she asked in a thin voice when Caelica came into the parlour.

'A – Anstice and I h-have m-much o-on hand, m-mamma.' As usual, her stammering grew worse under her mother's questioning and once she had thrust out the stubborn words, her mother gave her a long, hard look, lips narrowed and meagre eyebrows drawn together.

'M-Mr Curwen d-does not mean to impose up-upon our – our h-hospitality,' Caelica tried to justify Edward's visit. With every sentence, she grew less articulate. If only her mother would answer instead of just staring at her, knowing and silent. A word of acknowledgment – to seek encouragement would be too much – might lift her spirits and ease her speech. But her mother stayed mute, her features static.

'S-sir R-Rowley b-egg-begged it of our kindness,' Caelica remembered, leaving off her dusting to explain. 'I kn-know it goes ill w-with Kit, mamma,' she had the idea that she sounded more petulant than persuasive, 'yet Edward will have trav-travelled a fair distance W-would you have h-had father de-decline to w-welcome him to – to spend the night here?'

At once she reproached herself. Of course her mother had cause to be sad – so did they all.

'Your father extended his invitation to Mr Curwen as a pledge of his goodwill to Sir Rowley.' Her mother's words came sharp as frost in the sun-warmed parlour. 'Yet you appear to treat Edward Curwen's visit as an excuse for conviviality. That he is a personable young man I allow, but do you not see how inappropriate it is to entertain at this time?'

'F-father answered S-sir Rowley's request in good faith a-and be-before he knew of the Grand Jury's decision,' Caelica began, but catching sight of her mother's expression, the words she thought to say swelled to such a size that they became unmanageable. Stricken, she fell silent.

'Sir Rowley,' mused her mother, a knowing smile playing across her long face. 'I believe Sir Rowley has begged your father to put up Edward overnight so that he may have Mrs Whatmough's company to himself.'

Caelica clenched her hands to contain her curiosity. Her mother's observations were often enigmatic. It did no good to ask questions. She would only turn cold and scornful.

'Still,' Mrs Hearne continued, 'Some good may come of the young man's acquaintance – particularly if it leads him to take you off our hands.' Rising, she crossed to the window, and began to scan the distant English horizon.

Whatever her mother's misgivings, her father, it was clear, looked forward with high pleasure to the prospect of conversing with an urbane young man whose over-dinner talk promised to amuse. Realising he was as eager to see Edward again as she was herself, Caelica called to him as soon as she heard hooves on the pathway leading down from the drove road and they both went out to meet their guest.

The afternoon was mild and Edward had been riding in shirt-sleeves, his coat slung over the pommel of his saddle. As he pulled up, the sun caught the fine fair hair on his forearms, turning it to spun gold. Abashed to find herself staring, Caelica turned her attention to his horse. Sturdier than the iron-grey gelding which had baulked over crossing the old bridge that day last autumn, it was no less elegant – a liver chestnut with dark yellow dapples on its flanks and a flaxen mane. Robert, who liked horses, left off repairing the herb garden wall and came to look the beast over, shading his eyes and nodding as he marked the deep chest and powerful hocks.

Her father told Edward to leave his beast for Robert to rub down and to come at once to the house. Following the men at a modest distance Caelica heard him talking all the while, quizzing Edward about his journey, enquiring after the health of Mrs Whatmough and asking whether Sir Rowley would mind if Edward showed them the plans for the new steam engine.

Once he had had a chance to wash and eat and drink, they took him through to the parlour, which Anstice had cheered with a posy of gilly-flowers in a silver vase on the walnut wood table. Having greeted Caelica's mother who condescended at least to rise from her place by the window, Edward sat back on one of the stiff straight-backed chairs, extricated the engineers' specifications from his saddle bag, and began to describe the action of the pistons and pump-rods.

'Ah, so this is how Sir Rowley proposes to keep his workings dry, is it? And will he find fuel enough for his behemoth hereabout, do you think?'

Her father was entranced. Plainly this absorbing, male conversation afforded him infinitely more pleasure than her own diffident overtures. Here was sure testimony, should she require it, of Edward's solid worth. Before long, from discussing the dimensions of the cylinder and rate of coal consumption, he began to ask about her favourite literature and music, approving her tastes with hearty zest. It gave her some surprise to discover how many books and poems she had read which he had not.

Her father broke into their discussion to remark that it would do his pupil no harm to raise his head from his studies and do the amiable for a change. Although there wasn't much society as Edward would comprehend it in Llanmichael, nevertheless they could do more for him than a modest family meal. Having given Robert a note to deliver summoning Thomas to dine at the parsonage, without waiting for the answer, he told Anstice to expect one more at the table that evening. Caelica doubted there would be much fellow-feeling between the two young men, but it was so rare to find her father happy these present days she made no objection.

She was outside the kitchen fetching herbs for Anstice's dish of spring lamb when her tutor arrived, sombre, his cloak damp from Vaughan's coracle.

'Good evening, Miss Hearne.'

'A good evening to you, Mr Russell,' she said. 'You know there is to be company at our table besides yourself.'

'I do. Tell me, Miss Hearne, what manner of man is Sir Rowley Curwen's son? Is he suave and well-learned? Or rustic and boorish? How do you find him?'

'Gen – Gen –' Genial, was what she tried to say. She meant to add that Edward Curwen had views on every subject under the sun, but Mr Russell's question sounded so sour she couldn't find her usual fluency of speech with him. Instead, her hands grew laggardly as her tongue. Fumbling, she dropped her rosemary together with the knife she had been using to cut it.

'Come, let me help.' He bent forward, his rigid expression melting as he gathered up the silver green shoots.

Taking them, breathing their rich scent, she looked at him closely. Here he was, bidden to share a meal that would surely surpass anything he would have to eat in his lodging, and yet he came inconspicuous to the back of the house, his cheeks pale and his manner brusque.

Whatever sort of a parson would he make? The question had no bearing on the evening ahead, but she couldn't dismiss it. He would not condemn the people for their faint hearts and backsliding or their small arrogances and disobediences with the same zeal as her father, nor yet berate them from the pulpit for their ignorance. When they came to him with their worries and woes, he would listen and give what hope he could. She had the sense that in his preaching he would seek to cheer their hearts and fire their spirits. So why did he make himself so stern – his mouth straight, his voice dry, as though all the time he thought more than he cared to reveal? Why couldn't he be as unguarded as Edward Curwen, and let his face light with pleasure?

'Thank you.' Her voice was steady again and as she met his eyes, she saw his uneven smile begin to unfold.

In the event, the gathering delighted her. Through the dark winter months, they had kept themselves to themselves, and eaten with little ceremony. Now they sat at the table in a circle of light – from the fire on the hearth, candles on the table and the sun lingering on the western sky. Edward's presence at the table led her father to play the ceremonious host in the way he used to before Kit's imprisonment, and a faint flush of colour rose in her mother's sunken cheeks. She said little, but the sheen of jet at her throat and ears lent her face a rare touch of vivacity as she followed the drift of the men's talk.

'When did you say you were at Cambridge, Curwen?' her father asked. 'Ah, three years ago, was it? Your memories must shine as yet undimmed, sir. Maybe we'll engage you upon Homer later.'

But he must have seen Edward's grimace because as the meal advanced from soup through trout and towards the dish of lamb, rather than Homer he began to talk about the bridge.

Sir Rowley's scheme of soliciting potential designs he pronounced to be an extraordinarily clever way of arousing interest in the venture. Edward, nodding fervently at the compliment to his father, enquired how many entries there had been.

'Ten at least – perhaps twelve.'

'So many?' He sounded surprised to find the contest arousing such enthusiasm. Draining his glass, he gave a brief laugh. 'Well, Hearne, from so wide a field you are bound to find something good.'

Caelica thought of the crabbed, clumsy bridges in the sketches she had seen. What she had sought and missed in them was something approaching the bold simplicity of the figures she drew for her lessons in geometry. Might some geometric insight, she wondered, provide the vision – the beauty, even – that the drawings lacked? She was trying to find manageable words in which to ask about the relation between bridge building and mathematics, when Edward's voice, loud with a change of subject, interrupted her thinking.

'I met a fellow on my way,' he announced, pushing his plate away and sitting back, 'who maintained that the previous structure fell because it was, as he said, blighted.'

'Blighted?' It was the word Anstice had used. It caught at her father's wits like fire at a rag.

'So this fellow would believe,' Edward insisted, laughing.

'How so?' Caelica saw her father had put aside the liberal host and become once more his abrupt, probing self. Edward did not know him well enough to mark the shift.

'What manner of man was he?' her father rapped.

'A carrier, sir,' continued Edward, blithe and carefree. 'I passed him near the summit of that great hill between here and Carterford. He warned me that if I were heading into Wales, I should not be able to cross the river at Llanmichael short of fording it. Of course I knew it already, but since he was minded to gabble, I let him tell me about it. The cause of its falling, so he said, was that a young woman had done away with herself by plunging to her death in the waters beneath.'

Caelica watched as her father heeded this statement in silence.

'Some heartless gallant,' Edward went on, 'must have loved her for a while and then left her forever, caught upon the cusp of ruin.'

He looked round at them, confident of their agreement.

Under the table Caelica gripped her hands together hard, wishing she might make him aware of the perils of this subject before he took it any further. Thomas, freckled and serious, bit his lip as though he too wanted to utter some warning before Edward said anything more. All the liveliness had drained her mother's face and she stared, stony, at the fire.

'Proceed,' said her father softly. 'Say how the woman's drowning precipitated the fall of the bridge. Explain the link between the events.'

At last, Edward must have seen that something was amiss, for he paused as though taking stock of his listeners. 'There was more.' Evidently he decided that in the clergy view his talk must be unsuitable for female hearing because now, albeit without answering the question, he leant forward to whisper to the gentlemen across the table. 'What to my informant's mind magnified the evil of the original offence,' he confided, 'was the fact that some parson of the district – I know not whom, but, forgive me sir, the man must be known to you – actually accorded Christian burial to the woman's remains. Apparently he instructed the local coroner to dispense with the customary order about burying the corpse in unhallowed ground.'

'Now,' with a burst of his old assurance, his voice once more rose. 'I know little about the niceties of the law relating to self-murder, but to my mind there can be no surprise if such conduct gives rise to scandal. Here the clergyman surely exercised a most unwarrantable degree of discretion. Might not the explanation that you seek, Mr Hearne, lie in his bold defiance of church teaching?' asked Edward with a righteous expression. 'Whatever can have swayed his thinking?'

'Compassion.' It was Thomas who spoke, and Caelica wanted to thank him with all her heart.

'D-do not forbear to talk of th-these matters on my account,' she interjected, her composure returning. 'I-I was with

Mr Russell when he re-recovered the - the corpse from the river and later, I - I w-was on hand when my father here buried her.'

Edward looked from Caelica to Thomas and then to Mr Hearne. As he realised his error, a dark flush engulfed his face.

'You, sir, buried her?' he asked at last.

'I did indeed, sir,' the rector pronounced, 'and I acted, as Russell here intimates, from motives of godly compassion.'

'Sir, I can only offer my most profuse apologies,' Edward began, swallowing as he plumbed the depths of shame. By the candle light Caelica could see her father's lips spread as though in sardonic amusement at their guest's confusion.

But he was quick to compose himself. 'Now Curwen,' he said, brisk and purposeful as he cut short Edward's protestations of contrition, 'you did not know when you raised the matter, what parts my pupil and my daughter and I played in the events that followed upon the young woman's demise. I will not bandy words, with you sir, over the right and proper way for me to conduct my business in my parish. In recent days, I have more than once come across the superstitious notion that self-murder could have adverse consequences for our old bridge. This present occasion is hardly a fit time at which to discuss the error in logic and failure of reason, but all rational men would conclude that the bridge fell because it stood in so advanced a state of disrepair that its disintegration was unavoidable. It was a process conforming to the laws of physics, therefore all talk of "blighting" is so much mummery moonshine, would you not agree?'

Edward signalled his agreement with great vigour. Caelica saw her mother continue to watch the embers, while Thomas smiled ruefully, as though in fellow-feeling for anyone unfortunate enough to catch the rector on the raw.

'Yet Hope rises out of misfortune, even as she rose from Pandora's box, and bears blessings on her wings.' Her father's dogmatism was once more giving way to hearty liberality. 'The contest that we have in hand will bring a new bridge into being, the merits of which will no doubt far surpass those of its precursor.'

Thinking again of the dismal drawings Caelica marvelled at his optimism.

'Now, my good sir,' he rose. 'Before we dined I heard you ask my wife if she cared at all for music. I assure you that she does – she's very fond of it. Do you sing at all? Then let us go through to the parlour. Provided that your songs are well known, I am sure my daughter will be able to furnish an accompaniment.'

The music served to dispel any lingering tension. Edward proved to have a fine voice which served to redeem any stock he might have lost with Mr Hearne earlier, and the songs and glees he had committed to memory included many that Caelica knew and liked. Glancing from her place at the harpsichord to where her mother reclined upon the sofa, Caelica could see that her eyes were calm with peaceful sadness instead of brimming with a ferment of grief. She must be allowing Edward's fine singing and the restored good will of the evening to soothe her sore spirits. Then her father supplied the bass part to Edward's tenor in 'Castor's Lament' – it was one of his favourite pieces - and when they had finished, the two of them sat down together on either side of the fire to talk.

'W-will you sing now?' she asked her tutor, since he lingered by the instrument.

'If you wish.'

'Shall it be "Vital Spark?" ' she suggested, teasing him with a song that was almost a hymn because he was looking so solemn and thoughtful.

'Very well, then,' he answered, as though her suggestion was serious.

Careful, she played over the opening bars.

Vital spark of heav'nly flame!

he sang,

Quit, oh quit this mortal frame:
Trembling, hoping, ling'ring, flying,
Oh the pain, the bliss of dying!
Cease, fond Nature, cease thy strife,

And let me languish into life.

This accompaniment was so familiar beneath her fingers that she could play it while giving her thoughts free rein. She found Thomas a less spontaneous singer than Mr Curwen, but his voice was strong and true. It was strange that both men should sing in the same register and yet sound so different. Mr Curwen's music was airy and evanescent; it was pleasant while it lasted and then faded from the mind. Thomas' song would, she thought, stay with her rather longer. Of course the haunting quality came down in part to the sentiments, reflective and tinged with melancholy, but underlying his interpretation of them was all the gentleness, all the sensibility that he was at such pains to hide when he was teaching her.

Hark! They whisper; Angels say,
Sister spirit, come away.

These words were charged indeed. She had thought she knew them well, yet never before had she noticed their high intensity. Was it her imagination, or did her tutor allow his eyes to stray towards her as she played? For all the skill that he brought to bear upon the piece, she found that she could not, did not, want to return his gaze. It was best, therefore, since she had no music book on which to focus, that she should look past him to where Edward and her father continued to converse.

The world recedes; it disappears!

He was singing softly, very softly now.

Heav'n opens on my eyes!

She hoped that to outward appearance she remained detached, yet she could not help but see how the words, the melody and the harmonies in the harpsichord music all drew her towards the passionate heart of what, until now, she had taken to be a staid little piece that did well for funerals. Deliberately, she stared at where Edward, the firelight playing across his easy smile, chatted to her father.

My ears
With sounds seraphic ring:
Lend, lend your wings! I mount! I fly!

There was no question but that Mr Russell was looking at her. Fortunately, with her mother sewing as usual and with Edward and her father absorbed, she alone noticed.

O Grave! Where is thy Victory?
O Death! Where is thy Sting?

And without any tremor of transition, the words ceased to be high poetry and settled themselves back into the demure cadences of a hymn. How could she have imagined that sober Thomas Russell would sing with anything other than the utmost propriety, as befitted his future profession?

Once he had finished, Edward broke their silence.

'Ah, Russell,' he rose, 'your musicianship far exceeds my own. That was, beyond question, a fine execution of the piece. Mr Hearne, I thank you for this evening's many delights.' Satisfaction at finding things secure and upon friendly footing once more rang in his voice. 'Your daughter,' he continued, 'has a sweet, sure touch upon the keys and makes music with every grace. Miss Hearne,' he made a deep, respectful bow, 'I felicitate you upon your accomplishments.'

Sheer candour shone in his eyes. Besides her father's subtlety and even her tutor's unlikely artistry – what alchemy had he worked upon those dry words to make them quicken with such warmth and tenderness? This bluff frankness blazed like a beacon. Over dinner he might have laughed too loud and talked too much but he could not be blamed for failing to realise what an unhappy subject he had pursued. At least he dropped it as soon as he recognised his mistake. She hoped the incident would not discourage him from remaining on friendly terms with them, for his easy affability charmed her to the core. Looking to where he stood by the fire with one arm resting on the mantelpiece, she found his keen blue eyes resting on her and, smiling back at him, she felt herself possessed with sudden fire

Much later, after Thomas had gone home to his lodging and Anstice locked the doors, Caelica sat up in her chamber brushing out her hair. Outside, a gale had sprung up which lashed the windows with rain and made the panes rattle. Watching her candle flame dance, she knew she was in love with Edward. In terms of the logic and reason so beloved of her father, on so short an acquaintance, it should be impossible, but how far did the rule of logic and reason extend? Logic might hold the key to the true cause of the bridge's downfall, but it could not explain to her why she loved to look at him, to say his name, to feel him lighting the parsonage like the summer sun. She remembered the gold hair on his arms, the slow curve of his broad mouth; the nose so well-shaped for geniality, being neither thrusting like her father's, nor crooked like Thomas's, nor yet bony like her mother's and her own. Thinking about him made her breathe fast and hectic, and she found herself pushing her elbows into her sides to keep herself from untrammelling.

Soon, she would untrammel to her heart's content, breathing his name a thousand times over with only her dreams to hear. *Edward* – she tried it in a whisper. Her comb met a tangle, so she ran her fingers down through her hair to loosen the knot. How would it be if it were he who sat in a chair at her side with the comb in his hand, drawing it through each curl? How would it be if he should sweep the brush through the whole length of her hair with great rhythmic strokes, so that his hand touched it, and his body pressed warm against her own? How would it be when he picked up a lock of it to hold in his hand? How would it be, to lie with a man? Hannah Hallet had known. She had lain with Kit in a corner of sunny pasture, and once perhaps the sight of him coming across the fields had made her tense with anticipation just as Caelica tensed when she thought of Edward. He had touched her shoulder when he bade her good night. Kissing the place, she deliberately put her comb on the linen press, turned back her bedcovers, snuffed out her candle and settled herself to think in the darkness.

Chapter Nine

As Summer drew on, they saw much of Edward Curwen, his father and Mrs Whatmough. Sometimes the three of them caused the minute congregations at Sunday matins to swell, which so cheered Caelica's father that he would urge them to pass the time of day or even stay for a meal at the parsonage afterwards. Sir Rowley's attentions flattered him immensely, while Mrs Whatmough's winning manner drew a little conversation from her mother, and whenever Edward spoke to Caelica, she had the sense of being drawn out from the shadows into the light of day.

One morning she was in the garden airing the household linen and trying to imagine what he might be doing when Anstice emerged from the kitchen door. Ever since the evening when the stone-throwing townsmen had attacked the house, instead of putting the parsonage sheets and tablecloths over the bushes on the hillside to bleach in the sun, they hung them in the herb garden. Draped across the stout hedge which ringed the beds of rue, lavender, sweet marjoram and feverfew – aromatics hardy enough to withstand the cold and wet Marches winters – they were hidden from prying eyes. Beyond the encircling wall, ran a path leading in one direction to the church and in the other up the hillside towards the wide track by which the drovers took their herds to market. While the drove road saw many travellers, few people ever had reason to venture along the steep path skirting the back of the parsonage.

Caelica shook out a sheet to spread across the hedge. Although it was clean, it was tired to the touch which made her think it must have lain unused for a long time at the bottom of the press. She wondered if there was enough breeze in this secluded patch to restore its crispness; feeling the light wind tug at its corners, she picked up a couple of clean stones to weight it down. A horse's hooves sounded from the stables and she heard her father thanking Robert for saddling the mare. A moment later, formal in wig, bands and clerical hat, he rode out of the front gateway and headed towards Menston.

Anstice, who had been spreading a heavy linen table covering out across the lowest part of the hedge, straightened and rubbed her fleshy back.

'Our menfolk reckon that housework is no work at all,' she said, looking at Caelica sidelong. 'Leastways, I can't speak for your father, but my Robert'll tell me how hard a day he's had when he's strapped both horses and put in an extra hour on tending the garden. He makes out that what I do – cooking and cleaning and scouring and such like – is nothing. But the weight of this cloth runs down my spine like a skewer. If you weren't here to help, Miss Caelica, it'd take me till the next shower came on, and then I'd have to fetch everything in again.'

'Well, I m-must make haste, Anstice, f-for Mr Russell is c-coming to give me a lesson in mathematics.'

'Book learning.' Anstice reached down into the shallow basket at her feet, took up one of the delicate roundels that Caelica's mother had embroidered, gave it a righteous shaking and hung it on the bay tree. Then she wiped her large nose on the back of her hand. 'Your father knows his business, I suppose, but to my mind, girls don't need mathematics – nor yet that Latin he has you read. Isn't it enough for him that you're kind and clean and pretty?'

'He knows th-that I en- enjoy learning,' said Caelica. Why must Anstice always be sparking off arguments? 'And he w-wishes, I know, to f-find some employment f-for Mr Russell by w-which to support himself.'

'Well, if you enjoy it, I suppose that's something,' but Anstice's earth-coloured eyes were sceptical. 'Though as for that Mr Russell, I reckon he'd be better off tilling the fields or repairing the walls and ditches – anything other than book work.'

'But he seeks to be ordained as a cl-clergyman.' It was vain to defend her tutor to Anstice when she had so little time for him. 'He n-needs to read much. Besides, my father, Mr Russell and I all h-hold our learning and our books dear.' She tried to laugh through her stammering speech so as to soften the implicit reproach. 'Th-there surely is no harm in our ge-geometry, nor yet in r-reading the old authors?'

Anstice pursed her lips and nodded wisely. 'I'd hardly expect you to say a word against your father,' she said, 'but I didn't reckon to hear you talk up for that red-haired solemn-sides.'

'A-Anstice—' Denigrating her father's pupil was insubordination and her parents would not wish her to tolerate it. Besides, Thomas had supported her father over Hannah's burial and helped ease things for Edward on his visit; on both counts she was grateful. Before she could think what to say, the old woman cut in.

'Now don't you go getting sweet on him, Miss Caelica – not for all his book learning. You'd be happier with Mr Curwen, wouldn't you?'

'A-Anstice –'

'Don't think I didn't notice the glow in your cheeks when last he was here,' Anstice went on in a knowing voice. 'Don't tell me you don't think about him all the time when you're alone. He's a proper man, is Mr Curwen, and he stands to inherit a fine, big house. You could be very comfortable, living there.'

'Anstice, Anstice, you –' but still the words wouldn't come.

'What's this "Anstice, Anstice"?' taunted the housekeeper, turning her back and looking at Caelica over her shoulder. 'You think over what I've said when you're reading your fine books. Maybe you'll see the sense of it. Mr Curwen'd make you a handsome husband.'

Anstice, as so often, was right. Caelica thought about Edward every hour of every day, but it was hot shame to hear the stuff of her thinking laid bare in broad speech. Should she try to take Anstice to task, her stammer would make a mockery of her words. Therefore, saying she had to go, she made an abrupt goodbye and walked back to the house. Behind her, she heard a sound like stifled laughter.

Thomas, apprehensive, waited for his pupil in Hearne's library. Looking out of the window, he watched the rooks squabbling among the branches of the great ash trees near the house. So potent, so all-consuming had his fondness for Caelica grown – fondness was far too tepid a term – he could keep it to himself no longer. Ever since he and she had looked over the bridge drawings together he had yearned to tell her of his love. When he had sung *Vital Spark of Heav'nly Flame* that evening Hearne invited him to dinner to provide some smattering of learned company for Edward Curwen, he had meant it for her alone. He had been tutoring her for over a year now, careful to observe the proprieties, always making himself reserved and distant in deference to her father's clear wish, but he adored her. To prolong his silence was unthinkable.

When she arrived, her face bore a ruffled, defiant expression as though seeking to compose herself. But she gave him a rueful glance of unspoken apology and went to her usual place on the long side of the oak table.

'Miss Hearne,' He beckoned her to the high window. 'Look at this before you sit down,' and he stood to one side so that she could see. One of the rooks had flown down and was probing with its dark grey beak at the ground beneath the trees.

'I believe he must be going after dor-beetles or worms– watch.' Where the bird was foraging, the earth was bare and soft. An ash-bough had come down in high winds the previous autumn, leaving a raw scar that was beginning to darken and moulder on the tree's trunk. High above in the surviving branches, other rooks rasped with restless voices.

'He's found an abundant supply of food,' she agreed. 'O –'

Perhaps it took fright at hearing her voice through the glass, for the bird paused in its meal, then spread its ragged wings in flight. Watching it flap a short distance through the air, then settle in another ash, this time closer to the river, she turned to him her eyes alight.

'To your geometry, Miss Hearne,' he heard his teaching voice insist as he went to the table's head and sat down. Watching the rooks was only a diversion.

'Secancy?' she asked opening the instrument box in front of her and taking out rule and compasses. He remembered having mentioned the study of intersecting lines and curves at their previous lesson, but he hesitated. In truth, geometry was a diversion too. If he should once start talking about arcs and angles, he would assuredly lose all resolution.

'Ah, yes – secancy,' he agreed after a moment's pause. 'But Miss Hearne.' Absently, he picked up her proportional compasses, and started to open and close them, unsure how to begin and conscious that the back of his neck and the palms of his hands were sweaty with misgivings. He could not think how to begin. He put the compasses down, half rose, sat down again and looked at her straight.

'Miss Hearne,' he must retain all formal courtesy, 'Miss Hearne, I have come to nurture high respect and regard for you. If – if I were to approach your father and secure his consent, would you consider agreeing to become to my wife?'

He knew these awkward words, so strained and circumlocutory, were not good. 'High respect and regard' was overbearing, and what was this indirect nonsense of his proposal to propose? But he could hardly stem the formal vein now.

'You know my likely prospects,' he went on, 'and you have known the pattern of life among the clergy from your childhood. I – I can say no more.'

Threads of thought spun in her mind. This - this was a proposal of marriage. It paralysed her with astonishment. For it to come so soon after Anstice's goading was a turnabout indeed. There was so little preamble to his words, only a few seconds of friendliness as they watched the rook together, then he put that question about becoming his wife so sharp it almost took the skin off her knuckles. She had supposed that if ever a man should ask her to wed, it would not be in the thick of the business of the day, only a few minutes after she had been airing the household linen. She would have been in far more propitious surroundings than her father's dusty library, with her rule and compasses all in a clutter on the table top.

And what – what would it be, to be his wife? Although today he had surprised her, she knew Mr Russell to be kind-hearted. He taught her with patience and humoured her moments of shyness and hesitancy with such grace that when she was with him she barely stammered at all. He might be over-grave sometimes, but he wasn't a sober-sides, whatever Anstice might claim. His amiability never failed and she liked the way he showed the servants the same courtesy that he showed her parents. He sang well and his verses and breadth of learning proved that he was clever – so did the speed and agility with which he parried words with her father. He had spoken of respect and regard, but what did these words mean? Did he mean that he loved her, but could not bring himself to say so? When he taught her, she liked him, ill-fitting clothes, straggling hair, angular eyebrows, crooked nose and all. But did she love him? Or did she take his part and believe the best of him because he was so often the butt of her father's contempt? And what would it be, to share his life, his house, his bed?

If he were so rash as to speak to her father upon the subject of their marrying, she could not imagine that he would find any favourable hearing. Her father had not given her books, provided for her to learn Latin and geometry, to draw and to play upon the harpsichord with the intention that she should in time marry his pupil who might hope someday to become another country clergyman. Her father and, more particularly, her mother were more ambitious for her, she knew.

And all the while – confound Anstice for her needling – thoughts of Edward Curwen transfixed her very wits. Recollection of his stature, fair hair and wide, ready smile floated - the fragments of an image - before her mind's eyes. For a second, she caught the exact timbre of his voice and felt his deft fingers twining the flower in her hair.

Thomas watched her, numb, telling himself it should be no surprise to see her look away in silence, her blushing too fierce for her fair colour. For all the ponderousness of his absurd formula – asking her if he might ask her father if he might ask her to marry him – he had been over hasty. Resting his elbows on the table, he felt waves of failure beat against him. Despite the open window, the air in which motes of scornful dust circled grew suddenly heavy, while the spines of Hearne's books loured their contempt from the shelves.

'I d-do not kn-know how to answer,' she began, her voice almost under control as, at last, she met his gaze. 'You – you would ask me to wed you? I – I -I do not – I cannot – that is to say – A-and I d-do not kn-know what my father's response m-might be. A-And he h-has gone from home this day and sh-shall not return till evening.'

He had desired to hear her speak for herself, had thought it a kindness to solicit her feelings in the matter before speaking to Hearne; now he abhorred the idiocy of this action. He should have foreseen that to spring such a surprise upon Caelica would not so much win her confidence as mire her in shock. Hearne might be a tyrant, but he was also her father. She loved him. For Thomas to probe and drive her towards answering giving his proposal without allowing her to seek the counsel of her parents was rank cruelty.

'I understand.' The phrase had a reasonable sound, although all he really understood was that he had behaved like the crassest boor. 'It would be well, would it not,' he went on, 'if we abandoned your lessons for today. Forgive my – my –' now he was stammering worse than she – 'my want of sensibility,' he finished, the words like ashes on his tongue. 'Well, good day to you, Miss Hearne,' and, though he knew it was abrupt to the point of gracelessness, he rose, gathered his books and left.

Caelica's lessons curtailed, time hung heavy upon her. When the library clock struck noon, she went downstairs for the mid-day meal, she and her mother facing one another in almost total silence across the dining table while Anstice, her brown face dour and shrewd, served them with cold pigeon pudding. Unable to swallow, Caelica longed to tell her mother of what had happened. However much she might struggle in the telling of her tale, the discipline of making an account of the proposal would – might – help her find a way through her present straits. Words, phrases with which to open her story would come into her mind, but as soon as she looked into her mother's wan face, saw the narrow lips compressed and the metallic eyes that stared steadfastly ahead, they would sink away again unspoken. The meagre repast done, Caelica's mother retired to her chamber.

In the absence of any clear task, Caelica went into the parlour. The room with its harpsichord at one side and the walnut wood table in the centre felt too still, as though it resented her presence. Even so, she sat down on one of the chairs by the fireless hearth and tried to read, but no book – not even poetry – held her attention. Walking over to the windows, she looked out into the soft day. Beyond the path that led to the town, the river glinted in the sun as it tumbled over the shattered stones of the broken bridge. In the past, there would have been packtrains crossing or waiting to cross, the ponies sweating with the weight of the ore on their withers and the buckles of their harness jingling in the still air. Now, except for a couple of distant figures walking in the direction of Pwllfechan, the road was deserted.

Listless, she went to the harpsichord and picked up a book of music thinking to improve her playing, but soon she lost heart. Instead of the music, she saw Thomas, thin-faced and intent, his colour verging from its usual pallor to the violent red of their earlier conversation. His unexpected half-laughter over the hungry rook, caught with such clarity at her ear, he might have been sitting in the parlour at her side.

She slammed down the lid of the instrument, and set herself to draw. Sketching fast with bold lines and defiant shading she embarked upon a portrait of Edward Curwen. Thinking of his ready talk over dinner at the parsonage, and the easy solicitous way in which he had offered her his arm as he

106

showed her the gardens at Menston, she thought she should be able call to mind the outline of his personable face, yet somehow it refused to come. She tried to sketch his regular squarish features, to catch the texture of his thick hair and the gleam of zeal in his eyes, but the task defeated her. She might summon a shifting, blurring likeness of him to her memory, but before she could delineate it on paper, the image would fade and dissolve.

Stubborn, she continued – page after page. If only she persevered, surely Edward's picture would emerge in time and he would smile up at her at last? Again and again she started to work up the broad brow, the guileless eyes and the genial nose, but her vision quickly lost its focus, and she would score through her handiwork and discard it. For all her shading and shaping, the faces she produced were fictitious - pleasing in their way, but nothing like Edward Curwen.

Miserable with failure, her right hand aching from her tense grip upon her pencil, she decided she must talk with her mother after all. Despite the all-consuming worry about Kit – a daughter's frets always counted for less than a son's plight – her mother would surely hear her out and bring some advice to bear upon the question of how Caelica was to respond to Russell's offer. Putting her sketching materials away, she crumpled up her wasted pages and threw them onto the hearth.

The room in which her mother chose to spend her days had once been a nursery; now it stood empty, except for a solitary chair and table. Outside the door, Caelica paused then knocked. There was no answering word, nor even a sigh and steps. No sound reached her except the faint rise and fall of breathing. Cautious, Caelica opened the door. Her mother sat upright on a narrow oak chair by the large east-facing window. She didn't lift her eyes from her work, but as Caelica approached, went on stitching steadily with black thread upon black silk. Infinitesimal stitches they were, small beyond belief, the needle in her skinny fingers advancing with inexorable speed.

'Mother,' said Caelica. With no reply, her voice began to shake. 'M-mother,' she repeated.

But her mother stayed silent, blaming her for not being Kit. There was no defence to the charge. With a sense of defeat, Caelica reached out and touched the thin arm.

'Mother, I-I h-have this day received wh-what I t-take to be an offer of marriage.'

Her mother barely lifted her eyes from the fabric. Caelica realised that all hope of hearing words of wisdom or encouragement was vain. Yet although her mother continued to sew, the pace of her stitching slackened a little and the grim line of her mouth crumpled meditatively.

'Well,' she said at last, her eyes still intent upon the sheen of the cloth, 'you are of marriageable age.'

'I-is th-that all you can say?' It was searing to find her confidence so roundly dismissed. 'D-do you not seek to to know what manner of man b-begs for my hand?' demanded Caelica. 'Do you not c-care to consider wh-whether I may be h-happy with him or nay? Wh-whether he m-might love me?'

Her mother still did not look up from the silken wisp in her hands. 'The matter of whom you marry and when does not concern me.' Clear as glass, her speaking mocked Caelica's stammer. 'I have no interest in you. Your father, I am certain, will give his consent only to a match that befits the standing of our family. As for your feelings for any man who may chance to ask for your hand, they are of no significance.'

'Bu-but -' She must speak out while she could, for soon her tongue would tie up once more. 'Ha-have you truly no curiosity, mother, over the man th-that w-would wed me? Do you not w-want t-to know the w-words in which he wooed me?' Her fracturing voice was rising, hot tears massing behind her eyes. 'Have you no th-thought for whether th-there might be any l-love between us or no?'

At last, her mother put her sewing aside. Turning to Caelica, she gave her a hard, appraising stare that soon turned into a look of boredom. 'No,' she said. 'I have no concern for these things. Once, perhaps, I might have found them diverting; now my only wish is to see your brother come home.'

For just a second, the faintest note of purpose entered her voice. 'But you will, I trust, acquaint your father with the fact that you have received an offer of marriage? Let it be his concern, not mine. Now leave me.'

Purposeful, she cut off her silk thread, though there was a good length left, threaded a new strand into her needle and resumed her work. Cold and chastened, Caelica left the room.

Chapter Ten

Caelica shrunk from the thought of telling her father, but once they had eaten and her mother retired early to bed, she went to keep him company in the parlour. With the curtains drawn and in the firelight, it no longer felt still and unfriendly. He was by the hearth and she took the chair facing him. Biding her time, she listened while he described the conditions of his ride home.

'All the roads in this district are bad beyond endurance.'

It was not like him to remark on the poor state of the thoroughfares. In all the years they had lived in Llanmichael unless his horse should have actually fallen to its knees and thrown him, he had endured rutted, stony, nigh-impassable lanes without a word of complaint. Promoting the bridge competition must, she supposed, have spurred this new interest in communications and ease of travel.

Murmuring in agreement, she waited to see whether she might turn the tide of their talk to the subject of the strange proposal of marriage she had received.

'Wh-when the town h-has its new bridge,' she began, bending over the fraying table cloth that she was mending, 'and finds itself on a great highway once more –'

'Hmm?'

'It will pr-prosper again, will it not?'

'Somewhat.' He reached up to take one of his long-stemmed pipes from the mantel shelf, extracted a pouch of tobacco from his coat pocket and started pressing it down in the bowl.

'It'll never be a place of much wealth, as I foresee. The small farmers live in modest comfort.' Bending, he took up a flaming splinter of wood from the fire and lit the pipe. 'But the men who scrape a living from the common lands face constant hardship, especially now the landowners are so hot for enclosure. Once we get our new bridge under way and see a turnpike sanctioned by law, things may improve for the folk who live by the trades that roadways generate. You know – inn keeping, ostlering, farriery, and such like. All the same, I can't see anything that promises to make the sons of Llanmichael grow great,' and he sat back, puffing meditatively.

Nothing in this speech bordered upon the theme of matrimony. As the smell of tobacco-smoke filled the air, her father frowned and fell silent. He looked drawn and weary.

'B-but,' she persisted, intent upon keeping the conversation alive, 'would you call Sir Rowley with his lead mines a benefactor to the people?'

'In a manner of speaking, I suppose,' he agreed before remarking, pipe in hand, that he could see nothing beneficial about the conditions in which the lead miners worked, or the state of the cottages that Sir Rowley leased to the labourers landscaping the grounds of Menston House.

'His son, young Mr Cur-Curwen,' she knew she would stutter over the name. 'Sh-shall he prove more – more –' No adequate word suggested itself, but a rueful grunt indicated that he had grasped the gist of her half-formed question.

'More enlightened, Cherry, would you say?' He raised his greying eyebrows. 'I doubt it. He was fortunate, when he dined here, to find us so forbearing. But he's personable,' he allowed. 'That much I grant you.'

Here was her opening. 'D-do you feel well-di-disposed to him, father?'

'Has he made you any offer?' At once he straightened, his eyes bright and keen.

'N-no, father. N- not he. B-bu...'

'Well, child?'

'Th-this morning Mr R-russell asked me - th-that is, he said h-he m-meant to ask me-. He hoped t- to ask you if he m-might take me to wed.'

'Russell did at last, did he?'

She had feared his indignation. In fact, he burst into loud laughter. 'Well, anyone could have foreseen that he'd think himself into a love affair sooner or later. I suppose I ought to find his choice flattering.'

To her dismay, she saw that he didn't understand at all.

'Of course there's no question of my giving him permission to ask for your hand,' he went on, pipe in hand. 'You know his father was a self-taught surgeon who died of drink?'

She knew nothing of the sort.

'He had a legacy from an uncle, so he told me,' at least her father's voice was more serious now, 'and he did well to spend it on putting himself through Oxford. Even so, he's not the suitor I'd choose for you, daughter. To be frank, the best I can say of his having lost his heart so near to home is that it'll be easier for me to snub him out of his lunacy. If he'd cast his cap at some girl of the town, we'd like as not have her parents doing everything in their power to promote the match, such is the hunger of Llanmichael people to claim connections with their betters. Then I'd have to lose my misguided pupil from an entanglement that demeaned his calling.'

A note of anxiety entered his voice. 'You haven't given him any encouragement in this business, daughter, have you?'

'N-no, father.' She shifted a little, as though she wanted to see her sewing more clearly by the firelight.

'No? That's just as well. I'll talk him out of his foolishness when next I see him, and tell him to mind his books with more diligence. Thomas Russell's going to end his days as a country curate – you mark my words. Just because your brother faces a criminal charge, Cherry, there's no reason why we should not find you a husband of greater wealth and standing.'

For as long as Edward could remember, it had been Sir Rowley's custom at the day's close to outline its events, good and bad. He would remark on which of his customers made prompt settlement of their account and which procrastinated; he would muse on how the market currently stood; he might even discuss the weather. Except that he never committed his recollections to writing, this act of nocturnal soliloquizing served him as a kind of account-keeping – a reckoning up of each day's worth.

At Menston that evening, after Alice Whatmough had withdrawn from the dinner table to write letters, Edward watched his father drain a full glass of port, place a weighty elbow on the table, lean his great chin in his vast cupped hand and begin to talk. Composing himself to listen like a minor lordling hearing out his king in one of Shakespeare's plays, Edward hoped his attentiveness might have the effect of putting his father in a serene, not to say forgiving state of mind. He had a difficult admission to make, and hoped he might make it without sparking a storm.

Taking advantage of the benign spirit brought on by port and pondering, as soon as his father's tally of the day was done, in a tone he judged to be both apologetic and deferential Edward confessed to having lost a packet. Once he had begun, the account of misfortune spilled from his lips with all the ease of familiarity. His conduct had been most ill-advised – to think of his foolish impetuosity was quite mortifying – allowed companions to lead him on – not entirely sober at the time – experience a harsh lesson indeed – he should never repeat such recklessness – profound embarrassment at having to appeal for funds in this way, but the sum of three hundred guineas was owing and his creditors pressed him at every turn.

It took a few minutes of close silence for Edward to see that far from finding the ready pardon for which he hoped, his self-reproaches had fallen on stony ground. The tender veal they had eaten for dinner, the fine claret they had drunk, the agreeable talk amid the light of many candles – everything that should have set the seal upon paternal magnanimity had somehow failed to achieve the desired end. His father's heavy features ground to a scowl.

'Debts, Edward? Creditors? Have I not heard precisely these sentiments from you many times in the past?'

It was quite true. Edward could not deny that he had often lost packets in recent years. The only details that varied were the packet's precise sum – though it was never less than a hundred guineas – and the place in which the loss had occurred which was sometimes Chester, sometimes Epsom, and sometimes, as on this occasion, Newmarket.

'Edward, you try me beyond all endurance.'

At least his father was not shouting. Perhaps Alice's presence in the drawing room close by curbed his choler.

'You settle to nothing. Think of it.' He gave the dining table a great thump, rattling the crockery and putting the glassware in peril. 'You've no head for business. You gave up the bar. You couldn't even make a go of schoolmastering. Either you idle away your days with dogs and horses, or you go off on a drunken carouse to the races and end up owing monies left and right.'

Agreeing that his father had every reason to feel aggrieved, Edward watched him reach out for the sturdy decanter, half-fill his glass, lift it, glower and then put it down without drinking.

'You know full well that I can't abide the thought of your creditors pestering me when they get no joy out of you, so you come whining to me to pay off this latest round of debts.'

Edward let that offensive term 'whining' pass. Insult was a small price to pay for the sake of finding himself solvent once more.

'Very well. I'll clear your obligations. But listen,' his father disregarded his attempted thanks. 'It is high time you made yourself useful. You can give up your race meetings and set yourself to manage the Menston estate. I want to see you leading a decent, sober life, married to a sensible woman and fathering heirs...'

'Father...'

'If you don't care for that as a prospect, you can consider this alternative. My old assistant Ezra Bragge has taken up employment in the East India Company. Deputy comptroller of excise he is. I've hopes that he'll act as my agent in Calcutta besides working for the Company, but that's by the by. Now, he says he needs a clerk to help in his counting house. Either I can ask him to take you on, or I can ask John to recommend someone while you turn your mind to making Menston profitable and finding an agreeable wife who'll curb your rakish spirits and bear you a mob of sons. Think about it.'

Calcutta? That swamp of fever where there was no hunting? To work alongside the yellow-faced Scottish misery-merchant Ezra Bragge? He'd sooner perish. If he went out to Calcutta, the chances were that he would perish, and that within weeks. There was no need to think about it.

'I don't care to be harsh,' his father continued, 'only to make a fair bargain. Provided you wed a woman who's good-natured, healthy, intelligent, and meets with my liking, I'll double your allowance – I can't say fairer than that. But I'm not prepared to pay off any more of your debts. These are my terms, Edward. Are they clear? Very well. Let us join Mrs Whatmough. Call Briskham for tea at once, would you, please? We have been keeping excessively late hours these past days.'

Rising early next morning, Edward went to the small east facing sitting room where Alice Whatmough was accustomed to read before breakfasting. She had furnished it in her favourite colours and her pair of azure sofas beside the fire looked comfortable and inviting. Still smarting from the exchange of the previous evening, he was too restless to sit and wait for her. Instead, he began to pace the length of her fine carpet, back and forth, fractiously tracing its intricate pattern of gentle browns and blues. Alice, wise, judicious Alice must share his views upon the utter unreasonableness of his father's scheme.

At last, she came in.

'Alice.'

Her smile was slow and full, as though she were surprised, but not sorry to find him there. It was also shrewd. Alice understood the ways of the world; it was why he enjoyed her company so much. With Alice, he never had to play the highbrow or make serious conversation of the type pretty little Miss Hearne had expected from him that leaden afternoon when they had been doing their duty by the parson.

'How fares my father?'

'Rowley is in excellent spirits and will rise shortly and take breakfast,' she said. 'Although I think he has less and less inclination to sit up late of an evening.'

'He – he – oh, Alice,' hang the formalities, he could not contain his outrage. 'He says he wishes to see me married – married and the father of sons.' The confidence burst from him in a mighty rush. 'Can you credit it? He declines to pay my debts unless I settle to manage the estate and get married. Then, he'll double my allowance, but otherwise he would have me go to Calcutta as clerk to Ezra Bragge, of all – Alice, are you laughing? How can you find it a matter for amusement?'

'High amusement.' She was convulsed. Well, perhaps his earnestness did make him appear somewhat ludicrous

'Oh, Edward,' she said through her laughter, seating herself and gesturing to him to sit down facing her. 'Is it so surprising that your father should wish to see you make a respectable marriage? You are a fine-looking affable-tempered young man, but you have yet to acquire your half-brother's settled habits...'

'I have no wish...'

'Yet because you are Rowley's true son, he wishes to see you perpetuate his line. And his name, of course.'

She extended her arm along the sofa's back to where the sunbeams glancing through the broad windows caught the pearl bracelet on her wrist. His eyes travelled on to her hands which, though lithe and slender, looked dry and worn. Noticing the wrinkles around her knuckles and at the base of her thumb, he trained his sight upon the shimmering pearls.

'I think,' she mused, 'while Rowley is fond of John...'

'Fond beyond question.' He breathed the sweetness of her perfume.

'Yet John is only his late wife's son by her previous marriage. He'll always be Rowley's stepson – John Phillips, not John Curwen.' Her musing tone gave way to something sharper. 'Now, Rowley longs for an heir of his own blood to take over the business in time and to keep the name and presence of a Curwen alive in it.'

Edward sighed. He found this insistence that the business needed heirs both wearisome and misplaced. Once his father was in his coffin, he would hardly fret over the question of who ruled the Curwen and Whatmough empire.

'Well, Sophy Phillips is still young,' he remembered. 'Her next infant may be a boy. He may not be a Curwen, but he'll be an heir, will he not?'

Would the son of a stepson be the grandfather's heir? It was a lawyer's quibble and not the sort of thing anyone could expect him to know.

'Sophy, if I read her aright,' Alice gave a sedate smile, 'has no intention whatever of losing her looks and health by bearing John more and more children. Her hopes of producing a son must have faded by now. Reflect – they have Isabella, Elspeth, Marianne, Cecilia and Sophia; five daughters and the eldest no more than eleven. No wonder that Sophy should dread her pregnancies. If she were to find herself with child again, I'd wager it'd be a girl like all the rest. Perhaps they'll all marry well in time, but what a drain on John's means they must be.

'Oh, forgive me if I speak too freely, but even if Sophy should produce a boy, it would not suffice at all in Rowley's eyes. It is to you – his son by birth – whom he looks to provide an heir. And I think that although he considers himself hale for his years and talks of entering Parliament, yet he is, perhaps, frailer than he cares to admit. That is why he urges you to wed. Is the prospect really so bad?'

It was all sound reasoning. Her sensibilities were, of course, too fine to permit her to make any mention of the possibility that were she to marry his father – something he thought highly likely – she must be past child-bearing age. It was an uncomfortable subject and not one on which he cared to dwell. Instead he told her how his father had offered to double his allowance, if he should like the wife he chose.

'Better to marry than burn, especially in the heat of Calcutta.' Alice laughed again. 'You need not think, my dear, that marriage will mean throwing over your old friends, or stagnating in domesticity. On the contrary, managing the

117

Menston estate will give you every chance to arrange delightful rambles in summer and winter balls. Now who, I wonder, would make you a good wife?'

He was about to protest, but she moved to sit at his side, so close to him on the small sofa that her white forearm brushed the fabric of his breeches. The cavilling died on his lips.

'What about Miss Hearne?' she asked.

'Miss Hearne?'

'Why so surprised?' She smiled. 'Think, Edward. She is very attractive, well-mannered and, I believe, drawn to you. She may have no fortune worth speaking of, but since Rowley feels his own lack of formal education greatly it would, I believe, please him to forge a family link with so scholarly a man as the Reverend Matthias Hearne. This match would beyond question win you your doubled allowance.'

For all her crying up the bargain, he wasn't sure how much he liked it.

'Miss Hearne is a sweet maiden,' he allowed, 'but she is over learned. Why, she must have read any number of books. When I dined at Llanmichael parsonage, she followed our talk about that tedious bridge business as if it thrilled her to the marrow. Were I to wed her, I should never keep up with her intellect. No, you must forsake all thought of my marrying Miss Hearne. We two should never fadge.'

'She is clever, of course,' Alice agreed. 'But now I think of it, her brother, so the servants tell me, is in gaol awaiting trial. The Hearnes are at pains not to speak of it, though I believe it is the source of the mother's melancholy. Of course, Rowley might not care to see you wed the sister of a man who may yet find himself convicted.'

'What's her brother's alleged crime?'

'Forgery, so they say.'

'A brother charged with forgery? That brings parson Hearne's heavenly girl down to earth a bit. I like her all the better for it. Alice, how should it be if I were to woo her and win her and convince my father that he likes her before he can raise a scruple of objection?'

'Oh, Edward,' her diminutive hand caressed his large one, 'that should be quite easy. I think she may well be somewhat in love with you already. When she came to Menston with her father and her whey-faced mamma, all the time you talked to her, she shone like a flame in a sheet of glass. I do believe the sun rises in her heart every time you attend matins in Llanmichael church. It would amuse me so much to see you win your doubled allowance with the sister of a convict for your bride.

'Besides,' she went on, turning brisk, 'A clergyman's daughter trained in parsimony and the arts of hospitality would make a good wife by any reckoning. What is more, Miss Hearne is quite innocent and trusting – you might be very glad, my dear, to have a trustful wife.'

What was she suggesting? A shaft of sun fell straight across her face; her eyes in the clear light remained inscrutable.

'Yet her conversation,' he objected. 'It'll always turn on more philosophical learned matters than mine.'

'All the more reason for you to wed her before she turns into a vapid old maid with her nose for ever between vellum pages and no thought in her mind for making life agreeable for those around her.'

Alice began to laugh once more and this time Edward found himself joining in.

It was mid-afternoon and all day the ash leaves had hung motionless in the still air. This was no weather for fretting; the stillness invited action. Leaving the parsonage by the kitchen door, Caelica let herself out of the gate from the herb garden, turned left and headed up the hill.

Walking fast, she soon reached the highest point at which trees grew. Despite the calm of the day, she hugged her cloak tight across her shoulders. The dismissive laughter with which her father had greeted the news of her tutor's proposal shouldn't have surprised her. Her father had never been given to magnanimity and she was used to the cynical amusement with which he took the world's foolishness. Wondering what her father might say to his pupil and hoping that his snubbing would not be too sharp, she let herself walk more slowly.

He would not laugh if Edward Curwen were to ask for her hand, and neither would her mother take news of his proposal in stony indifference. She should not, she supposed, think it unreasonable for her parents to set such store upon finding her a husband of mark and means. And Edward Curwen enchanted her. If he should seek her in marriage, she would not hesitate over her answer. She would accept him at once.

Not far from where she now walked, there lived a woman, an old, old woman who had kept house for the rector of Llanmichael before her father. Anstice had told her of the woman's skill in brewing draughts that would ease a sore throat, or dispel congestion in the lungs. She would even, so Anstice reported after the discovery of Hannah Hallet's corpse, make up a remedy that could put an end to an unwanted pregnancy. 'She uses savin,' Anstice explained, 'which does well enough, if you measure the dosage right.'

There were small signs in Edward Curwen's manner from which she thought that she could discern his growing regard for her. What else but dawning love should have made his eyes light when they had talked at Menston, and speak her name with such gentleness in his voice? Yet could she be certain that love would bring on a proposal? Surely there could be no vice in visiting the woman and begging her for something to encourage him.

The crone's poor primitive magic might change nothing, but Anstice had shown great confidence in her skills. In all likelihood, she would produce some crushed leaves boiled up in brackish water and give Caelica a few wild words to recite before she drank them down. But if the potion could serve to accelerate or make certain of Edward's asking for her hand, even when her brother was disgraced and in gaol, it would be worth her trafficking with the very forces of superstition that her father so despised. And if he ever found out what she had done, he would surely forgive her when he came to read the banns. She had a little money with her with which to pay for a love philtre. What harm could there be in asking?

The wise woman dwelt a little way off the drove road in a low-roofed stone cottage. It commanded a distant prospect of the river and the town, but had no view of either the parsonage or the church behind the hill's concealing flank. Walking up the track that led to the door, she saw how well-cared for the place was, how neat and seemly. Although the soil at this height must be poor and thin, a well-tended garden surrounded the cottage on three sides while a sow rooted in the ground on the fourth. There were curtains at the windows – not poor wisps of tattered muslin like Mrs Hallet's, but drapes of fine lawn through which she could see the flickering of a fire from the hearth within.

Having looked around and found no one at hand, Caelica waited by the doorway.

'Hollo,' she called at last, breathing deep to try to make her uncertain speech clear and even. 'C-come hither, I b-beg you, ma'am. It is Miss Hearne f-from the parsonage.'

'Aye,' a faint voice answered her from a gorse thicket somewhat higher up the hillside. 'Give me time and I'll come to ye.'

Caelica waited, turning to the airy hill where ravens circled and the small brownish sheep browsed. There was so little movement in the air that she could hear Sir Rowley Curwen's men from the far side of the river, cleaving the shaley ground with their picks and mattocks and shouting to one another in thin, urgent voices.

Turning to look behind her at the town far below, she could make out what remained of the bridge. She thought its rate of decay had accelerated since its fall, with the waters tearing constantly at the piers' remnants. The old structure never had much compactness; broken, it looked like a trail of rubble. For a second, she forgot her reason for calling upon the woman who dwelt in these heights, and imagined in the ruin's place a single great span, segment of a vast, generous circle, with the grace and scope of a rainbow arc, only shallower and wrought in stone. Not only would it be quite unlike the old bridge; it would be quite unlike any bridge she had seen. Her conception of it must have its origin in her geometry, though it was extraordinary to think that the stark, severe figures she drew in her lessons should beget so extravagant a fantasy. It was as beguiling as a dream, and every bit as insubstantial.

The old woman limped into sight, smoothing her bulky skirt with earthy hands. Raising her head with eyes narrowed as if, even in these grey conditions, the glare of daylight hurt them she gave Caelica a long, direct look.

'Caelica Hearne.' She did not sound as though she was enquiring whether this was indeed her visitor's name, but more as though she wanted to try the syllables over her tongue to see whether she liked their texture.

Caelica drew herself up. 'Yes, I – I am Caelica Hearne. I have c-come c-calling –' Now, of all times, she yearned to master her stammer. 'T-to make a –a request of you, ma'am.'

The woman waved this talk of requests aside.

'You are daughter to the present parson of this place – the man of learning who ministers in the church he would have us call St Michael and All Angels though it is properly Llanfihangel? And people make an ill match of the English and the Welsh and call it Llanmichael or Michael Church.'

Although it wasn't the conversational opening she had expected, she tried to voice her agreement. The dry, swift voice gave her no chance.

'He seeks to make us serve his English God...'

'W-well...'

'In his language and not our own.'

What fears could the English language hold for someone who commanded it with such ease?

'Why does he wonder that the people of these parts would sooner sing their praises from their hearts in the fields and hillsides, instead of sitting meek under his English eye? Have you come hither to ask why I no longer say my prayers in the dead air of his dusty church?'

'N-no.' She had lost all the words that, only a few minutes before, had been at the front of her mind. Trying to muster them, she saw the woman's face twitch with impatience.

'A-Anstice s-says,' she began.

'The goodwife who keeps house in my place for the parson? What of her?'

'Anstice says, ma'am, th-that you brew r-remedies and –' Was it after all the thought of her father's anger, if he should learn of this exchange, that made her tremble so? 'A-and – and s-simples.'

Her broken words met with only a bald stare. Wanting to bolt like a child, Caelica nerved herself to look straight into the hooded eyes, those slits of clear grey as cold as the hill streams and distant as the clouds, and hope for understanding.

'Why should the daughter of a priest talk of simples?' asked the crone. 'What about the pious supplications that your father must have taught you? Does God not hear them? Why should you think that I will do anything for you, when the Lord-Creator will not?'

This line of talk was not what she had hoped to find. Feeling that her quest was vain, Caelica prepared to make her farewell.

'Wait.' Despite her limp and physical feebleness, the old woman's voice was strong. 'Come into my house,' she invited. 'Sit by my fire. It will make your eyes smart, perhaps, and cause you to cough, but since you will listen while I talk that will not matter, for I do not notice its reek. From that purse hanging at your waist, I see that you have come prepared to pay me for the spell you want. You can pay me for advice instead.'

The inside of the cottage did not look smoky, but something was burning in the grate with an acrid smell that caught at the back of Caelica's throat. She did not know how far she might take this invitation to enter for friendliness, or whether the crone only wanted to taunt her. She motioned Caelica towards a backless settle on the side of the fire closest to the draughts of the doorway, then seated herself upon an upright chair opposite, resting her bony hands on its worn wooden arms.

'You're not a sour woman, Caelica Hearne.' She took a milder tone now, meditative as though she were speaking her thoughts aloud without shaping them for conversation. 'You visited me once when I was ill – I'd broken my leg on the ice one winter, do you recall? You came and read the psalms to me. I've had them by heart since I was a child, but it passed the time for me to listen out for which words you'd stutter over. Maybe the diversion helped me heal. There was damage, of course. Aye, a young man like that Mr Curwen of whom you think so much –' How could she know? Caelica had said nothing about him. '– or even a strong young woman like you would make light of it. I walked sound enough before, and even after my sixtieth birthday I walked to Pwllfechan and back between the sunrise and sunset of a winter's day, and though I'm no cripple, I'll never do that again. And you, Caelica Hearne, you held water to my sore lips so I should not have to stir from my bed; you brought posies of flowers for my table and tempting things for me to eat. Aye, parsonage food is a sight more delicate than what I find for myself now. White bread and butter you gave me, though I fettle well enough on the barley bread with lard and sorrel.

'You sought in your way to be kind. I've little use for charity, but it's worth more than a cold heart.

'You talk of simples. Well, listen. I can brew herbs together that may sometimes ease an illness. Perhaps they do no more than put a sick soul's mind at rest. I've taken something, he or she might say. I've done something to ward off the disease. I've taken a step towards fighting it. So I should recover. And maybe they will recover, though often they won't.

'But when I look into your eyes, Caelica Hearne, and hear the stammer that lies in wait between your tongue and your teeth to stifle your words before they take life, I know you weren't thinking of a remedy for illness. You want magic, don't you? Isn't that right?'

Caelica nodded, unable to trust herself to utter the truth in clear speech. The crone watched her, nodding in her turn. The sour stench of the fire grew stronger and its flames leaped higher up the chimney.

'Well, I have no witchery for you – priest's daughter with the name that means "heavenly".' The intensity of the old eyes' scrutiny stung worse than the smoke. As Caelica had to look away, the slow voice went on.

'But I know why you defy your father by seeking out hidden things, Caelica Hearne. You have a lover. Leastways, there is a man whom you seek for your lover, only he will not come forward to make a pledge of his affection. You hoped I could give you some draught to swallow that would melt his stubbornness and fire his cold heart.'

'But I have no power to soften proud spirits. Money might do that, but your father's not a rich man. Distinction might too, but your only distinction comes from learning – yours and your father's – and no man on earth ever sought to wed a wife on account of the books she'd read. Beauty should conquer him. Are you beautiful, Caelica Hearne? You're pleasing to some eyes, perhaps, but no more so than many a maid of your years. Maybe his idea of beauty doesn't run to brown hair and dark eyes against white skin, for if you were going to conquer him by your looks, it would have happened 'ere now. Are you witty in speech, and a graceful dancer, for these things sometimes take a man's fancy? No, for you speak slow, stammer much and I'd say you were far too shy to lead the sets. What's more, your brother faces a charge of forgery and people hold him responsible for making an innocent woman slaughter herself and her unborn babe beside. Why should Edward Curwen wish to marry you?'

She stood up, rubbing her old, stiff hands as though she sought to make them young and supple once more. 'If he won't ask you to be his, no power on earth can make him. Perhaps you'd live happier with another man – one who loves you with every breath of his being. Or you might live happier single than wed. Now, give me your money Caelica Hearne and go, for I've nothing more to say to you.'

Standing too, Caelica reached into her purse, extracted a number of farthings and a groat and placed the coins on the wooden table. At once she saw this action was wrong; the crone's eyes went to the pile of copper coins and the silver piece and then returned to Caelica's face while she continued to hold out her clawlike hand. Feeling sudden heat in her cheeks, Caelica retrieved the money from the table top and placed it in the palm where the misshapen fingers closed around it.

'You have me to thank for this wisdom, not my furniture,' came the grating voice. 'And you should have had these truths from your mother, rightly speaking. Now,' softening, 'since old Anstice set you on my path and you've paid me quite well, I'll do her a turn in kind. Wait.'

She went outside taking awkward, uncertain steps to return a few minutes later with leaves in her hand.

'There. I may be no witch, but I've skill enough to make herbs grow – even on this barren ground. Take her these with my thanks. There's tarragon, rue, vervain and gentian. She'll have some use for them. Now, on your way, Caelica Hearne, and don't trouble me again.'

But these lavish herbs did not, could not, grow out on the bare hilltop. They might not flourish even in the sheltered garden by the parsonage.

Meek, Caelica took them without question. 'I th-thank you, ma'am and farewell. Wh-what,' she must recapture a little courage, 'what, pray, is your name, ma'am? I – I must have known it once.'

'You do not need to know it. Perhaps it is better that you do not. Now be gone.' As she closed the door there was a scraping from behind it, like the sound of a turning key.

All the way back down the steep path, the crone's words rang, mocking, in Caelica's mind. It was true that she had few of the arts of pleasing – no amusing turn of speech, no very great skill in dancing, assuredly no wealth or legacy awaiting on her parents' death. Her looks might please some, but her mirror confirmed that she was no dashing beauty. Edward Curwen's taste might well run to higher colour and brighter eyes than hers, and it was only to be expected that he should not wish to marry into a family under the shadow of scandal. She had made a great fool of herself and it must have given the old woman much diversion. She would have done better to leave well alone.

It began to rain before she reached the parsonage, and when she entered the kitchen her cloak and her hair were soaked through and her boots muddied. But sweeping aside her stumbling attempt to explain how she had come by the herbs, Anstice hardly noticed.

'Where have you been, Miss Caelica, to keep you so long? Don't tell me now. Mr Curwen is with your father in the library. They asked me to send you to them as soon as you came in. Well, you might take off that wet cloak and hang it over this chair by the fire, but you must go straight upstairs to them.'

Entering the library, she found her father seated at one side of the table, on which burned no few than three tallow candles, and Edward Curwen lolling with every appearance of ease at the other, his chair pushed well back. Her father rose and held out his hand to her.

'My dear, Mr Curwen has something to say which will, I trust, make you very happy. Curwen?'

'My dear Miss Hearne,' rising and bowing, Edward Curwen addressed her in a solemn tone she had never heard him take before. 'Your father has given me his permission to sue for your hand in marriage. Will you do me the honour of agreeing to become my wife?'

Chapter Eleven

Meeting Edward Curwen's frank eyes, taking in his great height, Caelica wondered what humour of fate should have led him to propose in the selfsame room that Mr Russell had chosen for the purpose, and at a time which found her equally distracted? What worth now was she to place on the witch's words? The wise woman had known things that Caelica had never told her. Had she known by her art that even while they talked in the smoke of her fire Edward Curwen was bound for the parsonage to make his offer of marriage? Or had the crone power to shape events, so that despite refusing Caelica the love philtre, she had still brought it about that Edward should propose to her on her return home?

'She is overcome.'

Mute, she looked at her father, begging him without words to draw her out of the incomprehensible eddies of the witch's elemental power and restore her to a world of light and logic.

'Well, daughter?' He smiled his encouragement, but it was no help.

'I – I –'

If she were to recover, it would have to be through her own efforts. Looking to the plain clock they kept on one of the shelves, a volume of Donne's sermons leaning against it, Caelica struggled to speak. 'I –' again she failed.

The clock's hands were crossing the brazen lettering of the maker's name – Francis Abbott, London, 1690. She took a great breath and once more tried to speak out, even and steadfast as the time-piece. No words came.

'Have patience with her, Curwen.' Her father remained amiable. A faint smell of snuff hung in the air between Edward and himself. 'We have spoken of her speech trouble. It is my conjecture that a happy marriage might well go some way towards improving the condition – although I would not be so rash as to suppose that it will ever find a cure.'

As though on impulse, he rose. 'It may be that my presence checks your tongue, Cherry. I shall withdraw to see how Christina doth and leave you and Mr Curwen to talk. But I am eager to hear the outcome of your deliberations.'

At the door he paused, gave her a look of the most earnest supplication before leaving the room, his quiet steps on the wooden floor sounding full of satisfaction.

His term 'deliberations' proved wide of the mark, for Edward, it was clear, interpreted Caelica's hesitation as the flowering of modesty alone. From the way in which he took her right hand in his left and, placing his other arm round her shoulders, drawing her to him and kissing her on her mouth – lingering, savouring her like rare wine – he clearly had no notion that she wouldn't accept him. Yet she found neither this high confidence, nor the kiss, nor his encircling arm displeasing. Had it not been the hope or dream of conjuring his love that had led her to seek out the wise woman? To find her yearning fulfilled in Edward's possessive embrace, his substantial body powerful against her slighter form and her nose quickening to the luxurious scents of wealth – fresh linen, snuff and refined soap – that surrounded him was shocking, but it was hardly uncomfortable. When she became his wife, it would surely compensate her parents for her stammer, her shyness and all the other disappointments she had brought them.

She would have been happy for the embrace to last longer, but all too soon, he stood back and addressed her.

'My very dear Caelica, if I may now use your delightful name – delightful and apt, for you are the very incarnation of all that is heavenly. Your acceptance of my offer makes me happy beyond measure.'

At last, she managed to make some response.

'I-it pleases m-me to find that y-you t-take my ill- ill-formed words f-for acceptance,' she said, her voice uncertain and her pulse insistent. She was happy – of course she was. It was the very outcome she had sought. It was only because it had befallen her so fast that she stammered so much and her heart raced. Before long, her spirit would lift with joy, and she should grow blissful and serene.

'It would be harsh in me,' he was saying, 'to force you to more eloquence than the time allows you to command.'

She supposed he meant that he did not want to watch her struggle to make graceful speeches, which was further evidence of well-meaning on his part. As he spoke, he put his powerful arm around her once more. Conscious of her damp and rain-spattered dress, she gave him an anxious glance, but found no dismay in his eyes – only a misty detachment, as though having secured her acceptance, he was looking already to the future.

For the future promised well, did it not? Both at Menston and when he had visited the parsonage he had always been kind to her; he was by any reckoning a good looking man and complaisant beside. It did not often happen, she knew, that people married for love alone. Anyway, she was in love with him – she had been ever since he had dined with them. Besides, if the tension that caught at her wits to make them blaze were not love, it behaved so like love as to be love's true twin, indistinguishable from the thing itself.

'Sir,' she said in sudden calm. 'I shall be honoured to become your wife.'

From his pocket, Edward produced a ring with a large yellow-brown stone. It struck her, as she put it on and saw it hang loose around the fourth finger of her left hand, that hitherto it had been only to Mr Russell that she had ever managed to command such steady speech. And with her acceptance of Mr Curwen's offer of marriage, she had at a stroke distanced herself from Mr Russell for ever.

In the bustle of the days that followed, Caelica came to understand that her engagement had wrought a change in her standing. To find herself in the clear light of her father's favour was rare and pleasurable. Even Sir Rowley, despite his absorption in his park and his lead mines, accompanied his son to visit her at the parsonage. Indeed, once when her father was out on his round of parochial visits and Edward fetching something he had left by mistake in the Menston carriage, she found herself alone in his blustery company.

For all his successes and achievements, Sir Rowley appeared ill at ease as he stood in the dark dining room – the Curwens were to join them for their midday meal. First he looked up at the shelves of books and then into the blind eyes of Homer whose bust stood on the mantel shelf, and then round at the books again. Plainly, he was at a loss.

Making some inconsequential remark about the summer weather, Caelica wondered whether the books brought on this agitation. Despite the firm friendship he enjoyed with her father, he might well lack their ease in this place of poetry, philosophy and Holy Writ. Agreeing it was unusually dry and fine for May, Sir Rowley abruptly took up a volume which was neither in a foreign tongue nor expressly concerned with religion and rather to her surprise – she thought she was his hostess, not his audience - began to read aloud:

Glide by the banks of Virgins then, and passe
The shewers of Roses, lucky-foure-leav'd grasse:
The while the cloud of younglings sing,
And drown yee with a flowrie Spring:
While some repeat
Your praise, and bless you, sprinkling you with Wheat:
While that others doe divine:
'Blest is the Bride, on whom the Sun doth shine;'
And thousands gladly wish
You multiply, as doth a Fish.

By the verse's close, he sounded incredulous, as though he could not believe the heavy print under his eyes.

'Who ever could read this stuff for pleasure?'

'M-my father does.' For all her shyness, Caelica was determined to defend the book from his traducing. 'A-and I too am f-fond of poetry.'

'It must take a deal of thought to come up with that rhyming,' he allowed. 'At least I cannot quarrel with the last two lines.'

He gave a great guffaw, as though pleased with himself for having chanced upon verses that were so apt. Caelica yearned to say something that would show she was not so nice as to shrink from the poet's plain-spoken sentiment. But nothing came to mind and all her fire shrank into confusion. At last Edward's blessed reappearance with a wooden dressing box in his hand, her father eagerly following, saved her from fresh agonies.

Although Anstice was ready to serve a meal, they went through to the parlour. Edward it emerged had brought a gift for his future bride. To Caelica's surprise, even her mother now joined them. Stiff, black-clad, and silent, she appeared to think her daughter's engagement reason enough to lay aside her melancholia for a time, and unbend a little towards the flickerings of celebration, although she kept to her seat beside the window that afforded the best view of the road from England.

Placing the box upon the walnut wood table where only a few days ago Caelica had sat attempting to sketch his likeness, Edward opened it to reveal a set of ivory brushes. In wonderment she extracted them one after another, testing their cool weight in her hand and running her finger over the intricate silver pattern inlaid on their backs. For a long time she said nothing.

'I n-never thought to own such l-lavish a-a-acc-accoutrements,' she breathed at last, anxious lest Edward, or indeed Sir Rowley, should take her delay in expressing her pleasure for dissatisfaction.

'Ah, it delights me to see how much you like them.'

'L-like them? They are the f-finest I have ever s-seen.'

'Aye well, my dear. They'll be handy enough for chastising our infants, when the time comes.'

She was shocked. No man, surely, would anticipate punishing children before they were even born. Besides, a blow from one of these would inflict searing injury. She must have misheard him, she decided, stroking the hard, smooth surface with a tentative finger. Misheard, or misunderstood.

'Mrs Whatmough thought you'd admire them,' Edward explained.

For some reason, the idea of his seeking another woman's advice in this matter brought her up short. She imagined the dark head and the fair bending together over the brush merchant's wares as the two of them compared bristles and mountings. It was understandable that Edward should ask elegant Mrs Whatmough for advice about choosing a present for his bride, but Caelica wanted the gift to be his idea, not somebody else's suggestion.

'Alice has the keenest eye for quality,' Sir Rowley remarked, picking up an ivory brush and turning it admiringly between his powerful fingers. 'She hoped to be with us today, but she has a cold. I urged her to stay at home.'

'Ah, let us hope she makes a speedy recovery,' said Caelica's father. 'I recall the vivacity of her conversation with great zest. You said she was your late business partner's widow, did you not, sir?'

'Why, yes, Hearne. Forgive me if I overturn your conception of the rightful ordering of things, but to my thinking, her intellect was even sharper than his.'

'Oh, I have no dread of clever women, Curwen. I've always taken pains to see that my daughter should be provided with the rudiments of learning. Nothing like the education my son got at Eton, of course. Yet I would not have her grow up all ignorant. Her mother,' he bowed to where Mrs Hearne had risen from her seat at the mention of Christopher, 'has ever been shrewd, and I have, I hope, contrived to add a little polish to Caelica's native wit.'

'She is, good sir, the very acme of perfection.'

Edward's words were complimentary, yet to Caelica's surprise, he addressed himself squarely to her father, without so much as glancing in her direction, let alone giving her the fond look she expected. She smarted with regret, wanting more assurance of his love than his gift, for all its magnificence, could give.

With an effort of reason, she recovered herself. At this coming together of his and her families, unlike as they were, she and Edward were on display for inspection by curious eyes. The occasion was bound to make for shyness and strain. Were they to lock eyes in affection or exchange endearments, let alone a kiss, it might make only for awkwardness. Perhaps it was best that they hid their feelings in company, and saved soft words and fond embraces for when they were alone.

Hearne found himself thinking about Thomas Russell more than he was accustomed. The news that Caelica had agreed to become the wife of Edward Curwen would be a most effective reprimand for the unwarranted audacity which had led his pupil to propose to her himself. There was no real need for Hearne to upbraid the misguided young man for over-stepping the boundaries of decent behaviour, but a reminder about knowing his place and keeping to it would still be timely.

While the two of them said Morning Prayer together in an otherwise empty church, Mr Hearne, who was adept at pursuing ideas of his own while reciting the office, watched his pupil. Thomas's coat and breeches stained with river water from Luke Vaughan's careless oar-strokes, his face avid on his prayer-book as he uttered the responses in a serious, quiet voice. Hearne's scorn stirred.

After all his thankless years in this desolate Llanmichael, to find his wife's health failing and his son on the brink of disgrace, the news that his Caelica was to marry Sir Rowley's son gave Hearne the sensation of walking into a beam of golden light. Storm clouds loomed on the horizon, it was true, but the sun shone over his immediate path. Whatever might happen to Christopher, once the marriage had taken place, Hearne would be able to rest secure in his connection with the powerful, influential Curwen family, who were not, he reminded himself, impoverished nobility but belonged to the rising mercantile class whose wealth was far greater and infinitely more secure. For the young man at the litany desk – poor, maladroit and so laughably in earnest – to consider himself a fitting husband for Caelica showed a grievous want of judgement.

Having concluded the words of the grace, Hearne waited for a polite but extremely brief interval before switching from things of the spirit to practical matters. 'Russell.'

'Sir?' Was the hardening of Thomas's mouth meant to convey a reproach for concluding worship so fast? If he was going to turn priggish, he assuredly deserved whatever set-down Hearne could despatch.

'I find I cannot move the door without its sticking fast,' Hearne announced, as though it were a matter of the utmost importance. 'At first I thought it was only my idle imagination or perhaps that I bore too hard upon the handle, but I am growing convinced that it sticks. It would do no harm to take the door clean off its hinges and rub a little fat over the moving parts to ensure there is no friction between them. Perhaps you would give the matter your attention in the course of today. We would not want any new obstacle to deter the people of Llanmichael from attending their parish church.'

Let the presumptuous youth feel the rancid grease of parochial life between his fingers and perhaps he would presume no more. Hearne scanned his pupil's features closely. He wanted to know that he was irritating Thomas, wanted to see this young man from an undistinguished family who had the temerity to seek Caelica's hand cringe and quail under the full weight of her father's odium.

'By all means, sir.' Thomas did not appear irritated in the least. A ready smile played across his lips.

'My daughter,' one hand on the offending door, Hearne lingered over his news, in order to derive the fullest possible satisfaction from its announcement, 'ah, is to wed ere long.'

It would be too coarse, too much like vulgar gloating, to look Thomas straight in the eye while he scythed him down. Better to continue in the friendly conversation strain, which would foil any foolish notions of ill-treatment that the young man might harbour. Strolling into the graveyard, Hearne surveyed the river, rippling just beyond the churchyard wall.

'See – that pattern of light on water,' he remarked in his most benign manner. 'That must have been pretty much what Aeschylus sought to capture in that grand phrase "ἀνήριθμον γέλασμα πόντου." Of course he had his sights on the sea, yet wouldn't you say our river has a laughing look?'

Evincing no sign of dismay at the tidings of Caelica's engagement, Thomas agreed that the Greek words signifying the smiling ocean were indeed euphonious. He had the gall to add that since he had seen the sea only once in his life and that on a dull day, he hardly felt able to judge whether the metaphor could apply to the sunlit river or no.

Hearne saw no need to admit that he had never seen the sea in his life. Instead he reverted to the subject of his daughter.

'Yes, Caelica has accepted an offer of marriage from Mr Edward Curwen, Sir Rowley's son. You met him, d'you recall, when he dined at the parsonage. They have not known one another long, and yet they will, I believe, complement one another well. He possesses natural authority which she, with her habit of obedience, will assuredly relish.'

Was there a slight flaring of Thomas's nostrils at last? A momentary contraction of those emphatic eyebrows? Hearne rather thought there was.

'As yet,' he went on in his most nonchalant voice, 'they have set no date for the wedding, but I cannot believe they will wish for overmuch delay. Though they may choose to wait until the town has its new bridge. It would be wise.'

'It would indeed.' What business had Thomas to sound so cordial and pleasant? Hearne was telling him these things to punish him for his insolence, yet there he was, conversing with every appearance of goodwill.

'It occurs to me that you have amassed many competition entries by now,' Hearne continued. 'If you bring me all the plans, I shall take them to Menston. It wants but a few days before the competition closes, and Sir Rowley will no doubt want to appraise them before handing them on to Aislabie for judging. Yes, bring them to me tomorrow, and do your utmost, if you please, to ensure that they remain dry throughout your river crossing. It would be hard if any contestant were to forfeit his chance of winning on account of his plan getting wet. I urge you to take every care.'

'Oh, you may be certain that I shall. And please convey my wishes for the greatest future happiness to Miss Hearne and Mr Curwen.'

Having begged some mutton fat from Anstice in the parsonage kitchen, Thomas set about working it all around the cast iron hinges of the church door. As far as he could tell, it was not sticking at all. The stinking viscous stuff clogged his nails, got onto his clothes and somehow even into his hair. All the same, he could not entirely subdue his amusement at the brazen instinct for humiliation with which Mr Hearne had quoted Greek poetry while stifling his hopes.

Chapter Twelve

Now that her wedding was no longer a remote prospect but a certainty, Caelica's first thought on waking and last reflection before she went to sleep was of Edward Curwen. It was still with disbelief that she tasted the sweet thought that he should have asked her to become his life's companion – he, for whom she had such admiration, whose presence exercised such magnetism on her senses. Her happiness was of a species and abundance that she had never thought to experience. Edward, who had shown such admirable propriety in asking her father for his blessing upon their intention, now appeared in her imaginings like a bountiful deity, pouring his wealth, his home, his companionship and his love as blessings at her feet.

Her father, without offering any explanation, had put an end to her lessons so Anstice claimed more of her time for help about the house. With no Latin or mathematics to exercise her wits, she found herself dwelling upon Edward even as she folded the linen, gathered herbs to dry above the kitchen fire, or kneaded dough – whatever work the stout old servant happened to set her. How should this unlikely engagement have come about? How was it that he, in all his ease and with the polish of society so sleek upon him, should come to lavish affection upon so quiet a soul as she? It was a miracle.

He visited her many times in the long light days of the end of May and at the start of June, and while he was always courteous and attentive, perhaps he was a little over-courteous and maybe not quite as attentive as she might have wished. Her sole regret on these occasions lay in the thought that before they parted, surely, as an engaged man he ought to embrace her. She thought of the fervent kiss they exchanged upon his proposal. When he kissed her now, it was always on the cheek or the brow. Kisses of extreme propriety, they were decorous kisses of a man who desires not to offend.

Of his generosity there was no question. At about his third visit to the parsonage, he brought a string of garnets for her that had, he explained in his artless, good-natured way, belonged to his mother. It was a hot afternoon near the end of May and they were standing in the garden, the smell of hay from the pastureland mingling with the early roses and the pungent drying mud at the sides of the river. He held the necklace up at arm's length then poured it into her waiting hands.

The exuberant gesture delighted her, which was as well because it meant that she was able to hide her lack of real excitement over the pouchy, lustreless gems. It was the sort of elaborate, ugly piece of jewellery that she sometimes saw round the wrinkled necks of the older farmers' wives of the district. Remembering that garnets were supposed to have a special property of preserving the wearer from danger, she decided that she should be glad to own some for protection's sake. Besides, if these dark stones had once been his mother's, they must have especial value to him. A niggardly man would have left them in his safe to sell if he should fall on hard times; Edward had ridden over from Menston with them in his pocket so that he might fasten them around her neck alongside the heavy ring on its ribbon. Even though they might not accord with her ideas of grace and beauty, it didn't mean she shouldn't treasure them.

But as she thanked him and felt the warmth of his large hands at the nape of her neck working the flimsy clasp, she could not help noticing that there was more deliberation than zeal in his careful fingers. It was as though adorning his future wife was more of a duty to him than a pleasure. He was talking all the while of different subjects – the roads, the carelessness of his groom, Mr Rendle's latest plans for improving his father's park and gardens – all matters that had nothing whatever to do with their feelings for one another. As she answered his questions and smiled at his opinions she could not stop herself from wondering whether every man grew so detached and whimsical when conversing with the woman he was to wed.

Curious to gauge his thinking about the new bridge, she raised the subject of the assorted drawings submitted for the contest, which were now in a folder in the parsonage library. Whitsun, when the competition was to close was almost upon them and they did not expect many more entries now. Thomas had recently brought those he had received over from his lodging, his cloak wrapped round them to protect them from Vaughan's splashing, for her father to inspect at leisure before he took them on to Menston to await the judgement of Sir Rowley's engineering friend.

'Th-those that I s-saw – they d-did not impress me much,' she explained, wondering whether Edward might ask to see them himself. 'All the dr-draughtsmen p-portrayed bridges with m-many low arches, just like our old bridge. It-it w-was as though th-they feared to break with the past.'

Edward was watching a buzzard as it circled high above the town.

'Well,' he spoke without looking at her, but raised a leisurely hand to shade his eyes, 'this is a deep subject for a fair day, my love.'

'P-perhaps it is, Edward,' she allowed. 'Yet it interests me m-much. M-might you, do you think, sub-submit a drawing for the competition?'

It was open to all comers after all, not just proven engineers and she posed the question in all earnestness.

Edward only gave her a wide-eyed glance of surprise and burst out laughing. 'My dear Caelica – I know my father's keen to concern himself in the stone-and-mortar aspect of the thing. After all, it'll be a great saving to him to be able to despatch his ore to Carterford through Llanmichael without requiring the pack-animals to labour all the way round by Pwllfechan. But, for myself –' he guffawed. 'Well, I can't claim to find anything very exciting about it.'

'B-but Edward, such a chance – It could be so beautiful.' She thought of the visionary bridge that had formed itself in her mind when she had been waiting outside the wise woman's cottage, looking down towards the turbulent young river amid the bleak hills.

'To devise a bridge for this place would, I suppose, be quite a pleasing entertainment in its way,' Edward's offhand voice returned her to the present. 'were I able to find the time.'

'But sh-should you not relish the p-prospect of seeing your design brought to life?' she asked, with a rush of eagerness. 'Y-your f-father was saying that Mr – Mr Aislabie would s-select the drawing from which i-it most s-suited him to work. One that, b-be it never so modest – s-so lacking in the f-finesse that a true engineer w-would bring to his drafting – could st-still serve as a w-workable plan. B-besides the money, it would be p-prize enough, t-to my mind, to have Mr Aislabie bring his s-skill to bear upon any s-sketch of mine.'

Edward laughed again, as though it were her true intention to commit the bridge of her imagining to pencil and paper.

'My adored and beloved,' he said, derisive as if the glowing words were a snub, 'are women to undertake engineering schemes? It would be an affront to all decorum.' He leant back against the garden gate, folding his arms as though to close a subject that he found too ridiculous to contemplate. She said nothing more but she wondered why, if a woman were so fortunate as to have been born with keen, sharp wits, decorum should require her to blunt and muffle them.

'You gave her those garnets?'

Edward could not be sure whether Alice asked the question in disbelief or amusement. He had come before dinner to talk to her in her comfortable sitting room, already ablaze with light although outside it was barely dusk. She was seated on one of the blue sofas, examining a minute tear in a fan.

Sitting down opposite her, he caught a faint trace of her perfume through the hot wax smell of the candles. 'When I showed them to you,' he remembered, 'you said you didn't want them.'

'Well, garnets are hardly in fashion. I wonder whether I might be able to mend this rent.'

'I told Miss Hearne they had been my mother's.'

'Edward, dear boy, pass me my work-box would you, please? Thank you. Now be honest – do you have any recollection of your mother?'

'Direct recollection, no. How can I, when she died so soon after I was born? But both my father and John have often spoken of her...'

'A dead mother's jewels.' Having threaded a needle, Alice gave him her most captivating smile. She half spread out the fan by her side. By candlelight the silver in her hair and the lines upon her small hands were almost unnoticeable. 'A sentimental gift indeed,' she pronounced, her eyes glinting. 'Let us hope Miss Hearne is more sensible of the honour that lies in your dusty old stones than I would be in her place. No man could win me with such a gaud.'

'Alice...'

'You must forgive my blunt speech, Edward, but I have some news for you.' She paused to hold her brown thread against the fan, judging whether its shade chimed with the background of the picture on the leaf. 'It will not, I think, be any great shock to you to learn that I have agreed to marry your father.'

'My father? You? When he is so much your elder?'

But it was not really such a thunderbolt. After William Whatmough's untimely death, Edward's father had invited the widow to stay as his guest, first at the house in Birmingham and then at Menston. Whatever conclusions the servants may have drawn among themselves, they had raised no open objection to her presence. Edward knew his father liked her company and it was by no means unknown for widowers in late middle age to take younger wives. Nevertheless he couldn't help wondering why, if his father meant to remarry, he hadn't taken the mighty step long ago.

'Nigh on twenty years, I grant you.' Evidently happy with her choice of thread, she calmly started to sew. 'But his death is, I foresee, a long way off. Besides,' how she caressed the syllables, 'he has treated me all along with great kindness and liberality. He has, I think, taken upon himself the guilt that was rightfully speaking William's in the matter of failing to provide for me.'

For all her refinement, Mrs Whatmough lacked wealth. The rumour ran that in the weeks before his death her late husband had incurred large liabilities.

'So it's true that he died with debts owing?' Edward could not hide his curiosity.

'True indeed,' said Alice, looking at him over her sewing. 'And though I am not destitute, there are still some obligations outstanding and some of William's former associates who remain most pressing.'

'Had I the funds,' he tried to keep his voice cool. 'I should surely place them at your disposal.'

'It would be a charming offer,' her eyes were not so much blue in the candle flames as pure silver, 'but I should decline it.'

She turned her attention to the fan once more. It showed, he noticed, the judgement of Paris. With infinite care, she stitched the split swan-skin. It was fortunate that the tear should not be in any of the figures' faces. Even so, he found it strange that she should think it worth her while to repair this trifling trinket when she was about to wed so wealthy a man as his father. He could surely buy her a replacement.

'Does he look to you to give him the heir he seeks?' It was hardly a proper question, but he burnt to know the answer.

'Indeed I hope not, for the years in which I might have borne him children are past.' Alice, drawing the edges of the rent together so as to bring the handsome figure of fair-haired Paris under his eyes as she drew, did not appear to find the enquiry over-bold.

'Listen,' she went on. 'Your father has asked me to marry him and I have accepted him both because I wish to please him after all his generosity and because it will mean that I can live in greater comfort and security than I do at present. I do not enjoy contemplating the prospect of a life of near-poverty. Ageing he may be, but it will still be many years before his vitality starts to ebb. I shall make him a fine, stylish wife.'

143

Was she taunting him? Although it was not something that he cared to think about, he had a strong idea she had been sharing his father's bed on and off for months. The thought that she, so spirited and refined, should be the focus of his father's love-making brought him up so short, he found it hard to breathe. What price the pretty bookish maiden with the stammer besides a woman of Alice's pith and wit?

'There.' She spread the fan at a different angle so that majestic Juno and Mercury the messenger remained hidden in the leaf's closed portion. On the part open to his sight, shrewd Venus laughed at serious Minerva while fair-haired Paris stood beside the meticulous darn, glancing from one goddess to the other.

'That's a pretty gewgaw of yours. No wonder you should treasure it,' he remarked as she picked it up, and began to flutter it, looking at him over its top all the time.

But of course he should wed Miss Hearne; she was comely and amiable, it would secure him double his present allowance, and he could not bring himself to entertain the thought of going to Calcutta. The match was made and it might work out very well.

'I have every confidence that you and my father shall know great pleasure in one another's company,' he heard himself say. 'I offer you all my felicitations.'

Trusting that it was fitting for him in filial fashion to embrace her, he slid a broad arm around Alice's slight and pretty shoulders, ready to kiss her piquant mouth. But before his lips touched hers, affectionate stepson or no, he paused. Heavy footsteps sounded across the wide landing. The manservant must have finished dressing and shaving his master, who was now striding out of his dressing chamber to claim his consort.

Caelica tried to dismiss Edward's indifference to the bridge competition from her mind. She would have enjoyed showing him the drawings and discussing them with him. Were he to concur with her view that the contestants' liking for undersized

144

arches under heavy parapets was regrettable, it would have shown faith in her judgement. If, on the other hand, he weighed in on the competitors' side and argued the case for essays in squat stonework straddling river like ponderous beasts, she would enjoy trying to dispute it, so far as her stammer allowed. Husband and wife might dispute yet stay friends, might they not? She hoped Edward should not seek to enforce her agreement with him upon everything. Once he had gone, she went on impulse to her father's library, took the competition drawings from the folder on the mantelpiece where Thomas had left them, and spread them out over the wide table.

What had struck her about the early entries was their timidity. For the contestants' opportunity was immense. The river valley might be desolate, but it had a stark splendour that a bridge might well enhance. The old crossing of the Cistercians had had the appearance of growing out of the landscape, thrown across the lawless waters as though cast there by the will of the land, rather than proceeding from the mind and labour of man. But since the monks' time, the needs of the valley-dwellers had changed, along with their demands. Now, Sir Rowley was the power abroad in the district, and minerals, unlike crops and game, observed no season and took no thought for nature's shifts and changes. Llanmichael was no longer the place for a bridge that had the look of springing from the very earth. Instead, it needed a bridge that marked the sovereignty of the human spirit.

Looking once more at the drawings she had first seen all those weeks ago in Thomas's squalid lodgings, she realised that she detested the way that the contestants were set upon following the pattern of the past. They drew as though they were frightened – frightened of innovating, frightened of changing. Fear must lie heavy indeed upon the stagnant air of this forgotten place. Why otherwise should there be such fondness for cumbersome pointed arches with heavy cutwaters between them like a jaw of gaping teeth? Some entrants had bedizened their bridges with carved heads that scowled upstream; surely no one could be so foolish as to suppose that an ugly bridge could frighten the river into submissiveness?

Exasperated, she took up her drawing things. A form and outline had already suggested themselves to her; indeed so clear was her vision that it invited her – compelled her, rather – to give it expression without delay. For a moment, a sense of her own temerity made her hesitate. A woman design a bridge? Edward was, in a way, right. The thing was unheard of. It would amuse Sir Rowley immoderately, yet why should it be so risible?

Spreading out a sheet of paper, she wedged it with books and journals at each side – Euclid at the top, the *Iliad*, her father's favourite poem, on the right, a number of the *Tatler* to the left and Horace's *Carmina,* her old lesson book, at the bottom, all in substantial bindings. Preparation strengthened her resolve; now she had taken matters too far to abandon them. Her finished submission could surely be no more inept than all the others littering the table. Anyway, she knew she could draw well, and her mathematics made her all the bolder. The bridge of her devising should have the same clean lines and unassuming precision as the figures she had copied from the geometric tables in Chambers' *Cyclopaedia*.

Having previously sketched out the wide valley with the decaying little town at its heart for her album, it did not take her long to shade in the bones of the landscape. There were the gentle slopes of the pastureland, their grassiness giving way to heather and boulders as they neared the heights. Here was the river, entering the valley as hardly more than an overgrown stream with wide flat rocks at its side where she sometimes saw dippers. In its progress it deepened, thrusting its banks wider and wider apart, although it still retained some of its mountain stream capriciousness. To one side of it stood the low-roofed houses that made up Llanmichael straggling along their single street.

When she had drawn vistas and prospects in the past, it had been with an eye to producing some artistic or atmospheric effect. Today, she drew with an eye to analysing proportions. What, she speculated, was the greatest height that her bridge –

and it would be a high standing bridge, unlike all the grim, low-browed efforts of her fellow-competitors – could attain without dwarfing the nearest houses? To aggrandise itself by showing up the shortcomings of the existing buildings was not the effect for which she strove. It should blend with them, not shout above them. Of course, were it to be built in the local stone, the bridge would achieve a harmony with its surroundings that it would miss if they were to construct from imported material.

Now she sketched the single, rainbow arch soaring above the waters. As a draft, it conveyed her idea in triumphant style and if it interested Mr Aislabie, he could gauge the exact dimensions of the span. Intuition told her that a wide, flat arch would prove too heavy for the bridge's length; its lofty, rounded gracefulness did not only please the eye, but made also for strength and was therefore necessary for the structure's survival. On impulse, in the haunches of the arch, she drew piercings – three concentric tunnels running through the stonework on either side which gave the appearance of adorning it like jewels and heightening its ethereal lightness.

Finished, it pleased her immoderately. The way across it could, she judged, be made broad enough to accommodate both a file of packhorses and walkers passing them by at the same time. There were no piers in the river that debris might damage and no low arches for loose stones and branches to choke. If the water level should rise exceptionally high, her tunnels would give it an additional means of escape. The bridge would not impede the floods, but rather make allowance for them. It was, surely, both progressive and virtuous.

By the time she was done, the sun had almost set and she was working in near darkness. It was only with the final strokes of her pencil that she realised how much her eyes and her back ached. But her father kept a tinder box on the mantel piece and rising, she struck a flame with care, her right hand stiff with holding the pencil, and lit an end of candle, hoping he was not meaning to save it. Its light was defiant in the dusk, and once her sight had adjusted to its soft brilliance, she stood back to survey the fruit of her labour.

Her artwork was beautiful. Its beauty amazed her. The question, 'Did I achieve this much?' came unbidden to her mind. Years of hearing her mother instructing her to be humble, not to thrust herself to the fore, to give way before others and show polite appreciation of their talents however modest, made her hesitate to acknowledge the merit of her work. Yet to deny it would be a travesty. She let her tired eyes linger over the lines of the structure, marvelling at the way it combined elegance, which pleased the eye, with robustness to withstand the waters' pounding. If it were built, it would make endurance lithe and tangible; virtue in stone. It was her creation and she loved it.

She heard someone approach the door, someone with a brisker tread than her father, but not so light upon their feet as her mother. Suddenly shy, she looked round for some spare paper with which to conceal her handiwork. Before she could find any, Thomas came in.

She wished it was not he. Because her father had stopped her lessons, she hadn't seen him since the day of his proposal, and now with no word to him, she had agreed to marry Edward. Her father would have explained matters, of course – she hoped he had been tactful about it – but she could hardly feel proud of her conduct.

'M-Mr Russell, g-good evening.'

Her floundering speech must betray her guilt.

'A good evening to you too, Miss Hearne.'

His voice was friendly and bore no note of reproach.

'What leads you to sit here in the twilight? Ah, you have been sketching.'

There was no irony in his tone, none of the dry, edgy sharpness she remembered from their lessons, only cheerfulness and good humour. 'May I see your handiwork?'

Taking her abashed nod for an affirmative, he continued to talk as he picked up the drawing. 'I had no thought of finding you here. Your father had directed me to a passage in the writings of Richard Baxter and I came to look for the – Caelica,' it was the first time he had addressed her by her Christian name. 'This is drafting of no common order. And it is your work?'

All she could muster was another mute nod, her triumph of a few minutes ago spun away like river spray. Not only would she feel the lash of his reproach for having pledged herself to marry another man before giving his proposal the courtesy of a direct answer, but now he too would task her with indecorum and unseemliness for presuming to set herself up to design a bridge. Overcome, she put her head in her hands.

'But this is remarkable.'

His audible enthusiasm encouraged her to look up and compose herself. Stammer she might, but she would not shirk her moral duty. 'Sir – I owe – owe you –' she thought to say 'every apology' – before abjuring herself in the sternest terms, but he cut in.

'Caelica – you owe me nothing.' He faced her square across the table. 'If you are trying, under some mistaken sense of obligation, to explain the circumstances of your betrothal to that clown Curwen, then stop.'

But this was not the solemn young clergyman-in-waiting whom she suspected of schooling himself not to smile within a hundred yards' range of the church lest her father should think him frivolous. Here – the light of the candle was more powerful in the gloom than she had first thought – in the hollows of his face, in his mobile mouth and keen eyes was the flaming intensity of emotion which she had never seen igniting Edward's various bland expressions. And although he had no business to call Edward a clown, yet – yet she could see how it fitted.

'You will submit this drawing, won't you?' He was begging her in all earnest, and she had barely completed it.

'I hardly know.' Her voice was steady once more, for the first time, as she thought, in days. 'I shall have to ask my father.'

'If you must, you must, but you could slip your paper between the others in the pile, say nothing and avoid the risk of his finding some reason to forbid you from entering.'

She liked this different Thomas who made such shocking suggestions. She liked him exceedingly.

'No. In truth, I could do no such thing.' She adored the idea of smuggling her entry in behind her father's back – it made her want to laugh out loud. She hoped Edward would sometimes make her laugh and not just by playing the clown.

'Mr Russell – Thomas.' He, after all, had called her Caelica. 'I am sorry with all my heart for my want of courtesy towards you. It was a dereliction of all integrity to let my father speak to you on my behalf and decline your – your offer of marriage.'

He did not answer at first, but moved across to the window above the dark garden. 'Shall you be happy in Curwen's company, do you think?'

It was an inordinately forward question, but its directness made it easier for her to answer. 'He is affable, liberal and benevolent. These qualities should make for my happiness.'

'And good-looking besides?'

'Aye,' she allowed. Whenever would she have supposed her austere and scholarly tutor might tease her about being drawn to a man for his looks?

'Caelica,' he touched her shoulder. 'What I say now will sound like most arrant, contemptible jealousy, but have you no thought that you may, 'ere long, grow bored with a man who is content to wile away his time with cards, guns and dogs? What will you find to talk of with him? What premium will he place on your native wit?'

'I shall school myself to be as dutiful a wife as I have been a dutiful daughter,' she replied. That hand on her shoulder was no more than friendly warmth. To let it awaken misgivings was plain foolishness.

'Come,' he smiled. 'I have no business to tax you with these questions. Hold the candle for me, if you please, so that I may scan your father's shelves for the volume he wants me to read. Let us hope I may run it to earth without too much difficulty – ah, there I have it. Now I must leave you, for Vaughan attends me at the jetty unless impatience has driven him to his night-angling already.

'But, Caelica, be sure your sketch reaches Mr Aislabie. I have an idea it could interest him exceedingly. Sir Rowley too, come to that. Farewell to you now. God grant you all joy.'

'Goodnight, Thomas,' she answered, adding in a rush, 'th-thank you for your lessons. I enjoyed them much. G-God g-grant you joy too.'

It was not that her stammer had returned, but rather that a sudden vast surge of emotion she couldn't begin to understand had swamped all her words.

Chapter Thirteen

When Edward next visited the parsonage, Sir Rowley accompanied him. They headed straight to the library where Caelica was mending a quill while her father drafted a sermon. Having sat heavily down on one side of the oak table, Sir Rowley announced that he and Alice Whatmough intended to wed and that he had come to seek the parson's advice about the most appropriate timing for the nuptials.

'And where, exactly, does Mrs Whatmough currently reside?' asked Hearne.

Caelica found Sir Rowley's intention to marry no surprise; when they were dining at Menston Alice Whatmough had shown herself to be a deft and able hostess. Now she would be Edward's stepmother and, to all intent, Caelica's mother-in-law. That calm, searching question that her father had posed must arise from his sense that it was neither usual nor strictly speaking correct for the widow to live under the same roof as her prospective bridegroom. He looked intently at Edward and Caelica to signal that this conversation between priest and parishioner should be private. Edward either failed to interpret his meaning, or he ignored it and walked to the window. Although the quill was ready, Caelica stayed too, and sat down at the foot of the table.

'Has she family with whom she may stay up till the date of the wedding?' Hearne pursued.

Sir Rowley, his face already florid, flushed crimson. 'It is kind of you to enquire after her and show this concern for her well-being, Hearne,' he said awkwardly. 'Perhaps it was the example of Edward and your charming daughter that led her to agree to become my wife. As to family, she has no relatives near at hand. She,' He gave a forced laugh. 'That is to say, we planned that for the time being she should continue to reside at Menston.

'I wonder, reverend sir,' he hastened on, 'whether you would soon be so good as to read the marriage service over Mrs Whatmough and myself. I'll take a special licence, if you see fit, so that you may dispense with the banns and wed us without delay. We seek no show, you understand, it being a second marriage for both of us.'

'Without delay?' Did that bring her marriage to Edward all the closer? It was barely any time since they had announced the engagement.

'Second marriages are unusual.' Although it went against the grain with her father to deny Sir Rowley anything, Caelica could tell he did not entirely like this request. 'So are Special Licences.' He pushed his writing aside. 'I suppose from what you say there is no impediment to the union?'

Sir Rowley gave a hearty nod. 'No impediment. Most certainly no impediment.'

'Pray, how long has it been,' Hearne continued, very much the parson, 'since your late wife died?'

'Nigh on twenty years. Edward was but an infant at the time. He wanted for nothing – is that fair to say, Edward?' and Curwen raised an interrogatory eyebrow at his son.

'Oh, fair indeed.' So swift was Edward to support his father's assertions, she thought he must have been rehearsing. 'John – my older half-brother and I shared nursemaids and tutors until I was of an age to attend school. They took every care for our physical and intellectual well-being, and my dear father often chose to spend his scant hours of leisure in our company.' He beamed. 'It was, verily, as happy a childhood as any motherless infant could desire.'

He spoke with ease, favouring them all with that open guileless look that Caelica liked, though why did he insist on standing by the window and not sit at her side and perhaps touch her hand as he told his tale? He had barely spoken a word to her beyond his greeting. They were engaged to one another, yet since he arrived, he had barely glanced at her even though she wore his great ring on her finger and his mother's garnets round her neck together with a locket holding a lock of his hair.

She swallowed hard. She was being unreasonable. That was the trouble. For Sir Rowley to seek marriage was a momentous event. No wonder he was impatient to proceed. No wonder too that it should take Edward's attention away from her.

'And the late Mr Whatmough?' asked her father, his voice sufficiently casual for the question to sound conversational, while keeping edge enough to show he thought the answer important.

Sir Rowley's flush deepened. 'Whatmough died eleven months ago,' he said.

'Then it is somewhat soon, good sir, for his widow to think of wedding again.'

What might Edward, watching the older men without a flicker in her direction, say if her father insisted on making difficulties about marrying Sir Rowley and his Alice?

'Soon, that is, not only in the eyes of the Church but also in the opinions of most decent people, who like to see at least a year of mourning and then a year beside. Otherwise they gossip and spread slander. Sir Rowley.' Her father lowered his voice, 'I know what it is to be the subject of slander. Slander is vile. It will make unpleasantness for your Edward and my Caelica as well as for Mrs Whatmough and yourself. Was it, I wonder, for the sake of fleeing the comments of your Birmingham neighbours that you bought Menston and hastened ahead with its rebuilding? Was it to distance yourself from the talk of your old associates that you left your business in the hands of your stepson and started investing in lead? You are a deep man, Sir Rowley.' He laughed in the quiet sardonic way that he had for things which amused him but which he deemed not entirely fitting for the mirth of a clergyman.

'Listen, Curwen,' he sat up straight in his seat and folded his arms on the table. 'Provided you and Mrs Whatmough show due discretion, I'll ask no further questions about your domestic arrangements. You could, after all, find a parson of the Fleet who'd marry the two of you tomorrow if you wanted. Aye, and it'd be a lawful, valid union too, although there are always folk who want to pry into the reasons for a Fleet wedding. But if I'm to say the service for you, I'll have you bide a full two years from her late husband's death – no, two year and a little bit more. That way no one can make out you waited only the shortest possible decent time. 'Tis only a year and a month from now, but I'd sooner it were a virtuous year and a month, to appearance at least, so make discretion your watchword.'

Sir Rowley looked as though he wanted to interrupt; a look from Caelica's father quelled him. 'Since your son is going to marry my daughter, you'll be my family as well as my parishioner,' he went on, inexorable as though he were preaching. 'Now, I don't care to hear it said that my relatives lead irregular lives. Cutting the mourning short might well be taken for an irregularity; so might sharing the same house. Give it plenteous time, good sir, I entreat. And if, meanwhile, you and the lady were to pay some visits or travel a little outside the district, so much the better. Then once I have conducted your wedding, let us allow another month's grace before Edward and Caelica exchange their vows in turn.'

A year and two months. Time enough for Edward and her to come to know one another through and through.

'It will be a long engagement for them,' pronounced her father, still in pulpit vein. 'But waiting is good for youth,' he looked first at Edward and then at her. 'It teaches that most excellent virtue, patience.'

If she understood him aright, he had agreed to close his eyes to the likelihood that Sir Rowley and Mrs Whatmough were already living as man and wife in all but name. Friend of Sir Rowley or no, this forbearance was not entirely to his credit. He would have made no such concession to his humbler parishioners. But she kept her thoughts to herself.

On Whit Sunday Hearne preached twice over to a nigh-empty church, and fine, closely argued sermons he thought them. Dispirited by the way attendance at his church had fallen off, Hearne tried find some consolation in the company of his wife and daughter. Despite the warmth of early June, Anstice had lit a small fire in the parlour and by its light he watched his dear, sad Christina seat herself upon her favourite chair – the one with the flowers carved upon the thin wooden arms – and stare out into the dusky shadows. She had as usual taken very little either to eat or drink. Sighing, in the hope that music might lull their spirits he urged Caelica to go to the instrument and play and sing to them.

Obedient, she rearranged the candles, settled herself at the harpsichord and began. He did not notice what song she chose, intent instead upon his wife who sat like a carved figure of sorrow, hands open on her lap as though she were supplicating heaven for mercy. It smote him to see her so devoid of hope or happiness, especially when their daughter's marriage promised to bring such joy. Besides, when the town had its new bridge, the people would thank him for it and flock back to his church once more. Why would she not allow herself to draw some solace from these things? But she never would, not while Christopher's trial lay before them, its outcome an uncertainty.

Caelica, meanwhile, showing unusual want of tact, started to play the opening bars of *Vital Spark* – the song that misguided young Thomas had sung when they had entertained Edward to supper in the weeks before he and Caelica announced their engagement.

'Cherry – not that dirge, I beg you,' he expostulated.

'I –I like it,' she answered. 'A-and Tho - Mr Russell's singing of it moved me much.'

This remark was most ill-judged. 'Singing. All, I sometimes think, that he is any good for.'

'I think he tries to do good in his way,' she added with unusual stubbornness. Yet she must have realised the error, for she left off playing the piece and asked about the bridge.

'All the drawings that I have received I shall deliver to Sir Rowley tomorrow,' he told her. By mentioning that he would not be their custodian for much longer, he intended to silence her quizzing. Couldn't she see how tired he was? Anxieties, for his parish, for his son, for his beloved wife, beset him on all sides. Even his loyal daughter was grown too obtuse to see how provoking he found her harping on the wretched Thomas.

'Let us l-look at them to-together, father. Once m-more, b-before you take them to Menston,' she begged.

Whether her stammering appeal won him round, or whether he was too weary, too worried to refuse he did not know; whatever the cause, he let her have her way. She was not really provoking, his heavenly child with her grave eyes and uncertain speech. Loveable in her innocence, she was his recompense for the fate of Christopher. Edward might, after all, have wedded an heiress. That he should set his sights instead upon the gentle daughter of a country clergyman was most gratifying, and in the prospect of their happy union Hearne could take honest pleasure.

'Very well,' he agreed. 'Christina, my dearest,' he turned to his wife, 'you haven't yet seen the designs for the new bridge. Would you like to look them over? Tomorrow I shall take them to Menston for Sir Rowley's engineering friend to assess.'

For a moment, she looked as though she might rise to join them round the walnut-wood table. Then she shook her head. 'I am too tired,' she said. 'I'd sooner go to bed.'

'My dearest, we shall not detain you,' answered Hearne, sick at heart. The white hand that rested on the carved wooden blooms along the arm of the chair arm had grown almost skeletal. Brushing it with his fingers, he found it dry, papery and cold to the touch.

'Anstice will have aired the bed,' she told him when he exclaimed upon her chilled flesh. 'I shall do well enough. Good night, Matthias; good night, daughter.'

As soon as she had gone Hearne spoke his thoughts aloud. 'If only the judge at Christopher's hearing reaches a mild verdict.'

'Finds Kit innocent?' Caelica sounded surprised to hear him even hint at such an outcome.

'I cannot see that Christopher will avoid conviction – indeed, I am increasingly persuaded of his guilt,' Hearne admitted. 'And he shall have to frame his own defence, for I cannot afford to pay lawyers' fees. Let us hope the judge will give due weight to the fact that it is his first offence and that up till now his life has been blameless.'

He had no stomach for discussing his son's wrongdoing. 'Let us leave the subject of Christopher,' he declared. It was far better to make the most of his daughter's company before she married Edward and moved away. Rising to collect the drawings, he spread them across the table. Caelica lit more candles and then, in a gesture at once casual and deliberate, she chose one sketch from the mass and held it out.

Hearne frowned. The draughtsman had gone beyond his brief and had produced what was not so much an architectural plan, as a faithful portrait of the river at the crossing point and a new bridge over it.

But what a bridge. It almost defied Hearne's belief – a single vast arch spanning bank to bank with a leisurely stride, full of scope and grace. As though that were not audacity enough – was it feasible to think that a single span might extend so far and not collapse under its own weight? With boldness venturing upon outright bravado, the artist had drawn a trinity of tunnels piercing the gap between the sides of the arch and the surrounding framework of the structure; what Sir Rowley, who delighted in the arcane language of engineering, called the spandrels. Three tunnels on each side in perfect, pleasing symmetry, the bottom-most having, he would guess, about double of the diameter of the uppermost, and the middle one in between. As a geometric effusion, it was delightful. Truly a thing of beauty and drawn to perfection. As a bridge, he had not expertise enough to pronounce upon its merits.

'I did not see this submission among the others. Where did it come from?' he puzzled.

'Father, i-it is mine. I devised and drew it.'

'You?' He looked from the sketch to the young woman standing before him. Her statement defied belief. 'Is this true?'

'T-true indeed.' Despite the stammering, she looked happy, ecstatic even.

'It is hardly fitting for women to ape the role of architects and engineers.' Never before had she given him such unease. 'You are engaged to be wed.'

What husband could endure to live with a woman possessed of such eccentric fancy? And what would Sir Rowley think? 'Before long, you shall hold a position of authority in a large household.'

She appeared not to have thought of that.

'You will have servants to oversee and a husband to care for.'

He wished she had not shown him the drawing. 'I would very much hope that in a short time you will know for yourself the joys of motherhood – woman's true vocation, after all. Caelica, it is most unbecoming for you to step so far outside your rightful sphere.'

She read naked shame in his face. Once, she had known herself to cry at her set-backs, but this evening she was beyond weeping. Anyway, he hated tears.

'Father, I see that you do not care for my design.'

Dry-eyed, she took her drawing from his hand. Defiance steeled her spirit. 'I am no engineer, and I do not seek to ape men of achievement. But I have, I believe, crafted a bridge of greater skill and higher artistry than anyone else.'

She was his biddable child no longer. Indeed, for the first time in her life she found she could disobey her father's wishes and yet speak out without stammering. 'What I have drawn has come from my instinct and my heart. You may not like it. You do not have to like it. But at least let my drawing go before Sir Rowley's friend for his judgement.'

For all the shock in his eyes and mouth, no flail of recrimination lashed her soul. She had as much right to put her drawing forward as any other entrant. Her work had assured merit. If it did not meet up to the high standards of expertise that Sir Rowley's friend sought, she would have lost nothing. But if the great Mr Aislabie should chance to find something in it to praise, well, that would be reward indeed.

The blazing censure in her father's eyes sank down into smouldering vexation. He kept looking from her to the drawing as though he wanted her to disown it. But she had never cared for anything so much in her life. Her bridge was her creation and she would treasure it forever, fight for her right to place her drawing of it before the expert and let no remarks about womanly propriety stop her.

'I cannot allow you to submit it; it would be wholly immodest,' he said.

'Immodest? How so?'

'You are peremptory, daughter,' he rasped.

'I set as much store by the bridge scheme as you do yourself,' she said to reassure him, marvelling at her new-found eloquence.

'Perhaps.' The peevishness in his voice was acid. 'Caelica, you must think of your future husband,' he fretted. 'No man cares to think he has wedded a schemer – a scholiast – a woman more learned than he. Architecture and invention are, as I say, for men. How can young Curwen be content for his wife to surpass him in this field?'

'O, father,' what nonsense he was talking. 'My bridge is no slight to Edward. Why, he hasn't even entered the competition and to the best of my knowledge has no wish to do so. I ask only that my submission goes to Mr Aislabie for him to consider along with the rest.

'As you know,' she rushed on, 'I have few talents, but you in your wisdom have ensured that I should acquire some accomplishments in talent's place – not only art, music and needlework, but also Latin and Mathematics. Well, the discipline of these studies has left its mark upon my mind. I have devised a bridge which could, by my reckoning, meet this town's needs. I cannot say whether an acknowledged expert like Mr Aislabie shall find any merit in it – he may well dismiss it out of hand. Yet in all justice you cannot forbid me to put it forward for his appraisal.'

There was a long silence.

'You make very free with your desires,' he said at last. 'Sir Rowley might humour your notion, I suppose, and let Aislabie assess your bridge along with the others.'

It was grudgingly spoken and he refused to look her in the eye. She had no recollection of having brought her father to such depth of desolation before and she made one last plea for his understanding.

'But has it, to your thinking, any worth?' She begged like a dog seeking crumbs at the table.

'As to that, daughter, I cannot say.'

Chapter Fourteen

Hearne lay on his bed, fretful and sleepless. Had he been harsh to refuse Caelica the praise for her sketch she craved? He tossed, unable to settle. At his side, Christina slept like death. Once she had taken her nightly draught, her breathing grew so quiet it was inaudible and only the occasional sleepy shifting of her frail body signified that the tide of life still flowed through her veins. It was well that the Creator had endowed him with robust spirits, else how should he keep her from utter decline?

His wife sick, his son disgraced, his daughter turned contrary and unreasonable, in the stillness of the summer night Hearne began to pray. He did not make up his own words, but used the familiar phrases of the prayer book. *We thine unworthy servants do give thee most humble and hearty thanks for all thy goodness and loving-kindness to us and to all men...* But what goodness? What loving kindness? Estranged from wife, from son; perhaps even, from his beloved daughter, his parishioners having forsaken him, evidence of the divine benignity was thin indeed.

At last he lost patience. It wanted, he judged, no more than a couple of hours until daybreak. Rising, he went to his dressing chamber, lit a candle and put on warm clothes. Making his way to the parlour, he picked up the drawings. Over Caelica's remarkable sketch he paused. For a second, he thought of tearing it up and burning the separate pieces, his anger still hot at her presumption.

But anger gave poor counsel. He had been weak enough to indicate that he would take her submission along with the others. 'Sir Rowley might humour your notion, I suppose' was what he had said, and he would keep his word. To see Sir

Rowley take up the sketch, ponder it for a moment, utter some exclamation upon its novelty and then put the thing aside for evermore would be vindication enough. And then they could forget all about it. Caelica would marry that affable young man whose shortcomings of intellect she need never expose; the town, acknowledging him as the moving force behind its new bridge, would forgive him for the burial of Hannah Hallet; Christopher would be acquitted of his crime and leave the court in contrite heart; Christina would recover her health and they should all live at peace once more.

Tearing a leaf from his pocket book, he went through to the library and putting a quill to the ink, he wrote 'I rose before dawn to call at Menston. God's blessings upon you.' He left the message on the table where he hoped they'd see it. Entering the kitchen, he found a crust from the previous day's loaf on a shelf in the kitchen. Anstice always fed crumbs to the sparrows on her way to the well. Today, they'd have to go without. Hearne ate half of it himself and put half into his pocket for the mare. She had a longish way to go, but when they reached Menston, Sir Rowley's stable men would give her a feed of corn, a rack of hay and a good rubbing down.

Unlike some horses, she lay down to sleep, her legs bent beneath her compact body, tidy and supple as a cat. But she rose when she saw him holding out the crust, and came forward, eager and trustful, so that he could easily slip the bridle's headpiece over her ears and slide the bit into her soft mouth. In the dark, with unpractised hands, saddling and bridling took him longer than it would have taken Robert. His efforts to fasten the leather straps in the gloom were clumsy, but the mare somehow put up with his awkwardness, standing still and quiet even when he tightened the girth around her belly. She was a good, beautiful female who desired only to please.

He had put all the drawings in a leather bag, which he now buckled behind the saddle. There was no moon, but as he lead the mare to the stone mounting block, he saw that the sky was paler in the east than overhead where only sharp, unyielding star points broke the depth of blue-black. Fortunately, the mare was a sure-footed beast, and did not need much light to find her way along the well-worn tracks. He clasped his woollen cloak about him, glad of his hat, gloves and thick linen stock. With more deliberation than natural agility, he mounted, adjusted the reins and set off through the gate.

By birth a countryman, Hearne anticipated that he would find the last hours of night quiet – a time of respite between the close of evening revels and the start of the day's field labours. It was with some surprise therefore that he found he was far from being the only soul awake. Sir Rowley's mine on the flanks of the hill they called Allt Gwithel was stirring to life, men assembling around the crushing plant, or gathering at the head of the workings, called out greetings – some of them ironic – as he passed.

'Good morrow, sir – d'you seek to work with us?' came one voice.

'Don't you see it's the parson?' came another.

'Is one day's labour in the week too little for you, sir? You'd come and take the poor men's wages as well as his tithes?'

'Hush, he's here to preach to us,' said yet another, while a group of them doffed their hats as though in solemnity.

'The leader of the New Worship's good enough for me,' one loud voice complained. 'Mr Parry preaches out of doors in all weather and doesn't need a church building to keep his head dry. And he shares all he has with our sick and our injured to keep them from starving.'

Hearing, Hearne halted. 'Why, if you are too sick to earn your wage, do you not come to me for relief? I would show myself as generous as Emrys Parry,' he announced.

The man who had spoken spat at his feet. 'You're not one of us. You and your friend, Sir Rowley. You keep to your sort and we'll keep to ours.'

'But,' Hearne persisted, 'you must know that you and your families are always welcome in my church. And if you are in trouble, I would wish to give you whatever assistance I can. Do not spurn my charity, I beg.'

'Charity,' the man repeated in scorn, and Hearne began to understand. If Parry and the Dissenters could make charitable giving look more like friendship than the gracious generosity of rich to poor then people found it all the more palatable. Whatever Hearne's wishes in the matter, he knew he could never be a friend to the unlearned. They did not understand his scholarly speech and when he tried to talk in simple terms that they might follow, both he and they recognised that he was only playing a part. Given a minister who was one of them – a local man like Parry with the burr of the place in his speaking – they would accept his goodness as readily as they accepted the sun on their faces. But they would not accept bounty from Hearne.

Sombre, unable to think of any good way to take the conversation forward, he touched his hat and rode on in the growing light. Although Menston was about an hour and half's ride away, it would still be an excessively early hour for the household when he got there. But he had no wish to linger in these heights among the miners. Do good by stealth, he remembered, and hoped they might find it in their hearts to thank him when the bridge was built.

The track descended a steep, stony slope which the mare found uneasy going. Hearne gave her free rein and patted her neck in reassurance, but she stumbled so often that at last, he dismounted and walked alongside her shoulder until they reached level ground once more. Denied the feed that Robert always brought her at sun-up, the poor creature was quite lacking in spirit. By the time they reached Menston, man and horse were equally dispirited.

But the manservant who came to the door recognised Hearne at once and gave him a warm welcome on Sir Rowley's behalf. Promising that the grooms should give the mare food and water, he led Hearne to the library.

Although it was some relief to sit back in a soft chair and stretch his stiff hands towards the fire burning in the grate, finding himself obliged to wait did nothing to cheer Hearne's mood. Six months after his first visit and the library shelves were still near empty – how could Sir Rowley endure to see those desolate spaces that he might have crammed with volume upon volume? Not even the sight of a fine portrait of Alice Whatmough hanging above the fireplace in a gilded frame could dispel Hearne's gloom. The artist had done well, to be sure, and it would take a greater boor than he to dismiss out of hand the poise, the beguiling smile and the silver-blue eyes which even in the painting danced to their depths. But books were trustier friends than women. Since there was no sign of Sir Rowley, Hearne gave his attention to the ill-populated shelves once more and extracted Thomson's *Seasons*.

He had not read much when steps, lighter and more carefree than Sir Rowley's gouty footfall, sounded in the corridor outside. A moment later, young Curwen slouched in.

'Good morrow, ah, Edward,' he said rising. Before long, this imperious young man would be his son-in-law, one of the family. He hoped they would always accord well with one another.

'My dear Mr Hearne – a good day to you, sir. This is some surprise – whatever brings you to Menston at this hour?'

Would it not have been fitting for Edward at once to enquire after his beloved?

'First let me assure you, sir, my daughter is in good health and spirits,' Hearne informed him. 'She would, if she knew that I were here, wish me to convey her fondest regards to you.'

Lowering himself into a capacious arm chair, Edward let his expansive features settle to a satisfied smile. Hearne, seeing no need to mention his sleepless night, filled the ensuing silence by explaining how he had risen early on a whim.

'I had pledged,' he added, 'that this day I should bring the designs submitted for our new bridge to your father, both for his own scrutiny and for the appraisal of his distinguished friend Mr Aislabie.'

'He's bringing old Aislabie in on this bridge venture is he? I hadn't known.'

Old Aislabie? Yorke Aislabie was the foremost engineer in the country. At once, Hearne wanted to needle the sheer arrogance with which the young man reclined on that soft chair,

166

extending his long legs towards the fire. Needle it like a blown bladder, future son-in-law or no.

'You know Mr Aislabie?' he asked.

'I think I may I have met him once or twice.' Edward half raised his hand to hide a yawn. 'And everyone knows about his work at Lackenford and on the Borders Canal – not that I have any particularly strong recollection of the man's conversation, of course.'

'Am I to infer,' Hearne found it increasingly difficult to contain his irritation, 'that you have relatively little interest in Mr Aislabie's achievements?'

'My dear sir,' said Edward with a smile that stretched towards insolence. 'All my father's friends are men of achievement.'

To change the subject, Hearne asked if he would care to view the bridge drawings. Opening the leather saddlebag, he extracted the sheaf of sketches.

In secret, ever since he first saw them, Hearne had harboured many of the same reservations about the designs that Caelica had voiced. In truth, there were any number of dull bridges here which might serve, but which offered nothing in the way of vision or artistry. As Edward took the papers, Hearne watched to see what he might make of them.

Edward, as it happened, found much to admire. 'Oh see here,' he exclaimed, poring over a louring clumsy creation. 'Now that would suit well indeed. Look at the depth between the parapet and the arches.'

'It bears some resemblance to the town's old bridge and might for that reason prove popular,' Hearne allowed. 'But I fear,' he went on, 'it would soon suffer the same fate as its predecessor. Those low arches would choke with branches and debris all too easily and soon enough the blockage would bring down the bridge.'

At this self-evident truth, Edward's face clouded. He chose drew another drawing from the pile. 'What of this one, sir?' he asked.

Hearne took it from him, frowning. The draughtsman had portrayed a triple-span structure, with narrow piers between the arches.

'I am no expert,' he conceded, 'but by my judgement the weight of that ornamental balustrade could well prove too heavy for its slender supports. The man who drew this confection followed his fancy; his work is pretty enough but not, to my thinking, practical.'

'And yet it's highly decorative, wouldn't you say?' Edward persisted.

'It might do well enough in a rich man's park,' allowed Hearne, disappointed to find Edward so lacking in discrimination. 'It could grace a vista of woodland and water to powerful effect. But Llanmichael's no garden. For all the majesty of the hills around, the town itself is rough and plain. Its bridge will have ceaseless traffic of pack animals crossing it daily, back and forth. This dainty workmanship will not serve. To tell you the truth, I had hoped that some man of vision might point the way towards blending elegance with utility.'

For a time, Edward leafed through the submissions without evincing much enthusiasm. Then he reached Caelica's sketch. At once he hesitated. Hearne followed his eyes as they travelled slowly over the high, airy arch and dwelt upon the symmetrical tunnels. Suddenly, 'What about this?' he breathed, revelation in his face. 'Here, surely is a bridge that unites grace and strength in uncommon measure.'

'Ah,' said Hearne.

'See,' Edward grew more expansive. 'Not only will it meet the demands of the locality, but those tunnels are delightfully decorative - they frame the arch like jewels, do they not? And being but a single span, you would have little to fear from its becoming clogged. Whoever came up with this plan has something of the magician about him, I should say. This cleverness is more than human.'

'Oh, it's human enough.' Hearne gave a short, wry laugh. 'This design is the handiwork of my daughter – your future wife,' he announced. He wondered whether even now, for propriety's sake, he ought to rule Caelica's entry out of the contest and find some pretext on which to put it back in his saddle bag.

'Miss Hearne's?' Edward looked as though he had bitten into a maggoty apple. 'But building bridges is no business of women. Forgive me, sir – I do not set out to disparage your daughter, but it is – well, strange – to see her take strides in so unlikely a direction.'

'I tried to dissuade her,' Hearne admitted, shaking his head in recollection of their fraught exchange. 'For her to bring her talent to bear upon devising a bridge is, to my mind, a usurpation of the role that belongs properly to men. I told her so only last night. When the two of you are married, she shall no doubt find ample scope for her skills in running your household and managing your servants. For her to produce this design of a bridge isn't fitting in the slightest. At the same time, as you yourself acknowledge, it meets Llanmichael's needs in masterly fashion.'

'Well,' Edward rubbed his square chin. 'I can't claim to be pleased. For a woman to undertake engineering work is, surely, a reversal of all rightful order. And what might it portend for our future as man and wife?'

Hearne shrugged his shoulders.

'Yet,' Edward continued, 'the bridge she has sketched has unquestionable merit. How, sir, are we to proceed?'

All through his dawn ride, all the time he had been parrying the miners' insults, then whiling away the empty minutes over Thomson's *Seasons* and throughout his conversation with this shallow, callow, conceited young man, the question of how he should proceed had been twisting in his mind. It was only justice that his Caelica should be permitted to enter the contest, but it was manifestly unbecoming that his demure and biddable daughter should have conceived a bridge that was at once so daring and so innovatory. In honesty his dilemma had no simple remedy. He was on the point of confessing that he stood in a total quandary when Edward, full of resolution, made a suggestion.

'Let me pass off her drawing as my own,' he said.

Hearne stared. The effrontery beggared belief. At the same time, the idea wasn't entirely disagreeable. Hearne sometimes wondered whether, as a clergyman, he spent too much time among people who took every possible step to hide the excesses of their self-interest. He had forgotten how refreshing it could be to find himself in the company of men who, upon seeing something that they liked, reached and took it without pausing to dress up their actions in a cloak of polite morality. It was all very well to preach sermons on virtue, for virtue had its place; it brought people to church and encouraged them to pay their tithes. Of its value there was no question. Nevertheless, virtuous persons did not always make the liveliest of companions.

'You do not care for my proposal?' asked Edward, with a smile.

Hearne, to his amazement, found himself smiling back. He might not show much conscience, this handsome young thruster, but that wasn't to say he lacked charm. Even his impudence was winning.

'Well,' Hearne hardly knew what to say. 'It gives me some surprise, sir,' he admitted at last, 'to hear this suggestion.'

'You could, I suppose, say –' Edward's manner had such ease, such complaisance that Hearne wanted to like him after all '– that ever since my boyhood I have had a fondness for springing surprises.' As though recognising a fellow-accomplice, he gave Hearne a broad grin.

'My daughter will have no liking for this notion,' Hearne felt bound to say.

'Yet your daughter likes the notion of marrying me,' returned Edward the affable. 'And in the eyes of the church we shall be one flesh, shall we not?'

'Indeed, but that is not to say...'

'Come, Mr Hearne. You have indicated that you consider it improper for women to design bridges. "Not fitting in the slightest" – wasn't that what you said? So let me put an end to your embarrassment. Your daughter Caelica has planned out a most impressive structure which, you and I agree, does more

170

credit to her ingenuity than it does to her womanly grace. What I propose is that I adapt her drawing somewhat – put my own mark to it, if you like. Although the bridge will retain the full genius of her conception, it shall nevertheless take on an entirely new character.

'I have every confidence, seeing how her design stands head and shoulders above all those other rubbishy drawings, that Aislabie will make it his winner. When it is built, we'll have a stone engraved on it to say that it was I who was its originator. Then there shall be no more ugly talk about the woman usurping the man's rightful place.'

It was a way ahead, even if it were hardly fair-dealing.

At that moment more footsteps, ponderous this time, sounded outside the library.

'Ah, Edward – Hearne, a good day to you both.' Sir Rowley glanced from his son to his guest. 'You call at an early hour, reverend sir,' he observed. 'No – you have not put me out in the slightest; do not trouble yourself on that score. It is for me to regret that you should catch me playing the laggard. I rise early most days. You have brought the bridge submissions, have you not?'

He moved to the table where Hearne and Edward had been talking and looked over Hearne's shoulder at the sketches spread on its surface. The elegant buckles gleaming upon his broad leather shoes, the immaculate stockings and breeches, the easy cut of his waistcoat and perfection of the stock at his neck cowed Hearne, all too aware of the mud that clung to his own worn boots and spotted his coat. He tried to remind himself Sir Rowley hadn't started the day with a long ride, and since it had been a matter of duty rather than pleasure, he needn't blush for finding himself travel-worn.

But he could not argue away the uncomfortable warmth that clung around his neck, flushed in his cheeks and lurked behind his ears, and he knew that it owed nothing to his companion's stylish clothes.

Sir Rowley picked up one drawing after another and held each to the light. 'It's a pretty poor set,' he began. Then,

171

'Wherever did this one come from?' Frowning, he held up Caelica's entry.

'It is the work of my daughter, sir.'

'Is it indeed? And where did she learn such skill in working with stone, the baggage?' The thought of Caelica evolving a new type of bridge must amuse Sir Rowley hugely, for his dewlaps quivered with suppressed laughter.

'She has no proven skill in this field.' Hearne spoke sternly to hide his confusion. 'Though she has had some lessons in geometry which she found to her liking, and she's always had a taste for sketching, and,' he paused. 'Well, she has brought what I can only term her native intuition to bear on the problem of our old bridge's arches choking whenever the river was in spate.'

'I like that bold span,' Sir Rowley went on as though Hearne had never spoken. 'So will Aislabie. He has a taste for the heroic in ventures of this kind. Oh, it'd cause no end of pother if this bridge were known to spring from the mind of a woman. Still, it'll win the competition. I'll put my money to it, Hearne, never fear. Now what shall we say about its origin?'

'Father,' Edward spoke in his easy, confiding way. 'Mr Hearne and I have reached an accommodation.'

'Accommodation, my boy? In a fair, open competition?' Sir Rowley laughed out loud. 'I did not credit you with such shrewdness. Tell me about it.'

'The arrangement, father,' a shaft of sun lit Edward's face, making him look rapt and holy, 'is that we'll claim Miss Hearne's design as my own.'

'How so?' His father was captivated.

'I propose to adapt it somewhat – place a carved head on the parapet, perhaps, and consider ribbing the arch. Make small alterations that impose my own vision upon hers. Entries, I understand, may be submitted any time up till noon and the clock stands at half past eight. That gives me enough time to work up the drawing.'

'That shows a cool hand,' said Sir Rowley, sitting down. 'Well, if you ride pick-a-pack on the little lass's cleverness, you'll hardly be the first man to make other people's wits serve your own ends. Would your daughter mind Edward appropriating her design, Hearne? What do you think?'

Hearne's honest answer was that in all probability his Caelica would mind to a profound degree. In the face of Edward's manoeuvring and fearful of offending Sir Rowley he hesitated to be so blunt.

'How shall I explain the circumstances?' he asked instead. 'Caelica is fond of you, Edward, and bides the time until your wedding with much impatience. Yet she has, I think, fierce fondness too for that bridge of hers, and yearns to know what Mr Aislabie may make of it.'

'Come, Hearne. Call to mind the straits in which you stand. Your son, I hear, is named as the seducer of that unhappy girl who killed herself and stands charged with forgery besides. Your parishioners have abandoned your church in protest and threaten to withhold their tithes. If they make good their threat, I do not see how you can continue to live as you do at present. Assuredly when the time comes to build the new bridge, it will be necessary to recruit a labour force from outside the district, for no Llanmichael man will ever work on an enterprise connected with yourself.'

'Consider, dear sir,' Edward blazed in. 'These things all tend to the conclusion that you really must allow me to appropriate your daughter's design. Then although the townspeople will have no reason to associate you with its construction, once Caelica and I are married and the new bridge complete, they will recognise that their benefactor is one of your family – your son-in-law, no less. I am confident that with the excitement of a wedding in their midst and a serviceable bridge in Llanmichael once more, they will soon forget past grievances. Believe me, before long you will bask in their esteem once more. Surely your daughter, the sweetness of whose nature we all mark and admire, will see the merits of this course of action?'

'She might, I suppose.' A doubtful answer, grudgingly given.

'Take the sketch through to the morning room, Edward, and draw up the plan your way,' ordered Sir Rowley. 'We'll pass it on with the others to Aislabie. He has the task of making pen and pencil strokes work out in hard stone.' He paused and smiled. 'Ah, but I like the thought of a son of mine being credited with that fine bridge.'

'I'll make matters square with you, Hearne,' he added. 'I'll pay for the materials and it'll be my workforce who build it, so you need not think of the difficulties of recruiting labour from among your mutinous townsmen. What's more, I'll consider what we might do for your son when his case comes up at the Assizes. I don't care to think of Edward's marrying the sister of a convicted criminal. Now while he takes himself to the morning room, let us find you some refreshment.'

Summoning his manservant Sir Rowley requested him to bring coffee. Hearne looked worn out. Perhaps, Sir Rowley reflected, he had been too outspoken in his remark about criminals. But then everyone in the district knew that the son of the rector of Llanmichael was in gaol, and all the local people with whom Sir Rowley had dealings – his servants, neighbours and some of the larger landowners – seemed to know the boy's mother had lost her wits for very shame. Well, the children of clergymen were not supposed to kick over the traces. They were meant to be obedient, caring and courteous, like Hearne's daughter. Hearne was plainly ill at ease with the magnificent bridge that had sprung from the imagination of his quiet Caelica.

Perhaps, mused Sir Rowley, who had determined not to question poor, weary Hearne about his son again until the man was somewhat revived, the parson was right. Everyone knew how readily unrest sprang from small subversions of order and hierarchy. While in London, say, or Birmingham or Bath, a society delighting in novelty might well find something intriguing in the notion of a young woman's turning engineer, here people did not care to see disturbances in the pattern of their lives. They would have men for their leaders and for the initiators of new ideas. That was what they were used to.

The coffee when it came was hot and reviving, and Hearne marvelled at the delicacy of the china.

'This ware is most attractive.'

'Mrs Whatmough thought it would accord well with the style of her furnishings,' Sir Rowley set himself to play the genial host. 'The cobalt paint in which the craftsman has delineated the plumage of that bird – see there – catches her favourite colour. I believe it is because it chimes so well with the blue of her eyes, but were I to say so, she would protest that I was charging her with vanity.'

Talking about Alice Whatmough reminded him how far he stood in Hearne's debt. Not only was there the matter of the bridge in which Hearne was allowing Edward free rein but also, while it was plain that he did not care for the fact that Alice was living in her future husband's house and had, Sir Rowley strongly suspected, guessed at the way that things stood between the pretty widow and her protector, he had not stood upon nice clergy scruples and refused to marry them. Not all parsons would be so accommodating – not unless they were the ordained drunkards who officiated around the Fleet, demanding large sweeteners and disgracing their calling. Hearne wasn't that sort of clergyman. He had been magnanimous and Sir Rowley would endeavour to repay his kindness.

'How goes it with your boy?' he asked, sitting back in an expansive way ready to hear all that Hearne was willing to confide.

'My son, Christopher. Well, I am not surprised that you should ask.' Hearne looked and sounded quite wretched; when had the man last enjoyed a good night's sleep?

'Be assured, my dear sir,' Sir Rowley interposed, 'it is not vain curiosity that prompts my question. It springs rather from my wish to establish whether there is any way in which, by my offices, I might secure some remedy for the young man's plight.'

Hearne realised that talking through Christopher's trouble might be some comfort. He could trust Sir Rowley to keep the matter to himself. And if Sir Rowley were to venture an opinion of Christopher's conduct, it could hardly be more damning than

175

some of the views he himself had voiced in the past. Savouring the coffee upon his tongue – they never had it in the parsonage – Hearne allowed himself to smile at his host.

'After Eton, my boy Christopher set his heart on becoming a painter. Had he gone to Oxford, there were funds available on which, as the son of an Oxford man, he might have drawn for support, though I think Christopher would not have cared to be a scholarship boy, and have the gentleman commoners look down on him.

'His mother took his side and pleaded with me to get him indentured to a man called Le Marque. Christopher liked the sound of a Frenchman, though truth to tell, Sir Rowley, I could never distinguish his landscapes from those of his English counterparts.

'The term of his apprenticeship passed easily enough. As his father, I suppose I have some partiality in the matter, but I believe he was not without talent. Slender talent, I admit, but he had the ability to catch a likeness with a pencil and to set in pigment that mysterious light of dawn when you can believe the world looks like it did at the hour of Creation, or to capture the peace of a slow stream on a summer day. Naturally it pleased me to think that he might make a name for himself so I paid Le Marque with a good grace. I was only thankful the boy didn't insist on travelling round Italy.

'Once he was out of his articles, he touched me for a capital sum with which to establish himself as a portraitist in Brynwardine.'

'And your daughter, all this while?' interrupted Sir Rowley.

'My Cherry, poor tongue-tied lass, I kept at her books. Her stammering was always worse when she was among strangers, so we went abroad but seldom. I paid Thomas Russell – he's been reading with me this past year, while he prepares for ordination - to teach her a little Latin and Mathematics. He found her an apt and rewarding pupil, indeed – ' Realising it would be tactless to tell Edward's father about Thomas's absurd thoughts of marrying Caelica, Hearne reverted quickly to the subject of Christopher.

'But my son was hard-pressed to find enough business to support himself, let alone turn a profit. There were a few portraits, though never as much demand as he expected. In the end, he toiled round the big houses of the district hawking himself out as a drawing master. And all this time, his debts grew. Eventually, under pressure from his creditors, he forged his signature upon a bill of endorsement.'

'Well, what a poor use of his skill.' By the end of the rigmarole of woe, Sir Rowley could no longer hold back his laughter. 'Hearne, I was waiting for you tell me that he was passing off his landscapes as works of one of the Italian masters my Alice is so drawn to. No, I suppose it would be a bit much to expect anyone to believe that an oil painting of our Allt Gwithel might stand for a scene of Umbria. So, your boy did what any number of men have done before him in hard times, and stole from – who was it?'

'Bevan, the coroner – the father of one of his pupils,' Hearne replied, looking more hangdog than ever. 'Kit found the bill blown aside in the privy, or so he claims. Conscious all the time of his mounting obligations and negligible income, he pocketed it, then wrote "Pay Christopher Hearne" on the reverse. Once endorsed and hoping to raise some ready cash, he took it to Allardyce the corn-chandler. But Allardyce was suspicious and informed Bevan. Bevan hadn't even noticed he'd lost it, but it didn't stop him pressing charges.'

There was a great furrow between Hearne's eyebrows and the hesitant way in which he had been speaking put Sir Rowley in mind of Caelica's stammer.

'Had the boy ever shown any dishonest tendency in his life before?' Sir Rowley asked.

'Never,' answered Hearne in a weary voice.

'Nor, I suspect, will he ever act in any underhand way again. Hearne,' Sir Rowley seized his opportunity. 'Let me put your son on the way to taking a second chance. No man ever made anything of his life without a little backsliding. His term of imprisonment must have shown him the error of his ways –

177

aye, and satisfied your righteous wish to deter other miscreants from following his example.'

'My dear sir,' Hearne's usual poise had gone. 'He has not appeared before the judge yet. How can you talk of second chances when he hasn't even been sentenced? He may be transported – even hanged.'

'I shall find him a most eminent advocate.'

It shouldn't be difficult to find counsel for Christopher Hearne – counsel of such distinction and reputation as to scare any provincial assize judge into letting the foolish jackanapes off with a short and mild sentence, if not dismissing the case against him outright. It pleased him to make so munificent a gesture.

Hearne still looked uneasy. 'I cannot accede to your wish,' he flustered.

'My dear Mr Hearne, why ever not?'

'It would be an affront to justice.'

Confound the clergy conscience. Surely it was a most sensible course of action? 'Justice must needs find the temper of mercy – is not that what your church would teach?' asked Sir Rowley. 'By-the-by, would you like some more coffee? Shall I ring for Briskham?'

'No more, I thank you. *Blest are the merciful, for they shall obtain mercy* - is that what you would say?'

To encourage him, Sir Rowley nodded.

Still Hearne hesitated. 'I do not think,' he explained, his voice full of regret, 'that that verse entitles me to sanction any course of action which would enable my son to evade the due process of law.'

He was stubborn, this cleric. Anyone might think he wanted to see his boy consigned to fetters for years to come. While Hearne's daughter was a douce and decent maid, Sir Rowley would welcome her all the more readily into his family if her brother were not actually a convict at the time of the wedding.

'How does your lady wife view the matter?' he asked.

For a moment, Hearne was silent. 'Naturally, she desires to see her son have his freedom again,' he allowed. 'But it surely isn't fair to set such weight on the wishes of the mother of the accused?'

Sir Rowley leant forward. 'I don't seek to be fair,' he said, and though he never thought himself a demonstrative man, he deliberately touched Hearne's hand. 'I seek to be kind. Now, your son's not going to escape trial. What's more, his trial shall be as equitable as that of any other man who comes up before the Assizes. All I ask is that you allow me to furnish him with an advocate who can put the merits of his case in the finest light. I speak as a friend to you, sir, and one who is soon to be joined to your family through marriage. Let me do this small thing.'

'The trial will, you say, be equitable?' Hearne asked, anxiety making him twist his hands upon his lap. 'All honestly done? The only part you shall play, Sir Rowley, shall be to secure for Kit the service of an advocate to plead on his behalf? Does my understanding accord with your own?'

'Entirely, my dear sir. We speak with one mind.' A surge of friendship rose in Sir Rowley's heart. He always warmed to the people he helped. 'You have behaved most generously to Alice – that is, Mrs Whatmough – and myself. You have been kind to Edward too, allowing him to shape your daughter's excellent sketch to his own ends. I am honoured to be able to reciprocate your goodness by taking steps to alleviate some of your distress. I shall write this very day to Richard Endicott...'

'Endicott? He is one of Pelham's circle...'

'He is indeed. Some years ago, he commissioned a clock of a most ingenious design from me and professed himself well pleased with it. See – I liked it so well, I had a second, smaller version made to amuse myself. Here it is.'

Rising, he went to where a gilded clock stood on the shelves that he had no intention of crowding with heavy volumes. It was truly a thing of beauty. Its numerals were emblazoned in gilt, it had a square alabaster base and at each of the corners was a silver statue of one of the archangels – Michael, Raphael, Gabriel and Uriel – with their emblems. The art that had gone into fashioning the four commanding figures, justice and mercy bright upon each archangelic countenance, was nothing short of genius. He knew Hearne would admire an artefact upon which biblical imagery afforded such edifying embellishment. The sheer delicacy of the shimmering fins and scales of Raphael's fish was a source of unending enchantment. What pleasure, having won Hearne round, to be able to show him so splendid an example of Curwen and Whatmough's wares.

Chapter Fifteen

Edward knew he didn't have long. The morning room, with its wide desk, inkstand and blotter to hand was by far the most comfortable place for his task. With relief, he saw his father and Mr Hearne remain in the library. To have the gentlemen looking over his shoulder while he worked would only vex him.

Taking up Caelica's drawing, crumpled from its passage in Hearne's saddlebag, he spread it out flat where it caught the light. There was no question that she had a pretty talent for drawing. The closer he looked at it, the more it pleased him. There was such confidence in the drafting, such dash in the depiction of that great arch reaching across a span of – what? It must be well over a hundred feet from bank to bank – more like a hundred and twenty, he would estimate. Perhaps it was female fancy that made her envisage such a thing; even so, the fancy appealed so strongly to his taste that he was delighted to lay claim to it. And there was something decidedly masculine in its boldness.

Her dry old father had intimated that despite her bread-and-butter submissiveness, she might take great grief at Edward's ploy, seeing it as a sort of theft. No, Edward decided, pen in hand. Theft was too coarse a term. Just because Hearne was a clergyman was no cause for them all to look at the enterprise through a Claude-glass of crabbed and constricting morality. Edward was not stealing Caelica's sketch so much as appropriating it – appropriating it in the name of improvement. His own father had called it riding pick-a-pack on the lass's skills. Well, Edward knew much about riding – of horses and women alike. Before long, he should ride Miss Caelica Hearne and school her talents to accord with his expectations.

Once they were married, until there were children to occupy her time, she could always amuse herself by sketching the blooms in the garden or the crag above the waterfall in the high ravine beyond the house. Alice and he had explored it together only the previous day and it was, by any standards, picturesque. That should please his wife-to-be, who certainly showed a fine grasp of what made a fair composition. The sunlight on the page revealed the care of the cross-hatching with which she had caught the deepening shadow of the great arch. Of course, if he were to give the bridge ribs, as he planned, he would have to obliterate all that painstaking pencil work. It was rather a shame to doing away with her meticulous shading of the stonework, but if he were to set his mark upon the design so as to make it his, the loss of some of her fine detail was unavoidable.

Charging his quill with ink, he sat down and began to alter the drawing. To the underside of the arch he added stone ribs, some half dozen of them. He had no idea what function they served, but he liked their decorative character. At the arch's crown, he thought he might add a carved head. If a fearsome stone likeness of the gorgon Medusa, for example, glared down from the parapet at the torrent beneath, it would lend the bridge much distinction. Besides, the sight of the stone snakes springing from her scalp might frighten Llanmichael children into good behaviour and the fear of being likened to the bridge-hag keep the women of the town from nagging their menfolk. On a practical note, if anyone should inquire why his drafting was done part in pencil and part in pen, he would explain that mid-way through the work, he had switched to ink specifically in order to emphasise the more ornate features of his design.

The apertures with which she had pierced the bridge's haunches lent the structure an unassuming elegance. He wasn't sure that elegance was what folk looked for in a workaday bridge on one of the major routes between England and mid-Wales. Besides, for all their grace, against the grandeur of his new embellishments her chaste sequence of concentric tunnels on either side of the arch looked rather plain and rustic.

Puzzling – should he do away with them? Edward rose from his seat, and stared out of the window for a moment at the men hewing rocks with which to encircle Rendle's ornamental rill. Sighing, he returned to the inked-up drawing. Since time was short, he would leave the piercings as they stood. Inking them out would be a messy business and old Aislabie could always remodel the arch if he chose.

The reverse side of the drawing bore her name, the inscription 'Llanmichael Parsonage,' and the date of a day last week. He would leave the date. To make out that he had contrived to create so arresting a bridge in three short hours between nine and noon might give rise to tedious questions. Taking up his pocket knife – by great good fortune he had whetted its blade only yesterday – he scored away the surface of the paper where she had written 'Caelica Hearne, Llanmichael Parsonage,' trusting that Aislabie would not notice the thin rough patch on the page. The paper was not of the highest quality, being only what a country parson could afford. Thankful to find Caelica had spelt out the month – MAY – in easily imitated capitals, he wrote EDWARD CURWEN, MENSTON beside it, pleased he had been able to bring off his scheme with such ease.

For his journey home Hearne took a path that led through woodland in the valley bottoms, far away from the track he had ridden over earlier. Sunlight had broken through the cloud and the day was turning warm. He rode with loose reins, the mare's hooves quiet in the leaf-mould, her black ears moving back and forth to catch the querulous notes of the pigeons in the trees. Fording a stream, a tributary of the Llanmichael river, he let her stretch her coppery neck and drink deep. Once she had had her fill, she extended her stride and pulled hard, eager for home.

Giving her her head, Hearne's spirits lifted. It occurred to him that if he were to say nothing to Caelica about Edward's purloining of her drawing, she need never know the truth of the matter. In the coming week or so, Mr Yorke Aislabie would visit Menston, inspect all the drawings and select one as a basis upon which to build a new bridge for Llanmichael. For the comfort of Hearne's conscience, it would be happiest if he chose one of the clumsier, less adventurous sketches, but Hearne had to admit that outcome looked unlikely.

Yet even if Caelica's drawing won the contest as he expected, she surely need not know what Edward had done. It wasn't, Hearne reasoned, as though Aislabie was going to flourish the doctored sketch for everyone to see. All that would happen was that Edward stood to gain a cash prize. Even if, in time, she were to recognise her design in the solid stone structure, it would hardly matter. There might be a little coolness between Edward and her for an hour or so – a day, at most – but Caelica wasn't a girl to bear grudges. Besides, it was obvious to anyone with eyes in his head that she was so much in love with her handsome, good-natured husband-to-be she would allow him anything.

Two weeks passed. In mid-June Sir Rowley sent word to the Parsonage that Richard Endicott, Serjeant-at-Law, was willing to appear on behalf of Christopher Hearne at the Hereford Assizes. The Menston servant, evidently in a hurry with other errands to perform, gave her father the news in the hall. From the shadowy stillroom where Caelica was helping Anstice to make lavender and fennel infusion – it eased toothache and sore throats – she could hear him, circumspect as he relayed Sir Rowley's message. Neither the name of Endicott nor the term 'Serjeant-at-Law' meant anything to her, but she could not help catching every word of her father's ebullient reply.

'Endicott – well, if we have Endicott on board, we are home and dry,' and he drew in his breath with audible satisfaction. 'You may tell your master what I've just said, my good man,' he went on, 'aye, and give him my deepest thanks while you are about it. With a Serjeant-at Law to represent him, I do not believe any charge against my son can stick...'

'Sir Rowley bade me say that he urges every caution, sir.' The footman's voice sounded a note of warning. 'He asked me to remind you in all courtesy that the law's workings are often unpredictable.'

'Indeed they are. Yet with Endicott willing to plead my son's case – well, it's a most hopeful sign.'

Sealing the mouths of the full stone jars, Anstice paused and raised her eyebrows.

'Will not th-the essence evaporate and lose its potency?' asked Caelica.

In general, her father conducted his conversations quietly; unless his visitors were as forthright as Mr Bevan, it had the effect of encouraging them to speak as softly as he. His optimism getting the better of him, he couldn't be aware that his triumphant words carried through the whole house. Caelica didn't think he would wish his housekeeper to overhear this exchange.

It surprised her to learn how much Sir Rowley knew. Caelica thought she and her parents had reached a silent agreement not to speak of Christopher's plight outside the family. Yet if her understanding of the conversation in the hallway was correct, not only had Sir Rowley used his influence to obtain an able lawyer on Kit's behalf, but also he must have agreed to pay his fee. It was an act of extraordinary generosity.

'What is your father saying to Sir Rowley's man? What is that about pleading your brother's case?' Anstice asked, her head on one side, half a dozen jars ready to take their places on the shelves of the still room dresser, and the smell of lavender heavy in the air. Caelica hesitated. By rights, she and her mother should have learned the good news before their servant. Left to herself Anstice might well spread the tidings to Luke and Sarah Vaughan, to Gleeson the carrier and his silly daughter Catherine, and thence all across the neighbourhood. It might give rise to no end of harmful gossip.

To quell the questions, Caelica deliberately began to pound the celandine flowers she had picked before breakfast that morning. They grew well in the shady herb garden and her mother thought the juice cured warts. The clash of brass pestle against the mortar would blot out her father's talk.

'If your brother gets out of prison, it'll be something, I suppose,' said Anstice.

Caelica looked up from her work to scan the pouchy face. Was it her imagination, or was the housekeeper hinting at more than she cared to say?

'W-why do you s-say "something"?' she asked. 'F-for Kit t-to have his liberty again would c-count for much.'

'Perhaps, but it won't end your father's trouble.'

'H-how not? For Kit t-to have his f-freedom and no stain of criminality upon his n-name will bring great cheer to my father,' She tightened her grip on the shiny shaft. 'And even m-more to my m-mother.'

'It won't make things any easier for your father to have his son free again.' Anstice's face was expressionless. 'And I can't see your mother's happiness at his release lasting long either. Why did your father have to...'

'Stop!' This harping on the past, this ceaseless condemnation of her father's charitable decision to accord Christian burial to the dead mother and child was unendurable. 'Y-you mu-must n-n-n...'

'N-n-n,' Anstice mimicked her across the table. 'Oh, but I speak as I find and I've a straight tongue in my head which is more than I can say for some in these parts. I must not make out that your father's in the wrong – is that what you would say Miss Caelica?'

Unable even to mouth the syllable, 'Aye' Caelica nodded, her fingers stiff and stained.

'You nod, do you? Well, you'll learn in time. He can do wrong, even though he's a clergyman. I've said it before. It was burying that worthless girl in the churchyard that brought on all this hardship.'

'Anstice, h-hush.' Why should it take all her self-mastery to utter the two poor words? 'I kn-know you think this way.' These words were good – short and simple. 'But my father – my father wanted to show p-pity.' Breathe. Breathe deep and go on. 'Pity for mother and child. H-how could it be wrong?' Caelica demanded.

'Pity for mother and child,' repeated Anstice slowly. Her eyes, meeting Caelica's above the sealed jars flickered and her lips thinned. The lavender scent was overwhelming.

'All along,' she said, 'all along, I've followed your mother's way of looking at things. She could not believe that your brother would lie with a field girl and get her a big belly, and at the time, no more could I. But now I wonder. "Pity for mother and child" would you say?'

Again Caelica nodded. This time, Anstice gave a rough, joyless laugh. 'Come on. I can see it all now. Your father's put her in the churchyard because she was carrying his own kin. He wouldn't have countenanced any such thing otherwise. Her bastard babe was his own grandson or grand-daughter, wasn't it? Hannah Hallet was a foolish drab, but she knew who'd fathered the infant in her womb. And so, I think, did you.'

'Aye.' It came out barely louder than breathing. 'Th-this tale,' somehow Caelica managed to interrupt the grim mirth. 'I-it wou-would not be meet for it to spread. The sh-shame would not befall m-my parents alone, but the church besides...'

'Oh, you poor, frightened, milky little pigeon-heart.' Indignation flared all across Anstice's broad face. 'You urge me to think of the church? Are you hoping that all my years of cold worship will keep my mouth closed to spare your father, your mother and you from a lot of whispers and pointing?

'Listen to me, Miss Hen-heart,' her fleshy chin jutted forward. 'Why should you worry? You're set fair to wed that fine-looking gentleman, with his gilt watch and his fast horses. Once you're Mrs Curwen, you need never hear a hard word spoken in your hearing again. You'll be so great a lady that everyone in the district'll want to win your favour. As for parson and the mistress, your shine'll surround them like a heat-haze. People may not like them, but they'll still defer and talk respectful, on account of Mr and Mrs Hearne's being Mrs Curwen's kin.'

'An-anstice – why do you talk like this?' The question burst out like fire, but Anstice only grunted and shook her head.

'I like to see things plain,' she said.

Anstice always made free with her opinions. She held views on every subject under the sun, from the parable of the talents – 'Aye, you make your way in the world by hard graft, not squirreling things away so's you forget what you've done with them,' – to the best wine for a syllabub – Canary, as it happened, with milk straight from the cow – which she shared with everyone she met. Having once hit on the truth of Hannah Hallet's tale she would talk wherever she went, and soon the stone-throwing would start all over again. There was no helping it. The Hearnes' secrecy was vain.

When Caelica told her father about the old servant's reasoning, he brushed her fears aside. They had outfaced the men of Llanmichael at the parsonage before; had she forgotten? Caelica need not fret. What with the excitement of hearing the winner of the bridge competition named and then seeing the bridge take shape, the scandal would soon lose its tang. Once the town had its trade again, it should find itself ready to forgive. Caelica wished she shared his confidence.

Two days later, Mr Aislabie was due to announce the winner of the bridge contest, and Caelica was going to accompany her father to Tobias Greene's inn to hear the result. Helping her get ready, Anstice was dour and short-spoken, as though she thought it all a waste of time. She had wrenched at the cord of Caelica's stays and twisted her hair hard, but at least she said nothing more about Christopher.

Once she had gone, Caelica took up Edward's garnets. Even in the soft evening light, there was something sullen about them, as though they begrudged their own dull red sheen. Of course she'd wear them, after all they had belonged to his mother. Perhaps he could remember pulling at them as they hung round her neck; she'd often seen children play with their mothers' necklaces. The thread linking the stones looked old but when she gave it a tentative, experimental tug, it held secure. Working the antique clasp with great care, she fastened the heavy necklace in place. Once Edward saw the garnets he would smile at her again, perhaps offer her his arm and lead her off to a quiet corner where he would say wise things. He had not visited her these last few days, nor yet invited her to Menston. For an engaged couple, the two of them were almost strangers.

Caelica's father declined the services of Vaughan and his coracle. The river had been quiet all day, which made for safe fording, at least, on horseback. If he took the cob, he wouldn't have to pay the boatman to wait at Llanmichael jetty for the duration of the meeting. Caelica could gather her skirts up, ride pillion behind him and they should do very well.

Sure enough, she scrambled up into the saddle from the stable mounting block, put her arms round his waist – she was no more confident around horses than he – and they set off.

'You're taut as a bent withy, daughter,' he remarked as they went down the track that led to the fording place. 'Are you afraid of falling?'

She denied it, but something, a loose stone perhaps, made the cob stumble. With a most un-clerical curse, her father touched it with his whip causing it to throw its large head into the air and snatch at the bit. Caelica grasped him all the harder.

The Menston party had arrived before them, for Sir Rowley's carriage was visible in the inn courtyard through the square archway. Once both Caelica and her father had dismounted, he tied his horse to a hitching post outside Greene's stabling and they entered the narrow room, now lit by many smoking candles. There was quite a crush, for the contest had stirred much local interest. Caelica sat by one of the windows that looked onto the street and looked round for Edward, hoping that he would come and join her. Her father waited on the threshold, glancing from excited group to group, as though he was wondering which knot of garrulous townsmen – all of them members of his congregation, once – would show him the warmest welcome.

Caelica could not see Edward, but Sir Rowley stood by the great fireplace at one end, his head almost touching the blackened beams, talking to a slight, weather-beaten man at his left hand side who must, she guessed, be Mr Aislabie. The muted light entering through the deep-set casements together with that of the candles threw Sir Rowley's gnarled profile into relief. Since he was engaged in conversation, Caelica let herself stare at him, tracing the rugged outline from the high forehead, over the predatory nose to the belligerent chin. It was not an unpleasing face – the indomitable features commanded something close to admiration – but no one could call it compassionate. Would Edward, she wondered, come to look like his father in time?

Just then Sir Rowley's voice interrupted her thoughts. 'Miss Hearne – ah, Edward cannot have realised that you and your father are here. No doubt his parishioners will welcome the opportunity to talk to their rector once more – church attendance has, ah, declined somewhat I hear.'

If her father had told Sir Rowley about his congregation's desertion, he must have been frank indeed. But Sir Rowley did not wait for her answer.

'Allow me to introduce you to Yorke Aislabie. Aislabie – this is Miss Hearne to whom Edward is betrothed.' Before Caelica could assimilate the significance of the fact that she should find herself in the company of the greatest manufacturer and the greatest engineer of the age, the thin, weathered man had turned to her with an unexpectedly gentle smile.

'So this is the young woman to whom your son is affianced? Your servant, ma'am.'

She felt rather self-conscious as he took her hand. While the attention of these gentlemen was flattering – she liked Mr Aislabie on sight – she could not help but remember that until Sir Rowley had broken off his conversation on observing that she was alone, they had shown every sign of contentment with one another's company. She should be with Edward, or he more correctly, he with her. Why didn't he come and claim her? For there he was, on the far side of the room, talking to Mrs Whatmough, who contrived to sit gracefully, straight and poised, on one of the inn's hard benches.

'When is the happy event to take place?' Mr Aislabie's question hung in the hot air. It was Sir Rowley who had the readiest answer.

'In about a year – a year or just over. Of course,' he paused and smiled as though a pleasing notion had struck him, 'there is some chance, I should say, that we shall have our bridge by then.'

'If all proceeds to plan.' Perhaps Mr Aislabie's ventures had a way of taking longer to complete than people first thought. It was no surprise that he should be cautious.

'If all proceeds to plan, as you say,' Sir Rowley corroborated. 'That should be a fine thing, Miss Hearne. You'll be wed in your father's church in full sight of the new bridge. Llanmichael will have cause to rejoice twice over.'

Stammering a great deal, she tried to say her wedding would be of interest only to the immediate families, when at last Edward came to her side.

'My dear Caelica, I have been unpardonably remiss.' Rather briskly, he kissed her hand. 'Pray come and sit with me and Alice. Father and Mr Aislabie have had the pleasure of your company for far too long – forgive me gentlemen, if I bear her away.'

Going with him, she heard Sir Rowley laugh and sensed that he and Mr Aislabie, unhindered by any obligation to entertain her further, must have returned to their previous discussion.

To ask her father to address the company was courteous in Sir Rowley, but it was a mistake. All around her Caelica saw the signs of growing impatience as the men of Llanmichael, hungry after a day's work in the fields, tried to make their ale last. Weary, they shuffled and grunted with discontent. They did not want to know that *pontifex*, the Latin word for a priest, meant also bridge builder. They did not care to hear their rector remind them that their previous bridge had been built to serve a community of God-fearing monks. They already knew that their new bridge would be a triumph of human ingenuity and that they were indebted to the munificence of Sir Rowley Curwen for financing it and providing a team of labourers – drawn, someone heckled, from outside the area – to build it. Having to raise his voice above their restlessness, her father began to sound annoyed. Edward hid a yawn behind his hand; Alice Whatmough, noticing, smiled.

'...have every cause to be deeply thankful that Mr Yorke Aislabie should accord us the benefit of his experience and wisdom,' the fluting pulpit cadences insisted.

'O father, make haste,' begged Caelica in the silence of her heart.

'Mr Aislabie – May I now call upon you, sir, to address the people of Llanmichael and to announce to name of the successful contestant.'

Aislabie, keeping to the dingy corner in which he had been sitting now rose. He looked for a second to Sir Rowley for encouragement perhaps. There was a hesitancy in his eyes, as though he were not at entirely at ease in front of this fretful crowd, so clearly bored with clergy effusions. Oh, but let him say something in praise of her bridge and she should be more than happy, whether it was his winner or no.

Despite his apparent reserve, he proved a compelling speaker, his manner bluff, his voice powerful and unaffected. The people fell still and listened.

'The medieval builders, ladies and gentlemen, did well. They possessed no shortage of skill and showed a high degree of understanding as to how best to use the materials available to them. Their cathedrals will last till the end of time.

'But bridges serve changing needs. Once, only shepherds and drovers would have used the bridge of this place. Now convoys of ore come here to cross the river. Heavier traffic calls for a stronger bridge. Besides, by our energies we have contrived to change the way the river behaves.'

'Shame,' called the heckler. A few heads turned in Caelica's father's direction to see if he would utter any admonishment, but although his face darkened, he said nothing.

'It rises and falls,' Aislabie continued, 'not only according to whether there is rain or drought, but also in response to man's activities. For we are no longer content with the bounty our land yields us for the asking. We enclose it, so as to make crops and herds thrive in a way they rarely do on common ground. As for minerals, we don't just claim what we find in screes and crevices, but we tunnel after them with pick and mallet.'

''Tis wrong,' the disputatious voice insisted.

''Tis change,' Aislabie returned. 'If by any skill I can soften the pain change brings, that pleases me. But I cannot and do not stand in change's way.

'Now, gentlemen, through the good offices of my friend Sir Rowley and the parson here, I have chanced to see the different plans that some of you have put forward for a new bridge. For your inspiration you have gone almost with one mind to the past. In your drawings I see a wish to cling to the familiar. Like so many children, you would hold on to your mother's skirts rather than face the bug-a-boo unknown.'

The townsmen murmured at his insults, but Aislabie took no notice. 'Well, take heart and take courage,' he said. 'Your old bridge – I have seen it in pictures – served you well once. But you cannot expect it to meet your new needs.

'Forget, therefore, about replicating those manifold dark arches. The branches, animal corpses and other debris that that current bears along will only choke them. You would not wish to find yourselves bridgeless again.'

There was a grudging buzz of assent.

'The bridge I shall build for this town has but one arch – one single, great span that will leap from bank to bank.'

Caelica felt her heartbeat grow fast and urgent; surely everyone in the room must hear it? She stiffened every muscle of her face so as to reveal nothing of her thinking.

'With this bridge,' Aislabie's voice was steady, 'tunnels will run through the masonry on either side of the arch, as though a vast needle has pierced holes through the bridge's spandrels – haunches, if you will. You might take them for no more than ornament, but, I tell you, the design has sound purpose. Were

193

the stonework solid, its vast weight could well serve in time to twist the structure askew. Oh, not at once maybe; in fact, years might pass without any sign of trouble, but there'd always be a danger.'

She had not realised that her tunnels should serve so practical a usage. She had drawn them only because she had liked the way their symmetry framed the great arch. To hear Aislabie find they had other merits was quite unlooked for.

'Moreover,' he added, 'when the stream bursts its banks, which at times it will, the flood waters'll pass clean through the piercings, rather than batter down the stonework.'

She saw the crowd nod at his words. All this acclaim for her sketch – her spirits rose so high she thought she soon should take flight.

'The design from which I intend to work is not without defects...'

It was only to be expected that an engineer of his renown should find fault in the drawing of a girl like herself.

'...and on account of these shortcomings and at Sir Rowley's suggestion, I shall not exhibit it to the company here assembled.'

Oh, but she could not preserve this constricting mask of composure much longer; something in her must give way, must break open, or burst out in delight.

'You will all see the bridge soon enough, and I have every confidence that its fame and the fame of its creator will endure for generations to come.

'The winner of your contest, ladies and gentlemen, is Edward Curwen.'

'Look to Miss Hearne,' came a voice. The last thing Caelica registered was the sight of Alice Whatmough placing a white hand upon Edward's arm and smiling up at him. Knowing, as the blood sang in her ears and vermilion light flooded her eyes, that it should be she, his future wife, not Mrs Whatmough his future stepmother who offered this gesture of affectionate congratulation, she felt herself fall forward, powerless to withstand the elemental force that thrust her down to cold, filthy flagstones of the floor.

When she came round, it was in the open air. While she was unconscious, they must have carried her into the courtyard and laid her down on the mounting block. Her father and Edward were standing on one side of her, Mrs Whatmough on the other. She looked round at them, uncertain, guessing what must have happened.

'A faint – so foolish, at the second of Edward's high success,' she gasped. Pushing herself into a sitting position on the wide, raised surface, she let her stockinged legs dangle down like a child's. To have imagined, even for an instant, that the great Yorke Aislabie would have any regard for her bridge was a great mistake. Since she could not be his winner – and it had been arrant foolishness for her ever to think that she might – it should please her beyond question to find his choice light on Edward.

'Dearest Edward,' she smiled up at him, 'I fe-fe-felicitate you wi-with all my heart.' Edward, who had been so languid and undemonstrative with her, now leant forward to kiss her cheek.

The utter want of any charge in the embrace came like a dowsing with cold water. At once, she regained total command of her thoughts and feelings. It was not that the kiss was detached – on the contrary, it was full of careless enthusiasm. But Edward had kissed her in the same manner that he might kiss any girl who needed comforting – provided always that she had passing good looks and her breath was not sour. It was a kindly kiss, to be sure. It told her to cheer up, and rouse herself; it did not tell her he loved her. Even now, he was looking over his shoulder through the inn's open door as though he wanted to go back inside.

'My dear Miss Hearne,' Mrs Whatmough's voice was like silk. 'Whatever could have caused your affliction?'

'Dear daughter, I believe you fainted for pure joy.' Her father, perspiration glistening on his brow, supplied a convenient answer. 'Edward's success is an astonishingly happy outcome to the contest,' he continued, looking round them all. 'Only let us hope Sir Rowley takes the news of his son's achievement on stable feet. A faint for man of his years and bulk would be no light matter.'

'Let us indeed,' Mrs Whatmough agreed, as Caelica slid down from her perch.

'Sh-shall we go and join him and Mr Aislabie now, f-father?' she asked. 'To b-be sure, I am quite recovered.'

'Edward, the people ought to have the hero of the hour with them to celebrate,' announced her father, taking charge. 'But it would, I think, be best for my daughter to go home at once. While she is strong and not given to fainting,' Caelica had never fainted before in her life, 'I cannot believe that re-entering the stifling heat of the inn will be good for her. Yet for myself I dearly wish to stay in the thick of things. Besides, I have many questions for Mr Aislabie.'

'I am certain your concern for Miss Hearne's health is well placed, sir,' Edward concurred, raising his hand to silence her interruption. 'Much as I cherish your company, Caelica, sense of duty compels me to echo your father's counsel. You are plainly fatigued and overwhelmed. A night's sound sleep should revive you.'

He glanced round the courtyard. 'Shall you go home now, my dear? I see your father's cob yonder. Hearne, would you say she's fit to ride?'

'I doubt it,' said her father, plainly wondering how he would get home if Caelica took his horse.

'I shall take Miss Hearne home.'

None of them had noticed Thomas approach. He made his offer with kind, quiet certainty. Even so, Hearne hesitated, as though thinking that he might do best to ride home with her behind him and then return to the celebrations.

Before he could bring himself to speak, Edward, jubilant, leapt in. 'That's accommodating of you, sir,' he said to Thomas. 'Oh yes, I recognise you. You're Hearne's pupil, are you not? We met that evening when I stayed at the parsonage on my way from Carterford, d'you recall? Well, your suggestion is most timely. Good Mr Hearne has no wish to leave the company so soon.'

Numb, Caelica said nothing, content to let them arrange and talk and see her bundled back home while her future husband enjoyed his triumph.

'How fortunate, dear Miss Hearne, that this gentleman should be at hand,' murmured Mrs Whatmough. 'It was unusually close in the inn – I am not surprised that you should have fainted. Pray send word to me tomorrow, to let me know how you fare.'

With Thomas, her father was at his brusquest. 'Very well,' he said. 'You may escort her home. You should find Vaughan in hailing distance. I did not care to trouble him for the ferry this evening, but no doubt if you call he'll row you across the river for the usual fee.'

'You are right to remain here, sir,' was his only reply. 'People have every reason to be grateful to you at this time.'

Hearne ignored him, giving his attention to Mrs Whatmough instead. She had deftly placed herself between him and Edward, linking their arms through hers. 'Dear madam,' he exclaimed, 'What a fine trio you make of us. Let us visit the scene of rejoicing once more.'

'I thought it was to be my bridge,' Caelica said as they stood on the jetty straining their eyes for sight of Vaughan. There was no sign of his boat either up river or down.

'Look,' Thomas pointed to the far bank. 'Do you see that flickering? I think Vaughan must have mended his fire and gone inside for the night. You'll have to wait and ride pillion with your father after all – oh, unless I carry you.'

'You could not carry me over the river,' she objected, laughing. 'Well, you could, I suppose, but it would not – would not...'

'It would be the best way of getting you home to your bed and into Anstice's care. I'm certain she'll know plenty of remedies for fainting fits. And you're a deal lighter than Hannah Hallet, and no dead weight either.'

'Bu...'

'Put your hands on my shoulders and spring.'

Once she was on his back, he strode out into the water. No doubt it was cold, even at this height of summer, but she found the warmth of his upper body reassuring. Her thighs found their place somewhere around his thin flanks and her breast rested against the vertebrae of his spine, rough even through his shirt and woollen waistcoat. He was evidently sturdier than he looked, and soon instead of grasping his shoulders she let her hands rest on them lightly. Of course his stockings and shoes – she had an idea one of the soles was cracked – would be soaked through in no time, his breeches too, come to that. As for her skirt, its hem was sodden and stained, but since he did not mind their dishevelment and she couldn't have cared less, it did not matter.

She was on the point of saying something about how the night air was reviving her, when he missed his footing over the slippery stones of the river bed and slid sideways into an unexpected deep channel.

'Thomas...'

'Are you all right? There was a loose stone – Caelica, I believe you're laughing...'

'Yes.'

'Then I hardly need apologise for having almost dropped you. Here, let's get up onto that great rock before I lose my footing again.'

She slid off his back, onto a wide boulder and he scrambled up at her side. Despite his teasing words, his face by the light of the coppery half moon was quizzical and serious.

'It is not my business, of course,' he sat so close to her that the damp, rough wool of his clothing brushed the back of her hand. 'Yet can you – do you believe that Edward Curwen would hit on the clever design of Aislabie's description himself? Does his mind turn in ways so like your own that he might fashion your bridge's twin?'

He shifted so as to face her. 'Caelica, I was standing just inside the inn door, so I heard everything Aislabie said concerning the expansive arch with its pierced spandrels. These were the distinctive properties of your design. Am I honestly to think that these self-same innovations somehow suggested themselves to Curwen? And why did not Aislabie have anything to say about the coincidence of there being two plans so uncommonly alike?'

To hear him touch upon these troubling questions cut her to the quick. 'I cannot speak for Mr Aislabie,' she answered slowly, 'but I do not know how Edward came to produce such a design. When I asked him if he meant to enter the contest, he was undecided.'

'I suppose you must have shown him your design?'

'No – never.'

If Thomas should suppose that Edward had copied her drawing or taken it as a guide from which to model some artwork of his own, she could disabuse him of the notion at once.

'He took so little interest in the matter of Llanmichael Bridge that I saw no point in even showing him my sketch. You saw it of course. So did my father, who didn't at all want me to submit it for the competition – though he never quite forbade me to do so. But that was all. No one else to my knowledge gave it even a passing glance until my father handed it over to Sir Rowley.'

She spoke to him in just the calm, open way she used to in her lessons. Only they weren't in a lesson, but seated side by side on a vast boulder out in a fast-flowing river under the full night sky, with the scents of earth and water all around them. And for once, her voice was the steadiest thing about her.

'And are you happy that he should be named the winner?'

'Since we are engaged,' she said at last, 'I must rejoice in his success.'

'Come, Caelica – this is cold courtesy. Speak truth.'

She did not want to turn away, but she had to nerve herself to look at him. 'From everything that Mr Aislabie said, I thought it was my bridge he had chosen.'

That was all she could say and for a second she found herself blinking away tears, like a child caught out in a prank.

Meeting his gaze again, she found in his eyes only tenderness and complicity. Without her being aware of its happening, all the familiar contours of her thinking had changed, and she stood in a new country. She looked at him, dripping and earnest on the huge rock, his face sallow in the moonlight, and wanted to reach out and touch him – not just to perch on his back for crossing the river, but to knot her arms around him, breathe the sweat of his limbs and kiss and kiss his rueful mouth. It shocked her to the core. That such wild, confused, rash impulses should overtake her – she who set out to be quiet, biddable and demure – was surely wrong. Yet she never desired anything so much in her life.

She saw him watching her – did he, could he guess at her thinking?

He glanced to where the parsonage nestled between the enfolding hills. 'Come –' he bade her, sliding down into the cold water once more, 'we shouldn't linger. Get on my back again, Miss Hearne. How could I have been so incorrect as to address you by your Christian name? Your father would view my indecorum in the gravest light.' His teasing voice made it quite clear he did not give a fig for her father. 'I shall take you home, as I vowed. Anstice no doubt will find syrup of pennyroyal to seal your recovery from fainting and fetch warm stones for your bed.'

Putting her hands upon Thomas's angular shoulders once more, and looking down to where the careless knot of fraying ribbon with which he had tied his lank hair was coming undone, she let the truth rise and possess her. She loved him through and through, as steadfast and enduring as the stars in the sky.

Chapter Sixteen

Anstice met them at the parsonage door. If she read Caelica's high happiness in her eyes, she ignored it. Finding Thomas with Caelica and not her father surprised her, and surprise brought on all her sternness. She made no bones about holding him responsible for Caelica's fainting fit and at once swept Caelica into the kitchen to get warm by the fire.

'D-don't leave yet,' she begged over her shoulder. She could not tell Thomas anything of what she wanted with the old servant around them, so terse and unforthcoming, but she didn't want him to go.

Anstice bent down to the hearth to heat up two of the scrubbed stones they used as bed warmers. She looked keenly at Caelica, curious about the source of her elation, but Caelica hardly noticed. She had the sense that she was watching the scene from a vast distance. All of the old servant's care was meant for the girl who was engaged to Edward Curwen. It was Edward's future wife who should have the best place by the fire and hot stones in her bed, to help her sleep long and deep. To remember that Edward's future wife was none other than herself jarred like a discord. She loved Thomas with his soaked stockings and untied hair; all unknowing, she had loved him for a long time. To see Anstice fold the stones in cloth to make their heat last through the night was a stark reminder of the straits in which she stood.

Without saying anything Anstice left the kitchen. In a moment she returned with one of the dining room decanters. Silent, she poured some of its content into two earthenware beakers from the dresser and held them out.

'Port,' she said tersely and scanned their faces as though she wanted to read everything that had passed between them.

Before long, Thomas drained his mug and rose. Thanking Anstice, bidding her a courteous good night, he paused in the doorway and gave Caelica a slow twisting smile. Once they had exchanged goodbyes – Anstice's squat, brown presence precluded anything more than the plainest farewell – Caelica watched him vanish into the night to ford the river once more in his broken shoes.

The following day dawned grey, damp and unprepossessing. Waking, Caelica knew that whatever fondness she might once have had to marry Edward Curwen, it had proved to be a mirage, as insubstantial as vapour. She would still marry him – it was what her parents expected – but it was a marriage founded not in love, as she had once supposed, but in sheer expediency.

When she joined her parents for breakfast, once her father had muttered his accustomed grace, Anstice brought in bread and eggs, paused, drew herself up, motioned to the decanter on the sideboard, which was now rather less full than it had been, and explained what she had done the previous evening.

'Seeing as Mr Russell was dripping wet, I thought he must have carried Miss Caelica through the river,' she said in a righteous voice. She slid a glance in Caelica's direction that was neither precisely malign, nor entirely kind. 'What with her having come over faint, sir, and he like to take a chill, your port wine suggested itself.'

'I thank you, Anstice.' He frowned as he spoke. 'Your concern was well-placed and reasonable. A word with you, daughter, if you please,' and a knowing sliver of a smile flitted across Anstice's mouth as she withdrew.

He started on the subject without prevarication or delay. 'It was my intention yesterday evening that Russell should accompany you across the river in Vaughan's ferry.' Her mother raised querulous eyebrows raised and her thin lips grew taut with rising rebuke. 'Yet Anstice suggests that you allowed him to ford the waters on foot, itself a rash not to say foolhardy action, with you – on his back? In his arms? Daughter, what explanation can you offer?'

It was not outrage that coloured his voice and expression so much as distaste.

'I w-was o-on his b-back, father.' There was no reason to hedge or skirt about when her father pretty much had the truth of the thing from Anstice already. 'S-seeing the curtains of Vaughan's windows drawn and fire-firelight from within, and j-judging that he had retired for the night, Mr Russell and I agreed that he sh-should cr-cross the river w-with me on his back – m-much like I have seen Abel the tinker carry his wife over the water when it was sh-shallow and he s-sought a sh-shortcut. Th-then, we thought, we sh-should not have to call Vaughan f-forth from his cottage.'

It made fair justification to her thinking, although it brought down a veil of disbelief across her father's eyes, while his mouth pursed and went rigid.

'It was not as though you were asking Vaughan for a favour. You would have paid him, after all. I do not understand your reluctance to rouse him.' He gave a loud exasperated sigh.

'Now that you are engaged to Mr Curwen,' he said irritably, as though she were one of his more wilful parishioners, 'it isn't proper to allow another gentleman to – well, to perform such a service for you.'

She couldn't let him think it was Thomas's idea; Thomas had been living under the shadow of her father's displeasure ever since his proposal. 'I-it was my – my suggestion, father. My head was – was light s-still after my faint. I did not think,' she lied.

'Well, you should have known better,' he said. 'Still, it is, I suppose, understandable that fainting may have clouded your judgement.' It was a most grudging concession, and having made it, he blew his nose vigorously, his eyebrows bristling over his lawn handkerchief.

Her mother, who had listened to the exchange in marble silence, spoke at last, her voice cold and her eyes like shards of stone. 'Caelica, I will not have you talked about in conjunction

203

with that audacious and misguided man. Your father's pupil is less, bethink you, than a curate.'

'Y-yet, m-mamma, he is a man of l-learning and hu-humanity.' There was so little she could say in his defence.

'Do not speak as though you claimed to revere him. When he presumed to seek your hand, he overreached himself. Any courtesies you show him could be taken for fondness.'

Fondness - she loved him with all her heart, but she could hardly confess it to her parents. By what trick or grace might she hide her thoughts and restrain the blush she could feel rising to her face at her mother's words? Think of the river, the cold of it; think of the heights of the hills and the folk who struggle to live there. Think too of Hannah Hallet who is dead.

'You are to wed a man of position and wealth,' her mother continued. 'Your marriage will restore our fortune and our standing in this place. You will have the advantage of ample means and an exalted place in society. It will go some way towards enabling Christopher to clear his name. You cannot,' the stone shards sharpened to needle points, 'allow your name to be linked with that of a boorish buffoon.'

This asperity was too much for Caelica's father. 'All you say is correct, dear wife,' he said with a note of finality. 'Yet let us be fair. Let us treat the matter as a trifling error arising in consequence of Cherry's unlucky fainting fit and a foolish young man's uncurbed impetuosity. By-the-by, daughter, I hope you will be sure to take adequate refreshment before venturing out in future.

'Now, I should like to disclose to you a plan which Sir Rowley proposed last night. It has the merit of ensuring at once that yesterday's - how shall we say? - ah, indiscretion shall not recur, while giving Caelica a chance to buy everything she needs for her trousseau.'

The plan was that Caelica should accompany the Curwens and Mrs Whatmough upon a vast round of visits to relatives and friends. They should set off in a few days' time and traverse the nation from Edinburgh to Bath, for Sir Rowley had contacts everywhere. Apparently he hoped to renew his acquaintance with manufacturers with whom he had dealt in the past in the hope that they might purchase lead from him in the future. While he pursued commerce, Edward and Caelica would have the opportunity to taste the sweets of society in the gracious company of Mrs Whatmough, who would also advise Caelica in purchasing her bridal array.

'But the bridge?' Caelica asked at once.

'The bridge?' repeated her father, a piece of buttered bread in his hand.

'Aye, father. S-surely Edward wi-will wish to see how his bridge progresses under con-construction? It is no fit time for-for him to be away, ju-just when the men set about laying the f-foundation.'

'On the contrary, it is the best possible time. Edward knows that under the keen eyes of Yorke Aislabie and his resident engineer, his bridge will rise to completion without a hitch. Just as a wise father may, on occasion, allow his offspring to forsake his guidance and profit by erring somewhat, so a wise creator may be content to leave it to others to bring his creation into being, thereby reaping the benefit of their skills.'

Caelica fell silent. To see the bridge – her bridge – take shape; to hear Aislabie explain how he sought to modify its plan; to talk – she meant with Thomas – over each stage in its growth, these things counted for much. Had Edward played any true part in its creation, he would not think of absenting himself from its construction.

At Menston, Yorke Aislabie was breakfasting on gammon and kidneys with the Curwens. Alice Whatmough had not yet risen. In the gilded glass above the marble fire place, Edward caught sight of himself yawning. He would have liked to stay longer in bed, but he had had no wish to cloud the shimmer of paternal goodwill that he currently enjoyed and he knew that his father took early rising for a mark of virtue. Now he came to think of it, his priggish older step-brother John held rather the same view. Ah, he would have to endure a visit to John and his family before long. Edward swilled back a draught of coffee at the thought. If this engagement business demanded making visits to all manner of tedious relatives, then even for the sake of a doubled allowance it seemed a steep price to pay. As for his eventual marriage, he could not think of it without sighing. At least Miss Hearne was neither plain nor shrewish. He might have little to say to her – scarcely more, truth to tell, than she to him – but no one could claim that she did him any discredit by her manners or appearance.

'To take all precaution against the river's choking with refuse, I propose that under the great span there should be an inverted arch of stones without mortar.' Aislabie ate little. Crockery thrust aside he rested his forearms on the table, and smiled at Edward as he spoke.

'It sounds wise – aye, this scheme has a pleasing ring to it in your description.' Edward let his father answer with his mouth full. He had always been able to talk while chewing. It must be the legacy of years of hurry between one venture and the next.

'What do you think Edward?' Aislabie enquired. 'This bridge is of your contriving after all.'

'What do I think of what, precisely?' asked Edward. He did not see why he should be expected to hold any opinion on the matter.

'Let me explain,' said Aislabie. 'It is most improbable that a single span bridge of the width that we shall build in Llanmichael could ever suffer choking in the manner of the medieval structure, with its numerous small arches.'

Edward hid another yawn. Plainly Aislabie liked playing the pedant.

'Nevertheless,' he prosed on, 'I like to build to a good foundation. Therefore I propose to embed a half ring of stone within the bottom of the river. The ruin of the old bridge will, after all, provide us with ample material, and anyway there must quarries nearby. What would you say to our walling the river for some distance upstream of your bridge? To keep it in decent bounds, you understand?'

'It sounds a fine scheme,' Edward replied. He was going to look at a colt by Rockingham later that morning and having won the bridge competition he was sixty guineas richer than he had been. There was a prospect to cheer the soul. Perhaps if he agreed with all the great man's suggestions, this tiresome conversation would soon close.

'Very well.' Aislabie's eyes narrowed a little. 'There are two further modifications that I should like to make in the bridge's overall design.'

Edward didn't care what changes Aislabie made to the bridge in the drawing; provided that it reached a speedy completion in stone and the masonry bore his name somewhere in honour of his achievement. He gave a vague nod.

But his father's eyes gleamed. 'Aye, what alterations would you propose, sir?' he leaned forward.

'The ribbing of the arch,' Aislabie named it in a way that suggested he did not like it. 'Dispense with it.'

'Your reason?' His father was agog.

'It serves no useful purpose. Your piercing of the spandrels, Edward, will lighten the arch and hold the eye: the arch doesn't need ribs as well. They only look fussy, which leads me to my other point. Your head, sir: it must go.'

'My head?'

'Not your own head. I wouldn't be so facetious. The stone head of the gorgon screeching over the voussoirs. If you add that bauble to your stonework, I tell you, within weeks it'll fall into the wash.'

The older men both chuckled. Realising that they would dismiss out of hand any argument he offered for keeping the Medusa, Edward put on his widest smile.

'Oh, you show me the error of my thinking. Of course, I concur with you, Aislabie. I can't think what misguided spirit ruled my heart when I sketched that head – it was the sheerest folly. Provided the bridge bears its commemorative tablet, I shall do without the gorgon.'

'That would, I think, be for the best.' For a moment or two, Aislabie toyed with his unused knife, picking it up, laying it down and turning it over by turn as though he had some speculation in view that he wanted to dispel. He looked at Edward as though about to ask another question, then seemed to think better of it. Instead, he stared out of the window at the chestnut trees Rendle planned to fell because they hid the grand cascade at the foot of his rill. Abrupt, as though he could not contain the question, 'Edward, how did you come to conceive this bridge?' demanded Aislabie. 'What thought was in your mind when you drew the great arch?'

Edward was ready for the thrust. Frank and amiable, ever the man to make light of his talents, he gave a modest laugh. 'Ah, I have always had an interest in constructing roads and bridges,' he confided. 'And I must have learnt much over the years from observation – more, perhaps, than I realise.'

Why did Aislabie's expression stay so quizzical? Edward hoped the exchange wouldn't last much longer.

'That drawing, sir,' he asserted, 'is a triumph of instinct.'

'Sound instinct is a rare gift,' his father cut in.

'But now,' Edward could not trust himself to remain bluff and serene under Aislabie's incredulous gaze, 'with regret, gentlemen, I must take my leave.' He rose. 'This morning I've arranged to look over a colt I hope to purchase – Pollux by Rockingham. I'm going to ride over to Caldingleigh to view the beast.'

'Another horse? For yourself?' This time it was his father who quizzed him, none too gently and Aislabie looked sour as sin.

'Myself and no other.'

'Edward, we're about to make calls all around the country. We'll be away from Menston for eight – ten – months, if not a year. Yet you take it into your head to buy more horses. This is downright improvident. It isn't even as though you were planning to purchase a lady's hack for Miss Hearne.'

Edward spread his hands. 'I may never have another chance to buy into the Rockingham bloodline,' he objected. 'Look on it as an investment, father. Besides, it'll cost little to keep the colt at grass till our return. Then I shall seek out a quiet animal for Miss Hearne. For now, I must seize the hour.'

Closing the double doors softly behind him, he paused in the passageway, relieved at having extricated himself so neatly from Aislabie's probing. Taking out his watch, he saw he had ample time to spare before he had to leave for Caldingleigh. He would see if Alice was awake yet, and whether she might care to go with him.

Chapter Seventeen

Thomas decided that he had behaved like a Bedlamite. Here he was, without any patron or powerful friends, dependent for his hopes of advancement upon Hearne's goodwill, yet pitching himself against the rector at every turn. What profit was there in making himself stern with Caelica one moment, when he took absurd liberties like asking her to marry him, encouraging her to put her sketch into the bridge competition or carrying her over the river at the next? And yet, lying awake upon his bed in Gleeson's dark, damp house, he could never bring himself to wish he had left his fondness for her unshown. When he closed his eyes he would see her serious smile, and her quiet voice would come so clear to his hearing that more than once he had risen and gone to the door, believing she must be there. She never was.

About a week after she had gone away with the Curwens, he woke one night in great haste, thinking he could hear her saying his name. A hesitant 'Tho-Thomas?' sounded just outside his room. Blood pounding and the breath catching in his lungs, he sprang up. When he opened the door, it was not to find the hollow passage mocking his longing, as it had so often in the past. This time, a pale form loomed up before him like a substantial white ghost.

Only it was for sure no spectre. Gleeson's daughter stood leering at him, pallid and vast in the darkness, her hair loose over her shoulders. He had often noticed how, going about her work of cleaning and tidying his chamber, she would try to catch his eye, and pouted to make the dimples in her broad cheeks deepen.

'Mistress Gleeson, how now?' An alert, matter-of-fact address should tell her he was prepared for any surprise she cared to spring. 'What do you want?' he asked. 'What leads you hither at this hour? You know your father wouldn't care for it.'

'My father's not here. He had to take a load of hay to my uncle Riddock in Carterford and he is not yet returned. I am here alone with you.' She spoke in a high-pitched, pitiful voice, like a wilful child. 'But I cannot sleep,' she went on, 'and I mislike having only myself for company. Let me talk to you a little. Surely you wouldn't turn me away?'

'I would.'

Taking no notice, she pushed past him, planting herself on the chair by his table. Reaching into the darkness, he felt for his tinder box, and lit a candle. Better to see the expression on her large face – it was the size and colour of a young cheese – than try to guess whether she scowled or simpered.

'Take me to your bed,' she entreated.

He stared, unable to believe she could be so brazen.

Before he could answer, she lifted one of her plump hands to touch him. He dodged away, glad that he stood while she sat. At once she rose to follow, eyes wide in the uncertain light.

'Miss Gleeson,' he rebuked her, taking a step backwards. 'This will not do. Leave me, I beg. It's late and your must be tired. If you're lonely, I'm sorry for it.' Blunt speech might bring her to her senses. 'But your father won't be away long and I can't believe you'll come to any harm in his absence.'

'Take me to your bed,' she repeated, fixing him with her pale, excited gaze and holding out her hand once more.

Gagging, he recoiled. Word in the town was that Catherine Gleeson, known also as Cattern Glutton, would in time wed the baker. Perhaps it was true; or perhaps people repeated the tale because they wanted it to be true. Her appearance would be a constant testament to the excellence of his bread, would it not? They would be a fine pair.

'I shall not, Miss Gleeson. Your wits,' he told her, 'are disturbed. It's best that you go away at once.'

But she only drew closer still, laughing her whispering laugh and stretching out her wide white arms as though she wanted to hug him.

'Be gone,' he shouted, lunging at the glutton and as he did so, catching sight of her great thighs through her lawn shift. Since she evidently expected an embrace, the repulse took her unaware. Squawking, she stumbled backwards, her eyes bulging and her mouth open wide.

Seizing his chance, he swept her out of the door and slammed it hard. Panting, he leant against it, lest she should try to force her way in once more. Had it been no more than a nightmare, her visit would have been foul enough, and Cattern Glutton was no dream. He had felt her panting breath on his face, seen the clear outline of her gross breasts rise and fall, and smelt her greasy body. No phantasm grew hot, puffed and gave off such odour. No succubus wept as she was weeping now, sobbing great, tearing, windy gusts out in the passage.

After a few minutes, his relief gave way to shame. For all that she was foolish and lubberly, he had no wish to hurt her. At last her crying gave way to sniffs, then thick breathing and at last, silence. For a time, he continued to stand by the door, staring into the candle flame. When at last he judged that she must have gone, he blew it out and got back into bed. Deciding, after a few restless hours, that he wouldn't sleep, he rose, lit the candle again, sat down at the table, opened a book and tried to read. It was no good; the words fell dead on his wits. Pushing the volume away, he put his head in his hands, heard the clocks of the town strike two and waited, sore-eyed, for the dawn.

At daybreak, having sluiced himself with cold water and dressed, he read the office of matins and then out of habit set himself to English a portion of the *Georgics*, though it proved leaden labour. Once he had had a hasty breakfast of bread and cheese, still stinging with the previous night's embarrassment, he went into the town. Hearne, as usual, had given him no instructions, but he knew there was plenty of parish work to claim his attention.

Visiting the home of Watkin the churchwarden, he listened to Watkin's wife, who could no longer distinguish past from present, tell him how she and her sisters, whom he knew to be long dead, were going that very day to look for ripe blackberries. He called on Tobias Greene and listened to Greene's small daughter recite her catechism; he read over the end of the epistle to the Romans to Greene's neighbour Williams whose sight was near failing. Inclining his head to Williams as he left – the civility of the gesture pleased him, whether the old man could see it or no – and tucking his plain black Testament under his left arm, he paused to return the greeting of Emrys Parry, town schoolmaster and leader of the Dissenters. Hearne would have crossed the road to avoid Parry. To Hearne, a preacher who drew the people away from the English church and led them in worship in barns or farmyards or even out on the common pasture must be the enemy of wholesome order and an agent of destruction. Yet whenever Thomas had met Parry in the past, he had been struck by the man's quiet courtesy and warmth of heart.

Making his way back to his lodging around noon, he noticed a gaping bundle of his clothes against the house wall. At that second, a volley of books shot through his room's ground level window, flying open as they hurtled through the air. While he stood, transfixed, a second rush of books followed at great force, their pages flapping like crows' wings before they landed on the street's far side. Thunderstruck Thomas recovered a volume of Hesiod – Hearne's – from a steaming pile of dung.

'What,' he began.

'Oh, you've come back, have you?' Gleeson loomed purple-faced at the window. 'Well you can keep to the filth of the kennel where you belong. Don't you set foot in my house again...'

'Pray why?' he began to ask, then saw Catherine standing in the shadows. She must have spoken of the night's activities to her father.

'You know why, you hypocrite,' Gleeson growled. 'You walk through this town with a look on your face that says you smell the small clothes of every man of Llanmichael and thank the

Lord you are not as they. But look at you – you're no better than the rest of us.'

'Of course I'm no better than you. I've never sought to suggest any such thing – Oh, leave the books, I beg. They're not even mine.'

Trying to prise the three duodecimo volumes of Joseph Trapp's *Works of Virgil* from Gleeson's sweaty grasp, in his peripheral vision he saw curious onlookers gather. Typical Llanmichael people, their eyes gleamed with curiosity, but they kept distance enough to be able to disperse at will. Evictions made for good entertainment, but wise folk didn't watch at close quarters – they might find the homeless man asking for lodging.

Now Gleeson was scattering the leaves of every volume he could lay his hands on. A Greek testament landed beside one of the inquisitive little groups. Moving as one, they shuffled away from the sacred text, as though it carried some foul disease.

Cattern Glutton appeared at her father's side, bearing a sheaf of papers in her hands which she rested on the low window sill. Thomas recognised the manuscript of the translation of the *Georgics*. It had made scant progress that morning, but usually he found rendering Virgil's lithe hexameters into English both a comfort and a satisfaction and he had begun to think his work might even merit publication in time. Before he fully understood what was happening, Cattern Glutton gave him a mocking, pleased smile, took up some three or four pages, drafts and fair copies together, and began to rip them up.

To witness his work destroyed racked his eyes like gorse. 'Stop, I entreat you,' he implored. 'Whatever hurt I've caused you, Miss Gleeson, I repent it, but that writing is the fruit of long labour. It cannot hurt you – stop, oh, stop...'

'You've insulted my daughter,' Gleeson bellowed. 'And she as true and mild a maid as there ever was. No – keep quiet, you serpent of the sewer. Why, when I got home the poor girl was trembling like a new-born lamb.'

Solid Cattern Glutton ripping up ream upon ream of paper covered with his careful script hardly put him in mind of innocent lambs. Seeing her eyes dance, he reached in through the casement to rescue his work. She retreated, giggling, into the gloom.

'She isn't trembling now,' he said.

'Well, now her sorrow is spent,' her burly father returned. Weighing the pewter ink pot in his right palm, he slung it the length of Llanmichael.

'See here,' he turned on Thomas, hand on hip. 'My daughter's a good girl. I never thought she'd come to any harm with a man who means to enter the church. Yet she claims you tried to pull her into bed with you.'

'That is untrue.'

'She says it's true as holy writ. She'd never lie to me.' To underline his opinion, Gleeson picked up another book and began to pull it apart down the spine.

Thomas recognised the cover, appalled. 'My *Virgil* –'

If only he had his copy of the Latin poems intact, he could start the greatest part of his work over again. It would take a long time, and could never console him for Caelica's loss yet if by perseverance he might read English the verses once more, it would be at least something. But even as he tried to seize the volume, Gleeson rent the pages out of the binding and scattered them.

'My good sirs, whatever's amiss?'

The questioner had a lucid, Welsh voice – a voice at once kind and grave. Looking round, Thomas found Emrys Parry at his side. At the sound of disturbance, the schoolmaster must have retraced his steps. His expression was at once concerned and amused.

'I do not often find scraps of Latin poetry in the gutters of Llanfihangel,' Parry observed, picking up one of the broken books. 'The odd page, perhaps, put to use of necessity. Even then I would not expect it to be Virgil. Mausoleus now...'

Thomas reeled. What happy chance should have led this man, whom he barely knew, to seek to draw the heat from an ugly clash between landlord and tenant?

215

'Well, Hugh Gleeson, what bone do you pick with the rector's pupil?' Parry ran a deliberate finger along the volume's fractured spine. 'He may have his sight set upon ordination in the Established Church, but that is no reason to hurt his books.'

'Don't interfere, preacher. My quarrel is with that spawn of slime yonder.'

'But, Mr Gleeson,' Parry turned earnest, 'despoiling Mr Russell's property is surely no way to conduct your disputation?'

'He insulted my daughter.' Mention of the tender subject made Gleeson's scowl deepen.

'Cadi Glwth insulted?' Miss Gleeson's nickname sounded even coarser in Welsh, than it did in English. If Parry were minded to use it, he must be an ally indeed.

'And how did he insult her?'

'She won't say. And don't call her by that name.'

'Well, Cadi Glwth?' asked Parry.

Beneath his keen gaze, she only mumbled that she didn't want to talk about it.

Whatever the right and wrong of the business, Thomas decided, it was time to make amends. 'Perhaps I was over-brusque with Miss Gleeson yesterday evening,' he said. 'She was understandably nervous in her father's absence from home and approached me for reassurance. I was less than gallant with her, encouraging her to seek her rest when she craved for words of greater comfort. I may – for I have sometimes a curt turn of phrase – have uttered a needlessly harsh dismissal.'

'She says you stood before her in your night clothes.' But the purple of Gleeson's face was beginning to ebb.

'Aye, well, she came to me in her shift.'

While Parry struggled to suppress his laughter, Thomas assumed what he hoped was a most solemn clerical countenance – the look of a Pharisee able to smell the small clothes of every man of the town indeed. He reiterated his regret for any injury he might have caused to Miss Gleeson's feelings. It had never been his intention to distress her.

'There now, Mr Gleeson,' said Parry, composed once more. 'Mr Russell has made an apology, a handsome apology, to your daughter. But what are we to do about his books?' He picked up one of the volumes whose boards had come detached from the spine and held it together, as though trying to judge how easy it would be to mend. 'You have scattered their pages to the four winds – both his and Mr Hearne's beside. How will you explain it? 'Tis an ill thing for any man to unleash his wrath upon books.'

Gleeson muttered something to the effect of seeing no point in books. He could tally with figures and put his name to a letter; why did any honest man need more reading skill than that? Oh, the books were valuable were they? And some of them belonged to the rector? He had not known. As for the lost pages of Mr Russell's writing – well, it was too bad. He did not see what there was to be done about that.

At the sight of the large, awkward man turning his red hands over and over in confusion, so palpably taken aback by what had come to light concerning his Catherine's conduct Thomas felt the last grains of his anger evaporate. He could overlook the loss of his manuscript; rewriting might even improve it. But the ruination of Hearne's books was altogether more serious.

Parry gave Gleeson a searching look. 'No doubt Mr Hearne will understand the worries of a father where his daughter is concerned,' he said at last. 'He is, after all, a father himself, so he may make some allowance for the vigour of your wrath. And as for the books, I have some skill in mending worn bindings. I shall see what I can do with them.'

At his words Gleeson sighed, but his massive hands fell still and his scowl became less bellicose. Parry turned to Thomas.

'In the meantime Mr Russell, I should like to know more about your work. The titles of these poor scattered volumes make you out to be a learned man. Would Hearne, do you think, take it amiss if I were to invite you to dine with me this day? I have taken the liberty of asking Yorke Aislabie whom, though I barely know him, I met recently while he was surveying the site of the new bridge. Since he is responsible for its construction, I thought he might be able to explain it to me. I would have liked to include young Curwen too, since he actually devised it, but I gather he is away.'

The offer of companionship was welcome beyond words.

'I shall dine with you in good spirit,' Thomas assured him, picking up the bundle of his belongings. 'But could I ask you the favour, sir, of helping me to carry the damaged books – Hearne's and my own? Not to mention what fragments of my manuscript remain?'

Besides teaching the children of the district and leading what he termed the 'new worship' Parry was a smallholder, living some distance out of the town proper. As the two men took the road that led out of the town and towards the hills together, Thomas had the sense of leaving Hearne's close world of faction and dissonance behind and ascending airy heights of friendship. Before they had gone far, Parry, half a dozen or so volumes in varying states of repair under his arm, suggested Hearne's pupil might henceforward consider lodging with him. As he said, a return to the Gleeson household was unlikely to be comfortable in the circumstances.

'I had passed your window sometimes after dark and espied you working within,' he remarked to Thomas as they walked on. 'I had thought Hearne must have you write his sermons for him, so intent you looked.'

'Hearne would disdain to let any sermon be heard in the parish church but his own,' Thomas, touched by the offer of hospitality, assured him.

'Aye well, it is a good pastor who knows his people and what words may best meet their needs.' A more judicious reply it would be difficult to conceive, but the inoffensive words did not quite mesh with the shrewd smile that played across Parry's face as he ushered Thomas through a gate and into a wide, well-kept garden.

Parry's home which doubled as the schoolhouse was long and low, not unlike the labourers' cottages, except that it was larger. Since the hay harvest was underway, there were no pupils on hand. Bending beneath the lintel of the low front door, Thomas guessed that this building must be far older than the parsonage. The ceilings were low and blackened, the floors made of stone, the windows small leaving the rooms close and dark. Yet it was a place of some comfort. Parry's acreage and school must both have prospered. The house had fine furnishings and books – novels, Biblical commentaries, treatises on hydraulics and surveying, and volumes of philosophy, poetry and animal husbandry – spread themselves throughout the dwelling. They did not take their places upon tidy shelves like those of Hearne's library, but were lying on chairs, piled on tables, propped up on the window sills. Perceiving the sheer quantity Thomas swallowed with misgiving for the readiness with which he had accepted Hearne's view that Parry was barely literate.

'Ah, let us put Hearne's volumes somewhere where they shall not find themselves merging with my own,' Parry began. ''Tis well that Cadi Glwth and her father did no more than hurl them through your window and rip a few along the spines. As I say, these injuries we can repair, but as for the torn pages – what work have you lost, Mr Russell?'

'Oh -' He was reluctant to say much about his translation. 'I had set about Englishing Virgil and some of the other Latin poets for a diversion, though I have no great hopes for it.' At this point, a knock at the front door announced Aislabie's arrival, and they went to greet him.

Although they had not anticipated his company, Thomas found both men open and at ease with him, just as they were with one another. There was restoration of spirit to be had from finding himself among elders who were content to let him be young and forget his clerical leanings. Eating collops and bullace pie in Parry's compact dining room, they waited on themselves, which meant that they could speak freely.

'Poor Russell here,' Parry explained, taking a collop upon his fork, 'was coming home late morning from attending to Hearne's parish business when he saw his books all flung from the house where he was lodging and strewn along the street.

How could I not invite him to share our meal after that, Mr Aislabie, and offer him lodging in my poor dwelling beside?'

'Your dwelling is far from being poor, Parry.' Aislabie, no longer stiff with dignity as he had been when he announced Edward's success, ate with vigour.

'As you know,' he said, 'I've spent the last ten days at Menston, and that really is a poor dwelling. Its echoing emptiness now Rowley, his son, and his good lady – whatever she is to him – have gone to call on their fine friends – well, you would not credit it. Truly, Mr Russell,' Thomas warmed to Aislabie's friendliness, 'I am by nature a solitary soul. I could never wed, lest a woman's jabbering curdled my wits. But in that great square mansion with only the servants for company, I see all the sins of my youth rise before my eyes. Rowley thought I should put my time in his home to good use by drawing up some formal plans from that sketch of the bridge, but I can't make any headway with it at all. I shall leave for London tomorrow and see if I make better progress there. It is a sad thing to speak of, for Rowley has ever been a true friend and I've never spent an hour in his company that I had reason to regret, well...'

'Well?' prompted Parry as clearly as he could with his mouth full. He was evidently a man who could not endure conversational tags left to hang without seeking to tie them up.

'You bade me here to speak of the bridge; well, the bridge presents me with a puzzle.'

Thomas stopped eating. So Aislabie had qualms about the bridge too.

'A puzzle?' Parry had finished chewing and sat back in his chair as though to indicate that he wished to give all his attention to Aislabie's words. 'Tell us about it. But please say first how you came to light on young Curwen's design. What competition was there for that high youth's genius?'

'Little enough.' Aislabie speared a fragment of bacon on the end of his knife. 'As I said that night at the inn, in the main, the men who submitted entries to Curwen's contest showed themselves to be in thrall to the past. Since there's no merit in repeating old errors, I discarded their imitations of the old structure straight off. Then at last there was young Curwen's effort, or what I took to be young Curwen's effort.'

'Took to be?' Thomas heard himself ask, aware that Parry was watching him closely.

'Well,' Aislabie's slow speech gave no indication of whether he had marked the urgency of the question or no, 'I don't understand that young man at all. He has produced a most remarkable piece of workmanship, yet he takes no interest in it whatever. I was at pains to seek his approval for the alterations that I deem necessary for its perfecting – though it is, believe me, a conception of raw genius – yet all the while, Edward talked only of some horse he wanted to buy. It was as though the bridge were nothing to him at all. That a man should create anything so beautiful yet care for it so little defies credibility. Look at it.'

Watching Aislabie withdraw a much folded sheet of paper from the pocket of his snuff coloured waistcoat, Thomas knew for certain what he was about to see. Sure enough, the selfsame drawing that Caelica had shown him by candlelight in her father's library at the parsonage lay now in the engineer's agile calloused fingers.

'You see,' Aislabie straightened it with care and placed it on the table before them, 'the span is extraordinarily daring. Having made my own thorough survey of the site, I have calculated that it shall in total be one hundred and forty feet, no less. To my utmost knowledge, its length will exceed that of any other single-span bridge. The strength of the structure – and this is the most remarkable aspect of the thing – lies in the lightness resulting from the pierced spandrels, for that truly is an innovation of genius.'

Thomas hardly heard him. The pencil lines of Caelica's and he would remember forever the wonder in her face as she looked over her finished work. He had known Aislabie would delight in this triumph of her untaught skill. But snaking across her drafting ran lines of crass ink where some scapegrace had sketched crude ribbing below that lithe, bounding arch and

221

added a hideous head that stared out beneath the graceful parapet. So this was how Edward had contrived to set his mark upon her creation.

'What of these inked-in additions?' Thomas asked, with such severity that both his host and fellow-guest looked at him in surprise. 'They should not be there.'

'You are a man after my own heart,' said Aislabie after a slight silence. 'I share your view that they add nothing to the elegance or efficacy of the structure. I am pleased to say that young Mr Curwen has allowed me to persuade him that his bridge will be the better without them. Oh, this drawing is a conundrum – its pencil lines so wise and its ink so foolish.'

'Well, the ink is Curwen's and the pencil is that of Hearne's daughter,' and Thomas looked from one of them to the other, finding Aislabie's face full of kindly anxiety and Parry's caught between incredulity and irreverent amusement.

'I – I saw that drawing when first it reached completion,' Thomas explained, foreseeing their questions. 'It is the truly the work of Miss Hearne, at least, the skill of the draughtsmanship and ingenuity in the plan is hers. Small wonder if Curwen should feel little attachment to it, for he has only stolen it while it is hers by right. Listen,' with the shrewd engineer and the Dissenter who had proved such a friend he had no cause to hedge, 'I chanced to enter the room where she was sketching just as she finished,' he told them. 'The power of her vision amazed me. It was I who urged her to submit her drawing to the competition, knowing the interest it would hold for you sir,' he looked to Aislabie, 'aye, and Sir Rowley too. Miss Hearne is indeed to wed Edward Curwen in time, but I do not see that engagement entitles him to claim her design as his own.'

He sensed that although they heard him out in tactful silence, the vehemence of his speaking shocked these dispassionate, thoughtful men. He had no wish to appear the moonstruck lover, but if they recognised the true nature of his feeling for Caelica Hearne, he did not greatly care.

'Forgive me if I make too free with my opinions, gentlemen,' he said at last. 'But I have told you the truth.'

222

'Don't apologise.' Aislabie had cupped his face in his hand. 'If what you say is right, it goes a long way towards explaining Edward Curwen's curious detachment.'

'What he has done,' Thomas could not leave it unsaid, 'is an affront to all justice.'

'I share your thinking,' Aislabie told him. 'From what you say, it appears that Miss Hearne drew the bridge's best part and then young Curwen defaced her sketch. See,' and he turned the paper over to reveal the rough patch on which Edward had written his name. 'I would hazard the guess that there was a different name here first, and young Curwen saw fit to score it out and put his own in its place. Yet were we to challenge him with theft of the design it would not, I think, necessarily be to Miss Hearne's advantage.'

'You say they are betrothed, after all,' Parry interposed, before Thomas could object. 'It would be an ill thing to pitch the two of them against one another.' Since neither Parry nor Aislabie was in love with Caelica, they could view her injury with all the cool of detachment. 'For him to take out his annoyance upon her is not what any of us would wish to see,' he continued. 'But it's underhand, I grant you, and you don't have to be a principled young ordinand to see that.'

Parry sat back in his chair, smiling ruefully. 'It amuses me vastly to think what the Curwens have done,' said he, glancing innocently past Thomas, out of the window and towards the sky. 'No doubt Sir Rowley will find some mason to carve a fine stone tablet to adorn the keystone which will celebrate Edward's achievement in fulsome style. And do you know, Mr Aislabie,' he went on, in high seriousness. 'I find a fantastical charm in the gorgon head.' Despite the earnest tone, his eyes shone. 'Perhaps, Mr Hearne with his leanings towards classical antiquity, will admire her too. Indeed, it sorrows me to see how little you gentlemen like Curwen's Medusa.'

He laughed not unkindly and looked Thomas in the eye. 'Don't despair, Mr Russell. It may be that truth, the daughter of time, will show herself at the last. May I help you to another collop, sir? Or to some of the bullace pie?'

Chapter Eighteen

34 Layton Street,
Birmingham
11 November 1751

My most Dear Father and Mother,
I trust that my letter shall find you in good health. We are come to stay at the home of Mr John Phillips - Sir Rowley's stepson, that is to say, the son of his dead wife by her first marriage - who has taken command of his remaining commercial interests in Birmingham. Our travels of the past weeks have taken us to some of Sir Rowley's customers in Liverpool, to friends of his near Buxton – where, by-the-by we all partook of the waters and I thought their taste metallic and foul – and to his sister in Chesterfield who is many years older than he.

Mama, you task me in your letter with not having written to you before now. It is not true, for I wrote a most lengthy account of the concert we attended in Buxton, describing not only all the music but also the fiddle player the end of whose bow lodged in a fellow-player's button hole. Mrs Whatmough, who is the most vivacious of companions, said that she would think it impossible that any such mishap could occur, had she not witnessed it with her own eyes. But I have written this to you already. If my letter should have been lost or delayed I am sorry, but do not blame me for the misfortune. Perhaps it will reach you some time soon.

As for my host, Mr John Phillips, he is a proper warm-hearted hospitable gentleman. When Sir Rowley's carriage arrived at his house, he was on hand to welcome us – he, his wife Sophia who bids me call her Sophy and all their little girls beside. There are five of them, lively children and well-tempered in the main, though the little Sophia – they always give her the full name to distinguish her from her mama – is cutting her teeth and grizzles night and day. But Sophy is truly kind and will rise, whatever the hour, to take the infant up in her arms and comfort her. You might think she was near dead with fatigue, and yet while the gentlemen pursue matters of commerce she has escorted Mrs Whatmough and myself all over the town to choose material for my dresses, and never once has she shown herself out of spirits.

Caelica, seated at Sophy Phillips' pretty bureau with the inlaid writing stand before her, paused. Sir Rowley, Mrs Whatmough and Edward had accompanied John on a visit to the Assay office and while the children were playing in their nursery and Sophy going through the week's accounts with the housekeeper, it was a good chance to write to her parents. Knowing what affection they liked to find in family letters, she was about to say that Edward sent his warmest wishes, when she remembered that it wasn't true.

Since their departure from Menston, Edward had taken as little notice of her as he could manage in the course of their travel in the carriage's close quarters. He was always courteous, especially when they broke their journey at one of the inns along the way or arrived at the house or lodging where they were next to stay. Accompanying her to her room, he would inquire whether the windows were adjusted to suit her. When she joined them each morning he would without fail pay her some compliment upon her appearance. If they chanced to go walking, he would offer her his arm with every show of pride and propriety, but in all these civilities, she thought his heart lacking. Sir Rowley and Mrs Whatmough both had much to say for themselves, but Edward had initiated no talk with her, and made little response to her uncertain, stammering attempts at conversational openings. Assuredly he had said nothing to her about sending his regards to her parents. Should she, she wondered, as she fingered her quill and looked out of the window into the broad straight street below, mention this reserve and ask them if it was to be expected?

My dear Edward would wish me to assure you of his respects, she wrote, pleased not to be lying outright. *He is in excellent spirits* – but that was not strictly truth either; ever since they had arrived at the home of the John Phillipses, Edward had been behaving in a manner that was almost morose – *and pleased by the change of scene. Yet* – the sheer geographical distance that now separated her from her parents led her to think that she should be safe in posing to them the question that so ruffled her spirits – *I find him much given to unexpected silences. I should not, dear father and mother, even remark upon such a thing, knowing how objectionable it is to complain, were it not for Mr and Mrs Phillips' example. Sophy quizzes her husband in the most intent manner about all his plans, marking what he says and asking after his foreman, his assistant and any gentleman due to call at his works whose name she happens to remember. Her memory, I may say, is excellent and her acquaintance legion. He answers her with right good will and asks her how she is to spend that part of the day in which their daughters are with the nursemaid. This intimacy and companionship that manifests itself between husband and wife, each taking such frank delight in the doings of the other, I find pleasing. It is a sure source of great delight to both parties and overflows in the constant cheerfulness and tender considerateness with which they treat me, the stranger in their midst. To discover Edward so often mute, so little moved to questions and so taciturn* – she excised that word not caring for its overtones of discontent - *so grave*, she wrote in its place, *makes me question whether I am fitted to become his wife.*

Let her parents make what they would of that. She would not tell them how Edward always thawed in Alice Whatmough's company. To do so would be an admission of her dullness and want of spirit – shortcomings upon which her mother had often remarked in the past. Running her hand along the surface of the polished bureau, letting her sight trace the light and dark swirls of the wood's natural patterning, hearing the middle daughter Marianne singing in the nursery – she had a voice like a lark – Caelica felt an immense desire to love and be loved. It was revelation of a kind, albeit less happy than the vision of truth that had possessed her when Thomas had carried her across the river. To think of that time now would only confuse her. Her way led along the path of duty and she must take it with a robust heart.

She rose from her chair, went to the window and looked down into the street beneath. Since the John Phillipses did not live on a major thoroughfare, it was no surprise to find it empty except for a covered chaise travelling at great speed in one direction while a laden coal wagon, its horses straining in the shafts, came the other way. Putting her hands up to the glass, she set herself to make resolutions.

She would be a good wife to Edward, even if she did not love him. She would show herself warm-hearted, eager to please, hardworking, compassionate and cheerful. These things would stir up his native generosity and underlying good humour. Perhaps he was in a dull humour at present because he had a home-loving disposition and longed to return to Menston. Well, that was understandable, even if Menston had not in fact been his home for all that long, and she should make allowance. To have made herself acknowledge it was a start. As for any remaining anxiety, no doubt her parents would have some sound advice for her. The effort of describing her worries in words had had the effect of setting her well on the way to resolving them. She must give no quarter to self-pity.

Forgive me if my letter takes a low-spirited tone, she wrote, hoping that an explanatory sentence or so might serve to expunge any strain of vexation in her earlier paragraphs. *The weather here is most unpleasant, the skies dark with rain all morning and a strong wind that rattles every window of the house.*

As soon as Sophy has finished going through her accounts, she wants me to help her choose a gown for this evening's concert – it is to raise funds for the town's new Hospital. When first she suggested it, I urged her to ask Mrs Whatmough for I am sure I am not equal to advising any lady, let alone one who moves in Sophy Phillips' high circles, as to her attire. But Sophy only laughs at my protests, and tells me I shall find the experience a great novelty. Her company will set my spirits on the right road, so please lay aside any thought that I might be melancholy and wonder, rather, at the scope of the new orbit upon which I find myself moving.

Yet be assured – now she had to make her writing minute, and turn the page sideways to cram her words into its margins – *that my home shall always be most dear to me. In truth, I think of you every day. How doth Edward's bridge proceed, by the bye, and what manner of man is Mr Aislabie's resident engineer? I ask this question on Sir Rowley's account. He thinks Mr Aislabie has made Mr Mark Lyle his overseer and cannot recall whether he hath met this man or no. He might welcome some description to jog his memory.*

Now her right hand, grasping the quill, she added a parting question of her own. *How fares Mr Russell and his translating work?* She would have liked to ask what duties her father gave Thomas now, in what spirit he anticipated ordination which must be soon upon him, whether he was in good health and heart, whether he ever thought of her - but she could not write that and as she squeezed her question into diminutive script, her cheeks flared and her eyes pricked. In all likelihood her parents would leave it unanswered, but at least she had had the pleasure of writing his name. Sighing, in the tiny space left she wrote *your most affectionate daughter, Caelica Hearne*, and blotted the page.

Parry, the most hospitable of men, urged Thomas to stay at his house just outside Llanmichael for as long as he wished. The two of them, he pronounced, had recognised one another as friends from the outset; not only did the schoolmaster assist in mending the damaged books, both Thomas's own and the volumes belonging to Hearne, but also he proved to have salvaged almost the entirety of Thomas's translation of Virgil from Catherine Gleeson's thick, destructive fingers.

Although devoutly grateful, Thomas had no wish to outstay his welcome. Through the last weeks of August and September he had made himself useful with the harvest and in helping set the school to rights for the coming year, but, not without regret, he declined Parry's suggestion that he stay on and teach the older children. Instead, one light-filled early autumn evening while the two of them were angling in one of the river's tributary streams, he announced that he was going to leave Llanmichael and return to Oxford.

'Why?' Parry demanded, gutting the trout that he had just caught.

Pretending to be preoccupied with his own rod and line, Thomas said something about having changed his plans. Although he still meant to be ordained, rather than have himself licensed to a curacy, he thought he would seek election to a fellowship at his old college.

'Yet you show such leaning towards parish work,' Parry observed, busy with his knife. 'Has Hearne's talk led you to think the only true measure of a clergyman's worth lies in his learning?'

A trout rose almost at Thomas's feet, but he ignored it. In truth, it would be gall to remain in a place where every step he took made him think of Caelica and how, in the fullness of time, she would wed the double-dealing Curwen. Before long, Aislabie and his resident engineer would set about directing masons and builders in the construction of that vast, light arch with its encircling tunnels that she had conceived. If Thomas had to live henceforward without her, he would, he thought, achieve it with better grace if he moved right out of the district. Oxford, the only place besides his childhood Staffordshire home that he knew at all well, might purge his dejection and clear his spirits. There he might perhaps find calm with which to face the future. But he could not belabour Parry with this wearisome explanation, and besides, he had a shrewd sense that Parry might well guess the gist of it soon enough, if he had not done so already.

'It's just a change of heart,' he said, and then cast his line with great vigour towards the stream's farther bank to hide the inadequacy of his answer.

Parry's disappointment was plain to see. He said how much he liked Thomas's company and how sorry he would be to see him go. Thomas couldn't think what to say. At last, Parry tied a new, dark fly to his line and, sighing, offered to look after Thomas's belongings until his plans were more settled.

It was not until shortly before Christmas that Caelica received any reply from her parents. By this time, they were staying in a comfortable inn at Newcastle. They had agreed that since they wouldn't be in the city long, it would be sound thrift for Caelica and Mrs Whatmough to share one chamber while the Curwens, father and son, shared the room facing. Both apartments were on the first floor – warm, airy and clean.

Being a centre of silver smithing and jewellery making – trades which overlapped to some degree with his own – Sir Rowley knew many of the town's foremost men by reputation, if not by long acquaintance. Over luncheon, he expressed his hope that Mrs Whatmough would accompany him on a round of their shops and workplaces, arguing that it was only right for him to inspect the local ware to see how it compared with Birmingham workmanship. John made out that the Tyneside silver working was nothing very remarkable – but then John's pride in his own product might have blinded him to the merits of rival concerns...While Sir Rowley held forth on his intention of viewing all in the silver-smithing line that Newcastle had to offer, Mrs Whatmough yawned and fidgeted, evincing less than the keenest interest.

Sir Rowley's conversation – really it was more of a monologue – flowed on and on. He was telling them about how the London men had been discovered in the act of adulterating their silver with base metals, when he broke off midstream.

'My dear Alice – ' Turning, Caelica saw Mrs Whatmough's lips contract with the effort of hiding yet another yawn. 'The rigours of travel are telling upon you. Why, you are grown quite pale with exhaustion. I should have noticed sooner.' Throughout their travels, he had shown the most assiduous care for Mrs Whatmough's comfort and well-being. 'Lie down for what remains of the afternoon, ma'am. You will find your energies quite recovered by evening.'

Smiling, thanking him for the suggestion, she rose from her place and withdrew.

Their first plan had been to leave her resting at the inn, while Caelica accompanied Edward and his father into that part of the town where the silversmiths had their premises. Sir Rowley mentioned the possibility of hiring a chaise, but Caelica, stiff after prolonged travel, told him she would sooner walk. Rather to her surprise Edward agreed. Newcastle was a compact sort of place, so he had heard. They could easily explore it on foot.

She was about to fetch her cloak when one of the serving men came up carrying a letter. It bore her father's hand on the cover and had come to John Phillips' house; knowing where they planned to stay and thinking it might be important, he had sent it on by swift chaise.

Seeing Caelica seize it eagerly, Edward laughed and said while she read it, he would see if the inn servants had finished unpacking his portmanteau. Outside, the wind was cold and he wanted his greatcoat. Not wanting to hold them up, Caelica put her letter away in her pocket to keep for their return.

'Read it at once,' insisted Sir Rowley, guessing what she was about. 'Heaven knows how long it may have been on the road between Llanmichael and John's house, then John's house and here. Your mother and father may have all manner of things to tell you, my dear, and you really shouldn't make them wait any longer. I am content to delay our walk for a little – it'll be a chance to scan the *Courant* and take in the news of the town.'

He was so kind – kind with a sort of artless innocence that saw love in the simplest, strongest light. Her parents loved their daughter, he must reason, and she them. Therefore she should read their letter the instant it reached her.

Upstairs – letter or no letter, she still needed to fetch her cloak – she stopped beside a window in the long corridor to read by the grey afternoon light.

Llanmichael Parsonage,
Near Pwllfechan
8 December 1751

My most dear Daughter,
God's and your father's blessing upon you; I trust that this finds you in good health. You do not say whither Sir Rowley planned to move after his stay with his stepson; I must hope, therefore, that the young man – and from what you write it sounds as though he is of a steady sort of disposition – will take steps to ensure that this letter falls into your hands in time.

Your mother, you will realise, has written her own reply to those parts of your letter which, by hers and my estimation, appeared to address themselves to a womanly sensibility. While I have not, of course, read her advice to you, I have every faith in whatever counsel she sees fit to supply. Your dear mother may not enjoy every blessing that health and a cheerful disposition may bring, yet I have total confidence that by following her direction, you shall set your feet upon the wisest and most profitable course that your life may take. That is all that I had proposed to say about that portion of your letter which dwells upon Edward's habits, but it occurs to me, Cherry, that it might be as well if I were to remind you that happiness is a blessing, a privilege if you will, whereby God shows his favour to humanity. You express yourself in terms which give the sense of your demanding it as of right. I do not care to see this tendency – it smacks over much of petulance. While no father would wish misery upon his children, it offends me to see you harbouring resentment. When you write 'To discover Edward so often mute, so little moved to question and

232

so grave makes me question whether I am fitted to become his wife,' it suggests that an ugly shoot of peevishness has taken root in your heart. Nip it in the bud, my dear, before it ripens into rank spleen. If Edward, in these early days of your acquaintance, should manifest reserve, then it is no more than evidence of his tact. You may be sure that he will throw it off ere long and love follow upon marriage even as day followeth night.

Enough of this subject and let us turn to other matters.

Even from three weeks' past and around three hundred miles' distance. She could hear her father sighing with relief.

You are most fortunate to find Edward's family so congenial. Reading your account of Mrs John's household, it pleases me to think that you shall have the friendship and kinship of this sensible sounding woman throughout your life. I could not hope for two better companions for my dear daughter in the early years of her marriage than this good woman and Mrs Alice Whatmough. How doth Mrs Whatmough, by-the-bye? You scarcely mention her, yet it must be that you and she spend many hours together while Edward and his father discourse upon matters of commerce. It is rare to encounter a woman whose kindness is the equal of her beauty. Learn by her example in all things, my dear, and you shall profit greatly.

Despite a harsh season Edward's bridge, of which you make enquiry, comes on faster than I should ever have credited it. It is my belief that it shall be complete, or nigh complete, by the Spring. Much praise is due to young Mr Lyle who, you may tell Sir Rowley, shows rare skill in his commanding of the stone hewers, mason, and builders, cajoling and admonishing them by turn. Already a great lattice of wood stands abreast the stream that serves as a frame upon which the men may, as Lyle puts it, centre the arch.

Caelica paused and thought of the bridge for which she had cherished such hopes. From what Mr Aislabie had said, Edward's bridge was very like it. She read on.

Atop the frame is a derrick for hauling stones up to the crown. Besides using much stone from the fabric of the old bridge, he has established a small quarry at the side of the bank a short distance downstream from the town. Vaughan grumbleth that the quarrymen's noise destroys his angling, but Vaughan's speech was ever ungracious. I have told him that if he is so bestirred he may, for the time being, cast his line from the churchyard bank. This right is mine to bestow where I please and I owe him some generosity in return for his putting his boat at the town's service in our time of trouble.

Mr Aislabie visits the scene at intervals to direct Lyle. He has surveyed the site and with great skill devised fair, proper plans which give right dimensions for the bridge's length and elevation, and such like. It is well for the town that Sir Rowley, enjoying as he does the friendship of the most eminent men of the age, has come to live so near. That you should find yourself engaged to marry his son gives me the greatest satisfaction.

As to my pupil Russell, shortly after you were gone he changed his lodging to stay for a time with the schoolmaster Parry, that obstinate Dissenter. Then, once the harvest was done, he came to me to say that he wished to seek out a tutorship at his Oxford College, and off to Oxford he has now gone, though he tells me it is still his intention to be ordained ere long. If he remains in Oxford, the loss to the Church will not be great, for he hath ever shewn scant loyalty to the established order. Yet I see no great prospect for him in the University, he being so much the upstart. In truth, that young man is grown so conceited that were I to offer him my counsel, I doubt he would heed it. By my estimation, his time at Llanmichael hath been a desert waste of squandered hours.

I have writ enough, I think and it remains only for me to ask you to convey my respects to Sir Rowley, to the good Mrs Whatmough and to Edward. I hope and pray for your continued good health and look forward every hour, dear daughter, to your home-coming.

With the love of your father, Matthias Hearne.

Her mother's writing was far briefer; no more, indeed, than a note.

Daughter,

It would be well for you to remember that you wed as a matter of duty. Fate has decreed that a young man blest both with fortune and honour should ask you to become his wife. To cavil, hedge and raise spurious objections to his suit, making out that he is not so talkative and attentive as you might wish, is contemptible. His person is pleasing and his portion great. You would do well to reflect that the station of a clergyman's daughter is not so exalted that she will find desirable suitors thronging her path at every turn. That Mr Curwen should ask you to become his wife is a boon for which you should be hourly upon your knees giving thanks to Almighty God.

I have no more to say, save that now you are engaged, I think it a sorry breach of propriety for you to let your thoughts drift to your father's one-time pupil. Edward would not care for it and your duty is always to him.

Your ever loving mother, Christina Maria Hearne.

Biting her lips to hold in her annoyance, Caelica folded the letter once more and headed straight to her bedchamber to collect her cloak. In time, she would no doubt reason away her mother's sharp words. Opening the door, she saw Edward. He wasn't looking for his great-coat at all, but sat at Mrs Whatmough's side on the bed, one arm encircling her waist, the two of them absorbed in talk.

Caelica rooted where she stood, only looked at them. Her blood shrilled and stung with sensations too raw and deep to put into words. Every instinct told her this most tranquil scene resonated with wrong. Yet what wrong? In the eyes of the law Alice and Edward would soon be mother and son, well, stepmother and stepson. If there were affection between them, surely it was better than strife?

'My dear Miss Hearne – you look most perturbed.' Was there the faintest shadow of mockery under this outwardly courteous observation? 'Has something startled you?'

Of the two of them, Edward was the more flustered. 'Caelica, I thought you were keeping my father company downstairs.' His face, already ruddy after beefsteak pudding, grew darker.

'A l-let-letter h-had come fr-from –'

They watcher her, waiting for her explain her presence. Yet she – who had no reason not be there – couldn't manage it. Only with the most ponderous effort would the limping words heave themselves into her dry mouth. Still they watched, their eyes burning into her, Edward's sky-blue; Mrs Whatmough's blue-grey.

'Fr-from h-home. S-sir R- Row –' An intense pause. 'S-Rowley s-said I sh-should rea-'

'Read your letter from home – of course you should.' Mrs Whatmough might have been addressing a child – a child young and stupid enough to take the honey in her voice for goodwill. 'Come and sit down. Edward, the servants have had ample time to unpack your valise. My guess is that they will have put your coat in the wardrobe.'

Edward left abruptly, Caelica staring after him. She must still her hands before their shaking drew Alice Whatmough's attention to the letter she continued to grasp. She tried to take deep, steadying breaths.

'Fond tidings?' enquired Mrs Whatmough, scanning Mr Hearne's handwriting, minuscule grains of spite in her voice.

'F-fond indeed, ma'am,' answered Caelica, wishing the words came quicker. 'My fa-father writes with news of the bridge and it – it may be that Sir Rowl – Sir Rowley w-would fain hear it.'

'And I too.' She smiled with what should have been friendship. 'Dear Miss Hearne, I shall not ask you to tell me your father's drift when you find sustained speech so trying. Pray give me the letter instead so that I may read about the bridge's progress for myself.'

Seeing her beg like a lapdog brought Caelica up short. Bold with the knowledge that the letter was meant for her eyes alone, she put it in her pocket and buttoned the flap.

'I shall re-recover all - all power of speech ere long, ma'am,' she pledged. 'Then you may be s-sure I shall read you something of wh-what my father writes. Bu-but you had said that you are tired, ma'am, and th-therefore, I sh-shall l-leave you to-to take your rest.' Seeing her cloak where she had left it, she put it round her shoulders and left, latching the door deliberately behind her.

Retracing her steps along the passage, and trying to make sense of what she had seen, Caelica was at a loss. To be sure, Mrs Whatmough had done nothing amiss. Her appearance had not been in the slightest dishevelled – even her hair was smooth. Edward, ever the gallant, might have had his arm round her, but it was hardly as though they had been kissing, nor yet was the inn bedroom the scene of a lovers' tryst. Yet the meaning of the look she had seen pass between future stepmother and stepson as they talked could not be in doubt. Mrs Whatmough's probing remarks and scathing eyes had reinforced it. Caelica might have written about her 'dear Edward,' to her parents knowing how they would like the proprietorial strain, but he wasn't hers at all. What was more, she was nothing to him, nor he to her. He and Alice were utterly absorbed and secure in one another's affection. They had between them laced the delicate ties of family fondness into a firm fast, knot of deceit.

It wasn't unusual for a man and a woman to find themselves heading into marriage with little love between them. As her father had intimated in his letter, it was by no means impossible for a mild liking to ripen to love in time – provided, she found herself arguing, that that liking had not already found its lodestone elsewhere. Edward....Edward had never been unkind to her. There was little common ground between them for conversation, it was true, but that was not to say that she disliked him. He had good looks, good humour, good temper, good manners. To all appearance, he would make a good husband and their marriage would delight both her father and Sir Rowley. Wasn't that enough?

No, no, she wanted to scream. To proceed with the engagement and marry Edward when he was so much in love with Alice – Alice who was shortly to become the wife of Sir Rowley – changed everything. She wanted love, and all that the future promised was cold duty – duty to parents, to husband, to her new position as Mrs Curwen of Menston. She couldn't even weep, for there was nowhere in this inn where she could give free rein to her tears. All she could do was to retreat downstairs once more, rouse Sir Rowley from what looked like the sleepiest perusal of the local journal and wait for Edward to join them for their walk.

As they strode three abreast along the wide pavement, father and son conversed across her, as though she wasn't there. Her thoughts turned to Thomas in Oxford, set upon becoming a college tutor. The college tutors, so she had heard, spent their days reading books, writing books and talking about books. And they could not marry. When she remembered Thomas sitting next to her on the boulder, wet through and demanding that she 'Speak truth', to keep her countenance she had to stare hard at a pigeon as it picked at a crust by the side of the street.

Chapter Nineteen

Sir Rowley's attorney confirmed that when Christopher's case came up before the Assizes Serjeant Endicott neither required nor indeed desired the presence of witnesses to offer evidence as to the boy's general integrity. Hearne was rather disappointed. It would have been so encouraging to sound out people who were actually prepared to speak of Christopher's virtues. He had imagined Anstice as a character witness, perhaps. She might be a woman, a servant and an opinionated meddler, but anyone could see she was staunch and scrupulous. And then there were the men who had had the happy task of teaching Christopher at Eton.

He was indulging these reflections one morning as he walked home from church. It was winter, with rain falling steadily through the murk of a dark morning. Above the opaque grey of the river rose the new bridge, now so close to completion that the distinctiveness of the great arch struck him afresh each time he saw it. In fact, unless his path took him straight towards it, Hearne found himself making the utmost efforts to avoid it. Try as he might, he could not subdue his misgivings over allowing Edward to take the credit for Caelica's design. He would prevaricate with himself about it, arguing that it was fair exchange for Sir Rowley's securing a leading advocate for his son; that the husband should not allow his wife's abilities to eclipse his own and that the wealth that the Curwens were likely to bring to Llanmichael entitled them to public commemoration. None of his equivocations consoled him for long.

Downstream, like a fly on a pewter dish, Vaughan advanced in his coracle with the thought, no doubt, of seeing what fish there were to be had from the promontory bank. Hearne remembered writing of Vaughan to Caelica in the same letter in which he had endeavoured to quell her concerns about marrying Edward – why was it that everything served to remind him of this daughter who would so soon quit her childhood home for good? Even Thomas's absence from morning prayers made Hearne remember how the young man was sweet on her.

Hearne thought he had been a good father. He had enforced Caelica's obedience from earliest youth; he had allowed her to taste more in the way of learning than most girls – even the daughters of the gentry – could expect and then he had put her in the way of finding a suitable husband. Yet he couldn't rid himself of the idea that these things had never really added much to her happiness.

Reaching home, he found that while he had been in church, another of Sir Rowley's irregular communications had arrived. Watkin, having limped round with the letter, was drying himself at the kitchen fireside and getting in Anstice's way. He had wanted Vaughan to ferry him over the river, but Vaughan was fishing.

'He refused outright, Mr Hearne,' the old man complained. 'Said the fish came first and if I clamoured to go home before noon, he wouldn't heed me. As if I'd clamour – I've never clamoured in my life. D'you think you might have a word with him?'

At that expression 'have a word with him,' Hearne sighed. It was the parishioners' well-worn way of indicating their view that someone's conduct merited reproof by the rector. No wonder he was unpopular; not only did he correct their lapses towards God and himself, but also they would have him issue rebukes and scoldings for their slights of one another. Suddenly, this cheerless morning, he recognised that more than their respect, he wanted their love, just as he wanted the love of the daughter whom he had ended up wronging at every turn. Quietly, he asked Watkin whether, when the bridge was so nearly built, he might not humour the ferryman's cranks and quirks for a little longer?

Old Watkin muttered and grimaced, but Hearne ignored him. Pulling up a chair, he broke the seal on Sir Rowley's letter, eager to learn what tidings of his daughter it conveyed. He also wanted to see if Sir Rowley had any new information that touched upon his son's circumstances.

It emerged from the letter that the bridge would reach completion on the day of Christopher's trial. What better time could there be for the bridge's opening, Sir Rowley demanded, than the day after?

It sounded as though he had made his mind up, but the more Hearne thought about the way that the two events would come on hugger-mugger, the less he liked it. What appetite would he have for rejoicing if his son faced transportation? He thought of writing back to suggest they left a longer gap, but decided this view of things was craven. Instead, he would cling to the hope that Christopher would be released, and that the festivities should crown his homecoming.

Having a taste for public spectacle Sir Rowley planned to lay on music and flags, food and drink in the occasion's honour. He and Edward would lead the celebrations with Caelica and Mrs Whatmough in attendance. The townsfolk would undoubtedly come thronging and Hearne should make a speech.

Hearne nodded to himself at the prospect. He generally enjoyed making speeches and if he didn't seize this opportunity, Parry might address the crowds in his stead. Yet if anything should go amiss with Christopher's court case – if, for example, something occurred to prevent Endicott from getting there, or by some misfortune a perverse judge and stubborn jury hardened their hearts to his advocacy, what then? Christina would be inconsolable – indeed, it was doubtful whether the frail balance of her health would endure the blow. Turning his back on Watkin, Hearne went upstairs to his library to compose a letter to Sir Rowley offering agreement, albeit tepid, to his proposal.

Thomas had forgotten how much he disliked Oxford. He reached the city on an overcast October day and at once noticed its brooding stillness and damp. The whole place gave the air of being in the grip of corrosive sadness. In the past, he had thought the buildings beautiful; now they seemed to drift on a current of decay, the decay of flaking stone and rotting wood. It did not take him long to see that any hope of securing a tutorship was nigh vain. Dr Glaze, his own tutor, had died and when Thomas told Glaze's colleagues of his intention, they had shrugged their shoulders and shaken their heads. The regulations permitted him to reside in his old college, but for a man without connections, publications or references the university offered no opening.

At Serjeants' Inn on Chancery Lane, Richard Endicott SL looked through the papers concerning the case of the dishonest drawing master at which he was to plead at Hereford Assize. It was such a trivial matter, he would have declined the brief, were it not that the manufacturer Curwen was taking such an interest in the proceedings. On balance, Endicott decided not to call witnesses to testify upon the excellence of the defendant's character. In his experience juries gave little weight to such testimony. Besides, it was a desperate measure. It would afford him far greater satisfaction to secure the oaf's acquittal with a substantial legal defence.

As week succeeded week, Sir Rowley, Alice Whatmough, Caelica and Edward traversed the Midlands and east of England. Mrs Whatmough with her teasing smile took charge of Caelica's trousseau, taking pains to see that it fulfilled both Hearne's stipulations for economy and Edward's wish for a stylish bride. Bored with travel and homesick, Caelica let Mrs Whatmough speak to her of frocks, petticoats and stockings and submitted herself without excitement to the attentions of drapers and milliners. She hoped no one noticed her low spirits. There, under her shocked eyes, Edward and Mrs Whatmough continued their intrigue, of which to all appearance Sir Rowley remained quite unaware. She did not know what to do.

Shortly after they left Norwich, where they had spent a week at the home of one of the Canons of the Cathedral whose mother had been born a Curwen, they drove past an imposing half-timbered house with high gables.

'See the intricacy of those leaded panes, Edward,' besought Alice, pointing out of the carriage window with a thin, gloved hand. 'It shows such fine workmanship – the effect is uncommonly pleasing.'

Caelica looked sideways at the old house, and wondered whether Edward would include her in their talk.

But he had eyes only for Alice. 'Should you really care to dwell amid such antiquity?' he asked. 'I bet its rooms are full of dark old panelling, with low ceilings and uneven floors. You'd find it a far cry from the convenience of Menston.'

'Yet antiquity is so picturesque,' she murmured in reply. 'And the black and white outside has remarkable elegance. Were we to explore it, I've no doubt we should discover a orchard. What fruit trees, I wonder, flourish in these parts?'

'Apples, I should think, and pears – both for perry and dessert. Perhaps even your favourite apricots.'

Alice laughed softly. 'If I lived here,' she said, 'I might try planting peaches.'

'They would have to be grafted against a wall,' Edward was thoughtful, 'for protection from the winds.'

Sir Rowley, who had been writing in his pocket book throughout this exchange, remarked that it might be a good idea to wall in the kitchen garden at Menston. His son took no notice but Alice, who had been looking back at the Tudor house, threw him a quicksilver smile. Neither of them paid any attention to Caelica, although when they paused to change horses, Edward assisted her down from the carriage, as courtly as ever.

The full measure of her unhappiness broke upon her that very afternoon. It was still and cold, and they were travelling south on one of the featureless new turnpikes. The utter consistency of the horses' hooves on the road surface, the creaks and motion of the equipage and the colourless February fields and blank sky beyond the windows all tended towards melancholy. Her companions, silent after a heavy midday meal, looked close to slumber.

But her thoughts gave her no peace. Alice and Edward were so suave, so knowing, so adept at turning every chance to serve their ends, and they found endless ways of reminding her that to be Mrs Curwen of Menston was a very fine fate for a country clergyman's daughter. It might be that her husband's love was fixed on someone else, but why – provided he was not actually cruel – should she object? She would have the run of a fine large house with plenty of servants to do her bidding, would she not, and fine clothes to wear and books to read? Did not these things suffice to secure happiness among the meek and undemanding? It was as though she was the living proof of her father's objectionable sermons upon the theme of how God rewarded the man who accepted his earthly lot with a meek spirit.

Her spirit, this charmless day, was meek no longer, but straining under its stormy load. As she looked from face to torpid face, in her mind there arose a vision of her wedding to Edward in Llanmichael church. She, arrayed in town style and he an elegant bridegroom stood in front of her father beneath the broken windows of the chancel where swallows nested. Her father's voice, quite clear above the creaking harness and jingling bits, asked *Wilt thou have this Woman to thy wedded wife....Wilt thou love her, comfort her, honour and keep her in sickness and in health; and, forsaking all other, keep thee only unto her, so long as ye both shall live?* And Edward, now smiling in his sleep, gave the solemn answer *I will.* Then her father turned to her and asked *Wilt thou obey him and serve him, love, honour and keep him...?* And she shouted *No, No, No.*

What then? Assuredly no biblical vengeance would follow. The divine fire of judgement would not burn her; the walls of the church should not fall; the river should not rise to drown her, nor yet the mountains fall upon her head. There would be only the spectacle of a woman shrilling her denials while her family, Edward's family and any townspeople who were present, vilified her for a jade and a scold.

The rhythm of the horses' feet was inexorable – Marr-iage, marr-iage, marr-iage they demanded. The road led on to yet another town, where yet more people whom she did not know would inspect her, and make comparison between herself and Alice. Would Edward have proposed to Alice, had she not already accepted his father's offer? Had Edward and Alice slept together? The questions' boldness shocked Caelica even as they occurred to her, but once cast into words, they hung heavy in her mind. Closing her eyes, she thought of Thomas carrying her on his back and almost slipping sideways into the river.

Having given up all hope of finding a university post, Thomas decided to look for a position as a private tutor in some townsman's household. But Oxford brimmed with able young men down on their luck and seeking out promising appointments. It was as though events conspired to frustrate him at every turn.

As for the people of the place, he came up constantly against their cankered spirits. They were suspicious, dissatisfied and given to crying down good at every turn. In their midst, any small act of kindness, the retrieval of a dropped handkerchief, for instance, or his stepping aside to let someone precede him through a narrow entrance met not with thanks, but wary looks, as though anyone who showed even a small degree of kindness or generosity must be on the lookout for something in return.

With time hanging all too heavy on his hands, he tried to take up his translating once more, but his zest had gone. In Oxford, he was a fish out of water. In the midst of languid scholars drawling in dispute, he found himself yearning to catch the sound of insistent Welsh voices. He yearned to immerse himself in the rhythm of parish life once more; he yearned for Parry's quick humour and warm friendship. Above all, he yearned for Caelica.

Caelica, the Curwens and Mrs Whatmough had reached Bath. They went to the Assembly Rooms and while Edward led Mrs Whatmough to make up a set for the cushion dance, Sir Rowley talked to Caelica over the music. He had grown weary of travel, he said. He had had enough of inns and the houses of his friends. He wanted to see his mines again and sleep under his own roof. The sick folk who flocked to Bath disgusted him, and he scowled at the obese, the gout-ridden and the syphilitic invalids, sitting down the room's long side. Following his gaze Caelica noticed Edward and Mrs Whatmough, conspicuous in their health, strength and well-being, laughing as they bore the tasselled cushion into the middle of the ring. The question 'Do you not see what is afoot?' hung in her throat, but before she could speak, Sir Rowley turned to her with a thoughtful look in his hooded eyes. 'It pleases me so much,' he said, 'to see Alice and my son fadge along together. If they were to dispute – he to insult and she to scold, say – it would not make for pleasant times at all.'

It was not until the evening of the seventh of March – the day before Christopher's trial – that they reached Menston. In her most recent letter, Caelica had told her father that she would arrange for the coachman to leave her at the parsonage before he headed on with Sir Rowley, Mrs Whatmough and Edward. In the event, Sir Rowley thought of so many persons on whom he wished to call that instead of taking the direct route to Llanmichael, they approached form the north and came to Menston first. Given that a strong spring shower was falling as they drew up outside the house – they all had to run from the carriage to the portico – it made more sense for her to spend the night under Sir Rowley's roof. In consideration for Caelica's parents, he despatched a footman on a fresh horse to tell them of the changed plan while Mrs Lavery, the Menston housekeeper, readied a chamber for her use. Caelica, accustomed to feeling lonely in unfamiliar bedrooms, accepted the new arrangement without a word. She would see her parents next day at the court with her brother's fate in the balance.

'Come, sit here, my dear, where you shall have at least some view of all that unfolds.' Sir Rowley propelled her ahead of him into a great crush of people. 'And Alice – there is room at Caelica's side.' He had underestimated the time that the journey from Menston to Hereford should take and they had arrived truly at the eleventh hour. Entering the crowded public gallery, Caelica perched without much comfort on a narrow wooden bench with Mrs Whatmough, decorous in tidy brown worsted at her side. Edward and his father stood behind them.

Looking around she saw that her parents had found seats at the front. They must have persuaded Robert to rise well before dawn to secure such commanding places. The uneven wear of her father's wig – she had never understood why on the one side it should preserve quite a trim appearance while on the other it draggled so – was unmistakeable. His hands were white on the wooden rail in front of him and she guessed how they would be taut with the effort of maintaining a calm appearance. As for her mother, even at a distance, Caelica could tell how she had aged. Her face lacked all colour but there were lines – chisel marks on a stony surface – at either side of her rigid mouth.

Only when Caelica heard people talking about a murder trial did she realise that to most of the folk in the courtroom, her brother's trial was merely a side-show – a curtain-raiser for the proper business of the day. To herself, her parents and the Curwen party, Christopher's court case was a large matter; to the noisy crowd that had thrust itself into the narrow gallery the trial of a parson's son for forgery was no more than a tedious distraction.

She and her brother had never been close. Throughout their shared childhood, Christopher had teased her, used her and told her to leave him alone when he was tired of her. Yet despite this bullying, she had no wish to see him convicted. He was part of her family, part of her life's texture and there had been times when he let her join in his adventures. Besides, the prospect of hearing Edward's father decree, as assuredly he would, that he could not allow his son to marry the sister of a convict was hardly attractive. Edward having grown so distanced and detached from her would never defy his father to claim her as his bride; most like, he would find some way of despatching her home to her parents and never think of her again. She could wish their engagement at an end, it was true, but not in this way.

'Court rise,' grated the voice of an usher, and at once there was a surge like a wave through the court in anticipation of the day's entertainment. The jurymen must already have taken their oaths, for Caelica could see them seated in two long rows down the left hand side and the judge, red-clad, square-faced and short, nodded to them as he entered. Having taken his seat, he requested that the defendant Hearne be brought forth.

It caused some disappointment. Murderers were more interesting than forgers, so there was no eager craning of necks as two men whom she took to be warders led her brother to the dock. Christopher, whom she had not seen for over a year, looked older than she remembered, and by significantly more than a year. Perhaps it was because he had put on much flesh, with the result that his darting brown eyes did not look as though they belonged to his clumsy body. But he had taken pains over his attire – his shirt looked clean, at least at a distance, and the coat hung well, if straining a little across his shoulders, and looked as though it had had a recent brushing. While the buckles of his shoes might not shine, the leather bore no scuff marks and when he looked over the assembled court, it was with all his old swagger.

Giving Serjeant Endicott the task of pleading in her brother's defence when the evidence stood so plain against him was snatching at straws, yet she took some comfort in seeing the advocate so calm, so matter-of-fact as he gazed around the packed room. At least he looked clever – this broad-faced man in his coif – while Bevan's thinner, browner barrister had a venial face and eyes set on vengeance. While a clerk read the charge, Christopher's advocate sat back and smiled before taking up a quill and beginning idly to mend it.

'...did seek, by means of the falsification of an order of payment ratified by signature, to appropriate monies rightfully the property of the complainant John Bevan.' The clerk was young and nervous-looking, his soft voice easily lost. 'And how do you plead?' he finished.

'Oh, not guilty.' Did Christopher have any conception of the seriousness of these proceedings? So detached, so languid did he sound, it was as though he treated the trial as a mere bagatelle.

'There's Bevan,' whispered Sir Rowley, leaning forward over her shoulder. 'I did not care to say aught of it to your father, Caelica – though it may well come to light – but I wrote to offer him payment if he would but drop the charge.'

It was a most touching disclosure. Ignoring counsel for the prosecution as he rose to open the proceedings, she reached out, shy, and touched his vast hand in gratitude.

'S-sir Rowley, th-that was truly mag-mag-' the word magnanimous would not submit itself to her speaking –'truly good of you,' she finished.

'But he would not accept it', Sir Rowley added.

'How very short-sighted of him,' mouthed Mrs Whatmough from Caelica's immediate right. 'And unwise, since it is bound to emerge in evidence. The court won't care to hear that he has had an offer to withdraw his charge and rejected it. Your brother bears himself well, Miss Hearne.'

'Silence in court,' rasped the usher.

The thin, sharp-nosed local barrister raked the court with his eyes. 'All the evidence,' he said, 'points to the conclusion that, having by chance found the bill of exchange that the buyer Whitman tendered to Bevan in payment for a filly, instead of returning it like an honest man, Hearne appropriated it. He picked it up from the floor of Bevan's privy and put it in his own pocket. Having it in his possession, it was an easy matter for him to construct a passable similitude of Mr Bevan's signature under a statement purporting to endorse the bill in his own

249

favour. The profession of the defendant Hearne is that of drawing teacher and portraitist, although he has yet to achieve distinction for his artistic endeavours. Nevertheless, in the light of his occupation he would, I submit, find copying Mr Bevan's handwriting easy. Fortunately for the cause of justice, when Hearne, seeking cash, presented the defaced bill to a local tradesman – Allardyce the corn chandler – some strand of suspicion made the honest fellow hesitate. Telling young Hearne he must wait a day or so for his payment, Allardyce made enquiries of Bevan. And Bevan, who knew nothing about the statement assigning his money to Hearne, was aghast at this evidence of the drawing master's dishonesty.

'Vice of this nature, especially in a youth who has been blessed with every advantage that a happy home can supply, merits the sternest penalty.'

Christopher, Caelica speculated, might question that description of his upbringing.

'Think on this, gentlemen of the jury,' prosecuting counsel continued. 'Any grain of leniency that you show the defendant Hearne may, like the mustard seed of the parable, grow into a tree, a tree of risk that shall cast its large shadow over the lives of you and your children so as to block out the very light of the sun. How shall you sleep of a night when you know that the young gentleman whom you have appointed to tutor your stalwart sons and pretty daughters, might be a thief who is out to rob? If the son of a clergyman can prove a rank and craven criminal, how are we to trust other young gentlemen? Gentlemen from less pious homes who have grown up without the nurturing paternal guidance that lit the defendant's boyhood?'

The spectators were attentive now. These sentiments drew approving murmurs all around the gallery.

'Gentlemen, I abjure you. Do not believe that this defendant, being young, may see the error of his ways. My friend from London' – Bevan's barrister nodded at Endicott – 'may set out ingenious and fantastickal theories in the hope of swaying your judgement. But we countrymen are too shrewd to let the wiles of city-dwellers deceive us. Evidence against Hearne is plain and I invite you to convict him. Come tonight, you shall sleep all the sounder for the knowledge that you have maintained justice in Brynwardine.'

Tense, Caelica stared at her brother. Didn't he realise how provocative the court must find that assured squaring of his chin? Did he suppose that the jurors could not read the obstinacy in his eyes and the contempt in his fingers drumming upon the wooden edge of the dock between the metal spikes? Couldn't he understand how much it would please them to think that they had rid their society of an arrogant thief and trickster? Why couldn't Christopher show some sign of humility – even penitence? Why did he have to smirk as though he despised them all?

Looking ahead, she saw her mother's face had gone white. Perhaps for once her thoughts and Caelica's took the same course. Of her father's expression she could see nothing.

'E-Edward, wh-what is to ha-happen?' she turned to ask, but Edward, surreptitiously stroking Mrs Whatmough's slender wrist with his broad index finger, affected not to hear.

'Wait and see how Endicott shapes his cross-examination,' breathed Sir Rowley, confident and consoling.

There followed brief examination by the local advocate of Bevan himself who embellished his testimony with exclamations upon how mistaken he had been in his initial assessment of Christopher's character. Christopher's face all this while bore an expression that Caelica took for outright boredom. Did he not care, even now, to give some sign of remorse for what he had done? There was no question but that the court should convict him, but could he not see how, if only he were to evince less complacency, the judge might pass a mild sentence? It would not alter her fate, but it might sweeten his.

At last, Endicott rose to cross examine. 'Mr Bevan,' his voice had a confiding quality as though he sought to make the chill proceedings intimate, even conversational. Had Caelica not known it to be a trial, she could have believed that Endicott was opening a friendly discussion. 'In your evidence in chief,' he began, 'you told the court that the bill on which this trial turns was made out to you by one George Whitman on 17 August 1750. He had bought a horse from you, had he not?'

'A sorrel mare, Bathsheba by Kingmaker out of Ophelia,' Bevan affirmed, plainly delighted at a chance to talk about horses. 'Whitman wanted her to pair with a dun gelding in his stable. He thought the match'd look well in one of those new-fangled phaetons. And if ever she went lame, he could put her to stud.'

Endicott's eyes sharpened. 'So,' he resumed, 'Mr Whitman paid your asking price for this animal, - er, Bathsheba – or a sum that came close to it. Very well.

'Yet once you had his bill in your possession, Mr Bevan, far from banking it at once, you retained it for some considerable length of time. You allege that it found its way into the hands of the young drawing master whom you had engaged to teach your daughters, namely the defendant Christopher Hearne who stands even now in the dock. When Hearne presented the bill to Allardyce, it was October. Many weeks had passed since Mr Whitman made his purchase. How do you account for the delay?'

Finding the equine topic exhausted, Bevan fell to the silent scowling that Caelica remembered from his argument with her father.

'Well Mr Bevan?' interposed the judge, all civility. 'It's a fair question, by any thinking.'

Bevan's answer was inaudible.

'Come, raise your voice, Mr Bevan, if you please,' the judge requested.

'See here, I always meant to bank it,' Bevan admitted. 'I thought I had it safe. It wasn't until Allardyce spoke up that I knew what had happened.'

There were gasps and a little mocking laughter. To find the coroner at once so remiss about money and so resentful when his carelessness came to light was quite unlooked for. It would not, Caelica thought, change the jury's verdict, yet it might tell somewhat in Christopher's favour.

'Strange, is it not, sir,' Endicott took a new line, 'that you should decline an offer by a third party to make good your losses if you agreed to withdraw this case before its reaching the court? The third party concerned tells me he proposed generous terms. Yet you held firm to your course. You would go to court at all cost, you said. Why, pray?'

'I seek justice,' returned Bevan, sticking out his sharp chin. 'That can't be wrong, see. Nor yet to refuse the bribes of Sir Rowley Curwen, yonder.' He gestured dismissively to the gallery. 'He knows nothing of the ways of the people among whom he's made his new home. For a city man like him, a man who's got all his money by trade, look you, to start making terms with folk who have passed their wealth down from generation to generation is rank presumption.'

'Presumption is not a crime, Mr Bevan,' observed Endicott quietly, 'and to have taken up his offer would have saved the labour and indeed the cost of bringing this case to court, a cost which, sir, you may have to bear.'

''Tis the principle I would defend.' Bevan's defiant chin rose higher. 'The principle that a wronged man may see his wrongs given public hearing – aye, and see a meet punishment fall upon the wrongdoer. These are the things I seek.'

From outside came the sounds of someone arriving in great haste –cantering hooves, wheels on cobble stones, a slammed door, a chink of coin and running feet. Caelica thought the commotion must have some connection with the murder case. Endicott had done well, but nothing could happen now to secure her brother's acquittal.

The door of the courtroom opened to admit an excited looking young man. Whispering to the usher, he bowed in great haste to the judge before shouldering his way to where Endicott was half-rising as though in greeting, and thrust a journal into his hands.

'Found it at last, sir,' he pronounced.

'Is the court to understand, Mr Endicott, that this interruption necessitates an adjournment?' asked the judge. 'Or does the paper this gentlemen has conveyed here at such despatch concern the court's other business of the day?'

'Your honour, this paper is material to the case of Hearne,' Endicott announced. 'It is a copy of the *London Gazette*. I would crave a few minutes in which to acquaint the defendant with its import – I shall not need long.'

While Endicott turned the pages of the journal, found what he was looking for and showed it to Christopher, the court agitated, impatient. Suddenly Christopher gave a brash gust of laughter. There was a moment's silence in which Caelica, puzzled, looked at Sir Rowley. What possible bearing could a London journal have upon her brother's attempted forgery? But Sir Rowley only frowned in puzzlement of his own and shook his head.

Impassive, Endicott nodded to the judge, and the trial resumed.

'Mr Bevan.' Although Endicott smiled, it was a forced, fierce smile. 'The purchaser of your mare Bathsheba was one George Whitman, was it not?'

'Aye. I've told you that already.'

'So it was Whitman who made out the bill of exchange in your favour?'

'It was – just like I said before. You don't expect me to alter my story, do you?'

'Oh, no, not alter it at all.' Endicott gave Bevan a slightly fuller smile, then narrowed it again. 'You took Whitman's bill of exchange as payment for your mare on 17 August 1750. For weeks you were content to keep it in your possession rather than to bank it. Hearne, you allege, appropriated it and the first you heard of his crime was the following October when Allardyce drew the endorsement in Hearne's favour to your attention.

'Aye,' but Bevan's annoyance was giving way to suspicion, his pale eyebrows drawing together in a frown.

'Let me read you this notice from the *London Gazette*,' said Endicott.

'Whereas a Commission of Bankrupt is awarded and issued forth against George Whitman of Stokenbury Yard, London, Mercer, and he being declared a Bankrupt, he is hereby required to surrender himself to the Commissioners in the said Commission named, or the major part of them, on the 26th day of September 1750 at Three of the Clock in the Afternoon in Johnson's Coffee House, Pattern Street, London and make a full discovery and disclosure of his Estate and Effects....'

The red in Bevan's face faded, leaving his cheeks the colour of lime mortar.

'By the time the bill came into Hearne's hands, it had no monetary value whatever. You have spent this day disputing over the justice of your rights to a worthless scrap of paper.'

Chapter Twenty

The weeks following Thomas's solitary Oxford Christmas had been cold and dreary, but then, with the lengthening days, a letter came from Parry – a letter as warm and bright as the Spring sun. Running his eye across the pages of close-set, clear, rapid writing, Thomas could hear the cadences of the man's voice, even catch his intake of breath at each paragraph's end. It smote his conscience because, although he had written to Parry some months previously, his letter had been reserved and uncommunicative. Determined to say nothing of his disappointment with Oxford, he had ended up saying nothing much at all.

But Parry, incapable of resentment, had written back to him at vast, affectionate length and his letter brimmed and boiled with news. It told of the school and which children did well and which had fallen behind through illness; of how Cadi Glwth had wed her baker at last and how aloof Hearne had looked when he had married them; of Hearne himself – that he had taken a cold and grown very hoarse, though according to Joseph Watkin it hadn't stopped him from preaching a full sermon every Sabbath. And then Parry had reached the subject of the bridge.

In our inclement weather, he wrote, *the speed of progress in the construction hath been remarkable. Mr Aislabie – he asks after you, by the way, and sends his regards – has been here on a visit of inspection and to talk with his deputy Mr Lyle. He says that Sir Rowley plans to provide liberal quantities of food and drink for a grand opening ceremony, to take place on the eighth of March. Aislabie will not be there, since he must attend to his great drainage scheme in the Fens where he finds himself embroiled in dispute with the landowners. With neither he nor you on hand, I have little stomach to join in a celebration that has Edward Curwen's dishonesty at its root. I shall close the school for the day, for I would not wish to deny the children their chance to gorge at Sir Rowley's feast, but for myself I shall be content to spend the time setting my cabbages.*

Pray tell me more, friend Thomas, about how you go on in Oxford. Must I send your books after you, or will you return for them? It would please me so much to digress upon the world with you once more...

Thomas stopped reading, folded the letter with great firmness and decided he would put his meagre funds towards hiring a horse so that he might return to Llanmichael at once.

Outside the court, exhilaration swept through the Hearnes and the Curwen party like fire on a dry heath. Sir Rowley and Caelica's father thanked Endicott at the same time and with equal vigour, while he, saturnine and remote, waved their gratitude aside and prepared for his next hearing. Christopher, his earlier languor forgotten, submitted himself to his mother's tearful embraces with boisterous laughter although Mrs Whatmough found a moment at which to interrupt and introduce him to Edward, whose congratulations he accepted as though the acquittal had been his own achievement.

At odds with the mood of the moment and embarrassed, Caelica at last came forward and deliberately kissed her brother on the cheek in greeting. 'D-dear K-Kit, I am s-so very happy,' she began.

'Still stammering, eh, sister,' said Christopher, his brown eyes mocking her. He turned to Edward. 'See if you can cure her of that tendency, Curwen; otherwise, it'll drive you to Bedlam.'

Edward, indulgent, joined in his laughter. 'Come, Hearne. Your sister is blest by every grace. How pleased she must be to see you at liberty.'

She could feel the eyes of both of them hard upon her, as though they wanted to satisfy themselves that her spirits were as buoyant as their own. But merriment was incongruous in this grim stone street where beggars lounged against the massy walls of the gaol. Caelica wanted to get away from the town and see her home again.

'Father,' in the ascendant, Christopher's ebullient voice commanded the attention of everyone in hearing distance.

'Dear boy,' Hearne answered in a quieter tone which nevertheless overflowed with happiness. 'What is it you wish to say?

'You remember calling on me in gaol?'

'Indeed.'

'Well, at that time you taxed me there with all manner of questions concerning a young woman named Hannah.' Unable to help hearing, Caelica looked hard at Christopher. He spoke more quietly and pulled a long face. 'You bore heavy tidings,' he said. 'For you told me she was dead. And I, having no wish to find myself the subject of speculation among the felons with whom I lodged – denied that I knew her.' He shook his head in evident regret.

'That coarse great girl with her wicked accusations,' Caelica's mother recalled with rare energy while Sir Rowley looked on bemused and Alice Whatmough and Edward exchanged a long, curious glance.

'In recent days her face and form have shone clear in my mind,' he admitted, ignoring his mother's urging him to give Hannah no further thought. 'And it gives me true sorrow to know that she is dead, for I passed some sweet hours in that quean's ar – that young woman's company, I mean. In truth I think she had no eyes for any man but I.' As though to emphasise his sincerity, he gave a gusty sigh.

Caelica watched with disgust. How could he make such a confession out here in the thoroughfare as though Hannah's fate were a subject for idle chatter?

'I did not speak true to you that day in gaol, father,' Christopher avowed.

'Yet honest repentance wipeth every sin away,' said Hearne, very much the parson.

'I had thought,' Christopher continued, glancing at round to see if Sir Rowley, Mrs Whatmough and Edward were still listening, 'that a miniature portrait of her – pigment upon ivory in a silver frame - might make a consoling trinket for her parents. What do you think, father?'

Before her father replied, Caelica heard the iron of Mrs Hallet's voice as clear as if the woman stood at her side - *And you suppose that your apples can take away the sore I feel.* About to tell her brother that his idea was insensitive, distasteful – in short, just plain wrong, she saw Bevan.

He stood across the street and stared at the stones of the high gaol wall as though they held some extraordinary interest to him. How much of Christopher's disclosure had he heard? He must have heard the rumours that ran along the streets and sewers of Llanmichael. At that instant, he noticed Caelica on the edge of the lively group and strode up to her, his skinny face sour with resentment.

'I suppose you think today's events have served your family handsomely, young woman.' She tried to look no further than the myriad small red veins that traversed the dull whites of his eyes and avoid the venomous black of the pupils. 'See here,' his voice dropped so only she could hear. 'That girl who drowned herself in the river – she whose inquest I conducted at the parsonage – your brother fathered the babe in the womb, didn't he? So that's why your father wanted to bury her in his churchyard, is it not?'

Sir Rowley must have noticed Bevan, for Caelica found him at her side.

'The court has given its judgement, good sir.' His tone indicated that he would brook no discussion. 'No man can steal from an empty pocket. The jury has found young Hearne not guilty and there is no more to be said. To think that when I wrote offering to make good your losses if you would but drop the charge, you declined it – Now leave Miss Hearne alone and take yourself home, before I call the Watch.'

'Do you threaten me with the Watch, Curwen? See here, I've supported the cause of justice all my life, yet you get your way at the hearing by the merest chance. That wasn't justice, not by any means.'

There was nothing to like about this vengeful, leathery man with his bare longing to see her brother transported and her family humiliated, yet over the bill he surely had some claim to be in the right. Where, Caelica wondered, might his grievance lead? She had no doubt Mr Bevan had heard every word of her brother's admission.

'The proceedings,' Sir Rowley asserted, 'are now closed. The judge, if I mistake not, proclaimed you to be the author of your present misfortune by reason of your own delay in banking the bill. Learn by your error, sir, and be gone.'

Christopher, having caught wind of this exchange, thrust himself into the fray. 'I am minded to sue you for compensation in respect of the long months I spent in gaol,' he told the coroner.

'I can see how much that course of action might appeal to you.' Wistful, her father sounded as though he rather liked the idea too, 'but the wiser counsel would be to forbear and let bygones be bygones. Come, Bevan, we're near neighbours and we shall encounter one another often enough in the future. It would be folly to allow old enmities to sour our meetings for ever more.'

'You would talk of letting bygones be bygones,' Bevan retorted. 'You forget that I am out of pocket by forty guineas.' His skeletal hand closed around his riding whip. They were a countryman's hands, broad and hard, for all that he was a squire, a landowner and a gentleman by birth.

'Forty guineas, look you. Anyone'd think I'd wronged you – not your son wronging me. I'll not forget this day, Hearne. You're not in the right in this matter, and I'll not leave my scores unsettled.'

'Is there anything that he can do?' Hearne asked Sir Rowley, once Bevan had gone. Sir Rowley shrugged his shoulders.

'Refuse to cooperate with you in local matters, perhaps...if he resides in your parish, Hearne, I suppose he may withhold his tithes, or make his payment late. You've made an enemy of him of course, but in my experience, no one ever did anything of worth in this world without making enemies on their way.'

An enemy indeed, but Caelica guessed her parents must be happier than they had been for months, their beloved son a free man once more. If she were to tell them what Bevan had gleaned from Christopher's loud talk they would give it little heed. Her father might well accuse her again of giving way to spleen. Perhaps, once she was home she should broach the matter, but it was hardly the time now.

'Now let us leave this grim place,' urged Sir Rowley expansively, 'and prepare to rejoice at your son's release. By what means did you and your lady arrive here?'

Learning that the Hearnes had hired a chaise Edward proposed that he and Caelica use it to return to Llanmichael. He would, he claimed, relish the chance to make this journey in the company of his betrothed and the others could follow in the Curwen carriage. Mr and Mrs Hearne would surely wish to have Christopher's company to themselves for a few hours.

Caelica was amazed. In the course of their recent travels, he had been at such pains to avoid their being alone together, for Alice took pride of place in his heart. But Sir Rowley seconded Edward's suggestion with much hearty enthusiasm, and marshalled Caelica's parents and Christopher towards the Menston carriage. The road to Menston took them through Llanmichael and they would take the Hearnes home on their way.

'Now, my dear, if you would care to step up into the chaise,' Edward was half watching the carriage's departure over his shoulder. His command rang with formality and obsequiousness, but carried no charge. Despite the resolve she had just made, the echo of an amused, dear voice broke into her thinking, saying, 'Put your hands on my shoulders and spring.' Would Edward ever carry her over a river? No, for he would always have carriages, or horses or bridges. She stepped into the covered chaise and watched as he settled himself next to her, stretching out his long legs and sitting back, relaxed after the morning's drama.

As they set off he began to talk about the proceedings: how fortunate it was that Endicott's clerk should have laid his hands so readily upon the evidence of Whitman's bankruptcy; what a skulduggerist was Squire Bevan – truly, a man without the slightest apprehension of the way the world was changing – and how much he liked Christopher's frank humour and irreverence.

'I've taken to your brother straight away.' He gave a brief, idle smile. 'Ah, we view the world in very much the same light, he and I.'

'Y-yet, Edw-Edward, you must see th-that his in-in-intention' – she could not hide her opinion – 'w-was theft.'

'Oh, come, Caelica. Don't be such a little moralist. That careless old squire deserved every calamity that befell him. Were he a shrewder man, he'd never have laid himself open to misfortunes. The judge pretty well said as much. Don't waste your pity on him, say I. Rejoice rather in your brother's freedom.'

'I do.' True, the verdict had brought her parents mighty relief but it was harsh justice, and Bevan had overheard a choice morsel of information with which to feed his vengeance.

For miles they continued saying little. Edward moved restlessly from time to time and complained that his new boots were pinching. Seeing him fidget, as though trying to flex his feet, she tried to sympathise, but he silenced her, remarking tersely that it would please him to reach Menston without delay. Trotting along a straight stretch of road, he observed through the window that one of the horses was not pulling up to its collar.

'That sorrel mare's a lazy larrikin.' He holla'd to the coachman. 'Ply the whip more on the near side, sirrah. That idle jade hardly raises a trot.'

'She's a mite green, sir, and she's had a long haul already this day,' the man called back over his shoulder. 'I'd sooner not risk her wind.'

'Oh, very well.' For all his impatience, Edward was too shrewd a horseman to make light of the coachman's fears. But why should he be impatient when he was travelling with the woman whom he was going to marry? Surely they should enjoy every second they spent in each other's company?

Caelica interrupted his sighs. 'If your b-boots h-hurt so much, Edward, pr-pray take them off.' Here, surely, was plain sense. 'I have n- no ob-objection to your stockinged feet, you know.'

He looked at her with such blatant scorn, she wished she hadn't spoken. Unable to endure the silent censure in his expression, she stared at the grain of the wood of the floor. In the silence between them there came the self-same refrain that had mocked her when they were on their travels. Marr-iage, marr-iage, marr-iage beat the horses' hooves on the surface of the track. Because Edward said nothing, the pulse grew more insistent. The taunting rhythm made Caelica realise she had not grasped the extent of Edward's contempt for her before. She had not known that a man might have a talent for contempt, in much the same way that he might have a talent for running, or leaping or music. It was not so with Thomas, who could differ from her without despising her. Looking at Edward, she marked disdain in the set of his shoulders, the stillness of his mouth, from the proprietorial arm that circled her in ownership and most of all from the purposeful, damning, way in which he looked at her. It was like a surge of the Llanmichael river.

Since the chaise was much lighter than the carriage, it was clear that she and Edward would reach the parsonage before her parents, Christopher, Sir Rowley and Alice got there. Despite Edward's misgivings about the tarrying horse, they had covered the distance from Hereford at rare speed. They swung round a wide bend and paused at the top of a rise, for both horses were blowing. Edward removed his arm from around Caelica and stared straight ahead. Looking down, she saw his hands, large, gloved and motionless upon his cream clad thighs. She recalled the evening of his visit to the parsonage and how she had watched the light make gold of the hairs on the back of his

263

hands. Now, despite his embraces, he kept to his coat and his gloves, as though he sought to protect his body and limbs from making the slightest contact with her. Yet he had run his ungloved fingers across the back of Alice Whatmough's white hand as they sat in the public gallery of the court not more than three hours ago.

The coachman flicked his whip, ready to start the long descent towards the town. So as to see the familial landmarks as they approached, she leant out of the window.

'Take care,' warned Edward but, nettled, she leant out further. Next minute, she gasped aloud. There, where the river ran wide and fast among the huge boulders, was the bridge – unmistakeably the bridge of her drawing. For a marvelling second, her pent-up rebellion shrivelled and she turned to Edward as she would to a friend.

'See' she urged. 'See yonder – The bridge.'

It was a miracle. Aislabie, having derived formal plans from her drawing, had preserved the full daring of her great arch so that it leapt above the water's surface with all the grace of a rainbow. The threefold piercings of each haunch gave the structure pure, lithe delicacy. As she marvelled, a shaft of sun broke through the clouds to turn the dull grey of the masonry to crystalline pallor. Here was total enchantment.

'Oh, Edward,' she breathed.

'Ah, yes.'

How could such perfection leave him so cool? She looked at him, finding on his face a strange speculative smile, the like of which she hadn't seen before.

'Take a good look, Caelica, at my bridge,' he invited.

At once her joy evaporated. His bridge? When the distinctive outline proved it was hers? Edward, by some turn of self-seeking guile, must indeed have laid claim to her design as Thomas had suspected. Once she hadn't thought it possible; now she saw it for truth.

'H-how yours?' she asked. 'Th-the idea of the piercings was mine. I recall drawing it out one evening at dusk in my father's library. I drew till nearly nightfall, then found myself held, aye, quite transfixed, by what my art produced.'

Before he could reply, anger unleashed her tongue. 'When Aislabie described it at the inn, his words fitted my bridge exactly. Yet he made out it was yours. Even as I heard him, I could not see how the self-same device – the colossal arch and the tunnels – could suggest itself in both our minds.'

He tried to interrupt, raising his voice to talk her down, but hurt drove her on.

'This bridge is of my devising. If Mr Aislablie had its design from your hand, then either you used my sketch as a basis for one of your own, Edward, or you took up my handiwork and put your name to it. I cannot – I will not – credit that you could light on the same scheme as mine by chance. That coincidence defies belief. Besides, Mr Aislabie would have remarked on it. In truth, this bridge is mine.'

Edward was laughing – actually laughing – at her. For a moment, she thought of unfastening the door, leaping out of the chaise and running away – but where? Her only refuge was the parsonage, to which he would surely follow.

'Your bridge, would you say?' he asked. 'Dear wife-to-be, learn from your future spouse. As a married woman, you will own nothing. The law, as you well know, prescribes that all your property, be it land or funds, becomes mine on our marriage. In claiming title to that ingenious bridge, I am doing no more than making a logical extension of a well-established legal principle.'

'Yet if I do not marry you,' It was a wild fancy, but too sharp for sheathing.

'It will change nothing. All that will happen is that you return to live with your parents, helping the housekeeper, visiting the sick, attending every service in your father's church and hearing sniggers of people who remember that once you were to wed, but you broke off your engagement in a fit of pique. Believe me, Caelica, no man on earth will have you if you throw me over. Capriciousness is no commendation – eschew it. Come live with me and be my love, and you shall have wealth, comfort and freedom from the constraints of the parsonage.

'Coachman,' he raised his voice and leant across her to call his orders. 'Before you take us to Miss Hearne's home, let us pause here, if you please.'

The chaise stopped. Edward opened a door and handed Caelica out. They were quite close to the bridge, just a gentle stroll from it over the short grass where the sheep grazed. Ahead of them, a young man in town clothes was sitting on the bank, looking upstream and entering notes in his pocketbook.

Genial, debonair, Edward walked up to him, holding out his hand. 'Good afternoon,' he said at his easiest. 'I am Edward Curwen. You, I take it, must be one of Aislabie's colleagues. Allow me to introduce my betrothed, Miss Caelica Hearne.'

The young man had kind hazel eyes in his square, plain face. Caelica wanted to like him.

'Mark Lyle – resident engineer.' He shook hands with both of them. 'You've come to see the stone, I take it, Mr Curwen?'

'I have indeed. I want to show it to my wife-to-be.'

What stone could he mean? Before she found out, she wanted the answer to another question, one which was too pressing for her to contain.

'Wh-what,' she asked as soon they were out of Lyle's hearing, 'wh-what of your friendship with Mrs Whatmough?'

'Now, you surely cannot be jealous of our affection?'

'Bu-'

'Yes?'

Mute, she realised she had no word for what she knew Edward and Alice to be. Lovers? Not to her certain knowledge. Friends? But affectionate friendship was no sin. On the contrary, if a stepmother should find herself on good-natured terms with her stepson it was, as Sir Rowley had observed, preferable to malice and bickering.

'Listen, Caelica,' Edward could make his speaking voice quieter than a whisper, yet keep it clear as glass. 'You once thought it'd be a fine thing to wed me. Remember that summer day at Menston when you had your eyes fixed on me from the minute of your arrival till I blurred in your sight as the carriage drew your home. I read your face plain enough as you sat at my father's table and listened to my talk. Well, the wide-eyed child of the parsonage has got her heart's desire. And I am very happy that she should wish to marry me. If, meanwhile, I and my sweet Alice should find joy in one another's arms, what harm can it possibly do you?'

For a second, he gripped her hand hard, crushing it in his. 'If you should go – you stammering, white-faced, pious little moth – to my father, what tale can you tell him of Alice and me? None that is to our shame. Would you, basking in a little snivelling schoolroom cleverness, reveal your fribbling suspicions to my father? You'll destroy him if you do.'

Flexing her sore fingers, Caelica had to agree. Whatever outcome she might wish for herself, she did not want to destroy Sir Rowley. If he believed Alice Whatmough was in love with him, then God forbid anything should happen to disabuse him. The world was full of dreary wiseacres who liked to point up the folly of old men with young wives and she had no wish to join their number.

'Come Caelica,' increasing his pace, Edward led her along the path by the river. Soon she could see the marks of engraved script on the bridge's keystone. 'Read yonder,' he said, and looking up, she made out the words EDUARDUS CURWEN FECIT, 1752.

Chapter Twenty-One

Caelica stared from the stone back to Edward. The clouds had parted again, just as they had when the carriage had first drawn in sight of the bridge and this time, the sun shone on his hair as though to crown him conqueror. She could not let him conquer her. The dull garnets he had given her on the day of their betrothal weighed heavy round her neck. She reached for the clasp, but such a current of wrath ran through her fingers, she couldn't work the catch.

'I cannot wed you – I shall not wed you.' Shouting the words over and over, she pulled at the necklace with all her strength, broke the thread and sent the lustreless gems spilling across the common track and into the dung of the beasts.

'I shall not travel on with you,' she screamed. Could this scold's voice, shrill with choler, be truly her own? 'Not now, nor never again. I've no fear of living single till the end of my days. What I dread is living at your side. Go your ways, Edward Curwen. Go your ways without me.'

She picked up her skirts, kicked off the slippery shoes she had worn for attending the trial and ran, pell-mell in her stockings, towards the parsonage.

From behind her, she heard him call, 'Caelica, Caelica, come back.'

Ignoring him, she rushed headlong down the road they had just driven. She cared nothing for what Mr Lyle and the driver of the chaise might make of her flight but Edward she guessed might think twice about pursuing her under their eyes. Anyway, he wouldn't be able to run in his tight boots.

As soon as the parsonage door came in sight she accelerated, then hurled herself against it. The heavy oak would not yield. Trying the latch and finding it bolted, she remembered that Anstice always kept the door locked against trouble-makers. Still defiant, despite the tears gathering behind her eyes, Caelica went to the back of the house. The back door was fast too, so she knocked on the kitchen windows.

Inside, Anstice slumped on a chair near the fireside, her mouth open and eyes closed while flies moaned around the shoulder of mutton scorching on the spit. Behind her, Caelica could hear advancing steps, rather uneven. Edward must be stumbling along the track after her.

She knocked harder. 'A-Anstice.'

Edward surely wouldn't come right into the house to wrangle with her in a servant's hearing.

'Anstice, wake up.'

Inside the kitchen, the housekeeper yawned, stretched, saw the figure at the window and rose from her seat.

'What dost here, Miss Caelica?' Even after Caelica had been away for nearly a year, Anstice wasted no breath on words of welcome. 'And at the back door?' the old woman continued. 'Where are your mother and father? What news of your brother?'

'On their way. They will be here soon. Christopher too. Yes, he is free and found to have committed no offence. Oh, you may purse your mouth, Anstice, but let me in, I beg.'

Whether it was because she had spoken so much without stammering or that in her urgency, her breathy voice rose at every word, Anstice unfastened the door with something approaching haste. At once Caelica slipped into the hot, stuffy room and almost collapsed with relief.

'Where are your shoes?' asked Anstice. 'What are you do-?'

'Don't ask me to explain.' After her run, Caelica was out of breath and very close to crying, only she must not cry – not until she was by herself.

'But your clothes, Miss- ? What have you done.'

Edward must know where she was, for his footsteps had settled to a walk. Closer and closer they sounded outside. Soon he would be at the door.

'Listen to me, Anstice,' she looked the housekeeper full in the face. 'My mother is not yet returned so I am mistress here.' Surely she had never said such a thing in her life before? 'You are, I see, preparing a meal for my parents' return. They will be hungry after their journey – Christopher too – so pray continue with your labours. In the meantime, if anyone should come to the door, you must not admit him. Admit no one but my father, my mother and Christopher. Do you understand? Very well.'

'I suppose you've had some tiff with Mr Curwen.' Anstice's expression was at its most scornful and knowing, but when Caelica met her eyes stare for stare, the old servant turned away.

Soundless in her gaping, bloodstained stockings, she crossed the shadowy hall and began to climb the stairs. Might Edward have stopped short in his pursuit? But no – there were his crisp strides on the stone path that led up to the house. Caelica froze upon the landing. Those pinching boots must still trouble him, for his steps came *heavy, light, heavy, light* as though he favoured one foot above the other. There was the rap of a cane upon the front door followed by the rattle of Anstice with her keys and the scrape as she opened it.

'Where is Miss Hearne?' Edward demanded.

Since Anstice liked Edward, she probably wouldn't mind his peremptory question, or even take umbrage at his refusal to remember servants' names. She even might think it her duty to admit him to the parlour, before fetching Caelica downstairs for an enforced reconciliation. Caelica pressed herself further back into the shadows.

'I've no doubt she came here, and I wish to speak to her.'

'Be that as it may, Mr Curwen,' Anstice answered, 'my orders are that I should admit no one. Only the master, Mrs Hearne and Mr Christopher.'

Breathing silent amazed thanks, Caelica thought of Anstice, hands on hips, standing up to Edward, solid as a brick wall.

'But I am engaged to her. I must see her.' Despite having had his mother's jewels thrown in his face, he sounded more annoyed than injured.

'And so you shall, sir,' came Anstice's imperturbable voice. 'I don't know what you've quarrelled about, and I don't want to. But I'm not having you quarrelling here. Not with the master and Mrs Hearne away. You come back tomorrow, sir, when she's had time to come round to a proper way of thinking.'

Proper way of thinking? Caelica's thoughts had never been clearer in her life. Oh, but bless Anstice for being so loyal.

On the doorstep, Edward gave vent to an exasperated sigh. 'Very well, then, my good woman, since you would have it this way.'

'I would indeed sir.'

'Maybe your suggestion has more worth than you suppose.' It sounded as though he were thinking aloud. 'The bridge opening will hardly be an occasion for outbursts and petulance. Perhaps the presence of her parents and her brother, not to mention Alice and my father, will induce her to behave with her accustomed submissiveness. Good day to you,' and even as Anstice was bidding him good bye in return, the door closed with a bang.

Caelica crept on upstairs. She would thank Anstice and soon, but now she shrank from comfort and company. Reaching her chamber, without stopping either to change her ripped dress, or remove her torn and muddy stockings or even straighten her torn hair, she collapsed at the side of her bed and wept and wept.

Having once tasted what it might be to love and be loved, she could not endure the prospect of a marriage of silences and loneliness. Edward, to be scrupulous, was not intentionally unkind. His conduct concerning the bridge owed as much to an exaggerated sense of the dignity owing to him as Sir Rowley's son as it did to outright malice. He did not dislike her, only viewed her with the careless, idle affection that he would show to a pet dog – not a useful, spry gundog which he would treat as a respected accomplice, but an old, lame, quiet dog that he would suffer to sit by the fireside of an evening.

But she was not old – she had not reached even her nineteenth year. The folly of youth bloomed as bright in her as poppies in the summer pasture. Why otherwise should she have thrown her best hope of happiness away?

She would not go on thinking in this vein. It benefited her not one whit. At the least, there was needful work for her among her father's parishioners here in Llanmichael. The sick sometimes welcomed her visits; she should, perhaps, try to teach the younger children – not those of the dissenting families who went to school with Emrys Parry whom her father so disliked... Oh, but she had been too long her father's meek daughter, letting him direct her in everything, even to marrying Edward. It was high time she learned to think for herself.

Now that the storm of her crying had given way to more controlled contemplation, Caelica heard the house stirring in anticipation of her family's return. Anstice must have seen the lumbering Menston carriage approach, for Caelica heard her stumping up the steps and throwing open the windows. Finding fresh water in the ewer on the shelf, Caelica dipped her handkerchief in it, soothed her eyes and wiped away all trace of her tears. With great care, she combed out her hair and saw on the dressing tables the ivory brushes that Edward had sent her upon their betrothal. She had not taken them on their travels because they looked so valuable she had been afraid of their being lost or damaged along the way. Once, she had thought them elegant; now, they struck her as weighty and imposing, like the garnets. She would return them with more decorum than she had the necklace.

The exchange of greetings reached her from downstairs. Anstice was brisk over Christopher's homecoming, Christopher brazen in his turn. 'We totally scotched that sourpuss Bevan, Anstice,' he said, while her father's ringing exclamations upon the good fortune of Sir Rowley's finding so conscientious a lawyer drifted through her closed bedroom door. And what of her mother – still weeping tears of joy on Christopher's chest? But this ill-nature was contemptible; she must show herself willing to enter into the family celebration and then, when perhaps the time felt right, she should take her parents into her confidence, explain

272

to them how things stood between Edward and herself, and weather the chill of their disappointment as best she might.

Opening the door, she saw her mother approaching, full of purpose along the corridor.

'Mother?'

Even now, when Kit's triumphant homecoming should have delighted her heart, her mother did not smile. Instead, she stood quite still on the threshold of Caelica's bedroom.

'Mr Curwen returned some way along the Hereford road to intercept our return,' she remarked in a cold voice. 'He said you were in distress.'

'Mother,' the kinder name "mamma" was not solemn enough to use at this time. 'I have brought my engagement to Mr Curwen to an end.'

Her mother's thinning hair had parted across her temples so that the white of her scalp showed between the strands. Her face had grown so thin that her cheeks were concave and streaks of what Caelica took to be rouge extended beneath her cheekbones. But the wives of clergymen did not paint their faces, surely? The purplish tinge in the red pigment did not chime with her mother's sallow skin.

'And what makes you presume to think you may take this action without discussing it either with your father or myself?'

Caelica stayed silent.

'Answer me, daughter. By what right have you ended your engagement to Mr Curwen?'

'Because there is neither love nor respect between us, mother.'

'Love between you? Respect? What idiocy is this? I order you, daughter – send after Mr Curwen and tell him that you are mistaken.'

'I shall not.'

She knew that her mother would be vexed, but she could not understand why vexation should lead her mother to cross the threshold, take up one of the great ivory brushes from the table and then –and then – pain flared in her jaw and ran down her spine. The blow had been so sudden she had no chance of dodging it. Shock quenched all Caelica's thinking. Holding her left hand to her face, she found only naked rage in her mother's eyes.

'Mother – mother, why? Pray do not hit me again,' she raised her right hand to ward off the next blow.

'Of course I shall punish your defiance.' Despite her frail appearance, Caelica's mother had wiry strength and held the brush high. 'What else is it but defiance that should make your stammer of years vanish away?'

'Believe me,' Caelica found herself pleading, 'I do not seek to defy you. But surely you would not have me wed Edward when there is so little affection between us? I cannot marry a man who claims my creation as his own.'

'You mean the bridge, I suppose.' At once, her mother's rage passed its zenith and she laid the ivory brush down beside its fellow once more. 'Your father told me he was uneasy with the way Edward had adapted it,' she said, her skeletal features taut with self-justification. 'But I silenced his doubts. The man has the right, I said. Edward wouldn't want a wife who was cleverer than he.'

'I cannot marry him.' Despite the intense pain in her jaw, Caelica remained insistent. 'Do not hold me to marry Edward. Do not force me to spend the rest of my days pretending to be stupid so as to please him.'

'But you gave him your word.' Her mother was inexorable.

'Aye – and I drew my bridge in good faith that it should be taken for my creation. And you, you and father, and Edward and Sir Rowley – all you who make out that you are fond of me and care for me – you would say that it is Edward's work. Well, I cannot add my voice to this lie and marry him.' She fingered her swelling face, finding it hot and tender. Before long the flesh would darken.

Now that her choler was on the ebb, Caelica's mother's flesh had gone grey. It made the rose petal attempt at boldness look sadder than ever. To try to make peace, Caelica moved to give her an embrace of forgiveness, only her mother thrust it away with the same impatience with which she had refused her husband's embraces in the past.

'I want your obedience, not your caresses. I have my son back, so why must you bring me new woe and thrust fresh disgrace upon us?'

'Mother...'

'Don't try to plead with me, Caelica. I'll not strike you again, but I demand that you reconsider. I'll not have my family lose all dignity.' Both her natural colour and her self-possession were returning, although her eyes remained chill. 'You shall compose a fitting apology to give Edward on the morrow in which you shall tell him how deeply you regret your ill-judged words of today. And you need not think that, by your wiles, you might win your father round to your way of thinking, for he'll see things as I do.'

The meal that they shared when Caelica joined them in the parsonage's chill dining room was disagreeable, the mutton dry with neglect and vegetables flavourless from being stored overlong. By rights, Christopher's return should have evoked holiday spirits – why then should the servants' elation be so muted? Was it that having divined the truth of Hannah Hallet's accusation, Anstice had lost her uncritical zeal for Christopher's cause? She had professed herself pleased to see him, and Robert had shaken hands with him in his grave, taciturn way but neither of them showed much eagerness to celebrate his acquittal or welcome him home.

Indeed, at what should have been a prime celebration, there was a marked lack of conviviality. Caelica had arranged her hair in such a way as to conceal her swollen face, but she had no hunger and could hardly swallow. Her mother turned her head slightly so as to avoid looking at Caelica. Instead, she watched the son for whose return she had longed with such anguish and, consuming little, she sat back upon her upright chair and let her thin hands rest upon her lap. Seeing them tremble, Caelica wondered if the feverish motion was the only release her remaining anger could find, or whether it sprung from excess of joy at having Christopher at home once more, eating well and talking the while.

Before long, Mr Hearne turned his attention to the subject of the bridge's opening on the morrow.

'It will not,' and he looked round at all of them as though satisfying himself that each gave the matter due weight, 'be a ceremony of any high degree of grandeur. We shall make a grand crossing, all of us, in Sir Rowley's carriage, and then I shall address the people of the town.'

Caelica yearned to escape and hold rags dipped in cold water against her throbbing bruise. Her mother, it was clear, had said nothing to the others about her determination to end her engagement.

'I shall commend the felicity of Edward's design, the skill of Mr Aislabie in deriving the formal plan from Edward's drawing' – how could he traffic with untruths in this way? 'and the tenacity with which Mr Lyle has overseen the labours of the men at the site. We should all be thankful for the skill by which these men have brought the bridge into being.' This was nigh unendurable when he had taken pains to see that her own skills should stay hidden. 'Now when,' he mused, 'would it be most fitting for me to lead the people in prayer?'

'O father, forbear,' Christopher, picking his teeth, sounded bored. 'No one'll want to pray. You heard Sir Rowley saying on the way back from Hereford how he had provided four oxen for them to roast and ample ale to swill beside. They'll have their hearts set on the feast.'

'You are right, dear boy. Perhaps I should make allowance. Very well, at the close of the speeches – I have no doubt that Sir Rowley will wish to mark the occasion with a few words; perhaps Aislabie too – we shall return to the parsonage to dine, while the townsfolk feast on Sir Rowley's beef and beer. After all, there will be a service of thanks later. It will please me to see the church full once more.'

She was on the point of asking aloud how certain he could be that the people of Llanmichael would wish to attend any such service, but it would not do to cloud Christopher's homecoming further. Besides, her jaw ached almost too much for her to speak. If her father or Christopher should ask why it was swollen she would tell them she had blundered into her bedroom door.

'To return to the subject of the festivity, once, the formal ceremony and speeches are concluded, the bridge will be open to all comers.'

Was his pomposity greater than usual, or did every remark, be it never so innocent, serve to prick on her anger this evening? Under the edge of the table she clenched each hand, so that her finger nails dug into the soft flesh at the base of her thumb. When would she tell her father that she refused to marry Edward? By rights, it should be before she found herself sitting opposite him in the carriage on the morrow, watching him approve that lying stone tablet and pushing the truth of the matter to the furthest reaches of his mind with a knowing smile and a gracious wave. Yet it would be well to wait until her father were in less agitated vein than he was at present, with his quibbling over prayers and the matter of which carriage she was to travel in. Or was it only cowardice that counselled her to delay?

When the meal had ended, they repaired to the parlour. Taking Christopher's arm, Mrs Hearne made him sit at her side to tell her about his time in the gaol. The intensity with which she looked at him shut out her daughter and her husband. Christopher, long legs extended towards the fire, regaled her with his talk, assiduous as a courtier, his eyes glowing in the candlelight and never leaving her face. Caelica went and sat at her father's side. He said nothing, only followed Christopher's animated description of his fellow prisoners, pursing his mouth at intervals, or nodding his head as though to show he thought himself party to the tale, even if his son barely looked at him in the telling.

'Father, might I speak to you in your library,' she asked at last.

'But since Allbright always had ample funds...' It was clear that Christopher saw no need to break off his story.

'Daughter, in the name of all that is fair, no.' He sounded most put out. 'My son is newly come home to me,' he bristled. 'I cannot desert him now.'

'What is't sister? What nags at your calculating female mind when the rest of us are at peace?' Her father's riposte had forced Christopher to pause. 'Do you think this hour augurs well for persuading papa to increase your marriage portion?'

In the face of her brother's taunts, she would explain nothing. On the morrow, she would take her place at Edward's side and say as little to him as she could.

''Tis no such matter, Kit. Forgive my interruption.' She would say nothing until tomorrow night. After Sir Rowley's ale and oxen had put the people of the town into such good spirits that they might even smile at their rector and exchange his greetings, she would announce that she could not marry Edward. Edward himself, she gauged, would by then be so absorbed in receiving polite plaudits for what was supposed to be his creation, he would be in no mood to hedge and prevaricate. News of the severed engagement would seep out; at first, it might cause much curiosity, but once packhorse trains were passing through the town once more and trade returning to Llanmichael, interest in the marital fortunes of the rector's daughter would soon burn itself out.

'Father, mamma,' she said. 'I find myself sudden weary and would seek my rest. In this fatigue I cannot, dear brother, give my best attention to your tale.' If there her voice should harden, it would show what she thought of his clumsy teasing about marriage portions. 'I bid you therefore a good night, and may God's blessing be upon you.' Rising, she took up one of the candles from the mantel shelf and went towards the door.

'Speaking of calculating females,' Christopher went on as she crossed the room, 'hasn't old Anstice grown dour? I had looked to find more of a welcome from her at my homecoming.'

'Perhaps,' Caelica held her candle in one hand while resting the other upon the latch and answered him before her parents could speak, 'she discerned the truth of you and Hannah Hallet.'

Without pausing to hear her brother's reply, she sought her chamber to prepare for the hours of dark, sore sleeplessness ahead.

After his unhappy day in court, Mr Bevan did not go home at once. Having no wish to endure the prolonged gibes of the arrogant defendant, his slippery father and that old fox Sir Rowley Curwen, he lingered in Hereford. Even when he was confident there was no chance of meeting them on the road, he did not go home by the most direct means, but left the town by the circuitous south westerly route, crossing the river at Pwllfechan and heading into the hills above Llanfihangel as he always called it, although the English named it Michael Church or Llanmichael. After a time, he took a narrow path that forked off the main track and led up to the cave dwellings in the sandstone cliffs.

Stopping outside one of the caves, remaining mounted he raised his voice so that it would carry above the sounds of sheep nearby. Dusk was gathering all around.

It did not take long for the woman to come, the crone with the wasted body and claw-like hands that clung to the door as though she might close it in his face at any second.

'Well?' It was as though she grudged the single word.

If she were shrewish, he would be short. 'Wasn't your daughter with child when she died, mistress?' he snapped.

'Aye, what of it?'

'Didst ever know who fathered the child?'

'No – though whoever he is, I hate him.'

'You ask Christopher Hearne what he remembers of your daughter, mistress. Parson Hearne's son, new released from gaol. Tomorrow he will be with the gentry when they drive their carriages over that proud, new bridge that spans our river.'

Curiosity stirred in her sunken eyes. 'Why do you tell me this?'

'You have a score to settle, mistress, do you not? Think on it.' Setting spurs to his tired horse, Bevan rode off down the hillside.

Chapter Twenty Two

It was not much of a horse, but the small bay was the best Thomas could afford. When the ostler said the beast had stamina, Thomas wanted to believe him but the animal's narrow chest and protuberant bones gave him the gravest doubts. Given his meagre funds, he had no choice in the matter; the bay would have to suffice. With care, he fastened a bag holding some clean linen and the last of his savings to the saddle and mounted.

Leaving Oxford in the murk of a dank March morning was a reckless impulse, not least because, having left the place, he knew full well that he would never bring himself to live there again. Whatever he might once have believed, in truth he found the prospect of living out the rest of his life among complacent, gourmandizing, narrow-minded men detestable. All wisdom and sage counsel told him to stay secure in his disagreeable rooms, enduring Oxford for a little longer and see whether the coming summer might not bring a change in his fortunes, but wisdom and sage counsel had a way of turning crabbed. They weighed light in the balance of his thinking against the warmth of Parry's letter. In writing about Llanmichael, Parry had stirred up all Thomas's longing to see Caelica again, and – if it were not already too late – stop her from making a meek, dull, loveless marriage to Edward Curwen.

Parry wrote that the bridge's celebration was to take place on the eighth day of the month and his letter had not reached Thomas until the third. It wasn't long in which to travel, but now he at least he had an unkempt bay horse, currently shedding its scurfy winter coat in handfuls and lifting a wary, weary hind foot as though it were trying to raise enough energy with which to kick out. The best he could say for the beast was that it might get him to Llanmichael faster than if he set off on foot. It was a journey of around a hundred miles and it would, he knew, take all his humouring to induce the poor creature to manage the twenty-five he hoped to cover each day. If all went well, he could rest overnight at Chipping Norton, Evesholme, Worcester, Leominster and then reach Llanmichael on the fourth evening, which would be the seventh of March.

Having set off, the sky darkened and before he had got to Woodstock, the drizzle had turned to steady rain which soaked through his breeches and caused the stiff reins to slide through his gloveless hands. In all likelihood, Thomas reflected, urging the stubborn horse along the bare, treeless road beyond Enstone, Caelica would never receive any credit for her bridge. He disliked the thought of Curwen's reaping her rightful praise as much as the wretched beast, its dusty black ears flat against its neck, disliked the steady west wind and the cold. At the same time, Parry's belief that to name her as its creator would only provoke Curwen was well-founded and with Parry's assertion, that truth the daughter of time might show herself at the last, Thomas would have to be content. The hope of seeing her again was reason enough for his journey.

The morning after her return, Caelica kept to her room. Having washed, dressed, and arranged her hair so that it fell forward to hide the dark bruise on the side of her face, she sat quite still upon the chair by her bed, her hands folded on her lap, resolved not to move until the sounds of the Menston carriage reached her from outside. In the past her father, demanding to know what had caused her delay, would have sent Anstice bustling upstairs to fetch her down. Indeed, in the past it took little for his impatience to overflow and bring him knocking and indignant to her chamber himself. This day, the combination of excitement at Christopher's return and the thought of the speech that he was to make must occupy all his thinking, for he came nowhere near her. Neither did Anstice, whose mind would be fast upon the meal with which they were to regale the Curwens, and as for her mother – well, perhaps her mother did not want any reminder of the events of the previous evening.

Having eaten little the past day, she was hungry, but she didn't care. It only strengthened her resolution to have nothing more whatever to do with Edward.

From the library came the sounds of her father's pacing to and fro. He claimed that walking enabled him to compose with greater fluency than sitting still at a desk with pen poised over the glaring white of an empty page. Three paces, turn; three paces, back. His lips would be forming phrases as he went and his wig would slip down his brow as he frowned with worry. And what greater worry would it be for him to learn that she had ended her betrothal? To hear that she had broken with Edward, unscrupulous, easy-going Edward, and severed the familial connection with Sir Rowley would cut her father to the quick. His sadness would hurt her far more than her mother's blow. But she could not give way now.

Her mother's sharp voice rose from the kitchen, evidently in altercation with Anstice about dinner. Outside the house, the rooks were rasping in the ash trees. Of Christopher there was neither sound nor sign. Caelica supposed that he must still be asleep.

Hearing the sounds of the Menston party drawing near, she went to join her family in the hallway, resolved to be easy with them and complaisant, as though they had spent all morning chatting and preparing happily together for the ceremony. Pretence was necessary for survival and, so far as she could see, they were all playing parts today. Her mother was the gracious lady favouring loyal parishioners with her dignified presence, her father made like the well-beloved clergyman whom he must know himself not to be, while her brother, when at last he got up, came strutting about like the conquering hero with his hair powdered and sporting a coat of bright blue broadcloth that strained across his shoulders and midriff. He began to tell Robert what sort of horse he wanted to buy for the next season's hunting.

Robert, his hands in his pockets, did not act. He was blunt and downright. Of Christopher's blown talk of beasts with proven quality he took no notice. Instead, in a voice he may have meant for Christopher alone, she heard him say, 'You might buy one of Mr Bevan's colts.'

She couldn't help looking at Christopher. One moment he had been so vehement and brash, it was remarkable to see him flush and fall silent the next.

Sir Rowley and Alice Whatmough who had travelled over in the carriage gave the Hearnes a buoyant greeting. Edward, who had been riding at their side on a new black horse, dismounted, moved at once to Caelica's side and took her hand in his own. To keep things smooth, she let him kiss her, although she held her face immobile against the pressure of his lips. *Let my words stand. I will not marry you.*

From the way in which he hailed the carriage, Christopher had clearly recovered from Robert's snub and was set once more upon treating the day as his triumph.

'Oh, you can surely come closer,' he urged the Menston coachman, who was cautiously reversing the horses in the lane outside the parsonage gate. Although he had met the Curwens only yesterday, he gave Edward a loud salutation, struck a familiar note with Sir Rowley – a 'Holla to sir,' in place of a 'Good Morning' – and lingered over shaking Mrs Whatmough's hand as though he wanted to stroke it. While Caelica recoiled at this posturing, her mother gave a faint smile and her father fretted about whether the pages of his speech were in the right order.

Once they were all installed upon the carriage's plush seats – it was Christopher who directed them where to sit – and Edward had remounted, the party set off on the short distance between the parsonage and the bridge. Caelica's parents were opposite one another beside the window on the right hand side of the carriage. Christopher had placed himself between his mother and Mrs Whatmough facing the horses; Caelica, with her father on her left and Sir Rowley on her right, faced her brother. When Alice Whatmough smiled at her in a way that was at once both sweet and secretive, she found it hard labour to smile back.

On the far side of the bridge, people were beginning to gather in half-hearted groups. Sir Rowley, Caelica reasoned, should have foreseen how the local men would resent the way that Aislabie and Lyle had brought in their own workforce, instead of recruiting labour from the district. There had been the offer of a little unskilled work, it was true – jobs like quarrying, hewing and carrying fresh stone to the site. But the tasks that required more specialist knowledge of masonry and building – tasks which commanded the highest wages – had gone to individuals who had worked with the engineer or his deputy in the past. Small wonder, then, that the Llanmichael men should look on with glum faces and their women scowl at their sides as this carriage of self-styled grandees rolled towards them. Even the pledge of an ox roast and abundant free ale had not created any celebratory atmosphere in the town. What possessed her father, after crying down their pride and their errors in so many sermons, to suppose that he might buy back their love with a bridge and a speech? And in all honesty, it was Sir Rowley who had paid for the bridge's construction, yet he too must think the people simple indeed if he imagined that he could win them over with the gift of a meal.

Craning her neck at an extreme angle so as to look out of the carriage window, she caught sight of the bridge and its sheer beauty brought her a spark of consolation. Today's ill-conceived attempts at revelry would pass. So would her parents' annoyance over her treatment of Edward, who would surely find himself a more suitable bride before long. In time, the people of Llanmichael might even get used to crossing their new bridge without remembering how they had been expected to show fit and humble gratitude for its provision.

'Ah, now we approach – we, the first to make the crossing.' Caelica's father clasped his hands in excitement.

'Forgive my quenching your zeal, Hearne,' remarked Sir Rowley, 'but Lyle told me that he and his men took a stone wagon over a couple of days ago. To test the safety of the structure, you understand. And Aislabie, conscientious soul that he is, made a point of riding back and forth across it too – he'd never ask his men to take a risk he wouldn't take himself. In our ceremonious passage, we claim an honour that is not our due.'

Was it an accident that he should happen to catch her eye as he spoke? Caelica wondered. In their travels, Sir Rowley had always been kind to her.

'Yet ours is the journey that people will remember,' insisted her father.

'Perhaps, Hearne, perhaps,' Sir Rowley answered, his tone weary as though his zeal for the bridge had burnt itself out.

On the day he hoped to reach Leominster, Thomas did not get beyond Bramyard. His bay horse, poor beast, could go no faster than a snail. The stabling at the Worcester inn where he had spent the previous night had been filthy, the water dusty and the hay mouldering. When he went to saddle the wretched animal and patted its thin neck, it had put its ears back and swished its tail. He had cut a hazel stick from the hedge, but he used it sparingly, judging that if he whipped the creature, it might well turn lame out of spite or even die beneath him. Closing his legs around its sides in frustration, he realised it was most unlikely to carry him as far as Llanmichael.

Once on the bridge, Sir Rowley's carriage horses managed the pull to the crown of the arch without much difficulty. There they paused for the coachman to attach a drag to the rear axle so as to make for a safe descent.

While they were stationary Christopher, who must have noticed the commemorative tablet on their approach, slowly repeated its words.

'*EDUARDUS CURWEN FECIT*. It's a very worthy commemoration,' he called to Edward through the carriage window. 'I like the stately Latin,' and Edward on his black horse laughed and flourished his whip.

About to speak, Caelica thought better of it. If she might only be released from this marriage which had grown so loathsome to her, she would not lay claim to the bridge as well. Her protestations of injustice would sound like sulks and never sway anyone. She didn't much care for the bargain, but provided Edward didn't have her, he was welcome to her handiwork. Breathing deep, she offered her pledge to God or fate – whatever power might heed. Around her, her father's and Sir Rowley's hearty, pleased voices exclaimed upon how well the structure stood out in the surrounding landscape while Christopher observed to his mother that he might set up his easel nearby and paint it on the next fine day.

The wary groups, recognising that the speeches were a necessary preliminary to the ox roast, began to edge nearer. The carriage halted and Caelica's father looked round as though expecting applause. There was none, but old Mr Watkin the churchwarden limped up and offered to hold Edward's horse.

'Ah, Mr Curwen – what an honour you have done us, sir,' he said, taking the reins over the beast's head. 'A fine bridge it is to be sure. People'll come from far and wide to admire it. And you to wed our Miss Caelica too. See here, you people, Greene, Gleeson and the rest of you,' he called over a bony shoulder, 'let us have some cheering now for Mr Curwen who is to marry Miss Hearne.'

Caelica found herself manoeuvred out of the carriage and to Edward's side – of all places on earth the one where she least wished to be – embarrassed by the fervour with which Watkin tried to rouse the suspicious onlookers to cheers. Her hand in Edward's insistent grip grew slippery with sweat. Drops of it – not the honest perspiration of heat, but rank sweat of shame – clung to her brow and broke out on her cheeks like a rash. There was a feeble huzza from the watchers – no open jeers, but a ragged edge of irony to their shouting.

'We thank you, good people, for this display of your good wishes.' Edward's grasp tightened – he must know how much she longed to run away, but his clear voice rang out as fulsome as if their cheers had been full-throated and spontaneous. Was he crushing her fingers to punish her for yesterday?

Around them, sheep browsed at the smooth grass. Not far away, the chimneys of the straggling town sent their smoke up to the heights of the massive hills beyond. And before them stood the bridge in all its unassuming grace and strength. Her father came forward. Unfolding the pages of his speech, he took his place on a convenient flat topped rock and faced the sullen people.

'My brethren,' his sermon voice sounded thin in the open air.

'Don't be too long about it, parson,' came the inevitable heckle. 'We've oxen to roast, aye, and liquor waiting.'

'My brethren,' he said again, ignoring the gibe. 'We gather today to mark the opening of Llanmichael's new bridge – Curwen's Bridge as it shall henceforth be known, to commemorate both our local benefactor Sir Rowley Curwen who has paid for its construction, and his son Edward who conceived its ingenious design.'

Edward's powerful grip which had eased somewhat, clamped abruptly round Caelica's hand as though he meant to remind Caelica that her creation was his and she should not flout him again.

'Now the exercise of human ability in pursuit of the common good is the summit of virtue,' continued Hearne, hitting his stride. 'Edward Curwen, as this structure demonstrates, possesses skills of no common order.'

Any moment, the bones of her fingers would break.

'The engraved stone upon the arch is but trifling recognition...'

'Hold!'

One word, shrill as a scream and clear as glass, cut through her father's prosing.

A gaunt woman, her hair torn and her grey dress ragged, thrust her way past Caelica's mother, past Sir Rowley, Mrs Whatmough and Edward in their respectful little group, past Caelica herself and stopped in front of Christopher.

'What dost here, returning to the scene of your crime?' Mrs Hallet's voice, so chill and terse when she had refused the gift of apples was higher and rougher now. Everyone fell silent.

'And who might you be?' demanded Christopher, raising his eyebrows. Since she was somewhat taller than he, he had to look up at her.

'You don't know me, but I know you,' she rasped in reply. 'You're the parson's son, aren't you? The one who's just out of gaol.'

The crowd caught its breath.

'You may have escaped the law, but you shan't escape me,' the skeletal woman told him. 'You wooed my poor daughter, got her with child and then you wouldn't wed her. She did well enough to lie with behind the hedge but she wasn't good enough for you to marry, isn't that so?'

Hearne stepped down from his rock.

'I assure you, my good woman, I had no such intent –' Christopher began, rather red in the face.

'You must have known where your loving might lead,' she shrieked. 'When she saw her big belly'd soon tell all the world what you and she'd been about, she couldn't bear the shame.'

She started crying in dry, tearing sobs. 'My Hannah drowned herself because you were gone and she couldn't bear to go to the parish for money to raise the child. What of it, parson's son?'

Behind her, Caelica heard her mother's sharp indrawn breath. 'What of it?'

'What manner of accusation is this, my good woman,' replied Christopher. 'You tell a sorry tale, it is true, but you cannot blame me because your daughter chose to do away with herself.'

For answer, she spat.

At once, a stone, the usual weapon, scudded through the air and landed by the globule of saliva at Christopher's feet. A second, following, winged Mr Watkin's wrinkled cheek. Others came in their wake, flying towards the Hearnes and Curwens. The crowd surged towards them. From the corner of her eye, Caelica saw Christopher looking over his shoulder towards the carriage.

'Good people, I beseech –' her father entreated, but the stones continued to fly.

'Get the young whelp,' yelled the heckler, and from somewhere, Caelica could not say where, two men seized her brother by the arms while Mrs Whatmough dabbed at Watkin's face with a lace edged handkerchief and Edward and Sir Rowley held Caelica's mother to keep her from rushing to her son's side.

With the eyes of the swelling mob upon him, Christopher did not struggle for long. Between his assailants in their earth-coloured woollen garb, his coat looked garish and his hair ridiculous. He lifted his eyes to the sky as though in exasperation. Even now there was no shame on his petulant features. Aghast, Caelica could find only contempt for him.

'Well, what would you have from me?' he drawled. 'I cannot bring her back.'

'Stay by me, I beg you ma'am,' Sir Rowley muttered, taking Caelica's mother by the hand.

'Hearne,' he raised his voice, 'this is an ugly mob. It would be best for your wife and daughter – and Alice too, of course – to return to your parsonage until some calm is restored.'

'That's good counsel.' Her father had lost his colour and looked quite defeated. 'Go Cherry, with your mother. Edward and Sir Rowley will accompany you. I must stay with your brother now.'

His lips brushed against her brow, then he walked forward and placed himself deliberately between Christopher and the crowd.

'If there have been things done amiss in the past, then tell me of them in plain speech.' he began.

'You can spare her your prayers and prating,' called someone. 'Give her cash.'

'Aye, she seeks cash,' the usual heckler took up the cry. 'Not words, not prayers, not empty mouthings. Give her cash.'

'Cash, cash, cash,' shouted the people louder and louder. Still Caelica hesitated at its side, intent upon the slight figure in the thick of the seething vengeful mass, but Edward pushed her forward up the carriage steps and hoisted her inside like a parcel. Sir Rowley got in after, looking behind him as though he wondered whether he should stay behind. Another cry of *Cash, cash cash* fell on Caelica's hearing. She should not be running away; she should not indeed, but the coachman was whipping up his team and Edward mounting his horse even as she tried to open the door. *Cash, cash, cash.* Edward must have locked it, but she leaned as far out of the window as she could, training her eyes upon the throng, searching and searching for the two men it held in its maw. *Cash, cash, cash.* How should they fare? Would they emerge alive? And if it should spew them out unharmed, what then? But now they had vanished from her sight.

When they got back to the parsonage they got out by the stables. Edward stayed to unsaddle his black horse and Caelica, steeling herself to be hospitable, led the others through the herb garden into the house. There, they sat in the parlour trying to ignore the rhythmic, relentless cry from the far side of the river and straining after subjects for conversation. Declining her offer of refreshment, Sir Rowley sat sighing by the fireless hearth, as though he continued to reproach himself for abandoning the fray. Alice Whatmough, graceful on the sofa, watched him without speaking. Caelica's mother took her place on one of the hard chairs, but rose almost at once to look out of the window.

'Oh, they do not return,' she lamented. 'Still they do not return. Why does Matthias linger? And all over a foolish, blowzy girl. Christopher owes her mother no obligation, whatever those vile men of the town may claim...'

'Come, ma'am,' Sir Rowley tried to rally her. 'It is hardly surprising that the good wife should find herself distressed. These parish matters call for much skill in the handling. No wonder that your husband should tarry.' At one time it might have amused Caelica to hear Edward's forthright father speak as though he knew about parish matters, but now she had put amusement behind her. She did not think she would ever laugh again.

Thomas walked at the bay horse's side. A distance beyond Leominster one of his reins had broken. The stiff, cracked leather had fractured near the stud that held it around the ring of the bit. He had tried to tie it in place, but it was not supple enough for knots. Not wishing to delay or venture away from his westerly route, he thought it best to continue on foot and hope he might chance to pass a saddler's shop in time.

In the parsonage parlour, the shouts from the town had died away. There must be some negotiation in progress between the Hearnes and Mrs Hallet.

Alice Whatmough looked round with her enchanting smile. 'Dear Mrs Hearne,' she asked, 'I thought I saw early feverfew growing in your herb garden. May I take some leaves of it? The anxieties of waiting are making my head ache.' She was, Caelica noticed, very pale.

'My dear,' Before Caelica or her mother could reply, Sir Rowley intervened, his voice full of concern. 'Would you wish to rest? No doubt Mrs Hearne could make some quiet room available?'

'No, no,' she waved his solicitude aside. 'If I may just take the air for a moment or so, and pluck some leaves of feverfew, I am sure that it will suffice to alleviate the pain. I have great trust in the old remedies.'

'Of course you may, ma'am,' answered Caelica's mother. 'Though it surprises me that you find feverfew in leaf already. Let my daughter fetch it for you.'

'No, no,' answered Mrs Whatmough with great decision. 'I shall go myself.' Still smiling, she rose, her full silk skirt sweeping across the floor.

Time passed. Trying to make conversation to Sir Rowley, Caelica caught the faint smell of roasting beef blowing on the breeze from the far side of the river. The calls for cash had given way to the sound of harsh song. Whatever might be happening between her father, her brother and Mrs Hallet, the townspeople must have started upon the feast. Meanwhile, her mother fretted, taut upon her carved chair and deaf to the boisterous comfort of Sir Rowley's remarks about the parsons' duties towards their parishioners.

'Come, mamma,' Caelica appealed at last, thinking he would soon lose patience. 'Let us take up your embroidery. It may serve to pass the time.'

At first, her mother sniffed that she could hardly sew when that foul peasant harridan was saying harsh things to her ill-used Christopher and her beloved Matthias, but Caelica reminded her she had sewn much when Christopher was in prison, so she could surely sew now. Having fetched the thread box and tambour frame, she asked Sir Rowley – he was hardly likely to find much pleasure in the company of women at their needlework – if he would care to read in her father's library.

'Here,' she offered, seeing him rise at the suggestion, 'l-let me come with you and see th-that you have all need.' She led him upstairs and into the spacious room surrounded by shelves from which her father's books confronted them – Richard Baxter, Augustine, Henry More, Homer – the stern names that she had known from her childhood done in gilt upon their spines. The muted sun of an early spring afternoon had gone sufficiently far to the west to cast an arc of light across the table where she had sat to learn her lessons.

'See,' she invited. 'The windows c-command a fine view to the river, and – and the br-bridge. Edward's bridge.'

'Where is Edward?' Sir Rowley was in the very act of drawing out a chair, but at her words, he stopped short and put the question to her like an accusation.

'Settling his horse.' Alarmed by the stone throwing, it must have sweated up. Edward would calm it with wisping and gentling.

Even as she spoke, the reality of the matter broke upon her. Although she tried to silence it, some strand of knowledge borne of her experience over the past few weeks told her that Edward was with Alice Whatmough. That was the truth, and she had a strong sense that at last Sir Rowley saw it too.

Together they went downstairs, retracing their steps without a word. Ignoring her mother stitching in the parlour and Anstice demanding to know when they meant to eat because the meal she had prepared was fast spoiling, Caelica took Sir Rowley through the garden in front of the house and round to the stables.

'Edward, Edward,' she called, knowing there would be no answer. Then Sir Rowley called Alice's name over and over, his deep, confident voice torn by anguish when it found no response.

But their clamour roused the Menston coachman, who emerged from one of the stalls with a wisp and curry.

'Oh, he unsaddled his horse, sir,' he announced, addressing himself to Sir Rowley. 'But he didn't take long about it. I'm still trying to make the poor beast quieten. Got himself into a right muck-sweat, he has...'

'Thank you, John. And did Mrs Whatmough come this way?'

'Well, not that I've noticed, sir.' For a second, hope flared in Sir Rowley's eyes.

He led the way back, this time taking the path through the herb garden. Uncomfortable, she followed. Edward could have come this way and found Alice picking her feverfew. The gate leading onto the path that wound up the hill behind the house was wide open.

Sir Rowley and Caelica paused among the trim beds which, not many months before, had been green with sage, mint, sweet marjoram and fennel. Now they had died back, leaving the garden desolate, although the bay trees and rosemary bushes stood stalwart by the path, and sure enough, there were a few tentative shoots of yellow-green feverfew in a sheltered patch by the wall. Caelica crouched down by the new growth. It looked as though someone had recently torn away a handful of infant leaves. But Sir Rowley had gone through the gate and was heading uphill, so swiftly she rose and matched her steps with his.

They had not gone far before, as one, they saw a fallen tree some way above them up the slope. A few saplings screened it, but they were not yet in leaf and did not block the broad trunk entirely from view. Upon it, perhaps believing themselves to be hidden, were a man and woman – he fair, she dark. Their arms were fast around one another and their bodies cleaved together in hot embrace. Silent, Caelica glanced at Sir Rowley. But she could not bring herself to look long into the stricken face of this man so many years older than she, who had been so generous to her father, her brother and herself, and witness his heartfelt distress upon discovering that Alice – his adored, beautiful, vivacious Alice – was lost to him forever.

Instead, she turned back towards the house. At once she heard raised voices and the sound of shattering glass coming from the direction of the promontory. Looking towards it, she saw first tendrils of thick grey smoke circling towards the sky and then a flicker of orange flames; despite the distance she caught the acrid smell of burning reed-thatch in the still air. The fractious crowd had poured across their new bridge to turn their wrath upon her father's church.

Chapter Twenty Three

It was not the firing of the parish church, nor the attempt by mutinous parishioners to stone his loyal church warden that convinced Hearne he could no longer remain rector of Llanmichael. Late in the evening of that day for which he had harboured such hopes, he noticed dark bruising around his daughter's face.

'What injury is this, Cherry?' They were going upstairs, but on the half-landing, he paused short and moved his candle to where the light of its flame fell right across the livid mark. Beside his shame at his son, his sorrow for Sir Rowley who had been so open-hearted and was now desolate, his lament for the bare, stark church that he loved in his way and his pity for his wife who had been weeping ever since his return, his spirit quickened in compassion for his daughter. Not only had Edward deceived her but also, he judged, she was in pain.

'Tis nothing,' she said and added something about walking into the side of the door frame.

'That's not like you. You were never so clumsy, child. Besides,' he raised a tentative hand to her jaw and touched the bluish swelling. 'You would not incur such bruising when you were but walking – not at the base of your jaw. Did Edward ever strike you?'

'Not he.'

'Someone else then? Tell truth now, daughter.'

But she only shook her head and went on up the stairs. Following, he thought suddenly of his wife's mocking temper. On their return from Hereford Caelica had reached the house before the rest of them. He had thought that while he was undoing the thick coat he had worn for travel, he had caught the sound of hers and her mother's voices raised in hot exchange. At the time, he had ignored the clash, taking it for one of those female arguments which he preferred to disregard. But here, in his daughter's swollen face, was the result of his negligence. He could not imagine what perceived fault in Caelica could have drawn Christina to such a pitch of wrath as to lash out, so far as he could judge, with some heavy object. Why, she might have killed the hapless child – and Caelica only just home from her travels. Unsure of the facts and too sad to probe into the matter any further, turning towards his chamber he observed, as though he were following a new strand of thought at random, that it would be best for all of them if they moved away from this place with its profound and bitter associations. The next day, therefore, he would tender his resignation to the bishop. Then they could take steps to quit the parsonage and seek out convenient lodgings until something more permanent might be found. In future, the only link binding them to Llanmichael would be the lifelong monthly sum that he had agreed to pay Mrs Hallet in his son's name until Christopher was earning a wage that would enable him to pay it himself.

'Did the news please her, father?' Caelica asked.

'Well, she took it as her due,' he said, thinking of the lean grey woman consumed with grief. 'She uttered no word of thanks, but she heard Christopher out when at last he voiced his regrets and she let me tell her where she might draw on the monies before bidding me away. Her hurt, I think, will never heal.'

The following morning, before going to inform the bishop of his intention to resign the living, he bade her briefly into his library.

'What of you, daughter? The disappointment you must endure?'

'Disappointment?' He could not know of her changed feelings for Thomas, now so far away in Oxford.

'Over Edward.' Her father paused, showing rare patience for a man of his brisk temper. 'You say nothing of him, but you were ever quiet where your thoughts ran deepest.' His eyes, so often stern, were gentle upon her and rather sad. Caelica had been standing near the door; now she came right into the room where he sat at the great oak table, and took the chair at his side.

'I knew before yesterday that I could not marry Edward, father.'

'Before yesterday?' It was his turn for confusion. 'But, daughter, you and he always seemed to accord so well – he so very much a man for society and you retiring; he loving to talk, and you to listen...'

'And he so wealthy and enjoying such high station, and I but a country clergyman's daughter, would you say?' She did not wait for him to upbraid her blunt speaking, but tried to give the straightest explication she could find.

'Father, the bridge was mine, as you know – yet he claimed it as his own. If there is anything I desire in this life more than your affection, it is to live and to love without having to hide, cringe and conform my life to a pattern of my lover's wishing. When I drew that bridge, I cared for it as a mother for her own child. I didn't seek fame on its account, but I took honest delight at the chance of seeing my idea given solid reality. When Edward made out it was his, I knew I couldn't wed him.'

This avowal was the sort of talk he most disliked, so she changed the subject.

'I suppose Edward will marry Mrs Whatmough.'

Her father grunted with his old terseness. 'He'll have to accustom himself to plainer living than he's ever known before if he does. I hardly imagine that Sir Rowley'll care to settle anything on him now. Had I but known, daughter...'

'Had you but known what, father?'

But he only sighed, and rose without answering, except to say that packing up his books for a move would take an age.

Taking him at his word, she set herself to straighten the library. If they were indeed to leave Llanmichael, it would make the task of tying them into bundles for the carrier all the easier if they were ordered according to their size. As she began to move the taller volumes onto the wide shelves closest to the floor – her father had left many of them lying horizontal across the tops of the demi-octavos on the middle shelves – she could not help wondering if he had known the truth of Edward's bridge all along. He was a loving father in intention. According to his thinking, setting her on the way to marrying an affable man of means was a mark of that love. For all her life she had moulded and schooled herself to accord with his plans for her and now, in the matter of the bridge, she had rebelled.

She worked throughout the day, having no wish for either food or company. Her mother kept to her room and Christopher, at his father's behest had ridden out to settle some old debts. Late in the afternoon, she thought her father must have returned, for she caught the sound of his light knock at the front door. Anstice might be particular about keeping it locked at all times, but her hearing was not the sharpest and she might well fail to catch the sound of a bare hand on solid wood. Going downstairs to the hall, Caelica seized the heavy door by the latch and dragged it open across the stones of the floor. There, with the broken reins of a ewe-necked bay horse over one arm, hair untied, and his clothes spattered with glaring, greyish mud stood her father's recent pupil.

'Thomas,' he must have covered a vast distance to judge from the way the horse hung its head. 'But you are gone to Oxford, so my father said. Oh, I thought never to see you again. And,' It was far too frank and indelicate for her to mention it, but she had done with dissembling forever. 'And I br -broke my en-engage- engagement to Edward Curwen. H-he l-loves Alice Whatmough – she who was to h-have wed his f-father. But – but...'

In the past, he had been the only person on earth to whom she could speak without stammering. Now her voice was shaking so badly she could hardly speak at all. Now she would understand forever what it meant to feel the blood flowing backwards in her veins.

'B-but wh-what brings you b-back t-to Llanmichael?' she asked.

'You,' he answered.

When Hearne returned, he was mystified to find a knock-kneed, unprepossessing bay horse in his mare's usual stall. Puzzling over why it should be there and who it belonged to, he went in to the house to tell his family that the bishop wanted them to vacate the parsonage by the end of the month. Glancing, out of habit, into his library, he found the late sun lighting the shelves which were in a state of unusual tidiness. Marvelling and dazzled, it took him a few seconds to notice his pupil and his wronged, beloved daughter standing hand in hand at the window.

In that moment of seeing them together, he understood much that previously he had missed and it was a few seconds before he noticed that they were looking at something. At first, he could not guess what it might be, but when he joined them and let his eyes follow the direction of their gaze, he saw the last of the sun's dying beams gild the arch of Caelica's bridge.

Epilogue

In the autumn of 1756, a small family – husband, wife and infant daughter – were journeying from the Lancashire village where the husband had held a curacy to the Welsh town of Pwllfechan where he was to take up the living made vacant by the death of Dr John Aylmer. They had come through Birmingham and paused overnight at the house in which the woman's ageing parents lodged together with the drawing teacher son who supported them. Grandparents and uncle had welcomed the chance to meet the small girl who was respectively their grand-daughter and niece. The elderly servants had petted her and the visit passed off in good, if quiet, humour.

Beyond Birmingham their road wound west through the Marches – a tortuous route into Wales. The man and woman rode pillion on a sturdy young horse with the child in the woman's arms. Their progress was slow.

After some hours, they paused by a stream to let the horse drink and the child paddle. 'You know,' the man observed to his wife as they sat at the water's edge, 'that we are going to pass through Llanmichael.'

'I thought we must.'

'You shan't mind, shall you?' He looked at her in sudden concern. I mean, if you preferred, we might be able to find another way.'

'Of course I shan't mind. We both knew when you accepted Aylmer's old living that we should find ourselves near the town again. I've no fear of it, and you'll have the chance to go angling with Mr Parry again.'

For answer, he put his arm round her shoulders, and for a while forgetful of his clerical dignity, they dabbled their bare feet in the stream and looked for coloured pebbles to please the child while the horse grazed.

When they went on, the road improved somewhat, or perhaps it was more that the rest and the grazing revived the horse's energy. It did not take them long to reach the point at which a wide, snaking river drew a natural boundary between England and Wales. Approaching from high ground on the English side, they soon had an expansive view of the fast-flowing water, with the grey, mean little town on the far bank, the church on its rise near at hand and the square parsonage in a fold of the hills behind it.

'The church is roofed with slates now,' said she, looking ahead.

'Well, I suppose your father's successor must have seen that renewing with thatch would be asking for trouble in a stormy place like this. There Mary,' he addressed the child, 'that is your mother's old home.' But the movement of the horse and the comfort of her mother's embrace had sent the infant to sleep.

Another family would live there now. Another parson. The herb garden, insofar as anyone could see from the track, looked well-tended and cared for, the edges of the beds sharp, the plants free from weeds. The wooden gate in the low wall was securely bolted.

As yet, the one direction from which she had averted her eyes was to the south, towards the bridge. She had a fear that with the passing of time, it should look less to her than it had in the past. Now they were so near that short of closing her eyes, and this action she scorned, she could avoid it no longer.

The sky was overcast and there were no shafts of sun that might emblazon the supple arch, but beneath the grey cloud and against the pewter stream its grace was serene as ever. Hugging the sleeping child, she became conscious of great love rising in her spirit – love which somehow enfolded the bridge, the infant, her husband, the parents and brother with whom they had been so recently, and even the miserable, squalid town that had turned on them in hate.

Stocky and powerful, the horse made light of the ascent to the arch's crown where they paused to give it its head before making their cautious way down on the other side. Once over, their road took them into clear view of the engraved stone that purported to proclaim the bridge's origins. Steeling her determination, she stared at the tablet.

There were no words visible upon it at all. Incredulous, she leant forward.

'Stop, Thomas. Can you take the child if I dismount?'

It was an awkward business, this holding of reins in one hand while supporting a drowsy toddler with the other, but in recent months he had grown rather good at it. Forbearing, he watched as she slid down from the saddle, re-ascended the steep arch on foot, lent over the parapet at the height and felt with her hand across the face of the broad stone.

It had taken little time for rain and wind to wear the carved letters away. Where once the words EDUARDUS CURWEN FECIT had stood for all the world to heed, nothing but a few illegible indentations remained. Returning, she was on the point of remounting, only he, still cradling the infant, bent forward first to kiss her.

Notes

The song *Vital Spark of Heavn'ly Flame* which Thomas sings in Chapter Nine is Alexander Pope's translation of words attributed to the Emperor Hadrian.

In Chapter Eleven, the stanza which so confuses Sir Rowley comes from *A Nuptial Song, or Epithalamie, on Sir Clipsby Crew and his Lady* by Robert Herrick. The Greek phrase which Mr Hearne quotes comes from Aeschylus's play *Prometheus Bound* and means literally 'the infinite laughter of the ocean.'

As for the bridge, its original stands in Pontypridd, Rhondda Cynon Taf, and dates from 1756. It is the work of the Welsh stone-mason and preacher William Edwards, 1719-89, who styled himself 'a builder for both worlds'. I can but beg his pardon from beyond the grave for taking his remarkable design as the inspiration for my novel.

Victoria Owens, Bristol, 2013.

Acknowledgements

Many people have contributed to my enjoyment in writing this novel. On Bath Spa University's MA course in Creative Writing I had terrific support from my tutor Tricia Wastvedt, for which I am appreciative beyond words. Sabrina Brody, Dann Casswell, Matthew Hooton, Jane Panos, Joseph White and Ben Wright provided heartening feedback on the work-in-progress, while Richard Francis, Lucy English and Tessa Hadley also contributed much valuable guidance.

I'm grateful to John Freeman and Stephen Rowson for directing me to sources of information about eighteenth-century building ventures. All historical errors in the narrative are my responsibility.

Thanks also to Yvonne Barlow for her editorial flair; to the Hookline reading groups for their vote of support; to Carol Heaton for some excellent suggestions at the revision stage; to Katie Fforde and Lindsay Ashford for their encouragement; to David, Juliet and Rosy Owens for their vigorous and varied advice and to Sarah Duncan for her humour, shrewd instincts and steadfast conviction that writing should be fun.

About the Author

Victoria Owens worked both in the book trade and as a legal executive before reading for an English degree. PhD research on John Dryden's translation of the Virgil's *Aeneid* followed; she submitted her thesis about ten days before her eldest daughter's birth. She started to write fiction when her younger daughter went to playgroup and graduated with Distinction from Bath Spa University's MA course in Creative Writing in 2008. The following year, she won the inaugural Jane Austen Short Story Award. *Drawn to Perfection* grew out of her interest in the eighteenth century.

Lightning Source UK Ltd.
Milton Keynes UK
UKOW03f0347140913

217196UK00003B/18/P